THE SECRETS OF
THE TUMBLEDOWN

A Wilton-Blake Mystery

A DCI Jerry Blake and DI Rob Wilton Mystery

Laurence Cowley

Printed edition:
Also available in multiple e-book formats.

Published by:
The Endless Bookcase Ltd,
Suite 14 STANTA Business Centre, 3 Soothouse Spring,
St Albans, Hertfordshire, AL3 6PF, UK.

More information can be found at:
www.theendlessbookcase.com.

Cover Art by Michael Shorten
mikeshorten84@gmail.com.
Michael Shorten Ltd 2024.

ISBN: 978-1-917061-40-7

About the Author

Laurence Cowley was born in Cardiff in 1946. He will readily admit that he hadn't read a book from cover to cover until his mid-sixties, and even now no more than a few crime novels, so there are no outside writing influences.

'Secrets of the Tumbledown' is his fourth novel.

He is currently working on two new novels as well as a series of children's stories. Laurence says that everyone should attempt writing, it is very therapeutic, but as a story grips you…and often takes over your life…even though it becomes all-consuming, it is very enjoyable, very rewarding and very satisfying.

He believes that his books are not about academic achievement, or clever words, but about the story.

He says that his stories and characters are drawn from a varied work and business career, having worked as a salesperson, a manager, and a director, in more than one company. Having created his own textile business and having owned an up-market 'rosetted' country house hotel for ten years, he has converted many properties, been involved in financing other businesses, and has owned 13 funeral businesses.

He says that he may be called an opportunist or even a risk-taker by friends and acquaintances, but he's alive and kicking to tell the tale.

One small achievement he is very pleased with, which he says he is still 'milking' is that for his 70th birthday, despite suffering from chronic leukaemia, he completed the London Marathon (in 6hrs 20mins) and has the gong to prove it!

Acknowledgements

To my lovely Wife Tricia, my childhood sweetheart, who allows me to indulge myself writing, just for the joy of writing.

Thanks to my nephew, Mike Shorten, for taking the time out from his busy schedule to create the cover art for 'The Secrets of the Tumbledown'.

And to my endless list of friends from:

Bill and Sue Lindsay, who tell me that this book's a 'blockbuster'!

Nigel and Anne Tilley, who are ever encouraging.

Brian Purser, an avid reader, who tells me that this may be my best book to date.

Tony and Sue Hyde, who are just good mates and keep offering me alternative reading.

My sister Leona whom I have assured that there are no 'saucy' scenes in this book.

And last but not least, Morgana Evans for persevering with the proofs and Carl French for seeing the potential in my books.

CHAPTER 1

2020, Camden Estates

It's Monday and Jan and Phil Phillips make their daily trip to their property rental and maintenance business premises, based in Camden Lock, from their home in Huntingdon.

Jan is ever frustrated by the tedium that has become her working week and the business that she inherited from her father almost twenty years ago. She is using a break in the traffic flow to vent her feelings yet again, towards Phil.

"God, do you know what Phil, I am absolutely sick of working in London. I'm headed towards fifty years of age and I want to get out of here and find somewhere in the countryside that's peaceful and quiet and away from everything. I'm just sick of the morning slog, the traffic, the jams, the diversions, having to jockey for position every day, the buggers that cut you up. We've been doing it for almost twenty years now and I'm just fed up with the lot of it. Oh, how I wish we could just sell up and move, before we're too old to do it, or have run out of energy!"

Phil replied with some agitation. "For God's sake Jan, you've been saying that for more years than I can remember. Have you ever thought about it seriously? The upheaval, selling the house, re-locating or maybe selling our business, moving away from our friends and family. We need to consult them and consider what they want, too. Your aunt relies so much on you and my father is still alive. I mean, how would they feel if we were living as you suggest in the middle of nowhere? You're not thinking it through enough, it's just your fantasy, your dream. I suppose we all have to have one or two of those to see us through the weeks and years as they go by, or we would probably just stagnate and maybe go mad. You always seem to go through this when the business is struggling, or a client has let you down and you've lost a bit of business that you thought you had tied up."

Jan replied indignantly, "Well, that's it. As soon as we get into the office, I'm going to email some estate agents and get on the internet to see what's available in Devon and Cornwall and see what the prices are like and what they have to offer. The house prices up here, where we are, are so much higher than the Westcountry. I've seen some of those programmes where couples sell a tiny terraced house in London, or even where we are, and buy a mansion in Devon or Cornwall or the wilds of North Wales. We should be able to buy something fairly substantial and hopefully be mortgage free so we can start to enjoy our lives before we're too old to care. I wouldn't even mind a 'doer-upper' as they say on 'Homes Under the Hammer'."

As Jan turned the corner into Castle Haven Road, she spotted that their next door neighbour Dale hadn't taken his usual prime position in their small car park with its carefully allocated white-lined spaces. *Brilliant*, she thought. It was a rare thing to beat her neighbour, Dale, whose business premises were located directly next door to theirs, above the parade of shops that overlooked the Regents Park canal. *I must have beaten him in to work or so, unless he's lent his car to that blonde bimbo who's hooked her claws into him,* she pondered, as she made her way across the small courtyard at the rear of the row of shops along the waterside at Camden Lock. Dale waved from the first-floor window as she passed at the back of their premises. *Yes*, she thought, with a hint of jealousy, *lent his Porsche to that Barbie-girl!*

Jan and Phil had taken over a small property rental business some years ago from her father and managed to slowly build it up into a comfortable business. Jan didn't know her father well as he had died quite young and somewhat prematurely, as did her grandfather, whom she believed originated from Russia somewhere, but she never ever seemed to have the time to research her family history. She was just *far* too busy, trying to keep all the 'balls in the air' and all the 'plates spinning'. Their business was a mix of small commercial outlets, offices, shops, showrooms etc., and domestic flats. In fact, they managed the whole row of shops where their own premises were located. Even so, Jan had become somewhat disillusioned with the way in which almost all of these retail premises had garnered to the tourist trade and were now in-your-face trashy gift and takeaway shops. This was the core of their business but the add-ons, which they had cultivated over the years were as valuable as the rentals themselves. Each time there was a new tenant in any one of the premises domestic or commercial, there would be a new fee. To add to that, there would be an inventory report, a deep clean, or, in most cases, a complete redecoration of that unit or premises. Invariably the supply of new carpets, sometimes blinds or curtains, and occasionally a new or replacement piece of white goods, in the form of a cooker or a fridge or whatever was required. Part of their management percentage was also to provide insurance for each of the premises within their portfolio, on which, as they 'bought in bulk', would yield a handsome percentage. Because they had proved themselves to be efficient and capable, their property rental portfolio had increased in size and income value, year upon year, to the stage where it was gaining value as a potential business sale.

2020, UK Heir Hunters, Camden Lock

Dale Scott, Managing Director of UK Heir Hunters, a three-partner business, sat swivelling in his chair searching the Bona-Vacantia and Government Legal Department for this-weeks set of Wills and Probate, but more particularly, unclaimed estates. Dale and his colleagues had done extremely well these last few years tracing the distant relatives of those wills which were worthy of chasing. In other words, those with such a substantial net worth that he and his colleagues could take a good percentage from, usually twenty to twenty-five percent of the net value of that will, having invested heavily of their time to eventually have traced the inheritors or beneficiaries, of any said estate.

UK Heir Hunters was a three-partner business. Dale was the managing director and the driver of the business, with his partner Roger, a failed solicitor, or not so much a failed solicitor, but a bright chap that lost interest in completing his articles. He preferred to work and earn a living, rather than wait forever to get a senior job, or perhaps a partnership with a firm in the city. With his legal knowledge, he more than pulled his weight in the business. The third partner was Richard, an accountant. Although he was on the 'fast-track' with one of the big four accountancy firms in the city, he linked up with Dale and Roger as an equal partner and, as it happened, things were looking pretty good. The two younger partners were ten years junior to Dale and still in their late thirties. Dale was ten years their senior and now in his late forties, with itchy feet.

Dale had always dreamed of building a property empire. However, the closest he had come was buying his flat over-looking the Regents Canal and investing in three other flats in the same block, in which he owned his swish apartment, with a fairly substantial mortgage. But life was good, apart from the tricky situation he found himself in, with his much younger and much demanding girlfriend, Samantha, whose sole goal in life was to marry and produce a child. In which order, she wasn't bothered, but time was slipping away from her, so for her, it was a now or never situation.

Dale was always on the lookout for those substantial unclaimed estates that would yield a good above average return. If he and his colleagues could find them, then perhaps locate a distant relative, unbeknownst to them, that *was* a distant relative, then with a bit of jiggery-pokery, create a believable ancestral bloodline that they bought into, then they could sign them up as such and then yes, 'we're in the money'. It was then just a case of a brown envelope to their 'friendly manager' at the Probate and Wills Office to nod and sign off the estate to the new owner or the person who claimed to be the owner of the said estate, proven only by the heir hunters corroborating paperwork, substantiating and endorsing the claim. Couldn't do it too often, but every now and again it contributed cash into his and his two partners' holiday fund. Afterall, it otherwise would only go into the Treasury coffers and who would benefit there.

Having had his head down all morning, Dale decided he would visit his next-door neighbours, well actually just Jan, who he 'fancied the pants off'. Unfortunately, this was just a fantasy for him, forever searching for happiness. It was always nice to have a chat with Jan, to relieve the pressures of the morning, and besides that, Jan was a pretty face to gaze upon and she always cheered him up. She was quite petite and nicely shaped, she was always well presented as a business woman, favouring smart blouses under well pressed suits. Her skirt was invariably shorter than it should be, but Phil always complimented her on what he thought was a nice shapely pair of pins. Dale also liked the way she wore her rich chestnut hair in a bob which showed off the large earrings she always deemed to wear. He often wished that he'd beaten Phil to the base and met her first, but alas, it wasn't to be. Two marriages later and here he was at nearly fifty with a demanding thirty-two-year-old girlfriend, the envy of all his pals, but she was wearing him out and he was really feeling the pressure.

Business was no problem, they were getting their fair share of wills to chase and signing up plenty of clients. They seemed quicker off the mark than most of their competitors and his two partners, pals from their previous business of Estate Agency, all pulled their weight. They were a bit smarter than their competitors. Having a London base enabled them to send a runner to camp out at the Bona-Vacantia, Government Legal Department every day, and pick and choose what looked like the best unclaimed estates to prospect from the regular release of wills published as unclaimed.

In that respect business was good, income was good, life was good, but this girl was driving him mad. Although he wasn't a bad looking chap himself and turned a few heads in his time, and still turned the occasional one or two, he was still flattered when this good-looking girl he met at 'Stringfellows' Night Club showed some interest in him. Yes, she was a catch, and yes, he was definitely punching above his weight, and yes, it was great to be able to show off and have such a looker on your arm for all your mates to admire. Tall, almost statuesque, natural blonde, smart dresser, partner in a local solicitors practise, own money, own flat. Christ, what more could you want. Well, you wouldn't, would you, but the constant demand for sex and her need to have a baby with someone, and her mentioning marriage at every opportunity, morning, noon and night, was exhausting, it was all getting too much, just much too much. He'd done it twice before and swore that he would never do it again. Time to bail-out. If only he could pluck up the courage. At heart, he was just a coward and he knew it. But Jan would sort this out for him. She was a shoulder to cry on, an ear to bend, a nice hug, and Jan who always smelled so sweetly, he knew that she would talk to him and help relieve him of the pain of another bust up. Dale made his excuses to his two partners in their large open office and left his desk for next door, just along the landing.

Camden Estates Property Management

Phil Phillips was a studious, committed hard worker, sometimes lacking in fire or flare, but Jan made up for that in bucket-loads. Phil was a stocky five foot ten and at forty-eight, used to play rugby in his younger days, but now a bit stodgy and nothing like as quick as he was. He was frustrated, sometimes distraught, that he was seeing his hairline receding faster than he would like, showing more forehead than he was happy with, with his once blond hair, now thinning and drawn backwards to try and cover his balding patch. It was a misnomer that his eyebrows were still a dark blond colour, sitting over his watchful brown eyes, as was his neatly trimmed beard. But his smile when he did deem to smile, which wasn't often nowadays, could light up the room and it would remind Jan of the early days when they first met. She often cast her mind back to when she screamed on the touchline for her handsome young man sporting the number 15 fullback's shirt, with his broad chest and his muscular legs. Saturday nights at the club after a winning match were to be remembered in the dim and distant past with much affection. Sunday's relaxing, with Jan massaging Phil's muscular body, were to be cherished, leading to long-gone feats of sexual magic, which were also now a dim and distant memory.

The first sight they had of each other was at a Young Conservatives Dinner Dance, which they had attended both under protest against their respective parents, but in the event enjoyed the evening as they had met, and it seemed to have worked well ever since. Though the last few years had seen the lustre wear off a little. Jan had inherited her father's property rental business and the business that Phil and Jan had built up over the past twenty years was to be admired. By comparison, Jan was still a pretty thing, still able to turn heads, though not as many as she used to, at five foot two, rich chestnut bob and clear blue eyes. Still full of life, though the tedium of the workplace was beginning to tire her. She was without doubt the driver of the business and her pretty looks were certainly an asset when it came to negotiating with the men who dominated their client base.

Some of the corporate clients they had built up were to be envied. Four banks entrusted them to look after their properties, both locally and in the City, used for senior employees and visiting staff from overseas branches. This was great steady income with regular changeovers, so a maintenance charge each time and a new inventory. The accounts department of each bank just paid each invoice as they presented it; there was never ever a query, after all, it was only bank money. They were very wealthy operators and the invoices that Camden Estates presented were fairly modest by comparison to the invoices they received every day.

Jan and Phil enjoyed their business, but Jan, more and more, was finding the journeys into London progressively monotonous and soul-destroying. Tourists from all over the globe seemed to have discovered Camden Lock and even getting into their private parking spaces was a challenge. They had gotten to the stage where it was easier to take a cab to visit a client in the city or even out in the provinces, than to take their own car. Inevitably, on a regular basis, the entrance to their small car park would be blocked by a rogue parked vehicle, invariably leading to a fracas. Jan really was fed up with it. Even the journeys home were becoming more and more of a nightmare as the city and all the arterial roads became jammed up every time there was some sort of transportation strike. By the time they arrived home after the long slog, often an hour and a half and sometimes two hours later, Jan was too tired to cook so it was yet another 'chuck it in the oven' tinfoil or tray-bake meal.

The morning had gone by quite quickly, as always, and there were several changeovers today. The cleaning girls were in and out collecting instructions and keys. Their full time decorators, Paul and Dawn, a husband and wife team, had also been in to collect a different set of keys to be able to do a quick tidy up before the cleaners went in the following day. As the office cleared, the door opened and in popped Dale Scott from next door. *Probably in for some more sympathy,* Phil thought. As Dale entered, Phil, who felt quite inadequate in Dale's company, called out across the office, "Jan, I'm just out to the bank, won't be long."

Dale walked through the open plan office with three girls all tapping away and chatting at the same time. He tucked his way into the seclusion of Jan's separated office, she kissed him on the cheek and he gave her a hug, which lasted as long as he could make it last, and then slumped into the armchair tucked into the corner. Jan cheerily, but cheekily chastised him. "Well Dale, as if I didn't know what you want. Well, no more sympathy from me, I've told you what I think about your situation, you're digging a big hole for yourself. If this girl has your baby you are committed, and if it doesn't work out, I hate to say it but I doubt it will, the age difference is too great, then you are going to be paying for this child for the next, probably, twenty years, 'til you're in your seventies."

Jan stopped and took a deep breath and bared her teeth with a wide grin.

Dale piped up. "Ah Jan, you lovely creature, you're just like my mum, looking after me, and I appreciate that you are of course quite right and I came to tell you that I've heeded your advice and I shall be sorting the situation with Samantha tonight. However, that's not why I came to see you. Apart from to gaze on your loveliness—" Jan waved a finger at Dale suggesting he gets on with what he wanted to say, "I have a proposition for you. Now, I know your dad's name was Morris, so I guess that this was your maiden-name, and by coincidence there's an estate come up in Cumbria that we've been working on for several weeks with the same name, which is what prompted me to talk to you. My team and I have pretty much exhausted all our leads. It's not exactly an uncommon name, so the time spent in researching that name has been an enormous uphill struggle. In other words, we can't find any living relatives who might have a potential stake in this will. We have been around and around in circles. There is no-one. So, if we cannot find anyone to claim the estate, this reverts back to HM Treasury, and frankly, after all the work we've put in, not to get something out of that would be not only a tragedy, but a travesty. All that work and the estate goes into the Crown or The Treasury.

"But then I got to thinking. As you bear the same family name, we might be able to tweak your ancestry to show that you are distantly related to the deceased members of that estate and therefore can put in a claim. We are coming up to the twelve-year deadline for claims, I only discovered this after it had escaped the usual press announcements searching for relatives. It's ten years old, so to keep the claim alive, I would propose to create a family tree for you and tie this in with this estate which is currently intestate and with the Government Legal Department, or as it's known Bona-Vacantia. There, that's what I came to say. What do you think of that as a proposal?"

Jan had listened quietly to Dale's soliloquy and pondered the complexities. She cross-questioned him, "Woah, blimey Dale, that sounds like a helluva plan, but would this not be a case of defrauding the Crown, or The Treasury, of funds that were due to them?"

Dale replied, "Mmm, well technically yes, but if some distant relative finally turned up, then the estate would have gone to them anyway. There's not that much difference and the Treasury still get their dues in the form of death duties, which would be a big chunk of this estate. You wouldn't have to do anything. I can research your family and create a link, so far back, that even the best sleuth amongst the heir hunters would struggle not to find this as a valid claim. We have once or twice presented cases that were border line and tied up the estate for very distant families. The Legal Department of the Treasury tend to trust us heir hunters as we do a fairly thorough job on their behalf. It works!"

Jan replied hesitantly, "Ooh Dale, it sounds like a great idea, but I have reservations, it sounds far too dodgy to me. I wouldn't want to get into any trouble. Why don't I speak to Phil about it and come back to you?"

At that, Dale gave Jan another hug and took in her perfume. "Do you know what Jan, let's just keep this between you and me for the time being and I'll work on an ancestry family bloodline for you. In which case we could present a 'fait-accompli' to Phil, as if it were the genuine thing. Also, if there were any queries from wherever, which I don't think there would be, then you can blame it on me as your heir hunter, who got it wrong. That makes it risk free for you. What could be simpler? Now does that sound like a better proposition, go on tell me honestly, what do you think? And just for a bit of fun, if you give me a saliva sample, I'll send away a DNA test and see exactly where your family tree is extended to. I already have mine. I did it some years ago and I'm 'so English' it's not true."

"Mmmm Dale, it sounds like a bit of a plan, you obviously have such a cryptic mind, you could probably pull it off, but I am nervous. Why don't you create a family tree for me and show me how it would work and then I'll give it a bit more thought? Though I would be fascinated in a DNA test. Yes please, let's do that, thank you."

Dale smiled. "Promise me you'll seriously think about it. Also consider that this estate has around a hundred and twenty-three acres, possibly more. According to some old plans that I have managed to find, it has an old tumbledown house on it and has a stream running through it, large woods and has enormous potential. And, Jan, as far as Samantha is concerned, I will deal with that tonight, I promise. Don't forget, just think about it, we don't have much time. See you soon."

Dale left Jan's offices quite elated at the prospect of tying up something as large as this estate, and in Jan's name. As he took the short walk along the corridor to his office, his world was turning nicely, as it should. The sun was shining, the birds were singing, he could see folks chugging along the canal in their hire craft, trying to avoid canoeists and rowers. Office workers, hikers, mums with kids in prams, were enjoying walking the towpath, the world was turning nicely. *As it should*, he thought. He was a happy man. Not just contented, but more than that he felt elated and quite excited.

***

On his return from the bank, Phil seemed anxious and a little tentative. He sat at Jan's desk opposite her, to voice his concerns at the dialogue that he had just had at the bank.

"Jan, I don't know whether this is good or bad news. There is a new regional director, who has been looking at all contracts the bank has with small companies. They say that they have been approached by a much larger management company, who are prepared to halve the fees that they are paying us, for 'like for like' services. This also fits into their structure of less small accounts and more larger companies. Apparently, the new company are only interested in building up their management portfolio. They want us to contract to carry out all of our usual reports, inventories, decorating and all of the other jobs we undertake as well as adding their account to *our* portfolio. That actually means that we lose maybe twenty percent of our fee income from bank rentals, but gain possibly forty percent on add-ons, which as you know is where we make most of our money. Unfortunately, this wasn't a negotiation from our angle, it was presented as a fait-accompli, so I pretty much had to say thank you. There was not much more I could say as our contract with the bank expired many weeks ago.

The new management company, The London Real Estate Company Ltd, will send us their contract in the next few days. So, I am trying to put a positive on it, and treat it as it's sort of good news. We shall have to see."

Jan's day came and went. It was yet another hectic day, and she hadn't even had time to nip out to the Tesco Metro, just up the road past the lock gates, to pick up something for supper. Here they were again, having just had a screaming match, which almost came to blows, as Phil tried to clear the gates to their private parking by some lazy, inconsiderate tourist parked illegally, right outside their premises. And here they were as usual, jockeying for position in the outgoing traffic, 'snailing' along, trying to leave the metropolis. She was gripping the wheel as if her life depended on it and getting angrier by the minute.

"Don't start again," Phil rebuked.

As Jan grew more frustrated, she thought about the unclaimed estate with the tumbledown that Dale had spoken about. One hundred and whatever acres in deepest darkest Cumbria, an old house to be renovated and even a stream running through the property. *Oh bliss*, she thought. *Absolute heaven, peace and quiet at last.* Her thoughts were broken by the anxious bells of an approaching fire engine, coming from behind her. Miraculously, the dead-locked traffic parted, leaving a clear path for the big red beast that was in a hurry, to get to its destination. As soon as it had passed, all the traffic filled the space (like the miracle of the children of Israel having passed through the 'parting of the waves'), then it was back to gridlock and misery. She thought deeply about the conversation that she had with Dale but otherwise didn't mention it as she thought Phil would object somehow. Maybe she would chat again with Dale tomorrow evening when Phil had gone to his Ex-Round Table, Forty-One Club meeting at the Holiday Inn as he does every Tuesday just up the road. *I guess it suits me, as he thinks it gives me a chance to catch up on a few hours of paperwork. Actually, I guess it's a bit sneaky not telling him that I go out occasionally for a few drinks with my old girlfriends. It's just nice to do now and again, and it takes away some of the boredom, having a few drinks and a couple of laughs with your mates. I guess I can't really tell Phil, he takes everything so personally, I think he might be quite upset if I told him. Keep it to myself then, yes, but I might just give Dale a call and chat through this plan he has about this estate in Cumbria, or*

11

wherever he said it was. Wow, some dream, a hundred and whatever acres.

Yes, why not... I'll phone Dale. Jan closed her office door and phoned Dale.

"Good afternoon, UK Heir Hunters," Dale answered.

"Dale, it's me, Jan. The more I think about it, the more I am intrigued by your proposal or at least the conversation we had about that estate in Cumbria. Phil attends his Forty-One Club meetings on a Tuesday evening, so would that be a good time to chat? I could come to your place or would you like to meet in my office? It's fairly quiet here, I don't mind either way?"

Dale was pleased that Jan had obviously thought about the proposition and that he'd received a positive response. "Hi Jan, well yes, but come to mine, you've been here before and it's only another flight up and you'll like the views. I can see for miles along the canals either way and if the weather is as nice as today, we can sit out on my veranda and chat."

"Okay, that's a date then, I'll wait until Phil has left the office. That's usually around six when he goes off and meets up with his people, I think it's just an excuse to have a couple of drinks, though in fairness they do raise a lot of money for charity. Okay then, I'll come to you. I'll bring a sandwich."

"No Jan, don't bring a sandwich, I'll cook. Are you okay with salmon or chicken, in say a cream sauce, no allergies? ...And I've got plenty of wine here, so no need to bring a bottle."

"Right Dale, must go, see you tomorrow evening. I don't need to remind you *not* to tell Phil about your plot. He won't like it. I'll have to break it to him gently or I won't be able to get him on board. For better or for worse he's far too honest for his own good. See you tomorrow evening then. Bye." At that, Jan replaced the receiver, quietly excited at the prospect of potentially 'inheriting' a hundred-odd acres in the wilds of Cumbria and a house to do up. This was what she had been dreaming about for many months, if not years, and here it was, almost a possibility.

***

Tuesday went by slowly. Jan kept falling into a daydream and Phil kept asking what was wrong with her, she wasn't herself today. She'd just keep saying, "I'm fine, you carry on with what you're doing, I'm fine." The day kept dragging until she looked up at Phil who announced that it was five thirty and he was off to his Fort-

One Club, back for about ten, same as usual. He left with his usual goodbyes, telling her to have a nice evening and not to do anything he wouldn't do.

Well, what's that Phil? thought Jan. *There's not a lot you* would *do.* Jan was beginning to think that there were other things out in this wide, wide world. *Phil is getting monotonously boring. Time for a change,* she thought to herself. *No Jan, don't be ridiculous, grow up, you're nearly fifty for goodness-sake. You've got your twenty-fifth wedding anniversary coming up soon, stop dreaming.* At that, she looked up at the clock and it was finally 6pm.

CHAPTER 2

Dale was looking forward to having Jan on his own for a few hours, just to chat to and enjoy her company. They had been business neighbours for over ten years now and they had struck up a mutual friendship and an admiration for each other almost immediately.

Jan thought Dale was a nice-looking chap and had a very easy manner, warm and almost charismatic. He was friendly with everyone, had a great smile which showed a very expensive, much cared for, set of sparkling white teeth. He was probably the direct opposite of her husband who tended to keep himself to himself. Dale had a big personality and yes, she supposed in another life, she could fancy him. Dale was much like Jan who also loved people, but had found that many of the friends that they had, had dwindled away because of their commitment to their business and never being able to get away. Even weekends, when they thought that they could relax, there often seemed to be a crisis. And, who looks after crises when there is a problem, well the owner of that business of course and that was them, so their work-life balance was all out of kilter.

Jan knocked on Dale's front door. He called out, "It's open, come on in."

It was some years since she and Phil had visited Dale's flat, looking back she was remembering it must have been when Dale first moved in almost ten years ago. Wow, it looked different. Long gone were the small rooms off the entrance hall. It had been transformed into one large open space with huge sliding doors opening on to a veranda, decorated with foliage in the form of yuccas, aloe-vera and palms, even a banana tree bearing little green buds which might have been young bananas, who knows.

"Come in, come in. What do you think?"

Jan *was* impressed with the remarkable upgrade on his flat, it certainly had that 'wow factor', the type of place that made you feel good just to be enjoying this sort of space. She had made the effort as she always did to look good and Dale *was* impressed with her. He felt a missed heartbeat, a sudden flushing of his cheeks and a bead of sweat run down his back, even a stirring down below. My, she looked good. But they were here to discuss business. One hundred and twenty-three acres of business. Dale offered a drink.

"Red or a dry white, I've got a nice Merlot or some dry Sauvignon Blanc or I've got some Rosé in the fridge, or I can do a G&T, whatever you fancy."

Jan settled for a large glass of dry Sauvignon Blanc. Their conversation drifted into life's challenges and life's regrets and what they would do if they could start all over again. This of course was an ideal opener for Dale to chat through his plan to take on the inheritance claim of 'going for begging' hundred and sixty acres in Cumbria. He asked Jan to sit at the table that he had laid. He had already prepared a simple tossed green salad and the white marble table had been simply laid with the minimum of cutlery. Dale offered Jan a seat. He returned from the kitchen area with two plated deep pasta bowls, set with two chicken breast's stuffed with a mushroom duxelles, lightly masked with a mushroom, cream and tarragon sauce, sat on poached tagliatelle. "Hey, voila!"

Jan was further impressed and playfully remarked, "My, my, Dale. Are there no end to your talents? Maybe next time I think about getting married, I might just put you on my list. Mind you, you're going to have to compete with George Clooney and Brad Pitt. Now let's get down to it, and before you make any lewd comments you might regret, I am talking about your girlfriend. Have you done the deed?"

Dale answered triumphantly, "Yes Jan, I have. I told her last night that this was the end and that I wasn't prepared to be the donor to the child she so desperately seeks. She seemed to realise that I wasn't prepared to negotiate and she left last night, slamming the door behind her, breaking my lovely Lalique vase on the way out, as the slamming of the door vibrated the display shelf. But that's a small price to pay. I can live with that. So yes, thanks to your advice, I finally did the deed and my, it's a relief. I do feel a bit sorry for her, she is getting pretty desperate and I think that she might just settle for any port in a storm. There's some poor fella out there that is going to be dragged into her net. But, thank God, it's not me."

Jan's phone rang but she'd missed the call. She briefly listened to Phil's voicemail, letting her know he'd taken a room at the hotel.

Jan then responded to Dale, "Well young man, so you're saying that this is it for you for the rest of your life, a committed bachelor, I'm not so sure. I think you're the type that needs a good woman to keep you in order. And yes, to your earlier question, I would like another glass of wine and make it a large one."

***

"*That* Dale, was a very nice meal, I feel pampered and I haven't felt like that for a long, long time. I'm just beginning to relax – I think I'll flop on your comfortable sofa. Now tell me more about my inheritance, you know that big ol' place up in Cumberland or wherever you said it was."

Dale explained again how his company UK Heir Hunters worked, and that he and his team at the office would begin tomorrow on researching Jan's ancestry. They had already researched the Morris family tree on the Bona-Vacantia listing at the Government Legal site for unclaimed or 'intestate' wills, and were at a dead end. What he now needed to do was take as much information from Jan about her father's side of the family as this was the bloodline that they needed to research. Then Dale could create a link or a connection, an association between the two families as if they were one.

Jan had certainly had more to drink than she was used to and she stood up to be able to make her way over to the sofa. As she stood up, so did Dale and they stood face to face, she just trying to control her focus, he trying to control his ever increasing need to put his arms around her. Jan, (almost like a leaning tower of Pisa) slowly leant towards him until their foreheads were touching, just slightly. He was taking in Jan's lovely perfume and her sparkling eyes, the way her lip was turning into an inviting smile. She could feel his warm breath on her face and that heady aroma of a rich wine on his lips. They leaned together, their lips touched, his hands cupped her cheeks and they kissed (a full-blooded French kiss). She put her arms around his waist and pulled him closer. She could feel his body against hers, but she was married

17

and she couldn't do this.

She broke away. "Oh, Dale, that was very nice but you know I'm a married woman and apart from once before, a very long time ago, I couldn't cheat on Phil, it would hurt him so. Let's stay friends and if anything ever changes, you'll be the first to know."

Dale pulled away and the moment, no matter how lovely it was, had gone and he accepted that. Jan, now feeling a little light headed, realised she was not up to getting into her car.

"I don't think that I'm in a fit state to drive, so I am going to have to book a room in the Holiday Inn just down the road, I don't think I could drive home in this state. I'll ring now, Phil left a message to say he has taken a room, so I can stay with him." Jan found the number and dialled the hotel. She spoke to a girl on reception.

"Unfortunately, we can't locate a 'Mr Phillips' on our guest register, are you sure you have the right name? Perhaps he booked under another name?" asked the well-spoken young lady.

"No, there's no other name under which he would have booked. It is the right name – it's my husband, and you say it's not under our business name either?"

"No, unfortunately not."

"Okay, don't worry about it. I'll just have a single for tonight please and I'll be there in about a half an hour."

"I'm so sorry madam, but we really are fully booked, so I'm awfully sorry we can't help. Have you tried the—" Jan cut the call short, a little bemused.

Dale commented, "Jan that's crazy, if they can't give you a room, I have a spare room which has its own bathroom, so it's no problem, you can stay here. I'm sure one night won't hurt."

Jan rang Phil's mobile but it went straight to answerphone. She listened again to the message that he'd left earlier for her. The whimpering giggle in the background was niggling her. Maybe he made the message when he was in one of the public areas? She dismissed it without a second thought; she was in far too good of a mood to let a message upset her evening.

Holiday Inn

Phil had sat at the bar having just received a text from the chairman of his Forty-One Club, and in view of the recent sudden demise of one of their members, it was with great regret that he was cancelling the meeting. Phil sat on a stool at the bar pondering whether to give Jan a call or just sit and have a quiet evening on his own, a glass of wine, and a burger and chips. He sat there for ten minutes trying to decide what to do when he spotted Dale's ex, Samantha, coming in to the bar, though he didn't know then that she *was* his ex. She greeted him.

"Oh, hi Phil, didn't expect to see you in here. Where's Jan?"

"Ah," Phil replied. "Well, this is the evening for my Forty-One Club. We meet here every Tuesday, have a chat and a drink and organise meetings and charity things. I'm sure you know the sort of thing, no doubt you'll have done similar things in your time. But thanks for asking, Jan's fine, well as fine as she can be, if you know what I mean. Tuesdays are my evenings off, so Jan often stays at the office catching up on paperwork and though she doesn't think I know, I do know that she goes out for a drink with some of her pals occasionally. Who knows, it might be a fella, I think it may well be a bloke – we haven't been close for quite a while. She's taken to sleeping in a different room, saying she's too tired; it's a bit frustrating. But I'm sort of happy, it's nice to have an evening off once a week.

"Unfortunately, my meeting has been cancelled and as I phoned Jan, who didn't answer, she could be off with her fella, or some of her girlfriends, who knows. I guess I'm at a bit of a loose end. Can I offer you a drink?"

Samantha gratefully accepted Phil's kind offer. "That's kind of you Phil, a G&T would be very nice, thank you. Slice of lemon, no ice."

The barman served up a large G&T and Phil swiped his credit card in payment. Phil continued the conversation. "So, is Dale with you? What brings you to the Holiday Inn this evening?"

Samantha answered, a little emotionally, "Dale isn't here. We broke up last night and he was quite firm and said he didn't want to see me again. He insisted that I move out of his flat yesterday. So, I have the decorators in at my flat and I've taken a room here for a couple of nights. It's very nice and it isn't that far from where I have my office. I really thought Dale was the one, you know. But he turned out to be a selfish ignorant pig, like some of my other beaus. I'm very upset as my time clock is running out and we had

19

been trying for a baby and I really would like a baby before I'm very much older or I'm too old to cope. At this rate, I'll have to have a donor!"

She stopped and paused and started to shed tears which trickled down her face. She searched for a handkerchief. Phil was quick to offer his packet of tissues from his jacket pocket out of sympathy and his arms around her. It was a long time since he'd had his arms around so soft and lovely a creature and although Samantha was maybe ten or who knows, even fifteen years his junior, it didn't seem wrong. In fact, it felt very nice and he was getting as much out of comforting her as he was enjoying the warmth of her body close to his.

She spoke in appreciation. "Oh Phil, thank you for your sympathy, I didn't mean to burden you. I don't like to be such a wimp but I did need a shoulder to cry on and I feel much better having told someone of my woes. Thank you so much, you're such a lovely man."

"Let's have another drink and maybe we can share some supper and drown our sorrows together. I'd like that if you would?" Phil was more than happy to help, so his offer of supper wasn't hard to refuse.

They walked towards the restaurant along a wide carpeted corridor at the end of which was an impressive atrium, full of foliage. It even had a full-sized palm tree, hung with a glass ceiling and glass on either side, lining the walkway between the main reception, lifts and restaurant area. Samantha linked her arm in Phil's. It felt comfortable for both of them. The waiter guided them to a table and Phil ordered a bottle of Rioja, one of his favourite reds, without thinking to ask Samantha. She was more than happy that Phil had taken control, and was pleased and very grateful for Phil's easy company. She was already feeling much less distraught.

They chatted and enjoyed their meal and more than that they enjoyed each other's company. Phil ordered another bottle of Rioja, as the last one seemed to have evaporated, so he ordered a third. By ten o'clock, they were both getting very giggly and very happy. When Mantha, Smartha, Sam, Samantha, whatever, suggested that they finish the last bottle of red in her room, to Phil it seemed like the natural thing to do. 'Ah sod it, why not?' They giggled their way across to the lift, doing their best to walk in a straight line, amusing other guests who observed the tipsy couple. The lift dropped them off at the third floor and they giggled their way along to room 3008, thankfully not too far from the lift. Sam fumbled for the room card in her bag and eventually opened the door. The soft folds of the bed beckoned and they fell onto it. Fortunately for him, he thought he was awake enough to phone Jan and let her know that he'd had too much to drink with the chaps, as it was one of their birthdays and it was Champagne all-round, so he was going to take a room and stay for the night and that she should drive home. Also, could she please bring a clean shirt and clothes for tomorrow along with his electric razor.

When Jan rang Phil to enquire what room he was in as she thought she would stay the night also, 'as it was getting late and she'd done enough paperwork for tonight to sink a battleship', Phil's phone rang, but he didn't hear it.

The pair had fallen into a semi-drunken slumber and had crawled under the bedcovers. Phil woke about an hour later and gazed down on Sammy's half-dressed body. She'd removed her skirt and blouse and was left in just her pretty pink underwear. He couldn't remember having done it, but he had removed his trousers, though his crumpled shirt was still half buttoned and on his chest. He turned towards her and gently kissed her neck. She was still in a half-daze but awake enough to put her arms around him. They kissed and she unbuttoned, then removed, his shirt.

***

Dale showed Jan into the spare bedroom. It was as beautifully decorated as the rest of the apartment. He returned with a spare shirt for Jan to sleep in. There were plenty of fresh towels in the en-suite bathroom. Dale stood just inside the bedroom door and they embraced for what seemed like several minutes, until Dale kissed Jan on the forehead and wished her a good night's sleep, saying that if she needed anything in the night, just to help herself.

Dale and Jan said goodnight and closed their respective bedroom doors.

***

Samantha was enjoying the warmth of Phil's body beside her. He was awakening her senses and she was starting to respond. Maybe this was meant to be? She turned to face him, they gave in to the inevitable and it was enjoyable for both of them for different reasons. The sheer excitement for him, the love and comfort she needed from him, or probably anyone, whatever or whoever it was, it was good, and they fell heavily asleep.

***

Jan awoke in the middle of the night. The telephone message that Phil had left her was niggling and irritating her, more than worrying her. She listened to Phil's message again and there was definitely what she could only describe to herself as a disguised, whimpering giggle in the background, and if he wasn't in his own room at the hotel, where was he? She tossed and turned for an hour or so and then quietly opened her bedroom door and tiptoed around the corner in the half-light. The slanting rays of the moon gilding the polished granite tiles on the kitchen floor. Her mouth was dry, she ran a half glass of water from the tap. She stared at the door to Dale's bedroom. She took a deep breath and exhaled. She opened the door, took two steps towards the bed. The room was bathed in moonlight, she carefully lifted the satin sheets to gaze momentarily on Dale's body and slipped in below the sheets, feeling his warm skin. She undid the oversized shirt he gave her to wear as a night gown and discarded it on the floor. He woke as if in a dream, a wonderful dream, with Jan centre stage, but she was here, here in his bed and pressing her warm body against his.

***

Phil's mobile rang at his usual time of 6am. Allowing the early morning routine of bathroom and a light breakfast, they then had to jump in the car and be on their way by seven to make the daily journey to Camden. Phil could feel his head pumping blood around his fragile brain, which was banging against the sides and the forefront of his head, trying to get out.

He turned over to bury his head in the pillow. *Shit!* The realisation hit him like a sledgehammer. *Oh my God, what have I done? How am I going to tell Jan? How can I get out of this, oh shit, I'm in big trouble here. Fuck, I'm in trouble.*

Samantha rolled over and looked adoringly at Phil, her wonderful lover. "Good morning, darling. My, my, you're a dark horse. Where did you learn to make love like that, it was wonderful. I can't remember when I enjoyed sex so much. Wow, they do say it's the quiet ones."

Phil was dumfounded, he could hardly remember a thing and

my oh my, how his head pounded.

"Oh God, Sam, what are we going to do? I daren't tell my wife, if she finds out she'll divorce me, things are already shaky. I need to get dressed and get into work. She knows I stayed at this hotel last night, or that's what I told her."

Sam responded affectionately. "Phil, it was a wonderful evening, I loved your company, it was a lovely experience, don't go regretting it. And why would you tell Jan? What she doesn't know won't hurt her. It was a rare and precious experience. You truly are a lovely man and a very good kind and caring lover. I can't remember the last time I felt so loved. I would do it again, any time. Thank you."

Phil stepped into the shower and while he was in there relaxing under the warm shower, letting the warm stream sooth and reduce, if not take away, his headache. Samantha was pressing his very crumpled shirt using the ironing board from the cupboard. He stepped naked out of the shower, wrapping a towel around his waist. Samantha gazed at the strong masculine shape of his body as he dried himself. They started to embrace and she pulled him back onto the warm bed. It was over in minutes and they both fell backwards on the bed, very satisfied. But Phil's guilt was growing like Pinocchio's nose as was his resolve to sort out his marriage with Jan. He quickly dressed and phoned Jan. Jan's phone went straight into voicemail. Phil left a message.

Jan, it's me. I'm going to have some breakfast with the chaps that stayed last night. We made a bit of a night of it, so I might be in a little late. I'm sure the girls at the office can hold the fort. See you later, bye, love you.'

***

Jan was just about to get into the shower when she heard her phone ring. She picked up Phil's message noting that he was going to be late in. She dropped her towel and stepped into the inviting warm shower.

Dale stood just inside the bathroom door watching Jan covering herself with shower gel, creating swirls of soapy bubbles on her body, streaming down her neck, breasts, tummy and legs. He stood there mesmerised and in wonder that she had made one of his desperate fantasies come true last night. In the early hours of the morning, when all things were quiet and still in the outside world, their two bodies had melted into each other and they fell asleep as onc. Oh, that it could happen again. Dale hoped that it wasn't a one-off fantasy.

Jan turned to see him standing there. She felt completely at ease, smiled, slid the shower door partially open and stretched out her arm to Dale. Dale let his dressing gown fall to the carpet and he stepped in. Jan wrapped her arms around him and he put his arms around her soapy, slippery, sweet-scented body. He felt the shape of her back, his fingers up and down her spine. They kissed, with the warm stream of water pouring across their melded bodies. It felt natural, it felt comfortable. She turned away from him. She reached for the top of the shower cubicle and bent her body slightly forward. He responded, warm and luxurious against her soapy body. It was over in little more than a couple of minutes and they turned and embraced. Jan finished showering and stepped out of the shower. Dale followed and they both sat at the kitchen bar, looking at each other and holding hands, she in one of Dale's silk dressing gowns, Dale in his towelling gown. They enjoyed their coffee and decided that this was a one-off. A wonderful one-off. Not to be repeated as far as Jan was concerned. She needed to re-assess her marriage to Phil and their whole lifestyle.

She picked up her mobile to speak to Phil, but it went to voicemail. She left a message. *'Phil, it's me. I was up very late last night and I'm very tired, so I won't be going in today. I'm taking the day off. I'll see you tonight when you get home. Bye.'*

Dale was pleased.

***

At the offices of Camden Estates, Jan and Phil saw the remainder of the week fly by. It was soon the weekend and then Monday again in Camden Lock.

Dale had worked hard on the 'Morris' family tree, tying Jan's bloodline into the Morris estate up in Cumbria. It took all of his skills, to not only create a bloodline that tied in with Jan's family, but he had to create birth and death certificates as well as marriage certificates for the invented brother. He was one of the last Morris's to have owned and worked the timber mill.

Today was Monday and he couldn't wait for Tuesday evening, when he would not only present his findings and 'creations' to Jan, but be able, he hoped, to revisit the evening and night of passion that they had enjoyed last week.

CHAPTER 3

Camden Estates Office

Monday morning both Jan and Phil seemed to have had a cloud removed from their shoulders. They were both thinking about the unplanned and very pleasant diversions that each of them had had last week, not feeling the least bit guilty, nor thinking about confessing to their respective partner. Why should they? Nothing had changed, it was just nice to know that they were still desired in some way or other, it was a good feeling. A very good feeling. In Jan's mind, she was waiting in anticipation of Phil letting her know that he was thinking of staying overnight at the Holiday Inn again. He suggested he might, as drinking with the lads, discussing football and golf and rugby, was quite refreshing, after their Forty-One Club meeting. It seemed to have given him a new spring in his step. Jan was more than happy to play to his need for a bit of bonding with his Forty-One Club pals, particularly as she had hinted to Dale that a second evening might be on for them on Tuesday, if he was up for it. Dale needed absolutely no encouragement at all. He was all for a repeat performance, with supper.

It was coming up 12.30pm, lunchtime and Jan was doing her best to stick to a trimming routine, if not a slimming routine, so decided to nip out to the Deli for a tub of pasta salad.

As she was leaving the office she called out, "Anything for you Phil?"

Phil replied enthusiastically, "Yes please, honey, I'll have whatever you're having. Thanks."

Blimey, Jan thought to herself. *Phil's happy, that's the first time he's called me 'honey' in as many years as I can remember. Long may it last. And in front of all the office staff as well. It's probably the fact that I've let him off the hook and let him spend Tuesday night with 'the boys'. Maybe he's looking forward to it, and that's what's cheered him up.* Jan replied enthusiastically, "Okay, Sweetheart."

Blimey, Phil thought to himself. *That's the first time she's called me that in as many years as I can remember. Long may it last. And in front of all the office staff as well.*

As Jan left the office for the Deli, Phil, who was sat in the glazed office within their open plan office, closed the door. He furtively looked out on the staff, working and chatting away, generally minding their own business, and dialled Samantha.

"Samantha, it's Phil. I had such a wonderful evening with you last week, I wondered whether you would like to repeat the evening, I mean a meal, and or a drink. You know, even supper and a bottle of wine perhaps?"

There was a silence of what seemed like hours to Phil. He thought he was having a panic attack when his heart started pounding like mad, and his blood pressure seemed to be increasing with every fraction of a second the delay continued, in anticipation of a positive answer.

Samantha eventually answered, "Oh, Phil." Then paused.

I've blown it, Phil thought.

"Oh Phil, yes, that would be lovely! I thought you'd forgotten about me and weren't going to ask again. So yes. Yes, I'd love to."

Phil was taken aback with the positive response from Samantha. But nervousness and a touch of guilt crept into his thoughts.

"Oh good. That's wonderful. Do you still have a room at the Holiday Inn, or shall I book something?"

"Yes, Phil, my flat will take a few more days to be finished. The decorators are re-tiling the bathrooms as we speak, so I still have the room at the Holiday Inn for a few more days. Shall we meet in the bar at say seven, as we did last time?"

Phil answered, in a slightly more relaxed tone as it looked as if his feelings were being returned, and with some joy. "Okay Sam, that would be lovely. I'm so looking forward to seeing you again. Tomorrow evening then, seven o'clock. Bye."

Phil, from sitting on the edge of his chair, let his tense body relax, and fall back into the leather, office chair. He let out a sigh of relief, coupled with a satisfaction that came from achieving what he might have considered a week ago as being totally outside the grounds of possibility. He hadn't felt so good in a very long time. He kept thinking how gorgeous she was, and that it wasn't a dream he'd had last week after the disappointment of the cancellation of his Forty-One Club meeting. *Cancel away all you like*, he thought as he sat back at his own desk in the open plan office. *I've got better things to do!*

Jan had always had the private space in the glazed office for spreading her books and ledgers, and to complete the various contracts and adhere to her own strict accounting procedures.

Jan breezed through the front office door. "Lunch up!" she announced. "As it's such a nice day, I'm going down to sit on the bench on the lock-side. Are you coming?"

As she re-opened the main door to exit, Phil answered, feeling just a little bit guilty and self-conscious. "No, I'm okay here out of the sun, thanks. See you later, have a nice lunch. Bye."

Maisie in the office, nibbling away at her Ryvita and having taken a rather large bite out of a crispy green apple, remarked to Betty, sat opposite, and in a whispered tone. "Blimey, they're being so nice to each other. Either they're getting a divorce, or they're both having affairs, and neither one nor the other knows about the other one, if you know what I mean!"

As she spoke she splashed chewed apple out of her mouth onto the computer screen, and then wiped it with a paper tissue, smearing marks across the screen and getting a rebuke from Betty. "You mucky pup!" Betty exclaimed. Then she remarked, "Maisie, do you know what, I think you could be right."

Jan walked along the canal path and sat down on one of the wooden memorial benches that were bolted to the towpath, set randomly along the line of the canal. Most of these were dedicated to some couple or other whose favourite pastime was to eat their lunch together by the locks and watch the world go by. The canal was exceptionally busy today as new canal boaters had started their week's holiday on the weekend and then headed straight for Camden Lock, with the regular boaters and tourists who were walking the canals. There were cyclists, walking and riding and just stood or sat watching narrow boats steer towards the locks, channelling their boats through the massive wooden gates and on to the next section of waterway. There were plenty of willing helpers closing and pushing open the heavy beams of the gates. The scene was full of colour, as the many narrowboat companies painted their craft and their logos in different hues of reds, blues, greens and yellows, and every colour under the sun. Some were decorated with jugs and bowls of flowers, and praying Buddhas sat on the roofs. Random crews were dressed in T-shirts and jeans, striped tops and shorts and all manner of colourful holiday gear. They were wearing deck shoes, trainers or boots, and there was even the odd one wearing a pair of short wellies painted with skull and crossbones.

Jan basked in the sun, a gentle breeze licking at the stray hair on her forehead. She brushed it to one side, picked her mobile phone up from her handbag and dialled Dale. Dale answered. He recognised the voice immediately.

"Jan, how lovely to hear your voice. Where are you? I guess from the background noise around you, you're on the 'cut' and not in the office?"

Jan replied, "Well spotted, detective Dale. Tomorrow evening Phil seems to be planning to stay over at the Holiday Inn again with some of his new drinking buddies that he seems to have collected last week after his Forty-One Club. So, I thought we might have a discussion about my 'inheritance'. Perhaps at yours again? What do you think?"

Dale responded with some enthusiasm, "Jan, I couldn't think of a better way to spend an evening. My favourite person, coupled with my favourite subject, and how her bloodline is going to make us a small fortune. What's the plan?"

"Well, Phil usually goes off for his meeting around six thirty, so I'll be knocking on your door just after that. If that's okay with you?"

"Oh, Jan. I can't wait. Are you staying again?"

"Mmm. Maybe, perhaps, but only if you're a good boy! Must go now. See you tomorrow evening."

Jan rang off and Dale pressed the button on his mobile and disconnected the call. He adjusted his trousers that had been marginally somewhat aroused while talking to Jan and remembering last Tuesday evening, when she had come to him unexpectedly half way through the night. He sat in his office chair, hands behind his neck supporting his head and swinging back and forth feeling very good about everything, and in particular, his romance with Jan. Even if it were to be only brief, it was something he had dreamed of, and fantasised about, for years, almost ever since they first became business neighbours. His mission now was to create a platform to be able to add Jan's forebears to an ancestry bloodline which showed that she had a distant connection to the Morris estate that he had worked solidly on for several months and got absolutely nowhere with.

The twelve-year rule was coming to its conclusive end-date. It was frustrating that this had been missed by Bona-Vacantia listing and he had only had the files for less than two years and time was fast running out to be able to claim this estate for someone... anyone. So the next couple of weeks were both crucial and critical. He had more or less a month to create a bloodline, to key this into the Morris estate and to place a claim for the descendants of the Morris family. It was a happy and fortuitous co-incidence that Jan had the family name of Morris and that they had a certain connection with each other. Dale thought to himself that he could steal Jan away from that boring-arsed husband of hers. But then he thought, in all fairness, he was quite a nice bloke and he really shouldn't be thinking like that. *But then, who was it that said 'all is fair in love and war'? Was it from Don Quixote, do I remember from what little schooling I did? Whatever, first things first,* Dale thought. *Bloodline. Family tree. Connect my lovely Jan Morris to the Morris estate.*

As soon as he had put the phone down, he pulled out all the Morris estate files again, bloodlines, tracks, ancestry, documents, old photos, newspaper articles. When he had spread everything that he had acquired on the estate, he realised that there really wasn't that much to trace, but nevertheless, trace is what he started to do, in earnest. This was a big one and was very important. Not only that, probably the most exciting one he had ever worked on, given that there might be an outcome, never previously foreseen, with him and Jan in the centre picture, centre stage so to speak. *Just maybe,* he thought, *if I can pull this off, Jan will jump on to my white charger and we can ride off into the sunset, as in the movies.*

Then he rebuked himself for being so ridiculously romantic. *Wake up, son! Get a grip, just get the job done and stop fantasising!* He steeled himself to get on with the job in hand. He wanted to get some sort of proposal ready to present to Jan on his desk before tomorrow evening, when they were due to meet up.

***

Jan returned to her office having enjoyed a relaxing hour, she delivered a pasta salad to Phil. She then sat watching the amusing organised chaos on the canals, out across the road and through their windows, with boats coming and going through the locks, either down the Regents Canal headed east for the Islington Tunnel and on to Limehouse Basin and the Thames junction. Or, they were headed out westwards, towards the Maida Hill Tunnel and on to Little Venice and the Grand Union. This route connected almost all of the UK with its complexity of canals and river networks.

She couldn't relax, she seemed to be in a dream for the rest of the day, thinking about the conversation she had had with Dale and remembering the night of, more 'romance' than 'passion'. *Though the passion was pretty good,* she vividly remembered. Mmm, made her stir, with anticipation. She carried on her working day in a sugar-coated cloud, like candy-floss all around her, licking her dry lips every so often when she thought of Dale.

Phil worked his way through the tenants list and made notes of the shorthold tenancy agreements that needed renewing, while he picked away at his salad, not really interested in the food. Every few minutes he would find his thoughts drifting towards Samantha. At the same time, he was agitated about the meeting he had had with the bank's estate department. He was pondering what the final outcome might be, working with this new company, The London Real Estate Company, that the bank had transferred all of their substantial property and rental contracts to, which were formerly with their company, Camden Estates. He viewed this as a potential set back, given that the business set up by Jan's father twenty-odd years ago, was now playing second fiddle to another business, who had taken over a major part of their portfolio. He was disappointed but it was presented to him as a fait accompli. Unless he wanted to get into legalise and potentially litigate, which was frayed with unretractable cost and potentially unsurmountable challenges, then he had to accept the fact that, even though nothing had changed that much, they were now a minor player as far as the bank was concerned. They needed to make choices of where to take their business next. But they would definitely have to make that choice when it came to it. They daren't procrastinate for fear of the whole thing collapsing in a heap around them. He needed to have a meeting with Jan together with their accountant as well as their solicitor to clarify where they were in the career of the business. That was for another day. Meantime, his mind kept drifting towards Samantha. That beautiful soft-bodied creature that had made him feel so good. This lovely girl with the long angular frame that reminded him, as she glided along, of the movements of the most graceful giraffe, with those massive eyelashes, long legs and long elegant neck. *Why does this beautiful woman want to spend time with me*, he kept asking himself. *Oh joy. I have never been stirred like this before.* He adjusted himself in his seat, looking at the office clock which seemed to take hours, just to turn a few minutes. He was desperate for the day to end so that the new day and evening would start. Tuesday evening, a whole twenty-four hours away.

***

Samantha had been pleased that Phil had been in touch. He was such a nice man. No pretentions, no airs and graces, just a nice, kind, down to earth man, but with a very sensitive nature. Why hadn't she found someone like this before, instead of having endless bumptious, show-offs, who think they are all 'God's gift' to women. So much misery and heartache and then the highs and lows of meeting new men, boyfriends, potential suitors. Most of the time, they just want your body. They're all shallow. 'I'm really getting too old for this,' she told herself. *I just want to settle down with a nice man that loves me and with my baby, well 'our' baby, though frankly, if the man doesn't stay, I don't care. I just want my own baby, someone that I can love and will always be with me.* She sighed and went into a daydream at her desk until the daydream was broken by one of her legal colleagues calling out to her.

"Samantha, can you hand me the 'Simons' file please, we need to see if this is a bona-fide litigation claim, before we advise our client. Thank you."

Sam peered out of the window and viewed the crowds circulating around Kings Cross and St. Pancras Stations. So many people, like ants, or a swarm of bees over a honey pot, back and forth, back and forth, to and fro, to and fro, going about their business. Happy, sad, rich, poor, busy, broke, in love, lonely, travelling, living, dying, having babies, having families. *Which one of those am I?* she asked herself. *So many folks*, she thought. *But I have tomorrow evening and that lovely man to look forward to.*

She viewed the clock. It was five-thirty. She called out to that same colleague. "Tristan, I've had enough for today, I'm off. I'll see you tomorrow. Good night."

At that announcement, she picked up her bag and scarf and left the office, hailing a cab to Regent Street, in pursuit of some comfort shopping. Some fancy underwear and a couple of sexy nighties might be nice, in anticipation of a passionate evening with Phil.

CHAPTER 4

2020, UK Heir Hunters
Dale's notes

At the offices of UK Heir Hunters in Camden Lock, Dale had the Morris estate files spread across the large platform-desk. He tapped away at his ancestry records and came up with nothing other than the end of the line for Samuel Abrahams, followed by the Morris brothers Benjamin and Joseph, formerly Morritzstein, then Emmanuel Morris and Bryn Morris. That seemed to be the end of the line. 1970, fifty years ago.

He had made his mind up to add a brother, a second son to Benjamin Morritzstein, later to be known as Morris. The timing of the bloodline had to work in the Morris bloodline that was Jan's.

A suitable old-fashioned name would be logical, rational and sensible. Noah seemed like the sort of name that Benjamin Morritzstein would have named his son, along with a 'second' son Samuel, later known as Sammy Morritzstein, or Sammy Morris. (Dale thought this was a nice touch as Samuel Abrahams was the original owner before Benjamin and Joseph Morris…AKA Morritzstein)

Benjamin Morritzstein

Birth Cert: None. Not traceable. Eastern European birth date and country unknown.
Death Certificate: December, 1940. Age circa 67/68 years.
Benjamin Morritzstein, who was an Eastern European Jew, who came to the country with his brother Joseph Morritzstein, 1890, according to passenger list records from the steamship S.S. Lilley,

docking at Tilbury en-route from France. Arrived with his brother Joseph Morritzstein.

NEWLY CREATED FIRST BORN

(Dale Scott: Note to self to delete when birth, marriage and death certs are created.)

Noah Morritzstein (Son)

Birth Cert: Carlisle, 1902.
Marriage Cert: Carlisle.
Death Cert: TBA.
(DS: Note to self. Add in here. Albert Morris, son of Noah and…)

Albert Morris / Son. George Morris / Janette Morris

Jan's family tree.

Noah Morritzstein
Noah, Second Son of Benjamin. Married Violet.

Birth Cert: Carlisle, February 1902.
Marriage Cert: Carlisle, January 1902 (shotgun wedding).
Death Cert: Carlisle, February 1902. During childbirth.
There was no death certificate for him, and no death cert for his wife Violet, though there was a marriage cert in 1902. The death, was suspicious in itself, or needed further investigation and clarification.

Violet Morris

Birth Cert: Newport Wales. May 1886.
Marriage Cert: To Noah. May 1902 (shotgun).
Death Cert: None. 1902 (in childbirth).
Morris name adopted from Morritzstein. Circa 1902, on marriage to Violet.

Benjamin and Joseph Morritzstein

There were no records preceding that and it was assumed that the Morritzstein brothers had left Belarus, Ukraine or Russia.

Probably being hounded out as much persecuted Jews. Dale had written to the records offices in all of these countries and received nothing but negative responses. It was therefore assumed that there were no living relatives in any of those Eastern European lands.

Joseph Morritzstein
Birth Cert: No trace. Same as his brother Benjamin.
Death Cert: December 1942, circa 68 years.
Additionally, there had been a second cousin, a Bryn Morris, with no offspring. There was a marriage cert for Bryn and his wife Mary, though there was no death cert for Mary Morris.
Dale delved further back into the bloodline.

Mary Morris (Wife of Bryn)
Birth Cert: May 1922 Newport.
Marriage Cert: May 1940 Carlisle.
Death Cert: Not known. Suspected of murder. Disappeared circa 1970.

Bryn Morris (Son)
Birth Cert: Carlisle, August 1920.
Marriage Cert: Carlisle, July 1940.
Death Cert: Unknown date, 1970. (Murdered.)
(Note to self: research old newspapers.)

Dale continued to work on the family history to create the family tree for Jan, using her own family tree, back as far as her great-grandfather. And though he was able to trace back her family's history far beyond that generation, the challenge now was to create a credible link to the Morritzstein family, which is where this substantial estate had originated.

The challenge was to be able to add to the Morris/Morritzstein bloodline and tee-off a family connection from one of the offspring fathered by one of the two original brothers who first came to the country, in the early 1890's.

Dale had found a potential section of the Morris family where he felt he could add a name and therefore a branch, which would lead nicely into Jan's family. Her maiden-name was Morris, so it was a case of grafting the two bloodlines together to make a believable strain of the ancestry to follow.

He pondered and scribbled against the names on his notepad. He placed his forefinger on the family tree and traced the names, studying the bloodlines with thought, then searching and pinpointing what he thought was the ideal entry point. He set out Jan's family tree on the ancestry framework, working backwards.

The method that he had decided upon was to add an additional family member to the Morritzstein tree. An additional brother from where Jan's great grandfather had been spawned. Great, Great grandfather Noah.

Janette Morris

Birth Cert: July 1972, London.

Father:
George Morris (died young)

Birth Cert: December 8th 1920. London.
Death Cert: June 6th 1990. Huntingdon.

Grandfather:
Albert Morris (died young)

Birth Cert: TBC.
Death Cert: TBC.

Great Grandfather. Noah
Older Brother of Samuel Morritzstein.

Noah Morritzstein (Need to create birth cert, etc.)
Birth Cert:
Marriage Cert:
Death Cert:
Married to Eliza Morritzstein.

Dale sat back on his swivel chair in the office until almost midnight on Monday evening, going through the plan. The moon was shining through the office windows and most of the sounds of laughter and jollity coming from the canal had abated. He looked out towards the canal and cast his eyes on the lock gates, one side full of still water with the moonlight just bouncing off the ripples and reflecting against some of the tall glass buildings that overlooked the canal. He felt the warm summer breeze rustling his hair. The plan was coming together. There were still the occasional walkers treading the towpath, couples holding hands or walking a dog, lads returning from the pub and even the odd jogger enjoying a moonlight run on a balmy summer night. Lights still shone from some of the narrowboats moored up along the quay, ready for the assault on the locks at first light.

Dale closed the Morris file, pleased with his progress and placed it in his briefcase. He would try and tie up as many loose ends this evening as possible and present the file to Jan tomorrow evening. He was so looking forward to seeing her again, but for the time being, he was off back to his apartment to get a good night's sleep.

CHAPTER 5

Camden Estates Office

Both Jan and Phil had had a relaxed journey from their home in Huntingdon. Both had other things on their minds. The journey into London seemed to take no time at all this morning, even though there were the usual hold-ups, traffic snarls and roadworks, all adding to the delay of the journey. But despite that, both Jan and Phil were quite cheerful and looking forward to a working day. Phil was saying that they needed to get down to organising a meeting with the accountant and their solicitor, to see what the ramifications of this new company taking on the bank's main portfolio. He needed to know whether or not it left them exposed, financially. He had tried to put a positive turn on the situation or turn of events, hoping that the additional work that they would undertake for the new company, would compensate them for the loss of the main rental portfolio. He felt somewhat responsible in being neglectful, though he was mindful of the fact that he had not presented the bank with a new contract, to continue their long-enjoyed business. He thought the business with the bank was as safe as houses and didn't want to rock a very nice steady boat, producing a regular flow of fine income for many a year. However, here he was, wondering how the new company was going to hand out their contract work for cleaning, refurbs, decorating, the various certification reports and inventories required for the rental business. *We need a meeting with these new people, it's getting to that critical stage*, he thought.

As he held that thought, there they were, keys in the lock, opening up the office doors, ready for the start of a new day's trading.

The three office girls, Betty, Maisie and Rachel, trouped in and

Jan put the kettle on for the first brew of the day before the phones started to ring at 9am as they always did.

The day seemed to 'whizz' by as far as Jan was concerned, she busied herself all day, whilst drifting in and out of thinking about meeting up with Dale later in the evening.

Phil hadn't been so cheerful in a long time, going about his work as if he had just joined the firm, being extra pleasant to all the girls, cracking jokes, offering to make tea and even treating girls to sandwiches for their lunch. In between, his thoughts drifted back and forth to the face of the lovely Samantha. He was becoming quite clumsy through the day, dropping files, spilling water from the vase of flowers, jamming his fingers in the filing cupboard and saying boyish childlike things like 'Oh silly me!'

Maisie turned to Betty and commented. "Definitely in love. Mmmm, and not with Jan. He's definitely got a bit on the side, I'm telling you! Yes! And, have you noticed Jan, she's the same. I am telling you, right now, they are both 'at it', mark my words, it'll come to no good."

"Maisie, you are awful. But do you know what. I think you…are dead right!" Betty rebuked.

Rachel, who was twenty years younger than Maisie and Betty, looked at them both, tutted and shook her head from side to side by way of disgust, with the pair of old witches, brewing up and stirring their cauldron of tattle tales. Like something out of Macbeth.

By 5pm, home-time, the girls were switching off their PC's and saying goodnight. Jan was still tapping away at her PC in the back office and Phil was still tapping away at his PC, in the front open office. They kept looking up at each other to see what the other was doing 'til eventually Phil said, "Jan, I'm off to the Holiday Inn to meet up with the lads. If you remember, I said that I'd stay over as last time we ended up having a bit of a drinking session, if that's okay with you. I'll just claim the bill on the company account."

"Staying over? I don't remember you saying that, but sure, why not, it's good to have a night off occasionally. Go ahead, knock yourself out. I've got a bit of work to finish off here and then I'll get off home. I'll see you here in the morning then. Have a nice evening," Jan replied.

As Phil left the office, he was feeling very guilty. Jan was being so nice to him and he really didn't deserve it, but then Samantha was a hard choice to resist and he left with a smile on his face, almost having had the seal of approval from Jan, for a night off.

Jan shut down her PC and headed for the office door, pulling down the blinds and locking up as she left. She headed off to Dale's with a feeling of some nervousness, tension, and excited anticipation.

CHAPTER 6

2020, The Three Feathers, Denton. Cumbria

For Jerry Blake, life couldn't be better. After his two last cases, the *'Kings Ransom'* fraud case and the *'Art to Die For'* case, retirement had been most welcome. Making the transition from living and working in 'The Smoke', to retiring to the most beautiful location up here in Cumbria, was just like taking off an old well-worn pair of working gloves to slipping on a new, hand-made pair of kids gloves. Life felt that good.

Jerry had just enjoyed a big birthday. His police pension had just kicked in, and as part of his deal, he'd been gifted a new motor by the Mayor of London, for solving serious fraud within the Crown and Government Land Agencies and saving the country many millions of pounds. His working partner, DS Rob Wilton, had also received an ex-gratia payment for his sterling work on this case. They had both received commendations for bravery.

Gill, Jerry's new found love, just made everything in life seem as perfect as a life could be. Only two years before, Jerry as a Met DCI, had been seconded to help the local constabulary with a challenging case of what was originally thought to be drug smuggling, but in the event ended up as a trafficking and murder case. His digs at the time were a lovely old 15th century inn with a chocolate box appeal, The Three Feathers, where Jerry had fallen head-over-heels with Gill, the landlady, and she with him. This was now his home and his life, forever, as far as he was concerned. Life was good.

His 'partner in crime', working with him on both of these last cases was DS Rob Wilton, who was to his dismay, alas, still a working copper, a detective. However, Rob and Chrissie, who had known Gill from the time she and her now deceased husband had moved to the village and bought The Feathers, were now the best friends of Jerry and Gill.

It was eight o'clock in the morning and Jerry sat up relaxing in bed with his pillows plumped up nicely behind him. He was thinking that this was definitely the life, waiting for his lovely Gill to bring up their first morning cup of tea.

Gill slipped in beside him, her lovely thick blond hair falling nicely over her shoulders, revealing her soft warm shape as she leaned over to pass him his favourite mug. They enjoyed the warmth of the moment, just quietly sipping their early morning cuppa.

"Jerry, did you pick up that message left on the answerphone for you? It was from Rob Wilton. He didn't say much other than asked if you could you ring his number back urgently."

Jerry laid back, stretched out his arms, yawned and in his response told Gill that there was no particular rush. "Rob knows I'm retired, so if he wants my advice on something, that's fine. I just hope he isn't trying to coax me back to work. Having said that, he probably just wants to organise an outing somewhere for the 'Old Army Veterans Association' that he runs. I'll ring him later, when I've had my constitutional. Having said that, I'm not sure I want to take it. It just sounds as if I'm being offered a new case. And having worked all my life, it has taken me a lot of convincing in my own mind that I am now fully retired from the Met, so I'm in absolutely no rush to return this or any calls for that matter. Gill, my darling, sweet girl! I just want to spend the rest of my life quietly enjoying my retirement with you, working away together in this lovely old inn."

Gill dug Jerry playfully in the ribs and then planted a kiss on his cheek. "Jerry, I've gotten to know you so well, you're just an old waffler!"

Jerry finished his last sip of tea, swilling it around and draining the dregs from the bottom of the cup. He headed to the bathroom and peered into his eyes and reflected. Having listened to the answerphone message, he shrugged his shoulders and outstretched his arms in a questioning manner, half talking to himself. *Well, it is Rob, he has become my 'bestie-mate', so I had better give him a call.*

Jerry wondered as he was getting dressed. *So, you get an urgent message left for you by the local 'Bill'. Okay, well it is Rob insisting that you call back without delay. You've finally made your decision to retire gracefully with a half decent pension and start living a more sedate life with the lady of your dreams. Of-course you're intrigued, who wouldn't be? So, what's it all about. Why the urgency? Do you really want to know, when you're happily winding down after you believed what was your final case?*

He left himself with those thoughts, finished dressing and headed downstairs. He glanced at himself in the mirror as he entered the hall. *Mmm*, he pondered, *I wouldn't have seen myself in tweeds a year ago.*

He called to Gill, "Gill, Sweetheart, I'll be out with the dogs for the next couple of hours. I'll have breakfast when I get back. If anyone phones, particularly Rob, tell him I'll phone back later."

At that, the back door closed and Jerry headed to the hills for his morning constitutional. The dogs, two Irish Setters, obediently stayed to heel. Jerry took in the fresh, cold dry air of a Cumbrian morning, sun half risen and intermittently hidden, declaring itself occasionally between the fast moving, almost galloping clouds, as if playing hide and seek and teasing its worshippers.

Gill was a little bemused. She knew Rob well enough and wondered what he could possibly be wanting to discuss with Jerry so urgently. She hoped he didn't want him to become involved in another case.

Jerry enjoyed his hour-plus, often two hour long, walks on the moors with the dogs. He could completely lose himself in his thoughts. He had never felt as much at ease in his life than out here on the moors. Even more than that, he enjoyed his arrival back at the home he had made with Gill, in this wonderful part of the country. He still could hardly comprehend his delight at the way in which he had settled in here with Gill and the community that seemed to have taken him in as one of their own.

Jerry whistled to Gill's dogs, *their dogs*, the dogs that he had adopted as his own. It was a shrill whistle which was lost in the chill damp air in a rapidly changing sky. As the clouds moved over the horizon, the sun had decided to stop playing games and retire for the day. It was indicative of an angry breeze trying to rustle up a storm against a backdrop of craggy outcrops of rock and thunder-clouded mountains. The dogs came running back obediently, and Jerry attached their leads. He strolled back down the hill through the rocky paths, avoiding windswept clumps of heather, barely hanging on to their field positions by their wind torn roots, as the ensuing greyness started to form and cast out a fine mizzle. Jerry was looking forward to sinking into a comfortable armchair after his two-hour hillside recreational 'round robin' and back to the village.

He would never have believed that he could ever adapt to this change in his lifestyle since he had agreed to travel up to Cumbria on secondment, to help the local force with the *'Art to Die For'* case. But he had surprised himself in this, his happily converted state of complete contentment.

Jerry was London born and bred. Born within the sound of Bow bells, St. Mary-le-Bow, Cheapside, London, a true cockney. From Stratford in the East End he had lived, worked and walked every London borough from Romford, his first beat, and back again to working where he was born in the East End. A tough place to grow up for any kid. He thought of his home as Stratford, from where he had worked every job in the city and the East End that any aspiring young copper would want to be lifted. He'd either worked or been seconded to Camden, Islington, Hackney, as well as all the southern boroughs of Newnham, Southwark and Lewisham, and even special duties at Westminster. He'd enjoyed every minute of it.

There were one or two bad memories and regrets that we all have in life. The car accident in which his wife died. The heavy booze sessions in and around Soho, with the other young officers, many now senior to him, and the 'rap' he took for one of his colleagues, who would have been sacked, but for the fact that Jerry saved his bacon. But that was all in the dim and distant past.

Now he found himself in the rugged environs of windswept heather covered hills, glades, mountain streams and outbreaks of rock, whistling for two dogs that he didn't even know eighteen months ago. Yet here he was in his Barbour hacking jacket, thick brown corduroy trousers and Timberland hiking boots, tweed flat cap, hiding his normally slicked back greying locks. He now sported a tall walking stick. He held the v shaped top firmly between the thumb and the palm of his other hand, as if he had been born with it in his hand to support his bounding about on the hillside like a mountain goat.

But thank God, the modern world was still out there. His

mobile was a great way of tracking exactly where he was with its built-in GPS and mapping Apps that told him he was no more than 3 miles from civilisation and a hot toddy, when he got back to the Pub.

The Three Feathers was a 15th Century Inn in the heart of Cumbria's walking country, where Jerry had been billeted whilst on secondment to the Cumbria police on his last big case, was one of those lovely little pubs you dream about owning. It was nestled at the end of a small village, babbling millstream nearby, running over rocky outcrops, surrounded by trees, hills and greenery, old, late 1400's black and white with original beams, windows with small leaded lights, some of them bowed outwards with time. Tall red brick chimneys, just trickling out a spiral of wood smoke and one of those places, you just have to take a photo of because it's the photo you're going to send to Cadbury's for the cover of their next box of chocolates.

The sun was decidedly sinking into oblivion. It was late morning and the chill setting in. He was out walking far longer than he had planned, lost in the wonder of the beauty of the hills and mountains that surrounded him. Jerry's long, chiselled face was stinging as he disrobed his outer clothing in the outhouse, which doubled as a log store at this time of the year. The punters to which he affectionately referred, expected to see a nice log fire to relax in front of, while they were sipping at their local hand brewed ale or their G&T's, some a Hot Toddy and some a warming mug of hot chocolate. He quickly rubbed the dogs down before letting them into the bars. The smell of the pine-logs was sweet and heady and the scent of the wood-smoke started to circulate around the cosy rooms of the pub, lending a comfortable familiar homely feeling and offering a sense of belonging. He removed his tweed flat cap placed it on his knees and ran his fingers through his thick grey hair, sweeping it backward in the style that had grown up with him, since his twenties, swept back, but now slowly thinning.

The last of the summer season guests had booked out and there was a steady stream of those that were now arriving for the autumn winter hacking walks and moors tours, ancient monuments, letterboxing out to Laversdale, Scaleby Hill, Boltonfellend, Hethersgill and all the dales beyond. And that sort of healthy outdoor stuff that Gill had nurtured and had become a stock-in trade with returning steady and valued clientele.

Jerry was getting used to this way of life, thanks to Gill the land lady, whom he had fallen in love with head over heels and she with him, hook, line and sinker, whilst he was working on this now settled case which was gathering dust in his memory. But the criminal court case was still awaiting a date for commencement of a multi trial, involving several incarcerated rogues, vagabonds and indeed murderers. There would still be court appearances to follow up on and the giving of evidence, but that was just procedure and all of the hard work had long been completed many, many months ago.

Having returned to The Feathers, his nose was bright red and bristled and glowed with the warmth that was drawn toward him from the heat of the fire, which was now starting to take a hold in the big open hearth in the Snug. Jerry added a couple more logs to the crackling and spitting, roaring and rumbling fire as the draft drew the flames up the twisted chimney above the gnarled timber and charred bricks of the inglenook fireplace.

As the warmth radiated, Jerry gave a shiver as his body took on the welcome temperature change. The dogs had scurried straight to the fireplace and curled up ready for a well-earned rest having given their 'new' master a good run around the rugged Cumbrian hillsides.

This was the first time in probably the last twenty years that he had felt at home. He poked away at the fire, pushing fresh logs on to the iron in the hearth, again carefully placing some new logs on the glowing mass of reds and orange and blacks, in between the dark curling bark which flickered with delicate blue and green flames. He was careful to make sure that the iron rungs of the fireplace, kept any logs or large embers from rolling on to the old gnarled slate hearth and rolling over on to the well-trodden carpets.

***

Gill was in the kitchen supervising the prep for the restaurant for the evening. Felicity the new Cook and her two assistants Leona and Sjabena were well ahead of the game.

The great thing about a country restaurant is that nothing that is on the menu really needs a lot of prep on the night.

With stews, hot-pots, game pies, roasts and country fare, it's more of a case of serving than cooking. All the prep is done during the day and by the time it comes to serving, it was about taking it out of the oven and the vegetables out of the steamer. Gill made it sound so easy. It certainly appeared to be a well-oiled machine and everyone knew how it worked. Clockwork seemed to be the order of the day.

Jerry snuck around the corner and into the kitchen where Gill was just drying off a couple of large serving spoons. He slipped his arms through the back of hers just under her elbows and around her waist and gave her a big hug, kissing her neck and fondling her breasts to her infinite pleasure. She put her head back, feeling Jerry's warm breath.

They both broke out in a giggle as she turned around and they hugged and briefly kissed, like a couple of teenagers. A sniggering could be heard from the other end of the galley kitchen from Felicity and her assistants.

Jerry resisted heading towards the working end of the kitchen where the smell of 'Flick's' game stew wafted towards his ever-appreciative nostrils and tempted his taste buds, now bristling on his tongue. Before he was further-tempted he headed back to the main bar to check on the fires he had set, both there and in the Snug.

He sank into the big old well-worn leather hooded chair, stretching his legs. He reached for his work mobile and tapped the code to access and check his messages. Flicking through the endless copies of Met briefings, training session availability, vacancies at various levels he decided that there was nothing much going on, and thank the lord I'm finished with all that. He had pretty much discarded the phone as his eyes momentarily closed in the warmth of the room, when it started buzzing.

He answered, it was Rob.

"Hi Rob, what's up matey? Why are you leaving urgent messages for me? If it's work, you know I've given up, retired, done. Now if it's a bit of business for the pub, a nice lunch for your association then I'm all ears, but why do I think it's not that at all?"

Rob answered, "Yes, yes, yes, Jerry, I've heard all that before. I know you're retired however, I have just had the most intriguing case come up and not only do I need your help, but you're going to be fascinated by this one. Now are you going to listen or not?"

Jerry answered half-heartedly, "Go on then Rob do your

worst, give it to me both barrels, but the answer will still be no!"

"Right Guv, listen up. Some folks had inherited what was a small farm or more likely smallholding out in the sticks near Longmillbank, down on the B5299 apparently some hundred and thirty acres or so. Thinking about it from my childhood, it could be the old sawmill at Buckabank. Now, on the site according to old maps, was a stone farmhouse. The folks that own it, have been working on the plot for weeks apparently. They eventually cleared a wide path, big enough to get a truck down there and eventually found the farmhouse in a semi-clearing, which is now a complete tumbledown." Rob responded.

"Rob mate, I'm losing the will to live here, what's the bottom line, what's the payback story there must be a conclusion, given the speed you are talking."

"Yes, yes, yes, Jerry. Exercise some patience please, I'm getting there. As the many weeks have gone by and as they methodically cleared the old tumbledown, timbers, slates and stones etc., they eventually came across some cellar steps. The heavy old oak door's hinges at the bottom of the steps were rusted almost into the woodwork, but it appears that the bolt had been closed from the outside of the cellar. Now, here's the intrigue, the payback you asked for, the bottom line. Behind the door were three bodies, well skeletal remains, who had clearly tried to free themselves but eventually huddled together and died. So that was that, or as you would say in your neck of the woods, 'Goodnight Vienna', or they were 'brown bread'."

Rob continued, "Now then, the bodies or should I say the remains, were discovered this morning hence my urgent call to you. Right now, I have had my team secure the area and as yet I haven't visited. I'm not asking you to get involved as such, but I thought you'd be intrigued and might like to accompany me and throw in your expertise as my assistant. Well, when I say assistant, I mean my advisor or consultant if you like, no offence meant, and before you ask, no there's no money in it for you!"

"No offence taken Rob. No money hey, but my, Rob, you do know how to garner my interest, it sounds really intriguing. At least it's on our doorstep, none of that hiking up and down to London like the last case. Let me speak to Gill and you can collect me in the next ten minutes or so. We can go in my '4 x 4', if you say the ground is as rough as you say, and it took them that many weeks to get to the house, or tumbledown, as you called it. Okay, I'm in! I'll see you shortly."

Fifteen minutes later Detective Inspector Rob Wilton and the ex-DCI Jerry Blake were heading south towards Carlisle and out the other side further south along the B5299 to Longmillbank, and what Rob described as the tumbledown. They arrived at a small gated entrance off a narrow, unmarked lane that had long since seen a gate. The gate and its post had rotted and collapsed into the mud and disintegrated years ago, along with its sign that you could just make out as 'Buckabank Sawmill'. Two police 'blue and whites' sat on the verge, with 'Police Do Not Cross' taped across the entrance to the property and two of the four officers sat in one car.

CHAPTER 7

2020, The Tumbledown Investigation

Rob asked where the bodies were. One officer gave Rob directions, explaining that the recently forged pathway had been formed by the new owners to get to the old farmhouse.

The officer commented, "Though, it was originally a timber mill, so it would be designated a mill house, sir."

Rob thanked the officer for his input, wound up the window and asked Jerry to make his way approximately a quarter of a mile along the recently created mill trackway. Jerry drove gingerly, with care not to catch the sides of his new toy with any larger branches that would or might mark the big black Range Rover. He skidded on the wet ground and pressed and turned the mode button on to the 'Woodland' setting, they felt the suspension rise by six inches to avoid stumps and stones on the rough ground that had been cleared. It was already in 4 x 4 mode. The path wove, missing some big old oaks, over outcrops of stone shallowly covered by tufted long grass and mossy fibre. Some of the ruts bumped the vehicle up and down but were no match for the remarkable self-levelling skills of his vehicle. After twenty minutes of tortuous journeying, they could see a very muddied police squad car parked in a clearing, well away from the main building which wasn't much more than a pile of rubble, created by the new owners.

Jerry stopped the vehicle and they jumped out. Fortunately, Jerry still had his hiking boots on from his morning constitutional on the moors with the dogs. Rob stepped out into a muddy patch in his highly polished brown brogues and sank almost up to his ankles. The ground squelched below his feet and he cursed not having had the forethought to put his new green wellington boots in the boot of Jerry's car.

The two bobbies at the location had cordoned off the potential crime scene, awaiting instructions from their senior officer. Rob had said to leave calling a forensic team until he had a chance to pass judgement on the next step. Forensics would have to come in from Newcastle on Tyne. From what had been described to him over the telephone when he was first contacted, was a scene that had remained the same for many years, so nothing was likely to change in the next twenty-four hours.

The apparent owners, Dale and Jan sat in the cab of their old battered green Land Rover waiting to talk to the police who undoubtedly would want to talk about how the bodies were discovered.

Rob walked over to the two officers, bidding them good morning and introduced them to ex-DCI Jerry Blake, though they knew him by reputation. The situation was self-explanatory in that the owners had phoned the 'find' in, and the patrol vehicle had attended. As soon as they realised that this was beyond their pay-grade, they phoned the station and called the job in, at the same time cordoning off, what was a potential crime scene. Rob thanked them for their prompt and efficient response and their site management. Rob nodded to Jerry and they walked over to the old tumbledown property and tucked under the 'Do Not Cross' cordon.

Jan and Dale, sat on a pile of timber, helpless, while the two detectives walked the immediate site. They were shown the cellar by the local bobbies on site and viewed the remains of what fairly obviously looked like three sets of human skeletal remains. There wasn't much to glean from that, apart from noting that the cellar had been very secure, in that no roots had forced their way through the thick stone walls. Therefore, no animals could have been responsible for these sets of remains, apart from perhaps rats and mice, but no larger. The cellar, was so secure that a carnivorous animal wouldn't have been able to enter the unit. It was as near to hermetically sealed as you could get in an old building of this sort. It was noted however, that even though the frames of the old cellar door had just about been eaten away by woodworm, the solid oak door itself though covered in tiny woodworm holes, was pretty much intact and the big iron bolts, meant to keep people out, were firmly rusted into their rungs .They had kept these three people irretrievably locked in. The detectives rose up, the now, very shaky timber steps, down in the dark cellar and into the contrasting vivid bright sunlight, blinking their eyes as they became adjusted to the sun's rays again. Both Rob and Jerry dusted the lime-mortar, brick-dust and cobwebs from their sleeves, Jerry cursing that this was a brand-new Barbour tweed-jacket, and he wasn't happy!

After fifteen minutes or so, taking in the general view of the site, they walked over to Jan and Dale, sat there looking agitated. Rob nodded and spoke, at the same time offering a handshake to both Jan and Dale. Jerry greeted them similarly.

Jan was looking as attractive as ever, with just a hint of make-up, her straw-blond hair tied back with a sprung-comb, a beige linen blouson tied at the waste, with jeans, cut down to shorts length and a pair of steel toe-capped working boots, with a thick pair of socks, pulled up to her knees. Dale stood next to Jan, similarly kitted out for work, with jeans, unshaven, a loose shirt, sporting a dark hirsute chest and a red neckerchief around his neck, which was soaked in sweat. They had both managed to get good sun-tans in the period that they had worked on the site, together with plenty of scratches and bruises, which they regarded as badges of honour, for a couple of 'office-wallahs'. As they had stopped working they had both donned their heavier outdoor coats, wrapped them around their shoulders and huddled together on the remains of a large felled oak tree.

Rob addressed them. "Good morning. I'm Detective Inspector Rob Wilton of the Cumbria Constabulary, and this is my colleague DCI Jerry Blake, who is retired, but assisting me with this enquiry. And you are?"

Dale answered first. "Yes, good morning gentlemen. I am Dale Scott and this is my partner, Jan Phillips. Jan inherited the estate at the beginning of last month and we arrived here just over two weeks ago, to start working on the site. We had no idea what was here, all we had were deeds, some maps and an ancestry trail. Until we actually got here some weeks ago, we didn't even know what was here. We tried Google Earth but that didn't show any detail through the woods and overgrowth."

Rob nodded towards Jan and gestured the question. "Ma'am?"

"Yes, detective, that's correct. When we got here, we found what we thought was the entrance, because there was the remains of an old gate and style, but everything was so overgrown that we couldn't get any further than what we believed to be the opening. It was just a bramble jungle growing into the tall pines. Everything was covered in ivy, and buddleia and elderberry were growing everywhere, we couldn't see any further than a couple of feet into the plot."

Dale broke in, "We decided to drive around and see if we could find any other openings, but the hedgerows for miles and miles hadn't been cut back for a very long time, from what we could see. So we went back into town, booked into our B&B and decided that we would need to buy some working clothes and some cutting equipment, we exchanged my Audi for this old Land Rover and returned, geared up to do the job."

"So, who found the corpses, how did you discover them?" Rob asked.

Dale spoke again. "Well, officer. We had been working on the entrance and what must have been the original track, or the most obvious way in to the mill. After a few days, I decided that what we needed was this old Land Rover, to help carry the equipment and we didn't need to worry if it got scratched or scraped. So, bit by bit, we cut through the overgrowth as well as the undergrowth and after nearly two weeks, we got as far as the old mill house. It was pretty much fallen down, a tumbledown if you like, but we were curious and there was one part that was still standing, which I leaned on and it just fell onto the top of the cellar floor."

Jan added, "We could see that there was a cellar, from the damage done by the wall collapsing. So we went looking for a way in and found the steps, under all sorts of timbers and slates and rubble, it seemed that the whole house had collapsed on top of the cellar, almost as if it had a secret to keep. So, we both picked over the timbers, some were quite heavy, and Dale went down the old timber steps, very gingerly. I was horrified when he told me there were skeletons down there. I thought he was just trying to scare me, jokingly, you know. So, I went down and there, and there they were. That's when we phoned you at Carlisle Police Station."

"Did you move anything or touch anything?" Jerry asked.

They both shook their heads.

"If, as you say, you inherited this property and you have the deeds, then you may be able to tell who these people might be.

Additionally, then I guess that these people must be distant relatives. If that is the case, then we will need to use your deeds to help us establish who these people actually are or were. Where are the deeds now?"

Dale was quick to jump in with an answer. "Ah, officer. The deeds aren't here. They are locked in my safe, down in London, but I could get them back to you, as soon as we go back to London, if that's okay with you?"

"And when is that likely to be, sir?" Rob asked.

Dale, not wishing to give too much information away to the police, given the way in which the property was gained, nervously made, what he thought might be an acceptable reason.

"Ah. We don't plan to go back for quite a while. We have both taken three months off work, just to work on the estate. So, we can get it to you. But in the meantime, I can let you have copies of my ancestry notes which should give you a good indication of who these people might be. Will that help?"

Rob answered, "Okay, Mr Scott, I guess that will suffice for the time being, but we will need the deeds or at least a copy of those deeds to verify the ancestry tree. Thank you. You have been very helpful. We will have to cordon-off the majority of this area, until the forensics team have given it the once over, but I can't see that there will be much to gain, from locking down the complete site. For the meantime, if you could keep away from the area we will be marking out today please, until I can let you know, when you can start clearing your property again. It might not be too long before we can discover and reveal, the secrets of your tumbledown. Thank you again for your help." He nodded to Jan. "Ms. Phillips."

CHAPTER 8

1890, Tilbury
Ben and Joseph Morritzstein land in the UK

The quay heaved with people and commerce. Another ragged steam driven ocean boat billowing smoke and exhaling steam, created vast fast-rising clouds of mist mixed with specs of soot, seemingly disappearing into the ether then raining down on unsuspecting travellers like a fine black snow. The boat, rammed full of hundreds of European immigrants docked on the quayside at Tilbury and was disgorging its hold. The alien passengers had endured months of travel from all across Europe as well as some from the Middle-Eastern nations. Eastern Europe brought mainly White Russian Jews who struggled and endeavoured to escape hundreds, if not thousands of years of persecution. Middle-Eastern Jews leaving Jerusalem, the Holy Land itself in limbo, their origins and a country without recognition, its roots in a state of suspension and uncertainty, lost in the wild wind-blown deserted terrains of Palestine. Even from Egypt, where a new breed of roaming people called Gypsies emerged.

The quayside was littered with people and horses and all manner of goods being delivered for the outgoing sailings. Coal, timber, bales of fabric, fertilisers, fruit and vegetables in broken crates butchery, ale by the crateload. Foot traffic trod in manure and oil and grease and the remains of discarded rotting fish, with seagulls swooping down vying for breakfast or lunch, perching on the high and low storage and working sheds that lined the quayside. They were filled with goods ready to load onto the waiting boats. Trucks and carts arrived and departed constantly, bearing coal and logs for the steam boilers of those ships with both steam and sail. The noise was constant and the bustling and frantic movement of people and craft on the quay was never ending.

As Ben and Joseph walked along the quay, the smells they encountered from rotting fish and vegetation to the sweet smell of perfume mixing with the enticing aromas of chestnuts roasting with corn on the cob and baking potatoes and sausages frying with onions. The smells and the scents and the perfumes, with the food particularly hitting the senses turning intrigue in to hunger. But neither Ben nor Joseph had thought about the English currency. There was all of this wonderful food to be purchased and all they had was a pouch full of roubles, which no-one wanted, a few French francs and a few German marks, from the previous countries they had travelled through. They were hungry.

Labourers, dressed in working clothes, probably the only clothes they owned, with string tying their waistbands and cardboard or sacking tied with string around the bottom of their legs to guard them from the army of rats that might bite or nip at their ankles if disturbed under sacks or crates. The men hassled and hustled and bustled, shouted and bargained to get work, either loading vessels or emptying carts and trucks or offering to shift luggage to the many pony-and-traps waiting at the harbour entrance gates.

Times were hard and many of the folks that scraped a living in and around these parts were left bemused at the immigrants wanting to come to a country that was struggling to feed itself. There was word around that there was work up north, but no-one would want to venture away from their kith and kin. And anyway, they were seen as uncouth and uneducated up there in the north of England, not trained in the ways of the world like us southerners. There might be work up there but if they were that uncivilised, uncouth and uneducated, then how could you communicate. You wouldn't want to take you family up there just for a bit of work, and how long would it last? 'No, no, I'll take my chances down here' was the local working man's refrain.

1890

Benjamin and Joseph Morritzstein, aged seventeen and fifteen respectively, watched the porter pull their single large leather wooden and iron-strapped trunk, from the hold and dump it on the quay. It carried all their worldly wealth and belongings. There was two years difference in their ages. They had already lived a lifetime in their short lives. Joseph was the younger, but often wiser, where his brother Benjamin was the brother with the determination to succeed. It was him that had persuaded not only his brother to leave, but he had to convince his whole family that to leave their home. It was no more than a shanty on the outskirts of the nearby Vilnius in Russia, that in the long term they would all benefit, when the boys had created a new, good life and were able to send for them. Benjamin was tall and angular at seventeen, he carried no spare weight. At approaching six feet two he was as strong as an ox, from working the fields at home with his father and older brothers. But with another failed harvest, leaving only enough for their parents and may be his fourteen-year-old brother and twelve-year-old sister, then it was Joseph that had eventually convinced him that their fortunes lay abroad. Joseph had put on a little more weight than Benjamin. It was always Benjamin that seemed to get the scraps and left overs, if there ever were any, from his Mum. He was clearly the favourite. But again, he was used to working and never shied away from any hard labour. Joseph, like his brother was a hard worker, not quite as tall and more heavily built, some might say stocky for a fifteen-year-old.

They were good pals, did most things together, talked for many years about trying to live in another country, where there was less poverty. Working on their father's farm, which was his Father's before him and again before that, was soul destroying. Whatever they cropped was poor and left little to be sold and re-planted, they were only ever left enough to seek a meagre existence. The land was dry and when it did rain, despite their efforts to irrigate, became flooded and fruitless.

It was time to try another world, another country and England, from what they had read and heard was a strong and upcoming country, it had conquered the world and was still expanding, welcoming all-comers.

And so, it was. Benjamin and Joseph had worked their way across Europe to get to France and had made enough money to pay for their passage to England. They had enough money to last them just a few days, so they had very little breathing space. But they were determined to work and felt confident in their ability with just a few words of English to their names, they decided that they would learn as they worked.

Joseph hadn't managed to exchange any roubles for pounds on their journey across the channel. Nobody wanted a currency that they had never even heard of before, so their stomachs were turning and with no local currency to pay their way, then they were destined to offer themselves as workers for any job that was available around the port just to earn enough for a meal. By nightfall, there were no takers. Nobody wanted to take on foreigners, straight off a boat. You just didn't know where they came from and you just couldn't trust them could you. Best stick to your own and in any event the competition was fierce if a job came up, it was always going to go to the locals.

By midnight, the brothers had pulled a shawl and a blanket out of their trunk and found a corner of one of the vast open storage sheds and did their best to curl up and get some sleep. The following morning, they would try again. A new day would always look better and they needed some food inside them. The following day saw them scrabbling around for work, to no end. By now they would do almost anything for a meal and a mug of ale. Benjamin managed to get a few hours sweeping up and helping out at a bakery that also had a shop counter. It was the smell of the bread baking that had lured him in and with his limited amount of the local language, which he knew before they left home that they would have to learn to get by. They called it English, he was able to partly speak and gesture a meal in exchange for some work. But a day's work from 5am 'til 7pm for a few rolls and a loaf of bread was hardly a fair wage or was not going to sustain the two of them for very long. But their alternatives were few. Benjamin persevered. At least the owner of the bakery allowed them to sleep on the floor in the warmth of the back room, where the ovens were built in to the walls and they were also able to leave their big old trunk there while Joseph looked for work. They did manage to laugh at themselves when they realised after the first nights of sleeping in the backroom of the bakery, when they awoke to look at each other, covered in flour dust and looking like ghosts. They were more determined than ever.

Joseph walked the quay daily for weeks, nodding to the stall holders, the ropemakers, the chandlers, the fishermen, still no work.

Someone called out. "Hey, you! Yes, you."

Joseph turned around to see a man on the deck of a working boat, that even in Joseph's eyes had seen better days. The man stood with a walking stick rested under one arm, and it was not hard to spot, that he had one leg which had been replaced with a crude wooden alternative.

"Yes, you, boy. Do you want a job?"

Joseph was quick to respond, nodding in the affirmative and putting up both thumbs as seems to be the signal that made when you agreed with something or you did whenever something was good.

"Are you strong?"

Again, up went his thumbs, even though he had never been questioned about his strength as a young man, he was fifteen and he knew he was stronger than most of his age, given his upbringing and his toiling in the fields at home. But he'd never worked on a boat before like this one, he had been out in a small fishing boat many times with his grandad long ago. But that was not quite the same, but he needed the work, so he thought that he would let that count as a thumbs up. In any event he could soon learn.

"Well, be here before four in the morning, we sail at four. If you're not here then, no job. Have you got that? Do you understand?"

Joseph understood. On the quay four in the morning, sail on the tide. He was keen to tell Benjamin that he had got some work, but didn't think to ask for a job for his brother, neither did he think to ask how long they would be out working. He didn't even realise what the boat did as far as work was concerned.

***

Joseph was there on the quay at a quarter to four and climbed aboard the boat with three other crew to join the one-legged captain. The deep-sea working Coaster vessel was no more than a few years old but had seen a fair amount of work in its short history. The timbered decks were coarse and worn from the dragging of all manner of goods to the fore and rear decks. The hauling gear was heavy and the cables were smothered in thick whale grease. There was a central steerage cab and a huge funnel, blackened from the coal-fired engine below decks. The boat smelled of tar and oil and smoke, it was not cared for. There were old ropes and planks just lying about on the decks, seemingly detritus that had been trawled up from the sea and dumped on the side. He wasn't even sure if the vessel was safe, but he needed the work.

Benjamin had walked down to the quay to see the Coaster TY 1179, 'The Captain Stephen Manchester', as it was leaving the end of the old stone quay, just breaking into the morning light. Looking back, Joseph caught sight of his brother Benjamin and waved. Benjamin seemed pleased that his younger brother Joseph had got himself a proper job on a sea going steamboat. They were finally on their way he thought to wealth, in their newly-found world in this vibrant country. He strolled back down the cobbled streets awash with the smell of emptied overnight 'gazunders' and discarded animal bones thrown out for the stray and feral dogs onwards to the bakery that was giving him bread enough to sustain him and a few pennies as a wage and his free accommodation. Life was getting better and they had only been in the country for a month or two.

Joseph was not aware what his job might be on board this dirty old boat. It seemed that they were bound for another port called Cardiff in the west of the island, though apparently it was part of another country, called Wales to pick up a load of coal. On board their boat was endless amounts of timber. Tall lengths were stored on deck with pieces of timber sat between each layer. Down below decks were thousands of shorter timbers around six and eight-foot lengths, many were round, created from felled trees, many were square from sawn timbers. As the boat chugged out of the Thames the waves started to hit the side of the boat, pushing it back and forth like a see-saw. The further they got out to sea, the more the boat pitched and tossed. Joseph felt sick. His head was whirling, his stomach was turning and he felt dizzy. He could hear the 'old salts' laughing at him. They'd all been there before and learned a long time ago to cope with the undulating waves, the rise and the fall of the prow, the swell and the surge of the treacherous cruel seas. Joseph couldn't contain himself. He felt the bile in his throat, he felt his stomach heave and he vomited over the port side of the boat, whist holding on very tightly. He had never felt so bad. The small crew, including the skipper, laughed for ten minutes at his malady and indisposition. Until a small scrawny man, in oversized oilskins with a hat to match, slapped him on the back and said, "Never mind son, you'll get used to it."

At the same time, he handed him a freshly brewed jar of black coffee to take away the taste in his mouth and perk him up for the ongoing journey. The crew were a motley bunch. There was the one-legged captain, who introduced himself as Ephraim Manchester, though the crew always referred to him as Michael, the scrawny man, who had just helped him out. There was a man with a large paunch and a grey beard and whiskers, and another man, who they called Scottish-Dunny, or Dunny for short, was a bit younger and seemed to be the next best thing to normal. It seemed that he was hiding from the authorities having killed someone and had hidden in the depths of this boat. Every so often he would say out loud to anyone who would listen, "Aye. I never 'din' it." Joseph got to learn that this had been some years ago and he hadn't left the boat since, apart from to visit in the odd port or two, where he knew he could find a good time girl. Joseph looked around and including himself, that made just five crew plus the captain. If the ship was ever due to dock in Glasgow or Edinburgh, Dunny's hide would never been seen above deck, not for love nor money. The captain had learned long ago that the man that Dunny thought he had killed had recovered and was actually alive and kicking, but the captain thought that that was one way to keep a good man aboard his vessel.

Joseph didn't know nor realise that they were a coastal tramp ship. Their farm in his homeland was land-locked for hundreds of miles, so apart from when they got to France, he had never even seen a ship before apart from in childhood picture books. He didn't realise that they may not return to Tilbury for weeks, if not months, or even years. It was very much dependent on their loads, where they picked them up, where they delivered them to and if there was another return cargo to collect when they got to that port. If there was no load to collect, the skipper had two choices, either wait for a new load, or move on, in the hope there would be another load at a busier port. In any event, Joseph was stuck on board this vessel and was at the mercy of commerce, his captain, and his worst nightmare, the cruel sea. He had no way of telling his brother that he was okay, safe and working.

Every day Benjamin walked down to the quay before he

started work at the bakery. His English was improving and the widow that ran the bakery was giving him a single meal each evening, which was helping him build his strength. He was feeling good, but worried every day about his younger brother and wondered how he was surviving and whether he would see him again.

As Joseph got used to the toss and roll of the boat, he could see that they were skirting the coastline and sailing in a Westerly direction. His English was improving, though it had many influences from this small crew. One man said he was a German, another was a Cockney, which he had never heard of before and the 'murderer' spoke what the other called 'gentleman's English', but the others said he was a mad murdering Scotsman. The captain was a French-speaking Canadian and kept himself to himself, apart from to bark orders at everyone and to stop and drink a lot of rum. Between all of them Joseph managed to glean that they were on their way to Cardiff, a three-day journey, to unload their timber for pit props, destined for the coal mines in the Welsh valleys. Then they were to pick up a full hull of coal as a return shipment to Tilbury for the steam pumping station, which helped to power the new underground tunnel under the river Thames, from one side of the Thames to the other. This was designed by a man called Marc Brunel, was opened in 1843 for foot traffic and horses and carriages. The plan was to open as a rail link at Rotherhithe to Wapping and the coal was vital to feeding the steam pumping engine to ensure that the tunnel was maintained with good clean air flow and to avoid the risk of flood.

Benjamin worked tirelessly for the widow at the bakery, eighteen hours most days and was doing his best to save his few pennies until he could move on.

Joseph was stuck on The Captain Stephen Manchester, 'The Manchester' for short, though he often wondered why the vessel was named so, as the skipper's name was Michael, though most of the time the crew just called him 'Skip' or 'Aye-aye, Sir'.

After weeks of coastal hopping and only once returning to Tilbury for a few hours, only to be told by the captain that if he, Joseph left now, he would have broken his contract and wouldn't get paid, he persevered having been the equivalent of shanghaied into continuing working on The Manchester.

The Captain Stephen Manchester was a coastal tramp steamer. Joseph, as his trips of weeks and months continued got to improve his English of many dialects and was able to eventually ask one of the crew why The Manchester was so called. It seems that the skipper was on a ship called The Lexington as a member of the crew when his father, Stephen Manchester, was the master of the vessel. This was twenty years ago. It was seen as the fastest vessel for its time, but The Lexington would come to be known as the first great steamship disaster in history, having sunk just four miles from the shore. The ship's motto was 'Through the Dawn' and the reputation was built on its strength and resilience as well as the guarantee of a quick and therefore successful voyage for those who invested in her. These were the reasons that The Lexington was chosen for her fateful trip in January of 1840 from New York to Stonnington, Connecticut. It was known that she would face sub-zero temperatures, strong winds and high seas and though the master of the vessel, the skipper's father, one Stephen Manchester, warned against the trip, the owners were convinced that the vessel was unsinkable. At the time, the fragmented, unconfirmed news reports said that The Lexington was mid-journey on the evening of the 13th of January, when a cotton bail, used as a seat in the engine room, caught fire, setting all the cargo ablaze. High winds fuelled the flames and the vessel was sent drifting endlessly to the north. Apparently, the passengers who survived the fire by jumping overboard only prolonged their lives by minutes as the cold icy waters consumed them. The lifeboats that were launched were met with violent waves, capsizing and drowning all aboard. In the end it was said that one hundred and fifty-four souls were lost. Only four survived the ordeal, including the ship's captain and a young man who had drifted on a cotton bail through the darkness and another night 'til the morning. They blamed his father, the captain, but his father saved his son, Ephraim-Michael, who lost his leg due to frostbite and gangrene.

"So now you know why our skipper has a missing limb. His father died in poverty, he could never get another commission, not even as a crew member. Our captain eventually found his way back to England on a tramp steamer."

Benjamin walked the quays, day after day, week after week, month after month, with no news of his younger brother. He hoped and prayed that his brother was safe and well. There were many reports of The Manchester; some said that it was up north. Some said that it had hit rough seas and had sunk, and some said that it had gone off to South Africa as they had started diamond prospecting. But Benjamin knew that his brother Joseph wouldn't leave without him, so each day he visited the harbour and the Tilbury quays, becoming a familiar face with all who traded there.

Through the weeks he sat on the quay, watching horses and carts, slowly moving all the goods either in or out of the port. The daily comings and goings of port life, from the porters, to the sailors, to the girls looking for business from the guys who wanted a 'good time', Benjamin noticed a sign on a building, with a comfortably dressed man sat at a desk under the sign offering work and lodgings and a free passage up to Carlisle, he had worked out that this was somewhere in the North of the country.

The smartly dressed man sat on a high-backed rattan chair, smoking a clay pipe. His whiskers waved in the fresh breeze as he sat playing a card game of solitaire on a rickety table. He wore a well-worn, green velvet coat over a cream waistcoat with matching breeches, black half-calf length boots and a topper to match. Benjamin was curious and greeted the man.

"Good morrow, sir. Your sign offers work in the north, may I ask what work sir, and is it you I would be working for?"

The man replied, "Good morning, young man. No, it is not me by whom you would be employed. I am an agent for The Northern Mining Company and I am recruiting mine workers, for new coal mines being opened all of the time in the north. The pay is good and there is accommodation for single men. A good strong lad like you could soon make his fortune. There is a basic wage but when rich seams are found then bonuses abound. Yes, a good strong man like yourself could definitely make your fortune. Now if you want to sign up today, your train passage will be paid up to Carlisle and you will be collected to start work on Monday next week at the pit. How does that sound to you?"

Benjamin was indecisive. He'd been in the country for six months now and work around here for foreigners was hard to come by. He didn't want to leave the port area in case his brother Joseph returned and couldn't find him.

"Yes, sir, you say I would have to be at the train station on

Friday as you suggested. Thank you."

Benjamin was pleased, but wasn't sure if he'd done the right thing. He couldn't just wait around for his brother for months on end, he may never come back. I will leave my address with Ma Siddal at the bakery and if Joseph looks to find me, she can tell him where I've gone. So that's that. I'm off to work in the north and to make my fortune. But come the morning, he just couldn't make the decision to leave. His decision was to continue to seek alternative employment, or indeed any employment, here in London.

1892, Joseph, The Captain Stephen Manchester

The weeks and months went by for Joseph working away on The Manchester. Even though he kept himself pretty much to himself, the skipper, Michael, was a good enough boss – he was a fair and considered man, with a motley but loyal crew. They steamed from port to port picking up cargoes of coal, timber iron ore, rocks, sand and anything that would pay. When they did get to stop in ports, either overnight or for a few days, Joseph would go out drinking down the back street pubs, with the crew. But he always restricted how much money he spent, unlike his crewmates, where nobody stood on ceremony and the 'likes of his type', working boys would blend into the beer-soaked smoke-filled atmosphere of screaming, noisy, bawdy, whore-filled harbour side ale houses. At every port, wherever they docked, there was always lined up on the quay, the odd girl who would perform whatever he needed, for a few shiny coins, to keep his animal instinct well fed. In all he wasn't unhappy with life, but he did wonder how Benjamin was doing. He wondered if he was still at the bakery, still covered in flour and looking like a ghost every morning, or whether he moved on? *He might even be on a tramp ship like me*, he thought. *Whatever, I'm sure he'll be okay and when we meet-up we'll be able to tell each other great stories.*

While his crew were enjoying the many pursuits of dry land, mainly pubs and bordellos, it has to be said, Michael, their skipper was again negotiating a load to take them further up the coast to Newcastle-upon-Tyne, from where they were, the port of Kings Lynn in Norfolk. This was a live cargo of sheep, pigs and chickens, bound for the livestock markets in Newcastle. It wasn't the usual cargo that Skipper Michael was used to handling, as ever he had his reservations, but a cargo was a cargo. What he was unsure about was his insurance. The agent had insisted that he confirm that he had insurance in place for such a load, should the boat be caught out at sea or was delayed in delivering the goods. But a load was a load and there was risk in everything if you were at sea. What he didn't take into consideration was the noise, the smell and the amount of water he would have to stow, to keep all of these beasts from drying out. But it was a cargo and it was to be loaded tomorrow. The sheep and pigs would have to be placed in separate sections of the ship's hold and the chickens were all to be delivered in cages, a dozen to a cage.

Life on board

After two years of coastal hopping, with Joseph saving most of his meagre wage paid to him by Captain Michael, he was hankering after a steady job on land. The heavy physical work was turning him into a fit muscled young man, but he didn't want to see this as his future, even though he had no idea at all what his future might be. He'd heard that Newcastle was a fine up and coming industrial town, with shipbuilding and iron making at its heart and he favoured trying his luck on land, even though Captain Michael had been good to him, it was time for a change. He couldn't wait until the tramp ship returned to Tilbury, he needed to breakaway now, and he gave Captain Michael good notice and voiced his intent. Captain Michael accepted that the young man wanted to do better, so when they were to dock in Newcastle-upon-Tyne, then they would shake hands and say goodbye. His fellow sailors would be sad to see him go.

He was bright, strong and a quick learner. He worked hard, always pulled his weight, and could drink with the rest of them, though he couldn't hold it at all, but at least he tried. When they visited the bordellos, wherever they were, he had no problem in pulling some of the better looking 'ladies' for himself and his crewmates. They would certainly miss him. He had become quite adept at the English language over the past two or three years, though the dialects were so different from each of his crew mates, when he did talk to folk on land, they were never sure whether he was a Cockney or a Geordie or a Welshman or even a Norwegian, given the variety of crew members on board The Manchester and the influence they had on his Eastern European tongue. But whatever, he knew he would adapt to wherever he ended up.

The day came The Captain Stephen Manchester hauled to and slowly pulled alongside the quay along the mighty River Tyne.

CHAPTER 9

1893, Benjamin, London Euston

Joseph had been missing for several days before Benjamin was able to establish that he had been recruited to a life at sea on a coaster, sometimes called a tramp ship. From the sketchy description Joseph had given him about this job he had to start at four am, as far as he was concerned was for a few days on a boat called The Manchester. Apparently not named after a town in the north of England but a dead sea-captain, related to the current skipper. Benjamin had no idea where his younger brother was. Except that he was now a crew member of a working boat that travelled from port to port and often country to country, in pursuit of work by collecting and delivering cargo, to anywhere its agents required it. The fee for these journeys was invariably fixed and it was up to the skipper to negotiate for the delivery of the cargo and do this in the quickest possible time, so that he could collect another consignment from the next port. So, Joseph had gone, with no word left for Benjamin.

Benjamin was down at the quayside every day continuing to look for work. He continued to help out at the bakery, which had taken them in originally and allowed them to sleep on the floor for a share of the labouring and cleaning chores. For that they were eternally grateful had also been rewarded with fresh bread every day to keep the hunger away. Benjamin continued to look for work.

Early one Saturday morning. Benjamin was again at the quayside looking for work. Any work. Anything that would help him make a life for himself. That is why he left the 'old country', to get a better living and build a life in a different country that wasn't always savaged by famine and poverty and death. This is why he and Joseph had made the long, long journey across many countries, to get to England where they knew they could make a better life. What they didn't realise, was that so many other folks, from so many other countries and nations had come here for the same reasons. The dialogue and the many tongues on the quay, created a continuous babble of nonsense. Now and again, he could understand some words that were similar to his own, but so many dialects and so many people looking for work and prepared to work for a few pennies a day, just to buy bread. This was becoming an impossible task. Benjamin strolled despondently, along the quay, down as far as he could walk, where the timber and coal was stacked for fuelling the steamships, a man sat in front of a large recruitment banner. There, a small gathering was forming, listening to the recruitment man speak. He stood in front of the banner, which read. This was a different company to the one he had seen some months ago and it sparked his interest again.

WANTED: Good, honest, strong, hard-working young men for mine work. Good rates of pay and accommodation provided. **APPLY HERE.**

The gathering of men, seemed to be enthusiastically enjoying what the man from the mining company appeared to be offering. Regular work, with accommodation and good rates of pay for hard work. Why else would you want good pay, but for hard work? Benjamin asked himself. He wasn't in a great position financially, so he listened intently to the man in the suit. Another man, who appeared to be a clerk, was sat at a makeshift desk, in fact an old table, on which he had a pile of forms under a large stone, to keep them from blowing away. He was puffing away contentedly on a clay pipe emitting a sweet-smelling smoke which glowed each time he chewed on the stem. The brim of his battered brown bowler perched neatly on his head above a wringed face with a large drooping moustache, was lost to the world each time he exhaled, like a smoking gun. Those that could write, were filling in their own forms and those that couldn't were just signing with an X, (some say 'sealed with a kiss') where indicated and were instructed. If asked, the clerk at the desk was completing the very simple forms on the applicant's behalf. They had signed up about twenty men that morning, ready to become colliers or mineworkers.

The man standing in front of the banner suddenly called out, "Right, that's it. If there's any more of you that wants a job as a miner, now is the time. We're closing up until next visit."

At that, Benjamin quickly weighed up that this was a chance that he couldn't give up. It seemed too good to be true. He only had a few pennies in his pocket with no savings. It seemed that the chances of getting work around the Tilbury docks was remote, given that every migrant that arrived at the port was in competition for any job that was available and they would work several days for maybe a half-a-days pay, if they could get the work, just to get by.

Becoming a miner, seemed like a step forward. Good wages and accommodation provided. This was a new start, the start that he had been waiting for, indeed it was his lucky day. A day to start a new life.

He signed all the forms and handed them back to the clerk. The recruitment man gave instructions to everyone to be at the train station early Monday morning. Anyone not there on time would miss the train and his chance of a job.

The small ragged gathering of men, young and old, dispersed, going their different ways. Most seemed to have a spring in their step, knowing that they, like Benjamin, had finally managed to get some regular work, even though it might be a couple of hundred miles away. In these hard times, times of survival, work is work, no matter what it is or where it is, work is work. A couple of the older men, walked away, round shouldered, not knowing what they were in for and not knowing whether or not they would be up to the task of miner. But choice? They had none. They were all desperate for work and they had to give it a try, even if it meant leaving their families living in some slum or holed out basement somewhere near the river for shelter. They had to give it a go. Maybe they could send for their families when they had established themselves or perhaps, they could send some money back to London, to help out. Theirs was a desperate plight and now, there was just a little light at the end of what had been a very long dark tunnel, and frankly, still was a very, long dark tunnel.

That weekend, Benjamin took a last look at Tilbury, where he and his older brother Joseph had arrived in the hope of a new prosperous life. Now he didn't know where his brother was and here he was, about to leave the only place that they were both familiar with. He had no idea how to contact his brother and he guessed that if Joseph were at sea somewhere, he had no way of contacting his young brother, to even see if he was alive.

He would leave his new address with Molly the kind lady at the bakery. That was all he could think of.

Benjamin was now twenty years of age. He was no stranger to early mornings. He was used to being up early working at the bakery, so getting to Euston train station at 5am was no challenge. He had hiked across London, managed to get a ride on the back of a horse and cart going into the city and most of the way to his destination. He had walked the five miles in his new working boots. Because of an accident when he was a little lad, he always had to have his boots either made for him, or altered to fit his shortened right foot. But with little money in his pocket nowadays, a larger fitting boot than was necessary for his right foot, which had to be stuffed with wool to make it fit more comfortably. He walked and hitched the rest of the way to make sure he was there for the 6am train to Carlisle. He had left the bakery in Tilbury at midnight. His feet chafed on his new boots, but they would soon wear in he kept comforting himself. But a set of good working boots was a necessity if he was going to make a success of his new job. This was a new experience for him and he looked forward to in with an enthusiastic curiosity.

A large steaming metal and steel construction stood, hissing and blowing like a large wooden horse about to defeat the Trojans, by its power and size and might. These huge metal constructions, running on iron rails and blowing out steam by the ton to push their wheels around, had been around for some years now as 'railway mania' had hit the country and new railway lines were forming and joining all over the country. The train he was awaiting, was a GNWR train and he sat on his bag of meagre belongings, which had travelled all the way from the borders of Russia. He was greeted by a man in what could be described as a working suit. The cloth was a rough worsted tweed of greys flecked with black. It hadn't seen a press or a hot iron for a long time, the jacket was creased at the back and under the sleeves, and where his large hands protruded well beyond the end of his sleeves, the cuffs were ragged and worn.

While he had been waiting for someone from the mining company, Benjamin stood next to a map of the railway network that had built up over the very short time that the railways had been in being. There were clear lines headed up to Lancaster, but not many beyond. There were lines creeping up the other side of the country, along the east coast of the country from London and reaching Scotland.

The man put out his hand to greet Benjamin. His large hands felt like sandpaper and his nails, though he had made some attempt to clean them, were split and soiled and burdened with black streaks of oil and coal Benjamin assumed, from working in the pit. Under his cloth cap was a wrinkled brow and Benjamin reckoned his age to be not much in excess of his own. He had a ruddy, chiselled face, stubble growth and a mouth full of broken and blackened teeth. The man was slightly stooped and walked with a slight limp, but Benjamin didn't know if this was from a childhood illness…or from an accident. Benjamin hoped that this was not his future fate from working in a mine. He was already apprehensive.

He was ushered into a waiting room, joined about twenty other men, of various ages and in a variety of dress, but all headed for the Cumbrian minefields, in anticipation of making enough money, to keep themselves and their families. His reservations were skipping ahead of him. If this man was the sign of the success of a working man, then he started to wonder whether or not he'd made the right move. But he needed work and a steady income if he was to build a life for himself. He wished his older brother Joseph was here to talk to, so that he could see if he was making the right decisions.

Cumbria was a long way from London and Tilbury in particular, which is where they first landed in this country and where they made their first few pennies, found a place to lay their heads, and were able to earn enough to literally buy a crust of bread. He sat on his bag and rested against the timbered wall. He studied the map on the wall and stood up.

He ran his finger all over the railway map of the British Isles, noting some large conurbations that he might pass on the way. Birmingham, Manchester, Liverpool and Lancaster, where the line ran out. This is where Tam, the besuited foreman, had introduced himself to be and said they would be picked up by truck and taken the rest of the journey by road to Alston Pit, east of Carlisle.

The massive steam railway engine rolled out along the high ceilinged, cavernous red-brick and fancily decorated iron building. Along the station platform at regular intervals, were flower boxes filled with pretty plantings, adding to the presentation of the recently flag-stoned platforms, with their new wooden benches and painted walls. The train's giant drive wheels were as tall as any of the men here. The handsome metal sculpture stood hissing and steaming, puffing and blowing like a snorting high bred horse, straining at the bit, or a grand horned brown bull, desperate to get to work, mounted on a herd of cows at the other end of a field. The magnificent beast, as Benjamin saw it, was finely painted in dark green and gold livery, with fine black and red lines hand painted around the engine and the tender. Everything was shining like a new pin. The engines name, 'The Lancaster Castle', was raised in brass, with red and black lettering, on each side and on the front of the engine. The carriage doors were opened by uniformed guards, in matching dark green thick cloth-suits. They wore matching flat-topped, peaked caps, with the company's emblem emblazoned on them. GNWR. Each double-breasted jacket, was neatly pressed had similarly embossed brass buttons with the same initials. Benjamin, felt privileged to be able to experience this relatively new form of transport, at no cost to himself, and was looking forward to experiencing the journey.

Eventually the train, with its four coaches and two goods wagons, pulled slowly out of the station. Steam and smoke belched out over the newly painted, whitewashed walls, leaving black smuts everywhere, much to the annoyance of the station staff. Almost blinding people, they covered their eyes, noses and mouths. Much coughing could be heard as the train left the station. As the fireman shovelled coal into the burners, the driver released the pressure and The Lancaster Castle slowly pulled away, gained speed and was soon passing through the smoky streets of north London, rows and rows of red-brick houses with dark grey slated roofs. The train crossed big steel bridges and looked down upon roads busy with carts and carriages as well as goods vehicles, unloading their merchandise at small parades of shops.

The train was soon out into the countryside, fields and villages, farms and hamlets. As the train slowly rolled back and forth through the fields, passing meadows grazing sheep, and cows chewing the cud. Benjamin could see fields of early wheat. Small settlements, seemingly in the middle of nowhere, the tracks passed through forestry and rough pastures, passing the edge of small towns where it made scheduled stops for water and coal and perhaps a loaf of bread and some cuts of boiled ham at the larger stops. Sometimes there was a brew of tea available in a workman's shed, sometimes there were a few bottles of ale available from a trader's cart, where the train made station stops.

Benjamin was not amongst the privileged to have been able to travel on a first, second or even third-class seat, instead the men sat on wooden benches in the goods wagon, some sat on the floor, or on bales of straw. In the carriage was an iron stove on which a kettle was almost permanently 'on the boil' as each man, as well as the guardsman and engineer, brewed a cup of tea, drinking from much used, chipped white enamel cups, and water poured from a jug. The jug had been filled with water and was replenished at each stop, where there was water. At some water stops, where there were no other facilities, other than the large water tank which was set on tall stilts, the guardsman would take the jug to where running water was available. Sometimes that would be a nearby fresh-water stream. Similarly, alongside the water jugs, there was a small urn containing a small amount of milk to which they helped themselves, but had to be carefully eked out. These were supplied by the railway company for their staff and passengers alike.

Passengers who had paid for seat tickets, certainly for first and second-class, would receive a slightly better service. In the next goods wagon to theirs were some livestock. A massive brown bull, secured in a huge metal stall. It had a ring through its nose and was connected by two further rings, which slid up and down its cage so that it could rest. In addition to the bull, there were about twenty wire baskets, containing racing pigeons. These billed and cooed for almost all of the journey, but a carriage away, didn't cause too much noise or disturbance.

Even though it was a long tedious journey, the countryside was unspoilt and beautiful and Benjamin was appreciating seeing a part of the country that he may not have seen if he had stayed in

London. As the train went on chuntering through the countryside, folks would wave, from horseback, or from carriages, or if they were on foot. From stone bridges, where they stood, waiting for the chugging of the oncoming train and then cursing at the realisation, that this great metal monster, had covered them with a sticky steamy coal, dust filled smoke. The grass and the moorlands and the meadows were varying shades of greens and yellows and browns. They passed lakes and streams and bogs and rivers. Benjamin felt glad to be alive, all of this beauty to take in, and a new life to be built.

The six o'clock train had left London for Lancaster, those interested in the rapid growth of the railway networks, reckoned the rail would eventually stretch all over the country and this line, would eventually get to Scotland. But for the time being it stopped at Lancaster, and Tam, the man who was in charge of the gang of workmen, said that there would be a truck ready to meet them when they arrived at their destination. It seemed that most of the gangs building the railways and laying the tracks were Irish, which Benjamin was told was an island over to the west of this coast. They called them navigators or navvies, whether they dug ditches, filled embankments or laid track, or for that matter did any job on this amazing new form of transport. The government and private companies were investing untold millions of English pounds, and American dollars were also finding their way into the funding, all of them expecting big rewards. Not Benjamin's concern, right now all he was interested in was getting to the mines and making some money so he could build for a better life.

They eventually arrived at their destination. An expansive goods yard, lit with gas-lamps, secured on buildings around the yard. A dead end, which had a huge turning circle for the train and tender, the turntable an extension, attached at the end of the rails. All around them, in neat bays were piles of sand, grit, roadstone, coal, logs, timber, bricks and rocks. There were stacks of well-travelled large oil drums, coloured reds and blues and greens, with black stencilled initials and numbers marked on them denoting their contents, with chalk names added for their destination. They were filled with all sorts of industrial liquids with open lorries and horse drawn trailers, queuing to be loaded. The twenty or so men, Benjamin hadn't counted exactly, alighted the train, down the

CHAPTER 9

steps, onto the rough ground of the busy goods yard. It was 2am in the morning, and Benjamin was staggered to find that it was so busy. Most of the men in his party, had been sleeping for the last four or so hours. As they arrived there was what someone had called a 'milk-train' in the sidings, waiting to use the same line, back down to Birmingham. Their engine hissed and blew and when the guard had given the all clear, the engine chuntered up to the turntable.

Tired and hungry the contingent of men, ageing from fifteen years old to fifty years old, trundled along the goods yard. Stretching their arms and rubbing their eyes, their backs and shoulders, still aching and sore from the long journey. Sham, or the foreman, as the men had now started calling him, was Irish, his name being short for shamrock. Ben got to know was the national flower of that country, an island across to the west of England, chivvied them up to climb on board an open Foden wagon, which had been awaiting their arrival. This vehicle was used at the colliery to moved timber and other goods, back and forth.

Sham called out, in an accent that Benjamin could hardly understand. But he got the message.

"Mind your arses when you sit down boys, there might be some wood chippings or some splinters, and we don't have any doctors at the pit. So just watch where you sit!"

The group of men heeded Sham's word and climbed up on to the open truck, with just thick wires and uprights for safety, bolted at intervals onto the side of the truck's platform. They shuffled along, to either sit against the cab, though that was limited in space, or they sat with their legs dangling off the side of the truck and holding on to the steel wire rails.

A bumpy half an hour later, they arrived at the pithead. About a hundred yards away were several corrugated huts. There was one long single-story timber shed with about one hundred bed spaces, there were bunk-beds, but mainly single beds, set out in dormitory style, with just a few divisions between every ten bed spaces. At one end there was a makeshift kitchen, a thrown together affair of a small range fed by, sticks and coal alongside an iron stove and a couple of tables. Benjamin didn't like it. It smelled of sweaty bodies and smoke, a stale odour, with no sweetness to it and not much ventilation. Men, who he guessed were off shift, as he was told that the mine operated on twenty-four-hour three shifts basis, were either laying on their beds dozing still wearing their working boots. Some were playing cards with piles of money lying on a bed. Others were sleeping heavily, still wearing their boots. Several of them looked like black men, as they hadn't washed when they came up from the mine, just keen to crash out and not bothering to clean themselves up. Black clothes, black hands, blackfaces. To Benjamin, it was altogether, a very squalid scene and his first impression of the accommodation and its inmates was that of suspicion. A coldness that created a tense atmosphere. Suspicious eyes followed him along the long-house, each new member being a threat to any pecking order that might have been fought for, when it came to working the best coal seams and then food space and bed space. Benjamin tried to cut the tense atmosphere out of his mind.

Outside the hut were 'latrines' and running water was fed through some lead pipes with brass taps and into cavernous tin sinks, he assumed and was later told they were for washing themselves as well as doing whatever laundry they had. It was cold water. There was no running hot water. If they wanted hot water, then this had to be boiled. There was a very large two-handled saucepan, which could be placed on the old iron stove, but that would take maybe an hour to boil, so cold water was the order of the day.

Benjamin was now even more apprehensive than he was before. The way in which the workers were housed, it seems was not exactly the way that it was explained to him, when he applied for the job, at a kiosk on a platform, back in London. He could see that most of the men in the bunk-house were unshaven, He could see why. With no hot water it was an added tedium to have to boil water to be able to shave. But he had always set himself a standard, and if he had to, then he would boil water to be clean shaven and to always look as groomed as he could. Cleanliness was next to Godliness, he was always told, not that he had ever heeded that, as he wasn't a particularly religious man. But that phrase seemed to have stuck. But he was committed, there was no going back and it was a job. It was a job with a regular income, for as long as he wanted and he could save and move on and do something better, if and when the opportunity came up.

Sham, the foreman, directed his new team to where empty beds or bunks, were free. By now it was 4am and Benjamin was flagging. He chose a vacant bed, with some freshly laundered though, grubby looking sheets and a towel, stacked on the end, of the bed next to a dividing screen. He unstrapped his newly bought boots, stripped his shirt and breeches off, hung them over the dividing screen threw his bag of meagre belongings under the flimsy wooden structure they called a bed and collapsed on it. He was told that his first shift would start later on that day. Benjamin slept heavily.

In the hours that Benjamin slept, two shifts of men had come and gone and he eventually woke to a fracas that had broken out near his cot. He looked at a couple of familiar faces that he'd travelled with on the train up from London, who had established that territorial fights were not uncommon.

Benjamin looked around for his boots that he had shoved under the bed, to find that they had disappeared. He stood up and looked again. He looked around all the other nearby beds.

One of the newly arrived men spoke, in whispered tone, "They've been nicked mate. Big fella, down there, unshaven Irishman, red hair. I saw him. If you look around, you can see that no-one takes their boots off while they're sleeping. Best way to lose them, especially if they're new."

Benjamin was tall and fit, but my, he viewed the Irishman and admitted to himself that *that*, was a big unit and might be a scrap too far. He favoured diplomacy, his first stop. Firstly, he walked down to the kitchen area and drew a mug of water, swilled it round his mouth and spat it out. He then drew water from the running tap and swilled it over his face. It helped to wake him up. He turned around and started walking towards the big Irishman, the one with the big red beard. The Irishman rose from his cot, anticipating the aggravation, indeed, looking forward to showing the occupants of the long-house, who was 'boss' and who was not to be messed with. The man *was* big and heavy and as he stood up, wearing Benjamin's boots, he stood what felt like a foot taller than Benjamin and absolutely solid, from all of those years as a navvy working on the railways. This was one fight that Benjamin could not afford to lose.

As Benjamin walked slowly down the line of bunk-cots and

beds, stacked against one of the dividers were several tool handles which one of the men was using to repair his shift's working tools.

This was one fight Benjamin kept telling himself that he could not afford to lose. One of the men picked up a pick-axe handle and threw it to Benjamin. He caught the pick handle in mid-air as he approached the big man, the big man laughed and mocked the youngster, preparing to take on a giant. He could smell his stale body from several feet away. Benjamin told himself that this was just an animal that needed to be put down. The giant's stained, unwashed singlet vest seemed stuck to his sweaty torso. His eyes and forehead were tainted with coal dust from the pit. "Go on boy. Do your worst." And he continued to roar, laughing and mocking the boy. Benjamin thought of the story of David and Goliath that he had had read to him in bible classes when he was back home, in his own country. He steeled himself as he came closer to the big man. He got as close as he could and the ginger gargantuan lunged at him. Benjamin was nimble and quick and side stepped the man with ease. The man tumbled on the floor, grabbing Benjamin's ankle tipping him over. The man was up quickly, despite his bulk. Benjamin was quickly back on his feet had to be decisive. He took the pick-axe handle in both hands and with all of his strength, hit the man across his kneecap. The blow ripped open his coarse canvas trousers with the rough sharp edge of the handle. The man reeled to the floor, one leg outstretched and his hands and arms holding his damaged knee. His arms were muscled and bigger than Benjamin's legs. As the giant stretched out his uninjured leg, Benjamin brought the thick-end of the pick handle down on his other kneecap and the man screamed in pain. Blood oozed through his thick grey working trousers and mixed with black coal dust in an increasing dark red pool on the floor.

"Get me a doctor. Jeesus, get me a frigging doctor, Jeesus, oh Jeesus, get me a doctor!" And crying out like a baby, "Oh mammy, oh mammy, I want my mammy."

Benjamin, pushed the man over on to his side and put one foot on his massive leg, the man screamed out even louder than before, eerily, like a mythical banshee from his own land of Ireland. Benjamin undid his boots, pulled them off the injured babbling hulk and walked calmly back to his bed.

The site manager, Thaddeus Lock, was called, the foreman

was called. There was no fuss or recriminations. They just loaded the big, damaged, blubbering Irishman on to the open lorry and drove him off to the hospital in Carlisle. Benjamin went calmly about his business, with admiration from all quarters.

No-one, but no-one, ever approached Benjamin again, nor stole his boots while he slept. The last time the red-headed Irishman was seen, was on sticks, limping his way on to the Liverpool to Dublin Ferry.

Benjamin hated the mine. Hated being a miner, a collier. The dark damp sweaty, dangerous conditions, the dust the uneven surfaces that hurt his feet, despite his thick working boots. His workmates seemed to accept their lot as a way of life. Their fathers had done it before them, their grand-fathers had done it before them. There was no way out as they saw it and they accepted their fate. They liked the camaraderie, working with their pals and neighbours from the same villages where they grew up. Same school mates working together, brother married to cousins. Friends married to sisters. Fathers married to aunties. Just one big working family, all going nowhere, just existing and accepting that that, was where life was and where they were in it. But not Benjamin.

Benjamin hated it all. No one had any ambition to change anything. Most of all he hated the cruelty towards the donkeys that worked and lived and died in the pits. Up to their knees in slurry most of the time, they worked pulling heavy trucks full of coal ore, along narrow passages for fourteen and sometimes more hours a day. And when they had had enough, they just died there on the spot. Some of the men would then drag them off the truck rail-track and push them down the nearest redundant shaft, long since having given up its precious black gold. The smell from these old shafts was putrid, acrid and enough to make men heave and throw up, until the rats, deep down in those shafts had gnawed their way through the discarded, extraneous, working animals. Skinny ribbed insignificant, emaciated bodies, their hooves and knee-joints rotting, having been working in waterlogged shafts virtually all of their miserable lives.

CHAPTER 10

1893, Samuel Abrahams, Buckabank Sawmill

Samuel had worked the timber mill at Buckabank for more years than he could remember. It never got easier, all these years and still a struggle to survive on a daily basis and never enough time to do all the jobs that were needed. He felt old and tired. He didn't know how old he was, he reckoned that he was in his sixties, though he didn't need to know. Somewhere he had a marriage certificate, somewhere deep in a pile of faded records, deep in a drawer somewhere. But the marriage certificate had been there for what seemed forever. He'd shed many tears over the document, trying to remember the girl he loved so much, his teenage bride, who died within weeks of their marriage from cholera, prevalent in those parts for some years. Thousands died, she was just another number. He was a broken man. But that was long ago and his memory was thinning and the pain receding, but not diminishing.

Nowadays, loading a wagon with pit props took him almost all day, cutting them days before was a twenty-four hour a day job to keep up. There never ever seemed like enough time to re-plant new stock, which would be ready for cutting in anything from three to five years. *If I ever survive that long*, he thought to himself. He was struggling more and more to keep up with the demand for pit props for this and two other mines. But to get the work, he had almost quoted below his costs and certainly couldn't afford a full time or even part-time skilled assistant, opting instead to take on casual labour as he needed it. Today was one of those days when he needed his casual labourer, but the no-good drunkard had turned up so inebriated, he could hardly stand, let alone take the heavily loaded cart, drawn by two old but still powerful 'heavy' horses. So, Samuel had to part with the drunken Jimmy, a mentally damaged ex Scottish soldier, and probably a closet retard, before he even joined up. So, Samuel was driving the heavily laden pen truck with its load of pit props, supported only by four steel uprights either side of the cart and two uprights at the rear. Samuel did his best to coax the tired old horses up the steep incline, along the colliery entrance, with its large unrepaired holes and bump breaks in the tracks. Some of the pit props had dislodged and started to slip one or two at a time and disaster was looming. The brake handle had caught on the road as the wagon bumped its way up the hill and had snapped off, rendering itself useless.

As Benjamin alighted the mine for his half-hour lunch break, he saw the cart approaching the coal yard. He viewed the old man struggling, to not only pull his cart to the top of the tracks to the open yard, but to see the old man physically wheezing trying to complete his task. Samuel had climbed down now, to try and pull the horses along. Seeing the man struggling with the two heavily perspiring, horses, straining at the bit and snorting, like a couple of fiery-dragon, with Samuel cracking his whip at their buttocks, Benjamin could see a serious accident in the making.

He ran across the yard through the emerging crowd of miners being disgorged via the mine cages that led up from their shafts, their dark and dimly-lit hell-holes, the black circles that were their eyes still blinking at the daylight. He screamed at the old man, "Hold it, hold it! Just stay there. Don't move any further."

Most of the crowd of miners gathering, as each cage reached the surface, watched with a morbid interest, waiting for the horses to bolt or the load to spill or the bolting horses turning the wagon over. They watched their fellow collier Benjamin taking control of the bad situation. He took the reins off Samuel, who sighed with relief and slumped on a grass bank on the side of the incline.

"Boulders, brick, rocks!" Benjamin shouted at Samuel. "Get some boulders under the wheels!"

Samuel, as old and wise as he was, knew when to take instruction from a young man who without him, there would have surely been a catastrophe. He drew up enough strength to do as he was instructed and secured the wagon, with boulders under its front and rear wheels. While Samuel was undertaking this task, Benjamin was soothing the horses, talking to them in smooth but strong tones, so they understood that they were safe and could settle. His head and mind and memory took him back, momentarily to the family farm. There he would spend all day with the horses, ploughing the lifeless 'steppe' that they called a farm, where growing the meanest of crops took an immeasurable will of iron as well as skill and hard work. His mind shot back to his struggling family and he hoped his journey to England was worth it and he would be able to send for them one day. His mind was now set on helping the old man and his delivery of timber pit props.

Benjamin uncoupled the horses and led them into a rough fielded area, just a hundred yards away. Samuel was again slumped on a couple of tufts of greenery, just watching Benjamin, young and fit, and wished his bones weren't as grey as his hair.

A full yard of miners smoking and swilling bottles of ale, eating sandwiches and home-made meat and veg pies, more pastry than filling, some swilling their faces in the cold water in the horse troughs, stood watching Benjamin working at his extra curricula activity, their arms folded, some admiring him, some tutting, some thinking that they had enough work to do, without taking on extras.

Benjamin returned from tying up the horses. Samuel stood up and put his hand out to shake Benjamin's for taking control of a potentially bad situation.

"We need to get your wagon unloaded, Sir. I can help and perhaps, if you will agree to buy some of my work-mates a bottle of beer, we can get some help. What say you, Sir?"

The mine foreman was not at all happy and told the men to get back to work. His message was directed specifically at young Benjamin, whom many of the men took a lot of notice of, particularly when he was arguing the rights of the men to ensure their work breaks and shift changeovers. The foreman was a man not unlike the big red-haired Irishman that had tried to take Benjamin's boots, that first day that he had bedded down in the mine dormitory. Though big and ugly, the foreman was never going to physically challenge Benjamin. Instead, he would stop him regularly and fine him for any reason he could. Late on shift, late off shift, refusing to throw a live donkey down a shaft, that had collapsed from being worked to near death. Any opportunity, and here was one.

Samuel's smile said it all.

At Benjamin's offer of a free bottle of beer for the first twenty men to come forward, the wagon load of timber props was unloaded within fifteen minutes.

Samuel pulled out his purse and gave one of the men, enough change to go to the camp store and buy twenty bottles of the foaming brine, they called beer. Everyone was happy but the colliery manager, Thaddeus Lock, gestured to Benjamin. "Let's have a word, son."

Benjamin knew what was coming and before the overbearing Lock was able to sack him, Benjamin said, "Before you even open your mouth Mr Lock, I quit!"

There was a roar from the remaining crowd who were slowly shuffling back to the cages to take them down to the depths of hell, to finish their shifts. Thaddeus Lock. Nobody talked down to him. He was the colliery manager and held shares in the company, nobody spoke to him like that and got away with it. He was red-faced and swore vengeance upon Benjamin.

CHAPTER 11

1893, Buckabank Timber Mill

And so, it came to be, Benjamin had a new job. Samuel had a fit young assistant who was keen to learn all about the timber mill and its business.

As Benjamin steered the horses along the roads and the lanes back to Buckabank, through a pretty village of flint and slate houses, and stone and thatch cottages. They passed a small shop opposite a square with a water pump and a few shrubs placed neatly around a grassed over-green. Out of the corner of his eye, Benjamin noticed a pretty young girl, probably around his age, laying out fruit and vegetables in front of the shop, who waved and smiled as they passed. The wagon jogged on by a large pond, somewhat overgrown with bullrushes to the rear of the water and an area of yellow pond lilies, and in need of some attention, but nevertheless, it looked very pretty. He felt strangely comfortable and at home, as the horse's hooves echoed against the short rows of cottages, clipped and clopped as they passed, and even though he had never been here before, either to the village or the mill, he felt that this was where he belonged. Benjamin chatted to Samuel about his family back in 'the old country', it warmed Samuel's heart to think that they were from the same region of Eastern Europe, though he had never heard of the village, or even the town that Benjamin hailed from. As the horses jogged past cottages and houses, fences and fields, hedges and ditches, one or two folks raised their arms and tipping their caps, in friendly gesture. After all, Samuel had been a fixture of Buckabank, for more years than most could remember. His mind wandering back to the 'old-country', the place of his birth, he could not even remember how many years ago. He was suddenly overwhelmed, and felt a wealth of emotion washing over him in a torrent. The memories that he could never quite erase from his mind, the fear returning from when he and his family had to flee from the cruelty of persecution, the beatings, the robbing, the thievery, the rapes, the murders, the beheadings, the plight of Jews from thousands of years, from biblical times…and what had changed. *Nothing*, he thought. *Nothing*. Tears streamed down his face. He mopped them with his tired, worn jacket sleeve and felt the rough tweed material scratchy on his face.

"This is a miracle!" he said.

"The Lord has brought you to me in my hour of need. He has sent me a son that I never had, thank God! A son, I am indeed a happy, happy man. Oy, oy, oy. I am blessed. Thank you, God!"

Benjamin, was a little taken aback at the rejoicing of Samuel, but as the old man seemed to have placed himself in a very happy state, then who was he to upset the apple cart.

Samuel directed Benjamin to turn at the next opening, the entrance to the mill. Through a huge wooden seven bar gate, tied open with rough shipping rope, it was overgrown and neglected. The horses turned automatically without being guided and continued to plod along steadily, by this time knowing exactly where they were headed and knew that there was a trough of water at the end and some fresh hay. Their master would usually give them a brush down or in hot weather, wash them down with buckets of water, drawn from the well and brush them with the yard broom. Today however, was a day to take off the harnesses and just let them wander where they wished.

Samuel directed Benjamin to reverse the wagon into one of the tall wood-sheds, before he uncoupled and let the horses roam free. Samuel wandered over to the house, slightly bent over and holding one side of his back.

Benjamin surveyed the site.

The accommodation at the timber mill, seemed to have been neglected, for quite some time. A big old farmhouse, just about still standing, needed a lot of work. The roof, the walls, chimney, windows, were all in a poor state and had been in that state for quite some time. But the outbuildings which housed the giant steam saw and other cutting equipment was in good working order. A little paint might not go amiss, but otherwise sound and solid.

Clearly, the emphasis here had been on maintaining the mill, to maintain an income from an old established and ongoing business. Though even that seemed to have seen better days. Perhaps Benjamin could improve things at his 'new home', and this did appear to be his new home. And, as he seemed to have been adopted as the 'son of Samuel' in the last few hours, then he would try and be a 'dutiful son' and settle in as quickly as he could and work hard. He looked forward to making a success of this and this would be one of the first steps to help him to make enough money, to bring his family over from Lithuania.

We'll see, he thought to himself. *We'll see.*

This was a good day. The start of something new and good.

CHAPTER 12

1893, Joseph, Newcastle upon Tyne

Joseph was almost overwhelmed by the city of Newcastle, on the river-Tyne. The sun beat down on the quayside which was alive with boats and marine craft of every description, from the 'tramp steamer', and the crew to whom he had just said goodbye, to boats lining the quay, sometimes three and four deep. There were large vessels, loading coal by the hundreds of tons. There were ships unloading timber from the Norwegian states, fishing vessels, the stench of rotting fish, bringing the seagulls soaring above and around them, occasionally diving down and stealing fish heads and any scraps they could carry. The big cranes moved along the quay with ease, lifting huge loads, creaking and scraping along rusty rails, wheels screaming and wielding, under the weight they were moving. People and horses, and hand carts, and horses and carts, and porters carrying suitcases, and working men pushing sack barrows, stacked to their shoulders. It was an exciting and vibrant, dynamic scene.

The quayside was bustling with people moving back and forth, going about their business. There were frock-coated men, with their exuberance of matching waistcoats and contrasting trousers. There were sparkling women with full length gowns with vivacious, mutton sleeves and carrying parasols as the late afternoon sun beat down on them. There were men in elegant morning suits, with grey striped trousers and tall black hats. Maids pushing prams and parties of people waiting to board the Paddle-Steamer from the quay to Holy Island. Joseph was particularly impressed by the ship that was tied further up the quay, it was the SS Woodham, built in Hartlepool in 1869. His boss on The Manchester had never stopped singing the praise of this wonderful

Screw Propellor steamship on which he had travelled as a boy and was one of the first of its kind. He'd read all about its owner a William Schaw Lindsay. 'Marvellous man', he repeated every time he mentioned the boat.

He continued to walk and took in the pungent aromas and the smell as he walked along the quay, stepping over ropes and dodging porters moving baggage and sacks and crates. He was liking the feel of the hard ground beneath his feet. There were so many different fragrances, stinks, stenches and malodours, from horse dung to spices, to meat being cooked alongside the hostelries on open fire-pits, with burning coals. Vendors offering cooked meats, ember-grilled sardines smothered in mustard and baked potatoes and fire-cooked sausages and meat pies and mash, roasted chestnuts and toasted marshmallows. It was hard to take it all in. The whole scene was of chaos, but organised chaos. Everyone seemed to have a place to go and a purpose. The noise was that of a hubbub, a constant hum, an incessant, non-stop cackle of voices and laughter and shouting and whistling and, boy he needed a drink, a 'few wee drams', as one of his ex-shipmates used to say as soon as he hit land. Only *Joseph*, needed a very large jug of beer to quench his thirst.

He headed for the Nags Head, on the quayside. He was told, that this was one of the finest inns in the north of England and certainly one of the best in Newcastle. Taking in all of this activity had given him a thirst like a horse. It was late afternoon and he had completed his final shift, helping unload The Manchester. He had said a final goodbye to his shipmates and to his employer, someone he regarded as his friend, the skipper, Michael Manchester, his employer for the past, almost three, years. He was finally on dry land and couldn't help wonder where his brother Benjamin was. Once he was settled, he decided that his next task would be to try and locate his older brother Benjamin. This wasn't a very large country in terms of land mass, but it was a very built-up country and it was a very busy country. He wondered whether he would ever meet up with his brother again. The papers that he had been reading, kept talking about this 'industrial revolution' that the country was enjoying, and that Newcastle was the busiest city, second only to London. There were ships being built on the Tyne, Ironworks a plenty, employing hundreds of men, and feeding the massive shipbuilding industry. There was coal being mined in the county and shipped around the world, in fact he felt good about where he was in his life and was driven to wanting to make his mark. All he needed was a job and he would be on his way.

He entered the Nags Head Inn, having to duck his head so as not to hit his forehead on the low-lying doorway. The pub was packed with people, shoulder to shoulder, but there were plenty of staff serving behind the bar. Big busted girls, probably chosen for their bosoms and not their minds or for intelligent conversation. They sported bare-forearms, with gigot mutton sleeves and wearing mop caps. They pulled pints from a pump-handle on the bar. Others were serving double-flagon jugs, straight on to the tables and as they delivered their foamy brew, they were being slapped across the backsides by the clients, who apart from the odd 'painted lady' were almost all men of varying quality. Working men mostly, clerks, sea-farers, suited and bespectacled gentlemen looking both seamy and disreputable, the lot of them. All there for their own reasons, be it business, pleasure, skulduggery, self-indulgence or just plain mischief. Most of them were up to no good.

Joseph slowly shouldered his way to the front of the queue, taking his turn and reached the bar. He had already taken heed of his skipper's last words.

"Joseph, trust no-one but yourself, keep your money well hid, don't drink too much and watch out for the women, for they'll take all you've got."

"A pint of your best please landlord."

He gestured to the well-dressed stoutish man behind the bar, with rolled up sleeves sporting a red waistcoat and wearing mutton chop sideburns on his red-cheeked face.

"Not me bonny-lad, I'm just the barman. The guv'nor's never here, we do all the work and he just likes to rake in the money."

"How much do I owe you sir?"

"That'll be two and a half of your hard-earned pennies, bonny lad."

After a few jars of ale, Joseph was feeling relaxed and starting to feel his 'land legs'. Having been at sea for the last two and a half years or so, the adjustment back to terra-firma was not as unnerving as his shipmates said it would be. They were just trying to encourage him to stay on board and live the life of a seafarer. But no, Joseph had done his bit. It was time to look for new things to do.

He had saved his earnings from The Manchester and had placed it with the Liverpool and Manchester Bank for safe keeping. He had been parsimonious when it came to spending his hard-earned graft at every boozer in every port that The Manchester had stopped, unlike his hardened sailor mates. The crew insisted that their wages be paid on a weekly basis so that they could gamble on board and spend their cash on wine, women and song, as soon as they had docked and unloaded the ship's cargo, whatever that may have been, from their coastal hopping guv'nor's business. Back on board, they would enjoy singing sea shanties with one of the crew playing on a tuneless old Spanish guitar, with only four of its six strings left on the beaten old body. Another would play harmonica as a limited form of accompaniment.

The wise old skipper was more than happy to pay them their dues. He knew, that when they were spent up, he would always have a crew, willing to come back to the boat and work the next passage. Joseph knew that there were no flies on this captain. But he liked, learnt a lot from him and respected him and even thought of him as a wise and worldly friend.

Looking back, Joseph had fond memories of his adventures on The Manchester. From his first day when he was as sick as a dog, to the days in ports, many and varied, when he had had to save his crew-mates from being robbed and beaten and to hauling their sorry, drunken backsides back on board to let them sleep it off. From the time that he signed up as crew, when his English was only just passable, to getting to know the crew, one by one. The scrapes along the way, where crew men had to be dragged away from dubious gambling houses, where they had been duped into spending their hard-earned cash, gotten into fights and had to be dragged away screaming, before the police had caught up with them and banged them up.

He remembered the time when Scottish-Dunny, the skipper's mate, had disappeared for two days and after a lot of searching, they found him, about to get married to a woman that was more of a man than Scottish-Dunny was. He was completely off his head with the demon booze and he had been stripped of his worth, including his two gold teeth and his solid silver belt buckle. He was ever grateful for being saved from a fete, worse than death, he kept reminding everyone. It took a long time, before Joseph realised why they called him Scottish-Dunny. Whenever he went ashore, he always wore a kilt. Someone had explained that when the Scottish men went to war, they wore kilts with no undergarments, so that they could pee, or whatever, along the way without holding up the marching troops. He never got to the bottom of whether Dunny murdered someone or not. Perhaps it was all make-believe or bravado. He also got to learn that 'dunny' was a slang term for a toilet.

Supping at his third jug of ale, taking in the sunny day and the entertaining scenes of the movement of people passing his seated position, he was finally feeling relaxed about having left The Manchester. Days to be remembered. But here he was, sat here in an unknown city, somewhere in the north of England, where they spoke with a completely different accent. Some of the dialect was so strong that he had to keep asking folks to repeat what they were saying. He sat at a small, beer-soaked table, looking out through bull-nosed glass, enjoying the scenery. A voice greeted him in this new accent that he was struggling to understand.

"Why hello, pet. Are you going to buy us a drink then?"

He looked around, but could only see one pretty girl in front of him, just sitting herself down at his table. She continued to speak. "My, well you're a bonny lad and you look like you're a seafarer, just off the boats, I reckon. Are you needing somewhere to stay, pet? Where ya gannin after here pet?"

Joseph was bemused. But she was a pretty girl and looked pretty wholesome, unlike some of the wayward looking creatures he'd seen around and along the quays, plying their wares. "Aye lass. Sit you down. I'm happy to buy you a drink for some company, but where's your friend?"

"What friend is that then bonny lad?"

Joseph replied, "Well, you said buy 'us' a drink, so I'm asking where your friend is?"

"Ah, no pet. It's just something we say. I guess it's local and mine's a jug of ale."

Joseph got it, at the same time calling over to the bar for another large jug of Newcastle's best for himself.

"Yes, lassie, I'm looking for some accommodation for a few days until I decide what I'm doing and where I'm going. Do you know of anything?"

"Well now, there's a coincidence, my ma has a room she is looking to let, to the right person. I could take you there if yous like, pet? I'm sure she'll like you, bonny lad. She's gannin a bit micey ya-knows. You know, a bit in the head, but she keeps a good house. Would you like me to take you there?"

Joseph was weighing up the possibilities. The last thing his skipper had said was, "Trust no-one and keep your boots on with any valuables tucked inside them, or they'll skin you alive." Whatever that meant, but he got the general gist.

He didn't think that English folk were still barbaric enough to strip him of his skin, but he'd got the message. So, he was wary about this newly found friend being overly helpful. Having said that, he had already walked the quays, looking at pubs with accommodation and salubrious looking boarding houses. Most of them seemed to have signs with no vacancies. Or they may have 'No Blacks', 'No Irish', 'No Foreigners', 'No Dogs', or just, 'Full'. So maybe he should go and have a look at what her ma has to offer. If indeed it was her ma.

After chatting for another half an hour, Joseph said, "Okay lassie (a term he had picked up from Scottish-Dunny). Let's go and see what your ma has to offer?"

Though he'd been aimlessly chatting to her for the last half an hour or so, through several jugs of ale, he hadn't actually noticed what a pretty girl she was. His age or maybe a little younger, give or take. Under her white linen mop-cap, tied with a pretty blue bow, was a head of rusty colour hair that shone through glimpses of sun. When they stepped out into the sunlight Joseph couldn't help but admire her fresh creamy skin and green, green eyes, and her laugh and her smile were something to behold. This was a very pretty girl indeed and it wasn't just because he'd been at sea for weeks upon end without seeing pretty girls. This was just a very pretty girl and with a handsome figure to boot.

They had stepped out into the afternoon sun, glinting off every shiny surface, Joseph held his arm up to his face to shade his eyes from the light. Here he was following this pretty girl to who knows where and he was being led like one of the children following the Pied Piper of Hamlyn, one of his favourite stories. But having read the famous English book, he thought, like the story, this could end in disaster. They turned off the main quay and started to climb one of the cobbled back streets, which were suddenly quiet, with few people passing. His eyes were everywhere and he was dropping back, several feet now behind the girl.

He even realised that he had not even asked this girl her name, and here he was following her blindly, after all the warnings, which he thought he had heeded. She called out to him.

"C'mon pet, it's a canny way yet, we won't get there 'til dark if you're so slow. C'mon bonny lad, it's just this side of toon."

He stopped. She stopped. He wasn't sure whether he had become her 'pet' and if he was, how did that happen? They looked at each other. He suspiciously, her tentatively. She spoke. "You'll like it, I promise you. Ma keeps a lovely hoose. And I know she's gonna like you, So, stop yer ganderin and howay, up them dancers, as they reached the flight of stone stairs, it's just around the next corner."

Joseph turned back and looked towards the port. They were about a mile away now and there was only a feint sound of the port below them. He could see the whole width of the river and the bustling quays either side, the tall ships, the steamships and the plethora of fishing smacks. The odd shriek of laughter broke the silence and the sound of distant seagulls filled the air. Joseph felt a lot more comfortable now. If he was going to be turned over, then it would have happened by now, on the lower back streets, where the labyrinthine of back to back alleys and paths intertwined to make a good escape route for those that wanted to do evil. He just hoped that Ma's 'hoose' was all that the girl had said it was cracked up to be.

At a whitewashed terraced cottage, with a green painted door, the girl stopped. She pushed open the door and shouted loudly, "Ma, I've got a visitor for you!"

A matronly lady poked her head out of an open upstairs window, bent forward with her bust looking like a couple of powdered buns, popping out of the top of the ribbed bodice of her brightly flowered dress, running her fingers through her mop of greying blond hair and returned the call.

"What's all this yammerin? How many times have I told thee

bonny lass that I'm not deaf. I'll be down now!"

Within minutes, Joseph was sat at Ma's table in the scullery, at the back of the house, looking out on a well-cared for kitchen garden. The terraced cottage was immaculately clean, with scrubbed flagstones covering the lower floor, extending out to the scullery and kitchen. The scullery was a stone extension which had been added many moons ago. In it sat a scrubbed pine table enough to seat six, with crude heavy pine chairs neatly placed around the table. There was a small glass bowl of fruit on the table and white linen place mats, set ready for the next meal. On the iron range a large blackened kettle was boiling and on the side was a large teapot, with a floral design, in which Ma put four scoops of tea. One for each person and one for the pot. Plain yellow linen curtains hung at the rear window which looked out onto the cared-for rear garden.

"Now bonny lad, if you're looking for a room, like my bairn says, there's one or two rules you need to know. Firstly, I don't allow any drinking or drunken behaviour in my house. If you're not in by eleven at night, you'll be locked out. I expect a month's rent in advance and I charge extra if you want breakfast and supper. If you say you want breakfast and supper and you don't take it, you will still be charged. And there's no lasses allowed in the room. AT ANY TIME! If that's understood, the room is yours. Have you got any questions?"

Joseph had had enough time to assess Ma. She was a goodly woman and obviously kept a good house. She had six letting rooms it seems. From what she said, all rooms were let out mainly to business type gentlemen and as soon as she had a room available, she would send her daughter Alice, to select an appropriate gentleman to fill the room. In that way, her accommodation was always full and she was able to maintain a good house and keep the wolf away from the door. Joseph felt as if he had to ask at least one question, or Ma would eat him alive!

"Yes, Missus. Firstly, I'd like to see the room and I'd like to ask if you do any washing? I have been used to working on a boat and have done all my own washing and it would be very nice to be able to pass on that task to someone else. Otherwise, I have no other questions, you have covered everything very well thank you, Missus."

"And one more thing, young man," Ma replied. "Don't call me Missus! I don't belong to anyone. Call me Ma. Is that understood? And yes, we can do washing. But we charge for that."

"Yes, Ma, understood!"

"Alice will show you your room. And when you come down, you can have a slice of some of my fresh baked bread and some home-made churned butter, maybe with some of Alice's home-made blackberry jam. We do everything ourselves here while we can."

"How much will that be, Ma?"

"Now don't give me none of your cheek lad, or you'll be over my knee and out of here as quick as winking!"

They broke out in laughter.

"How much do you want in advance Ma? I don't need to see it. I'm sure the room will be adequate."

The deal was done and Joseph tucked into some warm, home-made bread, straight out of the oven, with butter running down his cheeks and sticky jam, all over his fingers. Life was looking good. In the morning, he would walk around the 'toon' as Alice called it and get to know the place and look out to see if there was some gainful employment to be had.

"Perhaps Ma, Alice could show me around the town and point out folks that may be looking for a hard-working, ex-seafarer to help with their endeavours?"

"Well aye hinny, only if she has a mind to, and by the glint in her eye, I think she might have a mind to," Ma answered.

Alice smiled and a tour of the working yards around the 'toon' was organised.

Bright and early next morning, after Joseph had feasted on home-cooked griddled eggs and fresh boiled carved ham for breakfast, followed by a large mash of tea. The breakfast was a long, long way off the deep-fried eggs that the cook of the day might have cooked on board The Manchester, the types that resembled a discus and were almost as hard. He and Alice set off around some of the Newcastle Upon Tyne working yards, where he might find himself some work.

CHAPTER 13

1893, Benjamin, Buckabank

We'll see, Benjamin thought to himself. *We'll see.*

Benjamin viewed his new home. There was plenty of it. It was spacious, even though some of it was broken down and badly in need of repair, there was land and woodland as far as you could see. He loved the smell of the pine trees and the sounds of the birds whistling and tweeting in the trees, the flutter of wings, the bark of a distant family of foxes, an intermittent tapping of what he assumed was a Woodpecker. There were valleys and hills and in the far distance he could hear a fast-flowing stream or even a small river. Maybe he could do some fishing. He was taking in everything around him and taking deep breaths of the wonderful fresh country air. He was mightily relieved to be away from the coal mine and the dust and the dirt and the mice ridden, rat infested accommodation huts, which they laughingly called dormitories. The mine bosses charged a fortune for it and that drained his and everyone's meagre earnings, despite all of the extra shifts he seemed to work. He was counting his blessings.

Samuel called out to him as he strolled across the large open yard.

"Benjamin, come. I have vittles for you and I have brewed some tea and I have a beer for after our meal. Come, enjoy, already. You deserve it, oy oy, you have worked very hard today."

Benjamin ducked under the elder tree that was growing out of part of the broken-down old house. He stepped down a couple of steps into a room with a grey flagstone floor, with piles of rubble from the part collapsed house in ruins, around the room. Two windows were covered up with canvas sheets to keep out the weather and there were old cans, bottles, piles of rags and general debris, pushed into the redundant corners of the room. Benjamin wondered whether he *had* in fact made the right decision to throw his lot in with Samuel, who clearly, was only surviving hand to mouth.

Benjamin sat down at a massive oak table, pulling up the chair, which was hand-carved out of solid oak. The old man dusted the chair off for him as he sat and he gratefully tucked into a tin plate full of beans and bread which had been freshened up by being placed in the stove for ten minutes. But it was food and it was simple and it was good. Neither man said a word while they ate, just looked up occasionally and smiled at each other, as if they had worked together all their lives. Each one appreciating the other and feeling comfortable with each other's company.

Samuel spoke. "Tomorrow Benjamin, I will show you around my mill. No! Our mill! I will show you my order book and we will get to work on satisfying some of the outstanding orders."

"How long have you been here Samuel and how did you acquire the mill?" Benjamin enquired. "It's such a large expanse of property and premises. It seems like you have lots of land and woodlands. But no help?"

Samuel answered, in dismay. "Well, it's a long story. But I'll tell you, because it's important for you to know what this place means to me. I am from Lithuania in Eastern Europe, very close to where your family comes from. When I was a young boy, not even a man, three years off my Bar-mitzvah, we left our home with our family. I was the second youngest apart from my sister's baby. I was eleven years old. Not only were we starving but the persecution of Jews in our towns and villages never ever stopped. So, we had no alternative but to leave. It took eighteen long months to track across all the countries of Europe, through scorching summers and bitter winters. One by one I lost all the members of my family.

"I was eleven when we left Vilnius which is the capital of Lithuania. We were set upon by robbers and thieves. They raped my sister, several times, while I hid. They took all of our clothes and working tools, so we couldn't cut hedges or dig ditches to earn a living. We slogged across land after land, looking for work, we would do anything, even beg, just to earn enough money not to starve. We were camped out in the bitter cold one night with almost nothing to cover us. We were huddled together around a small campfire to try and keep warm and keep the wild animals away. The wolves kept circling us, all night they howled, as the fire dwindled, getting closer and closer. I tried chasing them off with sticks and throwing stones, but they just got closer and closer and then three of them rushed us, stealing my sister's baby. She was distraught and couldn't care about anything. She had never recovered from the viciousness of the animal's assault and went headlong into the forest after them, knowing that she would probably never come back. The last I heard was her screaming at them 'give me my baby, I want my baby.' Then a distant muffled scream and that was the last I heard.

"My father was taken ill not long after that, he was so weak from hunger, he died one night in our make-shift shelter that we had made in the forest and my mother froze to death alongside him. I buried them in a shallow, makeshift grave, but I didn't have any tools, so I know the wolves or bears would have eaten their remains. This left me on my own, so I begged in the streets. One day I jumped on to a wagon full of vegetables and I hid in the back. It was going to I didn't know where, and I ended up in Paris. At the time there was revolution brewing in Spain and I was recruited into a militia, called the Carlists. I was thirteen at the time in 1846. After three years fighting, I ran off and managed to hide in the freight wagon, on the back of a train and after a lot of stealing and hiding, I found myself at the port, and stowed away on a steamer. I eventually found myself in London. I was begging on the streets, but it was there that I was recruited as a woodsman for the Cardew Estate. His Lordship, Lord Cardew-Petteril saw me on the streets and took me under his wing. I eventually ended up running the woods and the timber mill, which was left to me by his Lordship, so many years ago, oy, oy, I can't remember, so long ago. No one has ever questioned it."

Benjamin could hardly believe this story of astonishing, mind-boggling, overwhelming, traumatic events, that no-one should ever have to endure in ten life-times, let alone one. It left him almost speechless, with a dry mouth and choking back tears.

Samuel could see the effect it was having on Benjamin, so he thought he would just take the sting out a bit.

"Ahh. It was all a very long time ago now and I have managed to keep myself fed as well as fit and well, all of these years and now God has brought you to me. This will all be yours when I die. Until then, you must call me Sammy. Everyone in the villages all around here know me as Sammy. Is that okay with you?"

Stunned at the story and the fact that Samuel was on his own and would leave the estate to him, was hard to take in. Sammy, which Benjamin had quickly calculated was now at the age sixty and not a particularly well, or fit man any more, was still prepared to look on the positives in his meagre life. Life itself was his salvation and his means of survival. Now Benjamin felt he had to do everything in his power to help Sammy enjoy the last years of his life.

Benjamin slept well that night. He tucked himself up in a corner of the stone-built room it was dry and he wrapped horse blankets around himself. He liked horses. They reminded him of the farm at home. He'd always worked with horses he loved the smell and the aura they gave off. He felt comfortable wrapped up and even though the surroundings weren't familiar, it helped him feel at home in his new environment. Even though it was June, the evenings were still pretty cool and no sun shone on that part of the building in which he stowed himself, curling himself up into a neat ball, just like a squirrel or a dormouse, as if hibernating. Once he had finally fallen asleep, the events of the last couple of years churned in his mind, but mostly his thoughts turned to his younger brother, Joseph and where he might be. Was he still at sea, had he returned to the land, had he given up this new world and gone home to Belarus, was he dead or alive and married with a family. Benjamin woke up with a 'start' at 6am as the cock was beginning to crow. Samuel was already up and about, having fed the horses, thrown corn for the clucking hens and washed and spruced himself up in readiness for the day's work.

As far as Samuel was concerned, this was a *good* day, a *very good* day. This was the day that he would start to teach his new assistant Benjamin, the son he always dreamed of having, how the mill ticked over, made its produce and took it to market. He brought Benjamin a steaming mug of herb tea, of his own concoction.

"Here my boy. This will set you up for the day. I have the last of some salted bacon already cooking in the pan and we will enjoy a good breakfast together, before I start to teach you all about the sawmill and how it operates. Then we will set to and try and deliver some of the outstanding orders."

"Yes! Good morning, Sammy. I slept exceedingly well thank you."

Benjamin was exercising some of his skill in his new found English, which he had been developing over the last couple of years.

"Exceedingly well, and I'm looking forward to learning everything about the mill and its workings and I'm going to help you make it successful again."

Samuel beamed. A smile so wide it lit up their day!

After chewing and just about digesting a thick lump of sliced and fried salted bacon and some crusty, re-heated bread, he swilled down a whole enamelled beaker of herbal tea. Then the newly formed team of Benjamin and Samuel, or as far as Samuel was concerned, him and his 'boy', as in his mind he had already adopted Benjamin as his son and heir, set off to 'survey the estate'.

Samuel explained that the land area took in approximately (one) three hundred acres, though as far as he was aware, there were no deeds that showed the borders of his land. The acreage took a natural shape, in that the river formed one border, the road ways two more borders. The natural lay of the valley to the north, formed boundary with a fast-flowing stream, which doubled back through the middle of the Buckabank sawmill estate. None of this had ever been questioned. Samuel had worked tirelessly for the then young Lord Cardew-Petteril and his estate and had been gifted the mill when his lordship had died. His son, who was the current Lord Cardew-Petteril, was more distant from the estate and had many other interests. They were mainly hunting and shooting and spent much of his time at the Reform Club in London, with his best pal David Lloyd-George the MP, so was a rare visitor.

Samuel explained that in years gone by, the mill's output was committed to producing and supplying timber for the main estate, in the way of fencing posts, timber for outbuildings, post and rail for paddocks and cattle pens. Since metal versions of these items were now freely available and were a lot cheaper, then the demand had died down to just a trickle these last few years. Samuel had picked up some contracts with the collieries for pit-props. But as there were so many imports coming in from the Baltic states, where they could produce in vast bulk and even with their shipping costs added, Samuel's mill could never hope to compete with these imports, then Samuel even with his low overheads, had no choice but to quote at below his costs, just to keep his business running. Needless to say, he always hoped that things would improve, but they never did.

But here was a new day, a new dawning, all would come good. They would assess what they had between them and go forward with a renewed energy. Well, a renewed energy, supplied by Benjamin. This was a new start a new beginning.

As Samuel showed Benjamin the mill and its grounds, he quickly assessed exactly what was needed and the direction he should be taking.

If the mill was losing money on pit props, then this had to come to an end.

"I think we ought to look at new markets for 'our' timber Sammy. Please tell me what you think. It seems to me that the railway networks are expanding and as I travelled up here from London, every single track had a large chunk of timber every few yards, laid underneath it for supporting the steel rails. I think they call them railway 'sleepers'. There must be a huge market there, additionally, all along the tracks at intervals, were large poles with cabling. Mile after mile after mile. I think they call them telegraph poles. Could we produce these and supply them to these expanding companies, and then there's fencing. Cross bars and uprights. We could sell them into merchants instead of having to cart all that weight to the collieries?"

Samuel was astounded at what his newly adopted 'son' had come up with and replied with enthusiasm.

"Well, my boy, I have been supplying either the estate and more latterly the collieries with pit-props these last few years. Frankly I've had so little time to even think about where else to sell my timber, oy, oy, that the thought never even crossed my mind. But if you think that's where we might do a little better with our business, then you must try and gather that business in. The trouble is, some of my machinery is old and not sophisticated enough to cut fine fencing stays. We would need to buy new equipment."

Towards the late afternoon, after they had walked the estate and Samuel had shown Benjamin the mill sheds and the sawmill itself, Benjamin was thinking about the immediate income and his head was turning to the accounts and general bookkeeping. He looked back at the bakery and was now even more thankful that Molly, the widow at the bakery in Tilbury, had let him learn about the costs of running her business and how her books balanced. He started to apply the same principles to the mill accounts. Samuel had not had the time to think about the collection of debts, his focus was always to get to the mill and cut enough props to fulfil his current order book and as he was so cheap, the orders kept coming. This would be Benjamin's first priority.

The evening came around and Samuel had unwrapped a chicken kept in the cold storeroom, that he had slaughtered, plucked and de-feathered a few days before. They sat in the big old farm kitchen discussing where the business was. Every so often, Samuel would go over to the range and turn over the two halves of the chicken, which he had split and was cooking on the top of the stove with some onions and a little stock, before he tucked it into the wood-fired range's hot oven with some potatoes. Benjamin studied the mound of papers that Samuel had placed before him. These were 'the accounts'!

Benjamin was bemused and had no hesitation in commenting. "Sammy. These are a mess! This is no way to run a business. There are delivery notes here, where you have made deliveries to mines and you haven't even raised an invoice yet. From what I can see, you have hundreds of pounds outstanding. It's no wonder you can't afford to pay staff or replace or maintain some of the machinery."

Sammy embarrassingly protested. "But I have no help and no time to spare with cutting and loading and delivering. Sometimes I just come back here, unharness the horses, let them wander in the field and I fall asleep, not waking 'til next morning. I'm sorry Benjamin. Please don't scold me. I am worn out with it all and sometimes I am just so tired, I just can't think."

Benjamin was feeling guilty at scolding Samuel. "Okay, okay. I'm so sorry, I didn't mean to tell you how to run your business, but from now on. If we deliver an order, we deliver an invoice with a delivery note. We will not then make another delivery until the last one is paid. In that way, we will improve the cash into the mill. I will spend tonight marking all of these in the ledger and we will be able to see exactly where we are. I will write an invoice for every delivery and go to each or the three collieries we supply, tomorrow and ask for payments for anything older than one month, otherwise we will be unable to supply them further. This will be the start to our new prosperity. When I collect some monies, I will take it straight to the bank. You will need to give me a letter, allowing me to draw money, so that I can get some supplies. I've made a list of what we need."

Samuel felt a wave of pride flowing through his veins. God had indeed been good to him, in sending him the 'son' he had never had.

On Saturday, the following day. Benjamin put on the tweed suit that he had bought from a second-hand clothes shop in London some months earlier, having spent his last few pence, hoping that his smart appearance would help him get a new job, to no avail. But now, here it was, being put to good use and on his way to the colliery office to collect some outstanding debts and to deliver new invoices. However, it felt good to be jogging down the country lanes at Buckabank, on the 'Trap' even though he had harnessed the most suitable of Sammy's horses, it was still being pulled by a shire horse. It looked cumbersome and totally out of place to say the least, way out in the sticks and headed towards Carlisle and the collieries pay office. The trap, meant to be pulled by a pony or small horse, looked awkward being pulled by a great big Shire horse and it also made the slope of the trap sit up at an acute angle, but Benjamin was undeterred. He had brushed the horses main and tail and taken a shears to it to tidy up its appearance. He noticed several heads turning and heard muffled laughs as he jogged past. But he wasn't in the slightest bit bothered. He was on a mission and he knew success beckoned him. He felt the fresh warm breeze in his face as he jogged along, birds singing, trees just waving in the light breeze, the scent of the old-fashioned roses and newly cut grass as he jogged past thatched cottages and village greens. It was then that he remembered from a few days before, that pretty girl, outside the grocery store, who had smiled and waved at him. That pretty, dark haired girl, wearing a mop-cap and a gingham apron over her flowing, billowing skirt. *My*, he thought, *she's pretty*. And she had given him such a smile and a wave. He might take a detour. But not now, business first.

Carlisle bustled as he jogged through the edge of the town. Folks from the villages thronged the town. It was barely eight in the morning and the market stalls were alive with trade. The Farmers market being the busiest, offering fresh meat straight off the beast, hams and bacon, fresh vegetables straight out of the ground, fresh chickens and duck eggs, newly laid. Cream, cheeses in a huge variety, home baked cakes, thick-crusted game and pork pies, bread and biscuits, all doing a brisk trade. The other stalls, offering dry goods, hardware, pots and pans, clothes stalls offering 'the latest fashions' from London and the list and the line seemed never ending. Benjamin raised many a titter with his horse and trap, but he jogged on. Past the cattle market and the railway station and goods yard, until he eventually made the colliery offices. He stopped outside, tying his horse to a strong wooden rail. He pulled a bucket from the rack at the back of the trap and filled it with water from a nearby trough and pulled a bag of hay which he had tied to the back of the trap, and set that down for the horse.

Benjamin looked at his reflection in a big plate glass window, brushed himself down took a deep breath, gathered his file of invoices and took the two creaky wooden steps up into the offices of Whitehaven Colliery Company Ltd. displayed boldly above the premises in blue and red livery.

Like the steps, the floorboards creaked as he stepped through the door. He was met by a wooden counter with a glass façade, reaching up almost to the ceiling. Sat behind, was a lady tapping away at a typewriter who didn't look up from her shiny new black and gold Underwood, until she had finished the line she was typing.

Benjamin smiled at her. In his best broken English, which was improving all of the time.

"Madam, might I have the pleasure of speaking with the manager of your accounts department please?"

By this time, the other ladies in the offices had all looked up at this handsome young stranger, in his smart tweed suit with its London 'cut', curious to see what his business was with the manager of the accounts.

A portly chap, Mr Stelling, was called from the back office and Benjamin was invited into the inner-sanctum. He sat on a wooden wheel-back chair in a sub-office as the chap, the manager, Mr

Stelling, entered. Stelling looked him up and down, noting the file in his hand, and partially tucked under his arm, regarded him and acknowledged him with a nod.

"What business do you have here young man. How can I help you?"

"Good day to you sir," Benjamin replied. "I am the new partner at Buckabank Sawmill and my partner Samuel has asked me to collect some debts as well as deliver some new invoices."

Stelling was a little taken aback. "Debts you say, how so?"

Benjamin explained that until his timely arrival, old invoices had not been paid and there were new invoices that needed paying. He also outlined the mill's new policy of accounting, and that if there were bills outstanding for more than one month, the mill was not in a position to deliver further supplies.

"Outrageous! Remarked the indignant Stelling. Who do you think you are dealing with? Lord Cardew-Petteril shall hear of this. Such impudence!"

Benjamin was quick to reply. "You will see here sir, that some of these invoices go back over twelve months and I am afraid that that is not acceptable. I will need to collect these today."

"Ridiculous!" retorted Stelling. "Be off with you, before I have you thrown out."

Benjamin was quick to come back to the red-faced Stelling, while the girls sniggered in the background regarding this young man's stance. "Sadly, in that case Mr Stelling, I will be lodging a complaint with the magistrate for unpaid debts and ask for debtors court to be contacted."

At that Stelling almost exploded red-faced and collapsed on the floor, gasping for breath. Benjamin suspected he might be over-doing the theatrics.

"Get me my smelling salts, girl. Get them now." He continued to splutter and groan on the floor. "Get this impudent young man out of here and call the police if he doesn't move."

One of the girls said, "Send for his Lordship, he'll sort this out."

Benjamin refused to move and was still sitting patiently in the inner sanctum, when Lord Cardew-Petteril arrived.

After a further confusing hour where the old debts to Buckabank were shown as paid on the colliery accounts, it emerged that Stelling had been paying these to himself. Knowing or believing that Samuel didn't have the energy or the nous to chase the debts. What he hadn't bargained for was Benjamin to turn up, with genuine demands.

A further hour passed and Benjamin left the Whitehaven Colliery Company Offices Ltd. with a large cheque, signed by Lord Cardew-Petteril himself. The police arrived and Stelling was hauled away without ceremony. Benjamin headed to the bank, depositing the cheque and drawing some cash for supplies.

This was indeed a good day!

CHAPTER 14

1893, Newcastle upon Tyne

Joseph and Alice set off around the working yards of Newcastle upon Tyne, where Josh, as Alice had decided to call him, might find himself some work.

Alice was walking with a spring in her step, particularly as she had a 'new man' in her life. She had only known Joseph less than twenty-four hours. Yet there was something about the man that made her feel comfortable and safe. He was kind, courteous and had confidence in abundance, and his rugged looks were quite appealing too.

"So, Josh, why Newcastle?" Alice enquired.

It was the first time that anyone had referred to Joseph as Josh and he liked it.

So, Josh answered. "Why not? I had heard that Newcastle was second only in line to London for commerce and work, and it seems to me that I wasn't wrong. It's a busy, busy town and–"

"City, we're a city, have been for almost nine hundred years!" Alice interrupted him.

"Well, I'd heard it was a good place to be and this is where I have my bank!" Josh apologised.

Alice was taken aback. "Bank, you own a bank?"

"No, no, no. In London, I opened a bank account for my wages and they have a branch here in Newcastle, so this is now where I have my bank, and my savings. I didn't spend much money while I was at sea, unlike the other crewmates that were off at every port, large or small, drinking up all their hard-earned cash and throwing it back up the walls and gutters of every other place the boat docked. The skipper wasn't daft, he knew if they had no money left, they would always come back to their home on board.

But not me. I've always had ambitions to do something with my life. Sadly, I've lost my brother Benjamin, somewhere along the way and I would dearly love to find him, but I've no idea where to look. Someday, someday, I'm sure we'll meet up. The last time I saw him, he was working on the docks in Tilbury, just sweeping up warehouses and then a part of the day he would work at a bakery. The lady would feed us and supply a few sacks and the floor for us to sleep on. I then managed to get a job on the tramp steamer. That was three years ago and I haven't heard from him since."

Newcastle was a hub of activity. Alice looked suitably saddened and sympathised with Josh, as they walked along the streets chatting. They passed yard after yard as they walked further up the River Tyne. They passed shipbuilders, boat builders, heavy engineering, timber yards, cutting, milling, Joseph's wonderment at the massive bridges that crossed the river, particularly the Swing Bridge, the road bridge at low level, which swung open to let large boats enter the upper reaches of the river. Eventually, passing large timber gates, open to the main road with **'James Wrighton & Skinnerburn's Timber Processors'** emblazoned across the skirting under the massive corrugated roof of its main shed. A large sign on one of the doors read **'Skilled Cutting Machine Operators Wanted. APPLY WITHIN'**.

Joseph walked into the yard, while Alice waited outside. He strode across the busy yard passing open-back trucks being loaded with large timber telegraph poles. They were being winched and swung over onto the truck, while two men guided them into place, climbing onto them as the next layer of timber was added. Smaller trucks were leaving every few minutes loaded with sawn planks, traders were coming in to select large and small panels for building works. Machines could be seen in some of the other sheds creating their own wheezing, high pitched whining and cutting noises, pushing clouds of dust into the atmosphere. Other men were gathering off-cuts and throwing those into large hoppers, to be sold for log fires. The yard was alive with constant chatter. A hive of activity with comings and goings, shouting and laughter, and the sounds of folk working as if they knew nothing else in life was more important.

As Joseph walked across the yard, a suited man with a clipboard which he assumed might be a foreman, or yard manager, saw him and gestured his head towards Joseph, with a nod which had a 'I suggest you make your way over to me' look.

Joseph spoke, "Good day to you, sir. I am hoping you might find some gainful employment for a hard-working ex-Seafarer in your establishment. I am fit and well and have good digs not far from here and I have several skills to offer."

The man was well dressed for a foreman, with rough brown corded trousers over well-polished brown leather lace-up ankle boots, a multi-coloured checked shirt that looked more like a shirt that a farmer should wear, a brown tweed jacket and a brown, cotton work coat over the outfit, with several pens of varying colours displayed neatly in its breast pocket. He boasted a large clip-board under the arm of his five foot ten, comfortable frame and from his expression, hearing Joseph's soliloquy, had heard it all before. Times were hard for a lot of people, but he had no time for wasters. He looked up from under his wire framed half-glasses and replied.

He brushed his hand through his greying wavy locks, gave a wry smile on his ruddy face and asked, "Well bonny lad, I might have. What are these skills you say you have?"

"Well, sir," Joseph replied. "I've spent more than two years on a steamer, going from port to port. I've learned how to fix most things mechanical, from winches to engines, to nets. I rebuilt some of the working quarters on board with timber, making frames and securing these to the metal hull. I've tried to learn other languages while I was on board from my crew-mates and have a knowledge of Chinese and German as well as French and my own tongue which is mainly Russian and I…"

"Okay, okay, I've got it. Jack of all trades, Mr Handyman, a Mr Fixit. And you can speak to anyone in any language, as long as they are not Norwegian, or Swedish, which is a pity as it's where most of our timber is from. But that's okay. I think I can probably find a job for a big strong young man like you. I've always got timber that needs shifting." Pointing to his office he instructed. "Go over there and wait in my office. I'll take some details from you there."

Alice watched at a distance from just inside the big work-yard gates. And thought to herself, *Mmmm. I think this one is a real gem. He's obviously a worker, he's a real gentleman, he's got savings in the bank and Ma likes him. Well, she hasn't as like as told me so, but I can tell. She definitely likes him. Ma never gives three griddled eggs to anyone, unless they're really in her good books. I think I'll keep this one. He is definitely a keeper.*

As Joseph walked over to the manager's office, he turned briefly to give a thumbs up and to wave to Alice. Alice turned on her heels and walked off, with a smile, knowing that she had helped Joseph in his endeavours. Now she needed to reel him in.

Joseph sat in the office, waiting for the manager. It was half an hour before the man returned, apologising profusely about how he was so busy and exclaiming that everyone 'wanted a piece of his hide!'

Joseph was quick on the uptake. "It seems to me sir, that what you need is a right-hand man, to do all your donkey work, while you carry on managing this busy yard. When I joined my boat, The Manchester, the skipper struggled to keep his crew in order, but by the time I left, everyone had a routine and a specified job and the whole crew were a lot happier. Jobs were evened out, workload was shared and if one task wasn't completed, it was up to the other members of the crew to help out. I rotated all the jobs, so everyone took a turn in cooking and cleaning, swabbing the decks or mending nets. It became a very happy ship and everyone worked well together, consequently they all understood each other's jobs and appreciated each other's value."

The manager, Jim Wrighton, broke in. "My, you do some jawing bonny lad. Do you ever stop?"

"No sir, I'm very sorry. But if you were to train me up, I could do all the donkey work for you while learning the ropes. I'm a very hard worker sir, I promise you. I'm not a drinker, well apart from the odd pint and I'm reliable and honest. I wouldn't let you down. I promise."

Jim Wrighton stood there listening to Joseph, holding his chin with his hand and rubbing his fingers up and down in contemplation and quizzical thought.

"Mmmm, bonny lad. Perhaps you're right. Maybe I do need someone doing the running around for me. I can't be everywhere. What about your references? What have you got for me?"

Joseph reached into his inner pocket and pulled out a praiseworthy letter of introduction from his old skipper. He started to hand it to Jim Wrighton.

"No lad, my eyes aren't so good. You read it to me."

"To whom it may concern—" At the moment Joseph started to read, there was and almighty cry, a man's voice at high pitch followed by an almighty crash. There was the sound of falling timber as the side of one of the storage sheds split and heavy telegraph poles tumbled out, like a row of skittles. They spilled downwards hitting stacks of layered timbers, maybe twenty feet high, causing a domino effect and pinging and bouncing towards the office in which Joseph and Wrighton were standing. Before they knew it, untreated timbers of ten-foot lengths were raining down on them as some of them started to penetrate the wooden framed office, smashing and splintering glass everywhere and sending folks running for their lives. There was much shouting and crying for help, screaming to get them out and cries of agony. Joseph picked up Jim Wrighton under his two arms and dragged him out from under a timber which had rocketed straight through the cabin window, splintering wood and glass and sending it in many directions, trapping his legs. The cabin was collapsing as more huge timber lengths crushed the flimsy hut. Joseph managed to free him, dragged him through the side door coughing and spluttering as the wooden hut was crushed like firewood, kindling and into matchsticks.

The accident was all over in a few minutes but the noise and the ensuing chippings and sawdust cloud, hung in the air. Men were collapsed on the floor. Others were caught under the debris. Many were coughing and holding handkerchiefs over their mouths to keep from inhaling dust, while timber creaked and settled.

Joseph helped Jim Wrighton up. They were covered in dust, but relatively unharmed.

Jim spoke. "Well lad, I think it would be fair to say that you probably just saved my life, looking at the devastation around us. Are you okay?"

"Yes sir, I'm fine. Just a bit shaken. Can I finish reading my reference from my old skipper?" Joseph answered.

Jim Wrighton started to laugh. Amongst all the chaos, there was mirth. And they both started laughing, it was infectious. Loud raucous laughter. Joseph didn't really know why he was laughing but laugh he did and heartily. It relieved the tension of the last few minutes or so.

In between bouts of laughter which almost turned to hysterics, Jim said.

"No lad, no bonny lad, you've already convinced me I need an assistant. If anything, to organise the clear up of this lot, that's for sure. And frankly let me tell you, I will need you to get to the bottom of this, because it's happened before. I have my suspicions, but a new face might be able to seek out who is trying to kill me off, if that's the intent behind this. When can you start?"

"How would tomorrow at 6am be for you, sir?"

At that moment as Jim Wrighton continued to brush himself down, two small children came running up to him.

"Granddad, Granddad, we heard what happened. Are you alright?"

The children were beautifully spoken and beautifully dressed in the finest clothes, the little girl with flowing skirt and a straw bonnet and the little lad in a sailor's outfit. They burst into tears simultaneously. Within the minute a young woman, their mother threw her arms around the old man, as the children clung to his legs, and cried.

"Oh father, father. You're too old for this. You need to give it up. Please?" She pleaded. "We can't have this happen again."

It seemed that Jim Wrighton was the owner of the timber yard and his son had been killed in a similar accident not two years since. The police were still investigating that incident, but with no conclusions.

"No need now. I have this young man to help me. He saved my life this morning and he will be helping me in future. Now, please take the carriage out of the yard before that too gets covered in dust or even damaged. I'll be fine. Really, I'll be fine."

Given his assurances. His stepdaughter and his two bonny grandchildren, climbed back into the carriage, which the driver slowly turned around and carefully pulled out into the busy road. He cried out his instruction to the dappled grey pony, "Howay lad, howay," before jogging off out into the sunshine of the day.

The yard claxon had already been sounded for the half-hour lunch break. Jim Wrighton and his father before him were great believers in looking out for their workers. Looking after them certainly seemed to get the best out of them and a strong sense of loyalty to the yard. Some of the yard employees had been with the

Wrighton family as long as Jim was a boy learning the ropes. But there was an element of discontent within the new workers. Men who had come into the country from Africa and Asia as well as Persia and the Middle-East. They seemed to have a different agenda that that of the local lads and Jim had his suspicions that one of the Persians was up to no good. His family appeared to be acquiring properties and wealth through dubious methods and Jim believed that was an element of this family behind the last accident where his son was killed. Unfortunately, nothing could be proven and the police seemed to be at a loss, without any clues or leads.

As Joseph finished brushing himself down with the back of his hands, he reached out to Jim Wrighton and bid him fair-well with a firm shake of the hand.

"Thank you, Mr Wrighton. I shall be here at six in the morning to start. Thank you again for giving me the opportunity."

"That's okay bonny lad. Thank you for saving my life!" Jim replied.

At that, no more was said and Joseph left the yard as men were coming up to Jim Wrighton to see if he was okay and report on the disaster as they saw it from their perspective and how they would put the yard back together.

Joseph left the yard and headed for the river and the Crown & Anchor pub, to wash away the dust. He decided that one pint would be enough and then he would head back to Ma's place and catch up with Alice, to give her and Ma the good news.

CHAPTER 15

1894, Benjamin, The Timber Mill

It was Saturday. Indeed, this was a good day! Benjamin had returned and relayed to Samuel what had happened. He showed Samuel the bank deposit slip. He explained in finite detail that the manager, (one Alan Stelling) when the police arrived, that they had hauled Stelling away without ceremony. Benjamin had left the Whitehaven Colliery Company offices with a large cheque, signed by Lord Cardew-Petteril himself. Benjamin had headed to the bank, meeting the manager, depositing the cheque and drawing some cash for supplies.

It was Saturday. The sun was shining, Ben had just left the bank, having banked several hundred pounds and shaken hands with an English bank manager. It was indeed a good day. The bank, on trust, had allowed him to drawn sufficient funds for his, old Samuel's, and the mill's immediate requirements. He loaded up the bags of grain for the chickens, flour to bake with, some fresh and salted meats. He pulled off from the rail where the buggy was parked and started to walk the horse through the town. It was now late afternoon. The bells of St.Mary's were ringing and he could see a bride leaving in a white open carriage, pulled by four white horses, a small crowd was throwing rice and confetti and there was much cheering. At one of the market stalls he tied up and bought fresh home-baked game pies, and a jug of gravy in a hard cardboard carton, a large string of pork sausages and a large round of Stilton blue cheese. A few more steps away was fresh bread and cakes. Two large stone jugs of cider, he knew would go down well, with supper. Irresistible. And he didn't (resist)! Right at the end of the town as he walked his very unconventional, awkward looking horse and trap, there was a tobacconist. The shop was magnificent. It had a large plate glass window, decorated with gold writing and raised letters, offering different brands of tobacco and cigars. The windows surrounds were made from a rich mahogany wood and were polished to perfection. As he opened the door, the sweet smells of tobacco and rich aroma of fruit and cigars hit all his senses. The door bell rattled as he left, having purchased four separate ounces of tobaccos and a new briarwood pipe for Sammy.

This was indeed a good day.

Benjamin continued to enjoy the warmth of the late afternoon sun as he jogged back to Buckabank. But first a slight diversion. *I must see if I can see that pretty girl again*, he thought to himself.

He jogged through the lanes and the villages, trying to remember the route that Samuel had directed him. Pretty houses and cottages. Thatched roofs, climbing roses, sweet smelling summer flowers and there in the distance the small village green, with its small grocery shop. Its wares were laid out in wooden boxes, set out on top of other boxes, a bright red Post Box set in the wall next to the open shop door, he noted bearing this country's Queen's initials of VR.

Benjamin, pulled at the reins and the horse came to a standstill. He pulled the horse over to where he could tie it up checked his cargo and smiled to himself. He stood upright, brushed himself down, took a deep breath and breezed into the shop. Looking forward, straight at the pretty girl he had seen some days before, he hadn't seen the small white dog sat on the floor. The inevitable happened. He slipped and fell headlong into a large display of flowers set in water in tin buckets, spilling himself and the buckets into the middle of the floor, surrounded by folks initially trying to help but then spontaneously breaking into laughter. There he sat, embarrassed, red-faced. Covered in flowers and sat in a pool of water. And there she was, this vision of loveliness, frowning and giggling, covering her mouth, trying not to laugh. He had never ever felt so awful in his life and wanted the floor to swallow him up. As he started to stand, the sole of his boot in the middle of the pool of water slid from under him and he was again flat on his back.

And that's how they met. Benjamin and Daisy.

Daisy held out her hand and helped Benjamin to his feet. Benjamin full of apologies. "I'm so sorry. I'm so, so sorry. I'll pay for everything, everything and any damage, I've got money. I'll pay. I'm so sorry."

Daisy looked around as her mother came flying through the backroom door.

"What's all this racket? What's going on?" Daisy was quick to reply.

"It's alright Ma, don't worry, there's nothing broken, there's no damage and if there is, this young man—"

Benjamin broke in. "Benjamin, my name is Benjamin missus, and I'll pay for any damage I've caused."

"—this young man, as you can see, is going to pay for it."

Ma seemed okay with that. "Make sure he cleans it up then." At that, Ma returned to her quarters in the rear of the shop, with the smell of the cooking of fish wafting out and masking the previous sweet smell of cut flowers.

Benjamin and Daisy sat outside Ma's shop, on wooden crates, chatting, 'til the early evening, when eventually Benjamin realised that Samuel might start to wonder where he was.

"I have to get back to Buckabank. Can I see you again?" Ben enquired.

"Well, bonny lad, I dussna see why not. I'm here every day, but not tomorrow, that's chapel day and Ma has always been strict about that. Say hello to Sammy for me."

"Oh you know Samuel, I mean Sammy?"

"Why yes, everyone knows Sammy, for miles around. He's a lovely man. Sad but lovely."

Benjamin wanted to start another conversation with Daisy, but realised that he was running out of daylight hours to get back and cook for him and Samuel.

"Thank you. Bye, see you soon." Ben repeated several times as he slowly jogged away, "Byeeee."

Within a half hour, Benjamin turned into through the big wide-open space that was the entrance to the mill. He slowly walked his horse and trap down to the barn and uncoupled the horse. The horse walked over to the hay rack and immediately started chewing away at his supper. Ben opened the sack of horse pellets splitting it with his fishing knife, he had bought as a treat for the horses and his two stable mates wandered over and began placing their heads in the sack and snorting their delight at the treat.

Sammy was quizzical. Ben had been away virtually all day and he wanted to know everything. Sammy was overwhelmed. Benjamin showed him the bank account balance and even after he had drawn cash and bought supplies, there was still several hundred pounds in the account, with several more invoices issued, so there was still more to come. Now, they could start to look at running the business properly. They might even look at one of those new Avery or Massey or Underwood steam cutting saws. That would make life easier for cutting in the forests and then converting the timbers into almost anything you wanted. Sammy was becoming very animated, until he broke out in a very deep throated phlegm filled cough coming from the depth of his lungs.

Benjamin sat him down in an easy chair and poured him a glass of sweet cider told him to relax and they would talk about it after supper. But tomorrow, they would have a day off. Sammy needed it and it had been a very good week. The Ben would be able to tell Sammy about this wonderful girl he had met at the local shop.

***

The following day, Daisy was up with the lark, as ever. Her older sister Betty, was always in the back with her mother. She was lazy and was always at Ma's heels crying wolf about how ill she always was, just like Ma. Daisy often felt like Cinderella from that Christmas pantomime which they had been to see last year on a rare outing. A treat for Betty's birthday. Daisy from then on felt like the one always left behind when something grand was happening. Today as always, the shop was all set to trade at six-thirty in the morning as folks were headed into town to start work at seven. Most of the colliers would take home made sandwiches or perhaps a pie baked by the missus. But they still came into to see her for an ounce of baccy to see them through for a few days. After all, what else was there in life, but work a smoke and a beer.

Daisy was almost sixteen and had always worked in her ma's shop, for as long as she could remember, probably ever since she was a baby. She can even remember sitting in her pram, with all the women cooing around tickling her chin and coochy-cooing her. Then as soon as she was old enough to stand and walk, she would be fetching and carrying and then serving and taking money. The number of times she missed school because her ma was always ailing, were too many to count. When the teacher in school asked her what she wanted to do for a living and she said that she'd like to train to be a nurse. The mistress laughed and said, not if your ma has anything to say about it. And so, here she was at sixteen, still a shop girl and no doubt a shop girl she would stay…unless some handsome young man would carry me off on his white charger, or maybe even his horse and trap??

Saturday soon came around again for Ben and Sammy. Ben had started to take stock of what they had lying around and in between loading and delivering, each time he came back and every evening he would try and get the mill yard into a better shape. He could already see the 'wood for the trees' and had quickly worked out who were the customers he wanted to deal with; the regulars and the good payers. He had written a letter to issue to all the mills customers as he was going around and had this typed up in town. The bank was very helpful in this respect and they had what was called a paper copier, where they placed a document on a roller, turned it over a few times through some liquid or other and out came an exact copy of what was written. He couldn't believe in the advances in technology, it was a mini-miracle. And so, this was a wet and messy business, so he ended up in the Carlisle Bugle newspaper office, and had two dozen professional looking copies printed off.

Most of the regulars were wealthy collieries so had no problem with paying to order. Those that had to be put on a pay for your last order basis, grumbled like hell and had no choice but to pay up, if they continued to want a cheap product. But even that was to change. Ben wanted a quid-pro-quo for all their previous hard work.

Ben had now made several deliveries to his regular customers and repeat orders were coming in thick and fast. If they were to cope with all of this additional work, then the mill would need a motorised-wagon. Ideally it would need a small crane or at least a mechanical winch on its 'bed'. However, two weeks later Sammy and Benjamin had acquired an almost new long wheel-based cart coloured yellow and had printed along the side in red livery 'Morris and Abrahams, Buckabank Mill'. Benjamin decided that 'Morris' would be a much easier name to remember when it came to their business and for that matter for customers writing cheques and generally, making payments. Morris, was the nearest name they could think of to an English name, and as their life was here in England, then why not have a name more appropriate to their working environment. As far as their new transport was concerned, they had considered the cost of buying a newly motorised vehicle cart, but as well as being ridiculously unaffordable, it might be more trouble than it was worth. He'd rather spend the money on new cutting machinery. However, he made the right decision when he decided to build a winch on the back of the new cart for unloading. It took several days, but all of the strengthening with steel and extra timbers underneath the structure paid off handsomely. Whenever they delivered the accuracy of being able to deliver on any one given spot was invaluable, instead of just dumping a load in a pile somewhere in a yard and hoping they did not roll away too far.

Another Saturday rolled by and Daisy sat on a wooden crate outside Ma's shop in the early evening, wondering where her handsome young man was.

Despite his mind being fully occupied with all the new work coming in at the mill, Ben's mind regularly drifted to thinking about Daisy. In the interim, Daisy was being courted by Tam Lock Junior, whose father was the manager and a shareholder at the colliery where Ben used to be employed. Daisy was regularly forced to see Tam Lock Jnr by her mother who thought that their family's wealth was more important than her daughter's happiness or welfare. Daisy had to do her damnedest to discourage his advances. She found him surly and common, with few manners and graces and he had pocked skin to boot. They were a wealthy family and he was pushy and played up to Ma. Ma thought he would be a good match. She thought he would always have work. Times were hard for a lot of folk who could only get by working at lowly, low paid jobs, that's if they could get a job at all. Life was not good for a lot of people. Poor folks could be seen begging for scraps around the markets and in the town, selling pegs, selling heather, selling their souls, if it would get them a meal.

Ben had decided that he needed to see if there was any hope of seeing Daisy, for more than just a chat and as his future was now looking secure. He saw himself with a wife and a family and if it could be with someone like Daisy, then his lot would be complete.

He spoke to Sammy about his thoughts and Sammy was delighted that he wanted to settle down here at the mill with him and a wife. Sammy's first thoughts were, someone to do the cooking and washing and cleaning and have babies. Yes. Sammy was all for it.

Early on Sunday morning, Ben decided that he needed to see Daisy and the only way he could do that with Ma's approval, was go to their chapel.

He spent a half an hour brushing down the Welsh Cob, acquired a week after the collection of some of the mill's outstanding bills. It was ideally suited to the trap. The Shire horse that Ben had coupled up with the trap previously, meant for a pony, certainly filled his requirements on the day. But a pony, or in this case a Welsh Cob, which they had named Buck after the Buckabank mill, was the perfect height. Its beautiful black coat shone as Ben brushed out the dust and the straw. He'd carefully plaited the mane and oiled its hooves. He pulled the trap out from the big barn brushed it down with the big yard brush and then hand wiped it with an old shirt. He coupled Buck up to the trap, adjusted his jacket and cravat, climbed on board and set off to Cumwhinton Chapel, just ten miles East of Buckabank. He jogged along the lanes, nodding to passers-by, both walkers and riders alike, tipping his tweed cap to the ladies, both young and old in their Sunday finery, tippy toeing along so as not to drag their full-length bustled skirts in any residual horse droppings or anything else that may have been on the road or grass. It was a glorious day for hats and there were plenty as Benjamin neared the Chapel. It was a small brick affair built probably only forty or fifty years before, but now attracting a throng of people.

The chatter was deep, but respectful. There was no high-pitched laughter, just the odd wave and a hint of social intercourse. Many carried their own bible and as he drove closely enough to the chapel, he dismounted and tied the trap up to a rail, where other horses were tied, waiting patiently for their masters.

As he nervously entered the chapel he spotted Daisy almost at the front, seated in a pew with her ma and another girl who looked very much older and rather haughty, in a red and burgundy and gold dress and laced bodice top. She was looking around and peering through a monocle on a fancily decorated long handle. The chapel appearing small from the outside, was quite spacious and was well decorated, with religious artefacts and icons dotted around the walls. The place was buzzing with folk just quietly chatting and the smell of perfume was almost overwhelming, mixed with cigar and tobacco smoke brought in on gentlemen's clothes. Ben had never been in a chapel before and was fascinated to see how plain and simple the whole room was. Above a small pulpit was a 'minstrel's gallery' in which was slowly assembling a small choir.

The organist started to play 'Guide Me O' Thou Thy Great Jehovah' and the congregation stood. The twelve strong choir began to sing and the congregation joined in. This was followed by 'All Things Bright and Beautiful'. Some folks singing in harmony, some singing less harmoniously, but with great gusto and enthusiasm. The organist held the last chord for what must have been a half a minute, then stopped playing. The room went silent, just the odd person clearing their throat or another muffling a cough. The scent of the room, was that of a mixture of sweet ladies' perfumes and men's mothballed suits, tumbled with the smell of damp and mould, from timbers sat on the floor and the walls of the old building, that would have been built straight on the ground, with no solid foundations.

Ben checked his pocket watch, given to him by Samuel, just seconds or so to 10am. A door creaked in the left-hand corner and the room went deathly quiet.

The minister entered. He was a commanding figure, tall and slim with sharp facial features with a mixture of grey and dark hair swept back off his forehead. He wore a pair of half-glasses that were perched precariously on the end of his nose. He was so clean shaven that the light from the windows reflected across his face and to some committed chapelgoers, gave the impression of an angel entering their midst. He was dressed in a dark suit, with a white ruff and white half-stockings, highly polished black shoes with a silver buckle. Over his shoulders was draped a black cassock and he wore a chain around his shoulders, supporting a large cross bearing a silver statue of Christ. There were two lay preachers following behind with large bibles tucked under their arms, with leather book markers protruding. They all marched quickly and sternly to the pulpit. The Minister nodded to the congregation, which appeared to be more of an audience. Above him in the gallery, were heard three taps and the pianist and choir started to sing almost immediately, with the congregation joining in after the first verse. Ben was impressed. This man, tall and grey, with a sullen look to his face after two hymns, slapped the top of the pulpit and spouted what Ben could only describe as fire and brimstone or thunder and lightning. He shouted at the sinners with vim and vigour and a ferocity that Ben had never seen before. When he had finished, he nodded and the congregation all clapped. There was one last hymn and that was it, all over in exactly one hour. The minister left as mysteriously as he had arrived. Ben would not have been surprised if the man had left in a puff of smoke, like a genie of the lamp or a magician with his ultimate disappearing act.

The organ started to play a tune he recognised, though he didn't know the name of it until today. The choir started to sing 'Amazing Grace' in full voice. The little chapel filled with voices and Ben was so pleased that he had made the effort to try and see Daisy.

He felt quite invigorated and was brimming over, when Daisy stepped out of the chapel with her mother and the other young woman, he assumed was Betty, her sister. She stopped to say hello, but as soon as she stopped the young man who thought he was her intended, came up to her, not quite dragging her away, but certainly forcefully ushering her away, one hand underneath her elbow, half way through the conversation with Benjamin.

Ben was most put out and could see that Daisy wasn't at all happy. Ben couldn't help but voice his displeasure, stating to Tam Lock Jnr. That the young lady was happy to be engaged in a conversation with himself and did not wish to be bullied away, by anyone. At that Tam took a swing at Ben, which Ben dodged comfortably and landed Tam Lock Jnr. a punch right on the side of the jaw, downing him in one.

Daisy's mother and the other girl, each put an arm under Daisy's and hurried her away, tutting at the embarrassment. Ben could be heard to be saying, "I'm sorry, I'm so sorry. Daisy, I'm so sorry."

Mother could be heard to be saying, "We shall never hear the last of this. Who is that ruffian, fighting on a Sunday and outside the chapel, not that dreadful boy who kicked over the flowers in my shop, I hope. Goodness me Daisy what is to become of you? What would the Lord say? What would your father say?"

Daisy couldn't get a word in edgeways. *My father wouldn't say a word, would he?* Then, speaking out loud to herself, but not so loud that Ma or her lazy sister would hear, "No wonder he ran off, I don't blame him. So will I, soon!"

Some rough looking 'friends' of Tam picked him up and half carried him off. Ben tried to catch up with Daisy and her ma, but they had already stepped into a large black open carriage wore a grey suited gentleman sat inside, facing away from Ben. The gentleman wore with a grey matching top hat. Ben thought he recognised the man, but from the rear, it was difficult. The carriage quickly pulled away, it seemed with Tam Lock Jnr. also on board.

Ben was at a loss. This was a disaster. *She wouldn't want to see me now. She will think I'm a ruffian and nothing but trouble.*

Ben jogged home in the trap with his shiny black Welsh Cob looking every bit the part, feeling very despondent. How was he ever going to make it up to Daisy. He only wanted to talk to her.

At five the following morning at first light, with the birds singing and all the joyful sounds of the forest to behold, Ben was still despondent. He hadn't slept a lot. He harnessed-up the new long cart after he had finished loading, he called for Samuel.

Sadly, Samuel was not up to today's journey.

"You'll have to go without me today. I'm not well. My chest is wheezing and I can't clear my throat. Go without me. You'll be alright now you've added the winch to the wagon. I'll do some baking and washing. I'll see you later."

Reluctantly Ben set off on his delivery rounds. Three drop-offs this morning to three different collieries. The last being where he worked. Rumour had it that Stelling, the accounts manager in the town office, was in league with Tam Lock Snr., with Lord Cardew-Petteril and the local constabulary looking into the matter. But there was nothing that could be linked.

Ben arrived at the colliery and lifted his loads down into the storage area, with reasonable ease. Lock came running up to him and shouted, "That's not where I want it. It should be over the other side of the yard where I always have it."

Ben looked bemused. This was the fourth delivery he had

made here over the weeks and where he had placed it, was exactly the same spot where he had previously placed it.

"I'm sorry Mr Lock, but that's where I have previously delivered it and that's where it's going to stay."

Lock was busting for a fight, clearly, after his son Tam Jnr. was humiliated outside the chapel.

"In that case if you are not going to put it where I want it. The order is cancelled. Take it away, you no good foreigner."

Ben stopped in his tracks. He could do one of two things. Land the man on the deck or walk away and take up the case with Lord Cardew-Petteril, who seemed the perfect English gentleman. Though he had absolutely no fear of Lock, he thought in this instance the best plan was to walk away.

However, by this time a crowd had gathered, hearing what was happening they were spilling out of the pithead by the dozen. Lock called out again.

"Don't walk away from me you cowardly foreigner, come and fight like a man."

Ben felt he had no option. He calmly tied the horse to a nearby post and rail and walked calmly across the yard. He couldn't have known that this was a set up and no sooner had he brought Lock to the ground with a single blow, a half a dozen men rushed Ben, thrashed and kicked him, with the police looking on.

All the pals he thought he had made friends with at the pit cowered away in a corner, he later heard that they'd been warned off by Tam Lock and that if they came to the rescue, they would lose their jobs. The police, having been given back-handers by Lock, eventually realised that enough was enough, that they had to step in, as explaining a death would be a lie too far.

Three burley officers dragged Ben's damaged and partially broken body to their police cart, threw him on board and jogged off at some speed to the local Carlisle infirmary. Ben's bruised and battered body was dumped outside the hospital without ceremony or explanation, other than, "This thug was picking a fight up at the Whitehaven Colliery. Looks like he got what he deserved!"

Two nurses carried him onto a wheelchair and rushed him off to an emergency treatment room for the surgical staff to ascertain the level of his injuries. Indeed, he was battered and bruised beyond recognition. His face was black and blue, with red marks and cuts to his cheeks and forehead and eyebrows. His nose was broken and he had multiple rib fractures. With great fortune, one of the medical staff a young doctor, had recently returned from Yemen, where some of the British forces had been supporting the Quaiti tribes of Arabs who ended up defeating the Kathiri tribes. He set to on Ben's injuries with knowledge and skill, instructing the nurses to cut off Ben's clothes, and start to clean and dress the surface wounds. Having felt Ben's damaged body, for broken ribs, he set about wrapping Ben's chest in thick crepe bandages. He then heavily sedated his patient, stating that rest through long sleeping passages were the best cure for this type of injury.

Back at the colliery, there was much unrest. Two of the miners had taken charge of Ben's horses and cart and set off back to Buckabank mill. Jamie, a young Glaswegian and William a much older local man with no family, to speak of. Needless to say, Lock stated clearly and succinctly, in no uncertain terms that if anyone dares to go against him and move that cart and horses, they will be in breach of their contract and may not show their faces at this pit head ever again. The rest of the men that had been standing around cheered Jamie and William as they mounted the driving platform and headed out of the yard.

A very worried Samuel greeted the men as they pulled up into the mill yard and was horrified to hear the story. It didn't take long before every household in the surrounding villages had heard the story. Samuel knew that there was bad blood between Ben and Lock, due to the way that Ben had stood up for the men at the pit and forced Lock, the pit manager, to allow breaks and paid time as they entered the pit and not a half an hour later, when they eventually reached the coal seam. And the way that Ben resigned, some many months ago in front of a huge crowd of men, humiliating Lock. Yes, there was bad blood between them, but not so much that would warrant this sort of brutality.

Daisy got to hear about the beating and told Ma, that she was going to see the young man in hospital.

But Ma had said, "No! Absolutely not. Do you want to bring more shame on the family, after that ruffian picked a fight with your intended?"

Daisy stopped dead in her tracks. Her mouth opened in shock and her body froze, sending a shudder from her toes up her spine and to her head. She felt flush with anger. She regarded her mother's words and regaled.

"Whenever did that ugly pock-marked Tam, Thaddeus Lock's son become my intended? He's the last man in the world that I would consider marrying, even if his family do have money and a share in a mine. He's ugly and he's uncouth and he's always pawing at me, whenever he can get close enough. He makes me feel sick. I hate him more every time I see him. I would rather be dead than give my body to him. Not in a million years will I be betrothed to that animal!"

Daisy was shocked at what had come out of her mouth. But she wouldn't withdraw, not a word, not a sentence, not a description of that person or how she felt about him. She had said what she had wanted to say for as long as she could remember. She was bouncing on her toes and when she had spoken took a deep breath and let out the smallest of screams, almost a hiss, as if she had just taken a boiling kettle from the stove.

Ma recoiled. "Well, it's too late. It's all done. His father has already paid me a dowry for you and I've put it into the shop, and I bought a new carriage for Sunday's chapel, or we would have all ended up in Carey Street. So that's it. It's all done, you're to be married. All I have to do is set a date."

Daisy stormed off. Within minutes she had gone out to their stables, saddled her horse and raced out of the village with Ma screaming, "Come back! Who's gonna look after the shop? Come back you stupid girl. Come back!"

But Daisy was gone. Across the sun-dried fields, the corn waving in the slight breeze, out through the lanes past the village pond under the big spreading chestnut, past the mighty oaks, the sweet-smelling gardens, down the bridle paths. And before she knew it she had slowed down to a trot and was making her way along the main Carlisle Road, and to the Carlisle infirmary. And she had no idea why.

CHAPTER 16

1894, Joseph, Newcastle

Joseph left the yard and headed for the river and the Crown & Anchor pub, to wash away the dust. He decided that one pint would be enough and then he would head back to Ma's place and catch up with Alice, to give her and Ma, the good news.

"Good afternoon, Landlord. Just one pint of your very best, please."

"Just one, bonny lad?"

"Yes, sir thank you. I have to keep a clear head for starting work tomorrow."

"And where would that be?"

"Wrighton's Timber, a bit further up the river, from here."

"Aye, you've done well there, bonny lad. Old man Wrighton is a good man. But there is a story behind some of the troubles he's had over the last couple of years."

Joseph was curious. "What so. How do you mean troubles?"

Robert the landlord went on to explain. "Well, there seems to be too many accidents up at that yard for a start. There appears to be a move by several business traders in the town, to disrupt the business so that Jim Wrighton, will give up and sell his yard. But the yard has been there for two hundred years and has always been in his family or they have always had a big share in its development over the years. Jim Wrighton is stubborn. Even when his son Michael was killed in what they said was a freak accident, he wouldn't give up. He wants his grandsons to takeover, but they're far too young yet. He had a foreman last year who also met with an untimely death, unloading timber from one of the boats on Wrighton Quay. And all these accidents."

Robert shook his head and rubbed his chin, pulling his cheek to one side as he frowned. "I'm not sure I would want to work there, but they say he pays well, so he doesn't usually have a problem getting workers. But if you're to work there, you need to watch your back, especially if you're in charge of anything important, like machinery. These people in the city seem determined to buy that land and develop it. It doesn't seem to matter if they lose a few lives along the way."

Joseph finished his single pint and headed back up alongside the river and turned off to the cobbled alleyway that he had been slightly nervously led just a day or so before. Now it felt like home. He was thankful that, not only had he fallen in with a really nice family, but he was already stricken with love and now he had a job, which looked as though it might turn out to be something better.

The sun was shining, he felt good as he took in a deep breath of air. It was a mixture of summer flowers, oil, salt water, mud and the tar that some of the boats in the shipyard were being treated with. Seagulls were calling overhead and sparrows were chattering and flying in small groups, pigeons we billing and cooing on roofs, as he paced out the steep climb up to Ma's. She greeted him as he opened the small white painted gate that defined the front of her terraced cottage.

"Well bonny lad, how did you get on? Take a seat in the garden and sit down and tell me. I'll pour you an ale."

Joseph was happy to recall the events of the day and the apparent accident, which in effect helped him get the job. Ma was curious as to how he had ended up in Newcastle on the Tyne and where his family were.

"Well bonny lad, you should advertise in the London papers. That's where people advertise for missing relatives. I know it's a long way away, but the papers travel and the news travels. I'm sure it would be good for you to be with your brother again."

By the time Joseph and Ma had been jawing, the time had flown by and Ma was off to make supper, for themselves and some of her lodgers.

Alice had returned home with a large wicker basket, with the remnants of her basket of flower posies, just a few broken leaves and stems. She greeted Joseph and gave Ma a peck on the cheek.

"I've had a very good day today. That's thirty-four posies I've sold today, just walking along the quay. I'll have to get up early tomorrow to get down to the market and pick up some more."

Joseph was quick to offer to accompany her. "Well, I would love to walk you to the market in the morning and then I can stop at Wrighton's to start my new job."

Alice was pleased and proud. In all her seventeen years, she had never met another boy who could hold a light to Joseph. Good looking, six foot tall, mop of dark brown hair falling over his right eye, dark brown eyes, a tanned ruddy face, with a dimpled chin and clearly a young man who was keen to work and make his way in life. But there was a sadness about him. She could often see him in deep thought, frowning, before shaking himself and then smiling. She guessed it was him having left his own country for a new life and continually wondering where his brother might be. But he was a good man. Polite and kind. Witty and likeable. And if Ma liked him, then he must be an angel.

Early the following morning, Joseph was up with the lark, sat downstairs waiting for Ma to cut some bread. He wouldn't be so presumptuous as to enter Ma's domain, without her express permission. Alice came down looking as pretty as a picture. His heart thumped and his face flushed. Joseph had only known this girl and her small family just less than week and it felt to him as if he had been a part of the family forever. It felt like a well-worn glove and he felt settled and could see a future. He hoped that Alice might feel the same way, but for the time being, he would set off early and ensure he did a good job for his new boss Jim Wrighton. He aimed to make himself absolutely essential to that business. He took a last swig of warm tea to wash down his bread and jam, buttoned up his jacket, said goodbye to Ma and set off with Alice alongside him.

Joseph was nervous about asking Alice out. But as he currently felt pretty much on top of the world, it was now or never.

Alice swung alongside him with a light skip in her step to keep up with his long stride. He suddenly stopped, Alice looking quizzically at him. He drew in a deep breath and nervously asked, "Alice, would you walk out with me this evening? Perhaps we could go for a walk along the river? Only if you want to, or maybe up to the top of the town and look out over the rooftops and the river, I don't want you to feel obliged or anything, or maybe we could go and sit in the park...or..."

Alice broke in, "Why are you asking so many questions, pet? I would have said yes to the first one, I'd love to walk along the river with you. Maybe Ma would even put a few things in a basket for our supper. We can sit on the bank of the mighty Tyne, watch the boats go by and chat. I'd love to do that."

Joseph didn't know what to say. He was flushed with pride that this lovely girl said yes to his proposal. He strode on as Alice linked her arm in his and his heart boomed.

"Today will fly by then. I will be looking forward to this evening."

As they rounded the last alleyway wall, both the flower market and Wrighton's yard came into sight as they simultaneously said, "See you tonight. Don't work too hard." They both laughed as Joseph entered the yard and Alice carried on down the hill.

***

Wrighton's yard was already busy as the sun became more rounded in the warm sky. A tramp ship that had docked last night on the high tide had begun to unload its cargo of trimmed but uncut timber. The gantries were sighing under the huge weights that were being very slowly hauled. The timbers were being, hauled up from the grain store and from the decks and the number of timbers being carried in one haul were putting strain on the gantries. Joseph could already see an accident in the making. The cables were straining, the ropes were straining and the sections of the steel gantries were, almost visibly twisting.

Joseph watched the load being lowered into the massive bays which held the stock and then watched several men shifting heavy timbers which were barred up to stop slippage. He took the bull by the horns, with a slightly raised voice, "Men, men."

Around a dozen men stopped what they were doing, wondering who this man was, a new face at the yard with a foreign accent, was trying to get their attention.

"Gentlemen, I'm Joseph. Mr Wrighton asked me to help with the yard management, particularly as I have had several years of experience in handling ships cargoes. Before we start again, I want to say that unless these loads are handled differently, then one or two of us is in danger of being in a serious accident. And maybe we are putting ourselves in a position where one or more of us might get injured, maimed or even killed. If you would give me a few minutes, please?"

There was a measure of disagreement about how loads should be handled. The general consensus was that the more timbers carried on each transfer from ship to shore, the least number of loads, meant they could all go home before their shift ended and still get paid.

"Just listen to me for a few minutes. I suggest we stop using the largest gantry. Each time it is overloaded, it is being put under too much strain."

There was much opposition to Joseph's first suggestion.

"Just listen to what I have to say please."

The men begrudgingly settled down, listening to Joseph's commanding tone. He'd been used to this sort of mutinous behaviour on The Manchester, but his ex-shipmates all saw sense in the end, to their benefit.

"If we use two smaller gantries, these will take a lot less time to load and they will not put strain on the mechanisms. A smaller one will be quicker to unload and use less men. While one is being unloaded, then the second one can be loaded, making full use of everyone's time. I guarantee that we could save a third of the time unloading. I'm sure all of you experienced dockers can see the logic here. Can we at least give it a try?"

There was a general nodding of agreement and comments stating it made sense could be heard in quiet corners, so the men wheeled up the new gantries along the rail tracks to the side of the ship and started to put Joseph's plan into action.

As well as the time spent moving the big gantry and getting the two smaller gantries into place, the disgorging of the timber into the yard, took twenty-five per cent of the estimated time. And it took thirty per cent of what the men would normally take to unload a ship of this size with a similar cargo.

As the last load was stored and barred-up. There was a spontaneous outbreak of clapping. Not just for Joseph, but for the record time which it took to unload the timber cargo from one of their regular suppliers. All the men on the shift went home early and the ship sailed on the ebbing low tide, eight hours earlier than expected.

Most of the time that Joseph was initially communicating with the men and then persuading and cajoling them to adopt a new method, Jim Wrighton had been watching from his timber-built office a distance away, unknown to Joseph.

Jim Wrighton was somewhat bemused by how many men had come up to Joseph and shaken his hand heartily, as they collected their bags and sacks and left the yard. Joseph mopped his hands and his brow with his red and white neckerchief, tucking it into the breast pocket of the jacket that was now being held in one hand. As he walked across the yard, Wrighton called out to him, "Young man. Over here please, I want a word."

Joseph looked sheepish, felt sheepish. From the moment he had turned up early for his new job, he hadn't stopped working. He'd forgotten all about reporting to the governor, Mr Wrighton. Mr Wrighton was supposed to be a stickler for rules and here he was, making his own decisions to alter work practises without anyone's permission. *I'll just have to apologise and ask if I can start again, tomorrow. I'll keep my fingers crossed, I can't afford to lose a job, before I've even started properly. What will Alice and Ma think of me?*

Joseph arrived at the office as Jim Wrighton closed the open door and sat at his desk. He bid Joseph to sit. Joseph started to spout an apology. "Sir, I'm so sorry, I meant to come here and sign on, but I could see how dangerous it was the way in which these men were operating the gantry and the winches... I am so sorry, I didn't mean to interfere..."

Jim Wrighton cut in, "Well bonny lad. I said yesterday that you had the gift of the gab. Just put your tongue back in your mouth and shut your teeth down tight."

"Yes, sir, but I am sorry."

Jim Wrighton gritted his teeth and then gave a wide smile. "I said, when you came in here, that I might just have something to offer you. I wasn't sure what. As of today, you are my yard manager and my second in command, if you'll accept the position?"

Joseph was, for once, lost for words. He felt a wave of emotion building up in his chest, he thought his lungs would burst. His heart and his head and his eyes, the whole of his body's temperature rose several notches, but he managed to stop at tears. He took a deep breath and asked, "I'm sorry sir, could you just repeat what you said to me. It didn't quite equate?"

"No, I don't think so, bonny lad. I'm not one for repeating myself, it's either yes or no!"

"Well yes, sir. Yes, thank you very much sir, I accept. When do I start?"

"Well bonny lad, I think you made a good start this morning. I watched most of your communication with the men and I was very impressed at the way in which you persuaded them to change the way they have always unloaded the timber cargoes. They would never ever listen to me or my son, who tried to change their working practise. If that had been me, they would have downed tools. So as of right now, the salary we discussed previously is doubled. Just one more thing. My suggestion, if you are to be my second in command, please go to my tailor and have him fit you a new jacket, on my account. You will need to look like a manager if you are to represent me, when I am not around. You need to look the part. It's also good that the men have taken to you already."

Joseph's first day at Wrighton's Timber had flown by. He was aching and needed a bath. Certainly, if he was to walk Miss Alice out this evening, he didn't want to be smelling of timber and sweat from the day's toils. He couldn't wait to tell Alice and Ma his good news and good fortune.

CHAPTER 17

1894, Benjamin, Carlisle

Daisy rode her pony across the fields and through the villages the moment that she had heard that Benjamin had been attacked by Lock's cronies. She couldn't believe it. She was hot and perspiring as she slowed her mount and trotted up to the Infirmary. It looked neat and well cared-for with its white painted walls and grey slate roof, a set of black painted iron stairs, to the right which she assumed, lead to an upstairs ward. She tied her pony up in the front of the hospital and brushed herself down. Her face was flushed and she wondered how she looked, but thought to herself, *I don't care how I look I just need to see him.*

She was greeted by a petite young woman dressed in a blue uniform with a starched white peaked head covering, black stockings and polished black shoes. Her frosty frown, was as stiff as her starched bonnet.

"Can I help?"

Daisy struggled to get her words out, still trying to catch her breath from the exhausting ride through the countryside. She was still hot and felt her face throbbing from the blood rising through her cheeks.

"Yes. Yes please. A man, a young man. A young man, hurt in a fight, I believe. Is he here?"

The nurse answered, but with a question, "Are you family. Do you know this young man? We have more than one young man here?"

Frustrated, Daisy tried to explain. "Well, I'm not exactly family, but we are friends, we have been going out together, well not yet, but I'm sure we will. Oh, please tell me he is going to be alright. Is he?"

The nurse swept a loose gathering of hair from her forehead and pushed it back under her hat and readjusted the hair pin and replied, "Well, I think I know the young man you are talking about. But he's not very well, he has obviously taken a vicious beating and I don't think we can allow any visitors until he shows some kind of recovery."

Daisy's face dropped like a stone, her head started to spin and the nurse could see that she was about the faint.

"Come, sit here a moment. I'll get you a glass of water."

As she slowly recovered, she pleaded again, to see Ben. The nurse responded. Despite her severe, starchy look, she seemed to be kind and thoughtful and answered, "Well, I suppose, given the circumstances we could let you see the young man for a few minutes, I'm sure matron won't mind. Come along with me."

Daisy followed the petite young nurse whose walk was made up of very small neat footsteps. Her soles squeaked as they walked along the polished stone floor. They walked down two cool corridors to a closed ward and the nurse opened the door and pointed to a corner bed, where Ben lay, heavily sedated and in a drowsy, half sleep.

"Now you mustn't wake him. He will need a lot of rest and sleep to recover from these injuries. Whoever has done this to him, held nothing back. He's been kicked and punched and has cuts all over his hands and face. He has a broken leg, two broken ribs and three broken fingers. He may well have other injuries that we have yet to find. He really is in a very poor state. Frankly, we think that he's lucky to be alive. You can stay an hour, as long as you sit there quietly, but no more. Is that understood?"

Daisy nodded gratefully and pulled up a chair by the side of the bed. Ben's bandaged left hand lay on the top of the blanket. Daisy took it in her hand and kissed it. Ben stirred and looked at an image he didn't recognise. "Mama, Mama, is that you?"

Daisy kissed his hand again and said, "No, it's not your mama, it's me Daisy. Daisy from the shop. The shop on the green, Daisy."

He seemed to acknowledge the fact. But fell away into a deep sleep. Blood was still seeping from the bandages and Daisy started to sob. Saying under her breath, "It's my fault, it's my fault for telling that Tam Lock boy what I thought of him, and now look what I've done. God will never forgive me."

Ben stirred again and through a delirium said, "Daisy, is that Daisy?" and fell away again.

The news had travelled fast and Samuel was grateful that Jamie and William had gone to Ben's rescue, taking him by cart into the hospital. It probably saved his life. The following day Samuel took the pony and trap to Carlisle into the hospital to see Ben. Jamie drove, leaving William to look after the yard, suspecting that revenge may well come in more than one form of violence.

Jamie tied up the pony and trap and as Samuel climbed off the cart, he regarded the pony that was tied up alongside.

"I know that horse," said Samuel as he headed towards the steps of the hospital. They approached the front desk of the hospital to be greeted and questioned by the same efficient nurse, who eventually persuaded that Samuel was his father and Jamie was his brother. She guided them along the same cool corridor to the ward where Ben was sleeping peacefully.

They were somewhat surprised to see a sleepy eyed, dishevelled young lady sat at Ben's side holding his hand. The nurse was horrified.

"What on earth are you doing here? Who let you in this morning?"

A sleepy apologetic Daisy said, "No one let me in this morning, I've been sat here all night. I just couldn't leave him. It's all, my fault and I wanted to tell him, as soon as he woke up."

The nurse a little bemused, but sympathetic and understanding said, "This way young lady. Come with me."

Daisy, apologising all the way, thinking the worst and that she was about to be ejected, was shown into the nurse's quarters.

"Now," she said. "There's coffee on the stove over there and there is a sink through that curtain. I suggest that you have a wash. Pour yourself a cup of coffee and brush your hair and tidy yourself up. Otherwise, what will your young man think of you when he wakes up."

Sammy and Jamie took a seat next to Ben's bed, Sammy tutting and Jamie shaking his head back and forth in recognition of the beating that Ben had taken. They had heard that it was bad, but not this bad. Jamie's fists were taught with anger. "We know who it was and they are going to suffer for this."

Sammy wouldn't have any of it. "One act of violence will lead to another and another and another and so on. We must get over this and get Ben better. We must have no talk of revenge. Is that understood?"

Jamie was not happy, but he nodded in agreement to appease the old man, Samuel.

Ben was still dozy. He'd had a comfortable night's sleep and he was coming to. Through a haze he could see two seated figures, but couldn't make out who they were.

"Papa?" he queried.

Samuel answered, joyous that he thought Ben had recognised him, "Yes, son, it's me Samuel."

"Mama?"

"No," Sammy answered back. "It's me, Samuel."

His eyes started to open. He did his best to rub them with the one bandaged hand that wasn't strapped to his body.

At that moment, Daisy breezed back into the ward. Seeing Ben struggling, she looked around and found an enamel bowl, partially filled it with warm water and took a fresh linen cloth from a small open shelf.

She dampened the cloth and began carefully wiping Ben's eyes.

"Daisy?" he asked. "Daisy, is that you? What are you doing here? I am in such a mess. I didn't stand a chance. They jumped me, held me and when I fell to the ground, they kept kicking me. I must have passed out, because the next thing I knew, I was here in this hospital, being patched up. Argghh." He groaned as he tried to turn.

Daisy spoke as she mopped his face of dried blood smeared everywhere. "I came as soon as I heard. It's all my fault. I shouldn't have listened to my mother who wanted me to marry that half-wit. Just because his father has a share in the mine and she thought it would make a good marriage. What does she know? My father ran off as soon as he could and I don't blame him. My mother is a witch in Greengrocer's clothing!" she exclaimed. They all laughed. "And my sister's no better. I do all the work, just like Cinderella and I never get to go to the ball. The moment I heard that you had been beaten up, I knew that I had to come to you. I'm never going back to that awful woman again."

"But what are you going to do then?" Jamie tentatively

enquired. "If you can't go home, where will you go?"

"Oy, oy, oy, families!" Sammy cut in. "You can come and live with us. You can look after Ben until he gets better and then we'll see."

She had nothing planned and had ridden across to see Ben because her heart told her to. She hadn't questioned it for one moment. She knew exactly where she wanted to be and it was here by Ben's side.

At the end of that day, Jamie and Samuel rode back to the mill, angry, but content that Daisy was looking after Ben. She had been allowed to remain in the hospital for a week, while she looked after Ben, cleaning his wounds, changing his bandages, feeding him and encouraging him back to good health.

Exactly seven days later, Jamie had helped Samuel lift Ben's straw mattress on to the back of the short wheelbase buckboard cart, collect him and return him back to the mill. Daisy sat alongside him, in the back of the cart, all the way home, while Jamie and Samuel, rode the sprung box seat.

While Ben recuperated, Daisy helped him exercise. Samuel made him a beautifully carved walking stick and a pretty basic set of crutches. These weren't meant to be a permanent fixture.

Meantime, Daisy was cooking and cleaning and making herself not only very useful, but indispensable.

Each evening after supper she and Ben would go for a stroll, down to the stream and sit in the warmth of the evening. Ben loved to watch the trout 'rising' for the insects. He loved the rustling sounds coming from deep inside the woods, he loved the peace, the tranquillity, but most of all he loved just being with Daisy. The sound of the water trickling gently just a few yards from where they sat on their favourite rock. It seemed that this was fate. They were meant to be together. Ben was getting better with every day and was keen to get back to work. He finally managed to dispense with first one crutch and then the second and was now walking confidently with just his beautifully carved walking stick. Samuel was truly a gifted woodsman.

Samuel had remarked more than once to Jamie and William, who had been invaluable initially in helping Ben, but helping Samuel to continue the day-to-day business, he couldn't help noticing that that love was in the air.

"Those two were meant to be together," he had said on more than one occasion. So it came as no surprise that Ben, arm in arm with Daisy, returned after their usual stroll that Ben said that he had proposed to Daisy and she had no hesitation in saying yes.

"We're going to have to tell your ma, Daisy." Ben was insistent. Daisy wasn't keen as she hadn't seen her mother or sister since she left on the day that she had heard that Ben had been assaulted by the Lock's gang of hooligans and ne'er-do-wells.

Now that Ben was getting back to full time work, Jamie had decided that he was missing the camaraderie of the pits and his drinking mates. A few days later the news came back from the pits, that Thaddeus Lock senior had mysteriously been found at the bottom of a disused shaft and was as dead as the donkeys they threw down there when their useful working life had come to an end.

A grand funeral was organised at his local church. No one turned up, apart from his wayward son, a handful of family members and a few thugs and hangers on. But no one from the colliery or his village. The son, without the protection of his father had become a laughing stock and had taken to heavy drinking. Later, desperate for money to feed the drinking habits of he and his cronies, he had sold his father's shares in the mine, squandered the cash, and then sold the family home and its contents for far less than their value. He was now permanently drunk and headed towards being penniless and the workhouse.

The minister at the chapel was delighted to hear the news that Ben and Daisy were to wed. Ben had become a local celebrity, in that his determination to put his attack behind him and look to make himself fit and well again, showed his courage and was appreciated by all who met him. The minister would use Ben as an example of how to 'turn the other cheek'.

Ben asked Daisy if they could have the hymns that were playing at the chapel, the first day he had been there to meet up with her and her Ma. He particularly liked 'Amazing Grace'.

The Vicar was delighted and took ten minutes explaining about the hymn 'Amazing Grace' and what a wonderful tune it was. He explained, "This was written over a hundred years ago in 1772 I believe, by a reverend John Newton. Before this, he was a slave trader and was in trouble one day in the water I believe, thrown from one of his slave ships. One of his slaves saved him from drowning and from that day, he became an abolitionist and wrote this wonderful tune. Now doesn't that make your heart feel good!"

Ben and Daisy were suitably impressed by the vicar's knowledge and enthusiasm. They left the chapel, hand in hand and Ben helped Daisy up on to the buckboard and headed home to the mill.

CHAPTER 18

1894, Joseph, Newcastle

He couldn't wait to tell Alice and Ma his good news and good fortune.

Joseph felt on top of the world. He strode out of Wrighton's yard, with a chest that wanted to burst. Not only had he secured a job, but it was a job with real prospects. He had become 'a manager' overnight. Well not exactly overnight, but during the course of the day! Wrighton had obviously placed a lot of trust in him. But Joseph was made aware and was becoming wary about some of the devious 'plots' that seemed to be undermining James Wrighton.

But enough of that for the time being, he thought. *Let's just get back to Ma's house and tell her and Alice the news. But I didn't even think to ask what wage I would be getting. I'm sure the old man will see me right.*

Joseph stepped a long-pace with his long, strong wiry legs. The back ginnels and alleys with their rough cobblestones, leading up the steep hill to Ma's house didn't even cause a sweat, he took it all in his stride. He reached the summit of the hill, looked back on the town and down to the river and took in a deep breath of the salty sea air, rising on the warm breeze. He marvelled at the seagulls flying high above the town just gliding on the same warm breeze, crying and calling to each other as if to acknowledge their next meal being delivered on the incoming tide, then sweeping down on the fishing boats returning to port, knowing that their next meal was there for the taking.

He finally reached Ma's gate, sat on the wall, took another deep breath, then stood up and punched the air. He heard his favourite voice.

"Why aye, bonny lad, what's ganning-on pet, you look as if

you've just won the National Winners Sweepstake, hey…but Ma don't hold with gambling, so I hope you won big!"

"Well, Miss Alice, yes. I think I have won a sweepstake, but it's not through gambling, as you might have thought. Not only have I got a job, but Mr Wrighton has offered me the job of yard manager, yes, you heard that correctly, *yard manager*!"

Alice was astounded and leapt into Joseph's arms. As they both jumped for joy. He swung her around and around until they were both dizzy and then without giving it a moment's thought, he landed a big warm kiss on her lips. She responded without even thinking. The kiss lasted for what seemed like hours, but was only seconds. Joseph stopped, picked her small frame up into his arms and they kissed again, until Ma came out of the cottage screaming.

"What's going on here? What are you doing making up to my daughter in public. Where do you think you are down on the docks on a Saturday night? Put her down. Now!"

They pleaded in tandem. "But Ma, Ma, you don't understand."

"Yes, what don't I understand? I can see you making a spectacle of yourselves! What will the neighbours think, out here on the path, and you're not even betrothed." She took a deep breath, her face flushed bright pink with embarrassment, more than anger. "Alice…get inside now. I want to see what this young man has to say for himself." Turning to Joseph, she asked, "Well, young man, what have you got to say for yourself?"

It didn't take long for Joseph to explain the events of the day and calm Ma down. She was happy for him and she quickly forgave him for molesting her daughter in the street. But what came next was not only a shock to Ma, but he couldn't believe the words he was hearing coming from his own lips…

"But Ma, I love her and I want us to be married. I've loved her from the moment I saw her and though we've only been walking-out together a few times, I think she feels the same about me."

He looked towards Alice, who was beaming like a sunflower out at the height of a summer's day, hands together and swaying as if she were in a light breeze, in the centre of a field of fleur-tournesol in a Van Gogh painting.

Ma replied, "I need to sit down. Go and get me my smelling salts. They're in a green bottle on the mantle. Go on, go and get them. Now, before I faint."

Joseph dutifully turned to go into the house to see several faces up at the windows, smiling and clapping. The first person he encountered as he stepped back through the door was Alice and she leapt up into his arm, legs around his waist, with cries of, "Oh Joseph, oh Joseph."

He put her down as she thrust Ma's smelling salts into his hand and turned him around on his heels.

Ma gratefully received these and sniffed away, jolting her head slightly backward as the sharp carbolic-vinegar smell hit her senses and brought her back to reality.

"Well bonny lad. That, was a bit of a shocker. I had no idea. I could see you liked each other, but you've hardly been her more than a few weeks. How *can* you be sure?"

Joseph answered, with absolute conviction, "Well Ma, when you know that something is right. You know. It's as simple as that and I know that I love her and if she feels the same, I will ask her to marry me, with your approval of course."

Ma was taken aback. One who was never lost for words, was completely lost for words. She had been struck dumb. Joseph watched the expressions on her face, which seemed to range from quizzical to a half smile to amazement and a broadened smile and pushing her head slightly back and nodding from side to side in disbelief and ending her facial athletics with a mopping of her forehead with her duster and a great big smile.

"Well, well," she finally remarked, "that has come as a bit of a bolt out of the blue. So, I'll have to think about it and talk to my daughter. Now I must get on and finish preparing tonight's meals for my guests. Be off with you. Get out of my sight, you've almost given me a heart attack!"

Alice had heard every muffled word of the conversation between Ma and Joseph and was as thrilled as if it were her birthday or Christmas morning and she'd been given every present that she ever wanted. She ran out of the house and straight into Joseph's arms. He swung her around in his arms again and then they briefly kissed and went off down towards the town hand in hand, not taking their eyes off each other.

Two hours later, by the time Alice and Joseph had returned from their hand in hand stroll along the quays, the whole street knew of the young couples' plans. Alice was only fifteen years of age so as much as they were in love, they knew that they would have to wait until Alice was sixteen. As Alice's father had disappeared off the face of the earth, some years previously, then it was down to Ma to give her approval.

The following day Joseph arrived at Wrighton & Skinnerburns Timber Merchants and Converters at six in the morning. He had to wait another twenty minutes before Jim Wrighton arrived to open the yard.

They pushed the big heavy double doors open, with the massive initials of W&S in blue and outlined in red, set on steel rollers, to one side one heavy door at a time. Wrighton was pleased to see Joseph turning up early and knew he'd made the right decision, in taking Joseph on as his yard manager.

"Well bonny lad, if you're going to get here before me, then I had better give you a key to the yard."

"Yes, sir. Thank you for your trust in me. I won't let you down,"

And so began a long and successful working relationship, Joseph Morritzstein as Jim Wrighton's yard manager at the W&S Timber Yard. Within six months, Joseph had made it his mission, to know every supplier and every customer as every member of staff and each worker by name.

The more Jim Wrighton trusted to Joseph, then the more work and responsibility Joseph took on. But there was still a suspicion of 'dirty work at the crossroads' with undertones of sabotage around the yard. There was a determined consortium of the town's business men, trying to buy Wrighton's yard for waterside development. They wanted to see the business fail so that old man Wrighton would give in and sell up. As it was the business was growing stronger and the business and yard were becoming more valuable.

From day to day, the yard grew stronger thanks to Joseph, but the 'old man' was getting older and was only turning up for work every other day. Jim Wrighton arrived one morning looking tired and older than Joseph had ever remembered him. He opened the door of the office and sunk into an old well-worn arm chair, that was his Father's before him and Joseph waited in anticipation of his much loved and respected boss to speak.

"Joseph, you've been working here now for over a year and I'll be honest, without you, this business would have folded a year ago. You've allowed me to take stock of where I am in life, and at my age, I need to be taking life a lot easier. My daughter and grandchildren want me to sell up and stay at home, so they can look after me, or perhaps we can travel a little, to other countries."

Joseph was taken aback. He wasn't expecting this sort of, as far as he was concerned, bad news. "But sir, the business is–"

"Don't interrupt bonny lad, or at least, don't say anything until I've finished talking." Jim Wrighton gathered his thoughts again. "What I have to say is this. Thanks to you and your hard work, this business is now in a better state than when you arrived on my door, looking for a job. I knew that there was something about you when we met and I wasn't wrong."

Joseph kept raising his hand off his knee to try and stop James Wrighton's flow, but the old man kept raising his arm and waving Joseph down. Wrighton continued, "In view of that Joseph, bonny lad, I have decided to make you a director of this company and allocate a share of the business to you. I haven't spoken to my Solicitor yet, but that's just a formality. Now…bonny lad. You may speak!"

Joseph for once, was speechless. "Oh Mr Wrighton, sir, I don't know what to say! I'm, I'm, well I'm truly overwhelmed by your faith in me and I cannot stress how grateful I am that you are rewarding me in this way. Thank you, thank you, thank you so very much sir. I won't let you down."

Jim Wrighton smiled, but sank down in the chair and held his chest, get me some water lad, some water please. Ten minutes later, the old man was in a cab and headed for The Grange, his home on the outskirts of the town. As Wrighton had left in the cab, Joseph telephoned the doctor and asked him to go straight to The Grange, with all speed, as his boss was not in a good state of health.

CHAPTER 19

1895, Ben and Daisy

Seeing the Vicar was the easy part of making plans for the future with daisy, but he couldn't allow his bride, his wife to be, to lie in a tumbledown of a cottage, barely habitable for a couple of bachelors and an old man.

He would have to start rebuilding, not only the business of the mill, but rebuilding the old mill house which had been so badly neglected over so many years, that it could only be regarded as a tumbledown.

Daisy and Ben returned to Buckabank, excited about the prospect of their being together, but Ben seemed to have a heavy heart, hidden underneath the joy of having announced their nuptials and having the banns read. They had planned to marry in exactly one year on her sixteenth birthday.

Daisy asked, "Ben, something is troubling you. What is it? Please tell me. Do you really want to marry me or have you changed your mind? Or are you marrying me because I left home to be with you?"

Ben was horrified that these thoughts passed through her mind. He replied, "No, no, no Daisy. I love you so much and I can't wait for us to be married. What is bothering me, is that I haven't heard from my brother Joseph in years. I don't know where he is and we always promised each other that we would be the best man at each other's wedding and I don't even know where he is."

Daisy felt very sad for Ben, but straight away said, "Well, why don't we place adverts in the papers to see if we can find him. You also told me that he was on a tramp ship, was it The Sir Stephen Manchester? We could write to the various ports and ask where the boat is now or leave letters with each port authority."

Benjamin was staggered at the brilliance of his bride to be. "Daisy, that's brilliant. How did you think about all that?"

"Well, when my Pa left, after a year, Ma placed adverts all over the country, through her solicitor. She decided that if he didn't respond, then she would declare him dead and she would claim the business and the shop premises. And that's what happened. And we haven't seen him since. Personally, I think she worked him to death, just like she and my sister tried to work me to death!"

Benjamin gave her a big bear hug. "Okay. I'll start writing letters to the port authorities today and in the meantime, what do you think would be the best papers to advertise in?"

"Well, why don't we wait until we get a response from some of the port authorities," Daisy replied. "We might then have a better idea of where to place adverts to find him. And maybe, just maybe, he'll still be on the boat or, if he's moved on, then his old skipper will be able to tell us where he left the ship. What do you think?"

"Think!" exclaimed Ben. "With a brilliant girl like you for a wife, I won't have to think! That's wonderful. I will start writing today. And tomorrow, I will get back to helping Sammy and William build up our stocks and get some income flowing. And then my lovely brilliant Daisy, we are going to start re-building the house."

Benjamin did his best to avoid the bumps and ruts as he steered the old cart down along the track to the clearing and the barns. Sammy and William were sat outside at a rustic table made out of roughly hewn branches knocked together with some six-inch wooden pegs. Two glasses of beer sat on the large disk of sawn tree, the full width of its girth. Its age was well over two hundred years based on the numbers of rings that Sammy had counted, but his failing eyes had let him down so many times that he gave up and just guessed!

He rose to greet the young couple. *My son and daughter*, he thought. His family. He was indeed a happy man.

"Sit, let me get you a beer or some cordial for you Daisy. It's a warm day, come and sit yourself down and tell me what the Vicar said. Have you set a date for the banns?"

Daisy responded enthusiastically, but then tried to temper her excitement with the knowledge that they wanted to find Ben's younger brother Joseph. They had made a pledge when they were young that they would be each other's best man when it came to settling down and Ben just couldn't let his brother down. So, their quest was to find him. It was a must!

***

Early the next morning, Ben was up with the dawn chorus. The birds were singing, the sun was shining, not a cloud in the sky, the brook flowed through the nearside of the wood. Fish were jumping. A Kingfisher flew past him and nearly knocked off his flat cap, the pigeons were billing and cooing, squirrels were up and down the old oaks like demented, deranged clockwork toys, frogs seemed to be hopping and jumping on the edge of the trickling tributaries, a truly beautiful day.

As soon as Ben started up the big steam driven saw, the peace was completely shattered by the teeth of the big blade being pulled down and cutting into the tree trunk on the thick plate steel cutting bench. Chippings flew everywhere and the saw dust created a woody mist. William and Sammy came out to see Ben cheerfully whistling away as he cut into log after log.

Last evening, he and Daisy had written ten letters and had addressed them to the port authorities in ten different towns and cities. Ben was up early in anticipation of giving his letters over to the Albert, The Royal Mail delivery man when he rode up on his rounds, saddlebags filled with all manner of post for all manner of locals.

Albert finally arrived, mid-morning as Daisy had made thick salted bacon sandwiches for the boy's break, topped with a runny duck's egg, fat running out of the sides, with plenty spare for Albert, as they bit into them. A big pot of black coffee sat on the side ready to wash away the sawdust.

Albert sat for a while and jawed with the boys. The (not) unexpected death of Thaddeus Lock Snr, being found at the bottom of a mineshaft came up in the conversation. It was a bit sad that young Tam Lock, though he was a bully boy and a thug, was going to the dogs. Albert said that the police were not even investigating Lock Seniors death. He wasn't a popular man. No loss. Ben gave Albert his ten envelopes and gave him sufficient monies to cover the cost of postage, with the instruction to post them, no matter what the cost, and if he needed to pay more, then he would pay Albert on his next visit. Albert let Daisy know that her sister was missing her, as she had taken over all her work duties since she left and that mother was still sat on her backside in the back of the shop.

The days went slowly by as Ben re-built the business and the stocks at Buckabank mill. Ben's friendly laid-back character and reputation of fair trading and honesty and absolute reliability attracted plenty of new customers. Ben and William were slowly pulling down parts of the old cottage and setting out the stones ready to rebuild the main structure. The chimney was the starting point. Each morning Ben would cut table tops to be sold at Carlisle market. He'd recruited a market trader to offer them on his pitch as 'self-build' garden tables. He had cut small apertures in the underneath of what would be the table top and hewn three branches to fit together to form legs, with a triangular piece of thick timber to rest on the legs as they crossed over each other. Then these could be assembled by hammering the wedges that he had made, into the holes he had drilled. The 'self-assembly' rustic tables were proving to be very popular. So much so, that he was having to deliver twenty-five to forty, every week to his trading partner.

However, Ben's anxiety and disappointment was building as one by one, a trickle of replies came back from some of the ports. In the South West there was Plymouth and Portsmouth and Folkestone, nothing. London, nothing. Hull nothing. Liverpool, yes, The Captain Stephen Manchester docks her irregularly, but not for the last six months. A note has been made to give the letter to the captain of that vessel, the next time it is in port. Cardiff. Yes. The Manchester regularly uses this port and is due in with a cargo within the next week or so. Newcastle no response. Edinburgh no response. Felixstowe. Yes. The Manchester uses this port on a regular basis and will be due in again within the next four weeks.

He and Daisy seemed to be getting closer and closer to tracing his brother Joseph. It was a Friday morning when Albert brought the letter. Ben greeted Albert and took the reins of his mount and wrapped them around the fence rail, next to the water butt. The horse needed no invitation.

He snorted his approval. "Go on then Ben, open it. It's marked Cardiff and only seven days ago."

Ben carefully opened the thick, rough, buff-coloured envelope and started to read out the text at the same time scolding Daisy for her over enthusiasm. "Stand still Daisy, for god's sake stand still, let me read it."

"But I'm so excited this could be the letter we've been waiting for."

Dear Sir,

The Captain Stephen Manchester. Docked.
Queen Alexandra Dock.
The Port of Cardiff.
May 5th 1894

I understand that you have been trying to locate one of my ex-crew members, one Joseph Morris. This is to confirm that he was one of my crew until April 1893. He is a much-missed friend and former member of my crew.

Alas he decided to take his chances ashore and he left my employ when we docked at Newcastle-upon-Tyne over a year ago. I trust that you find him and that you convey to him, my best regards.

Yours faithfully,

Ephraim Michael Manchester
Skipper
The Captain Stephen Manchester

"Oh my god!" was the exclamation from Benjamin. "My brother! He's up here in the north. Newcastle on Tyne. We shall go and look for him!"

"Wait, wait," Daisy cried. "Before we go headlong into a big town like Newcastle, we first need to place some adverts and see if we can find him. Otherwise, we have no idea where he is and in a twelve-month, he could have moved on, or even jumped on another boat and be anywhere."

Slightly deflated, but reconciled to Daisy's wise words, he had to agree.

Samuel spoke, with some apparent knowledge. "There is a paper in Newcastle called The Post. I've often seen it on stands outside the newsagents in Carlisle. The next time we take a load into the colliery, we can pick up a copy."

Ben couldn't wait. "No. I'm not delaying. I'm going right now. I'll rig up the pony and trap. Daisy, c'mon let's go. We can do some shopping in town."

Within ten minutes Ben and Daisy were jogging through the lush countryside in anticipation of collecting their means to find his brother Joseph. They jogged slowly into Market Street and pulled up outside the post office stores. The news-stand had a fine range of papers, from London, to Scotland, local and one only Newcastle Post. Ben snatched it up and tucked it under his arm. Paper paid for, they headed back to the mill and as soon as they were back, laid the paper out on the rustic table which sat just outside the house.

They thumbed through the sections and found a suitable column that they thought might be appropriate to place an ad. They headed home and began creating an ad to try and find Joseph. They gave the ad to Albert the Post, the next day and asked him to take it to the telegraph office and forward the ad to 'The Newcastle Post'.

Albert duly arrived at Buckabank the following day, and to the delight of Ben and Daisy confirmed that the ad had been placed that same day, as the Newcastle Post had an agent for advertising in Carlisle. They were thrilled.

LOST & FOUND

Benjamin Morritzstein
Is desperately seeking
Joseph Morritzstein,
some times known as
Morris. If any person
knows of Joseph's
whereabouts,
Please contact:
Benjamin Morritzstein
Buckabank Mill,
Carlisle.

MISSING PERSONS

Benjamin Morritzstein
Is desperately seeking
Joseph Morritzstein,
some times known as
Morris. If any person
knows of Joseph's
whereabouts,
Please contact:
Benjamin Morritzstein
Buckabank Mill,
Carlisle.

Newcastle Post comment: Or please contact this paper.

A telegraphic message may also be conveyed to Carlisle Telegraph Office.

Now all they had to do was wait.

CHAPTER 20

1895, Newcastle

Joseph locked up the yard at five o'clock after the day's trading. His head was all over the place, with a heavy heart on one hand knowing that his boss's health was deteriorating fast and carrying exciting news to give to Alice and Ma. On the other hand, of the conversation with Jim Wrighton and his offer of a share in the business, though he didn't say what sort of share, and that he was to be made a director of the company.

He hurried along the busy quay. Late summer, and the evenings were starting draw in a little sooner. Now and again, there would be the signs of autumn and winter to come, with the breeze stiffening up occasionally and sending ripples across the water. Folks were starting to wear heavier clothes. Some women choosing to wear a day coat and some men even a heavier top coat.

The activity however on the river never waned. Trawlers coming and going, disgorging their holds. The seagulls squawking, crying and sweeping down, scavenging their next meal. Ships unloading their passengers from far off lands, probably including his own. There was a timber ship, just docking, obviously his first load of tomorrow morning.

He felt lucky to be alive, he felt privileged. It was now three years since he and his older brother Ben arrived at Tilbury Dock in London. Despite a struggle for work initially, he managed to do alright, but there weren't many days when his older brother Ben didn't cross his mind or run through his thoughts. Was he still in London? Did he get a job on a tramp ship just like he did? Was he still sleeping on sacks on the floor of the bakery? Was he even still alive, where was he? Joseph dismissed his thoughts as he took in the smells of the quays and the harbour as he walked along at a comfortable pace. The salty tidal river, the fish, the tar being slapped against the timber boat hulls, even the smell of the horse dung was acceptable today. He loved the noise of the river, the hissing of steam, the occasional blast of a funnel, the haggling and bidding for loads. Men looking for work, the hubbub, life! He regarded it all and thanked god he was alive and that he now had some great and joyous news to convey to his, as yet to be officially announced, fiancée.

At the top of the mount, before he turned off into the alleys and walkways leading to Ma's house, he briefly turned and took it all in. It had been worth the trauma of leaving home and one day he would bring the family across to England to live with him.

Alice sat waiting for Joseph. She looked as pretty as a picture, as ever. She jumped up and gave him a big hug. He squeezed her petite body, until he realised that if he squeezed any more, she might break in two. He put her down gently.

"Right Missy, bonny lass! I have some good news for you. But it's for your Ma too. I think she'll like it."

They walked inside the cottage, Joseph ducking his head through the portal meant for fisher-folk of long ago, when the average person was a lot shorter.

"Now," Joseph ordered. "Both of you, sit down here at the table I have something to tell you."

Joseph told Alice and her Ma of his good news and good fortune. Unfortunately, nothing was written down and old man Wrighton had been taken ill and the doctor sent for. As of yet Joseph had no idea of the outcome, but this evening, before supper, he would walk up to The Grange, his boss's house, and enquire as to his health. As he understood it, the house was about four miles outside the town, but clearly visible on a hill a prominently placed house for a prominent citizen, which was built by his grandfather and passed down. If Joseph stepped up at a decent pace, he could make it in an hour or thereabouts.

It was dusk by the time that Joseph arrived. He had been following the view of the house for the last twenty minutes or so as he climbed the hill closer to the mansion. He entered two huge stone pillars with two huge iron gates sat open alongside. His footsteps crunched along the loose stone carriage drive until he stopped at the main entrance. Four huge Ionic pillars supporting a semi-circular portico.

Joseph stepped up to the entrance and pulled a large brass pull stop. He could hear the bell ring, inside the house. Within the minute a butler opened the door asking, "Yes, sir. How may I help you?"

"My name is Joseph Morris. I've come to enquire as to the health of Mr Wrighton. I am the yard manager at Wrighton and Skinnerburns Timber Merchants, where he was taken poorly yesterday."

"I'm afraid the master is not receiving visitors currently. He is not well enough," the butler replied.

No matter what Joseph said, he couldn't persuade the butler to let him see his boss, Jim Wrighton.

Joseph continued to run the business on a daily basis, but he wasn't able to make payments to the major suppliers. There was enough cash coming through the doors to pay staff and casual workers. But some shipments had to be paid for up front, or there were sixty and ninety-day bills, to be met as Joseph now understood, from when a consignment was purchased on an 'Freight on board' basis usually referred to as an 'FOB' contract. In other words, a signed agreement to pay for the goods within the specified period after the goods shipped, legally known as Free on Board. Unfortunately, that was not part of Joseph's remit.

At the end of the trading day, two weeks later. Joseph locked up the premises and made straight for the Grange. This time he would not take no for an answer. He needed to clarify arrangements with his boss, Jim Wrighton.

Joseph managed to see firstly his daughter, who was saddened that her father had not improved over the last two weeks and then he was shown into the old man's bedroom.

The daughter called out quietly, "Father, father, it's Joseph Morris, the yard manager."

"Send him in," came the weak reply.

Joseph stepped into a room the size of the arrival's hall at Tilbury docks. It was vast, as far as he was concerned. He had never experienced anything like this. Such opulence. James Wrighton was sitting upright in a four-poster bed. He was wearing a silk heavily patterned smoking jacket and propped up by heavy tapestry cushions. The bed around him was hung with deep burgundy crushed velvet drapes and tied with gold-coloured knotted ropes, the thickness of Joseph's wrist.

"Joseph, come in my boy. I'm sorry you've had to find me like this, the doctors have confined me to bed for a while. But I'll be up and around in a few days. How are things at the yard?"

"Well, sir. Everything is ticking over well, but I am worried, or should I say anxious that there are bills to be paid and unless these are paid, timber loads in particular will be held up at the docks and we won't have sufficient stocks to trade. As it is I have had some very odd propositions from business suited gentlemen offering me well paid jobs, just to leave the yard. But you saw the potential in me and I will stick with you, but I do need to get these bills paid on time. Also, sir. You said that you would gift me some shares in the business and for me to be a director. If this was the case, it might make life easier for your recovery, if you didn't have to worry about the business on a day-to-day basis."

Jim answered, "Yes, yes, I see that. I will get hold of Jenks, my solicitor, and get him to draw up some papers. Meantime, I will have my accountant pay the outstanding FOB bills and anything that is necessary. As soon as I am better, I will take you down to the bank and make you a signatory on the trading account. How does that sound to you, bonny lad?"

"Yes, sir. Yes. That would be fine. I wish you a speedy recovery so that we can discuss some of the ideas I have to expand the business of the yard."

Joseph reached out and held the old man's hand, the old man kissed his forehand and thanked Joseph for coming to see him. He offered him his carriage back to home, or, as close as he could get and Joseph gratefully accepted the offer. He turned on his heels and took in the surroundings. He had sunk into the rug on which he had been stood. The windows were only partially drawn, dressed with a dark blue velvet against a lighter blue wall. There were magnificent paintings of agricultural scenes and paintings of ships and castles and cows in meadows. The lamps, some of which were lit were heavily embossed with gold leaf and glazed chintz covered the rest of the bed, if the sun were to be let into the room, everything would gleam and sparkle. But there was a smell of death in the air. Of old bones and rotting flesh, poor air circulation didn't help. The windows needed to be thrown open. But the doctor's orders were a dark bedroom and peace and quiet. He couldn't even see his grand-children.

Joseph arrived back at Ma's cottage somewhat distressed.

The first words he spoke, as he sat at the supper table were, "I don't think he's going to make it. He's a very sick man and he doesn't know how sick he is. I've seen this in my father before he died. He became weak and then delirious. He didn't know where he was and then he died groaning in pain. It was a merciful release. And when I was there, I saw one of the men who is part of the consortium who want to buy the yard and the waterfront for development. He looked as if he was wooing the daughter, so I don't know what's going to happen."

Ma and Alice sat with Joseph and while Joseph ate his evening meal, Ma casually said, "Oh, I meant to ask you. What is your brother's name?"

"It's Benjamin, well I've always called him Ben. Why do you ask?" Joseph answered.

Ma flattened a piece of newspaper in front of him pointing to a column. "I saw this ad a few days ago, when I was clearing the fireplace and put the ashes into it. As I was doing it, I saw this advert in the 'Lost and Found' column, it did strike me as a bit strange. So, I dismissed it as the name was Morritzstein, but then I thought about it, it could be your name, shortened to Morris, which plenty of people do when they come into this country because it's easier to understand. What do you think?"

Joseph almost fell backward of his seat. "Oh Ma! This is my big brother, Ben. He's alive and he's okay and he's looking for me, I can't believe it. How old is this paper? Look, here on the top of the page. It's two weeks old. Look there's an address, I must go there straight away. But I can't. There's no one else to run the yard. If I leave it for more than twenty-four hours, there's only the women in the office and I could see some of the workers would be helping themselves to all sorts, in fact anything that's lying around, if I wasn't there."

Alice came up with the solution. "If you go to the yard, you could use this newfangled telephone thing and speak to the newspaper and maybe they have a contact that can get a message to your brother. At the same time, you could write and then as soon as the yard closes on Friday afternoon, you could hire a mount and ride to Carlisle. From my geography lessons, I know it's about sixty miles from here. If you leave Friday afternoon, you could get half way across in two or three hours. If you find a chandlery, you could hire a horse for the rest of the distance and be there by midnight. On the way back, you can collect your horse fully refreshed. How does that sound?"

"Wow! *That*, sounds like a wonderful plan! But I won't write, I'll send a telegram. I've sent them out from the yard before. They deliver them the next day via the Royal Mail. I'll go to the telegraph office now. There's one on the quay. C'mon Alice, you can help me send it."

The couple came back somewhat despondent. The office only opened in the mornings. So Joseph decided that the morning would have to do. On the stroll back, Joseph spoke about where they would live now that he had a good job and was becoming a director of the timber yard, with shares in the business. They would start small and then he would buy a big house like The Grange where old man Wrighton lived and his father before him and his father before him going back three generations. Life was good and getting better. Maybe his brother could come and work for him at the yard. He could make his brother Ben, yard manager!

Joseph opened up the yard at six thirty as usual. By ten o'clock, the yard was buzzing again. Timber in timber out. Cranes unloading from their dock, straight into the yard, the gantry cranes swinging their lighter loads over and into the specially built bays. With the expansion of the telephone system throughout the country, there was massive demands for telegraph poles, which was now making up twenty-five percent of their business.

Joseph left the yard and made his way down to the telegraph office. He created a short message to be telegraphed to Carlisle and for Carlisle to deliver this probably tomorrow or the day after. Friday. The message read:

READ YOUR AD. STOP. YOU HAVE FOUND ME. STOP.
WILL BE WITH YOU FRIDAY OR SATURDAY. STOP. YOUR
BROTHER JOSEPH. STOP.

In between work at the busy yard, Joseph managed to hire a horse and with the help of the stables, was able to locate a chandlery, part way across the Newcastle Road to Carlisle, where he could swop over and rest his own horse.

And so Friday morning came and went. Ma and Alice walked down to the yard with some food and a flask of beer packed into a rucksack, wished him luck and went home.

At dead on four o'clock, Joseph closed the big gates of the yard with W&S painted heavily across each door and climber onto his horse that he had tethered outside.

CHAPTER 21

1895, Buckabank

Waiting can be boring. Waiting can create anxiety, waiting can be exciting, but mostly, waiting leaves you in limbo and Ben didn't like limbo. Why was there no answer to the ads he had placed in the Newcastle paper?

"It's no good, I'm going to have to go across to Newcastle to find him. On Saturday morning, I am going to pack a bag and ride to Newcastle. That's the end of it, I'm going! Meantime, let's get on with felling. We will need to start building our cut stocks for next year and the years to come. When we've done that, I want to cut planks and pit props. We still have unfilled orders."

Two days went by in the flutter of an eyelid. The weather seemed to be getting much cooler, the boys were now donning heavy jackets to working and travel in. They delivered most days of the week and business was steady and every evening Ben would spend a bit more time organising the boulders and rocks that they had taken down from the old cottage as he prepared the timber for the roof joists.

He had less than a year to build up sufficient of the old cottage for him to feel it suitable for Daisy. Up until now, they hadn't shared a room. He had allocated the best room in the cottage for her with Samuel more than happy with his accommodation in a corner of the kitchen, where he was happy with a straw mattress on his home-made wooden bench, covering himself with horse blankets.

But now, thought Ben. *I will have my best man, as long as I can find him and I can fulfil my dream of getting married to a wonderful girl, and in less than a year's time.*

Joseph

By late Friday evening, Joseph had covered over half the distance to Carlisle. The last Milestone showed 27 Miles to Carlisle and 33 Miles to Newcastle.

It was still only eight o'clock in the evening and Joseph hadn't pushed the horse, they'd just trotted and cantered steadily, taking a break every time that they passed a horse trough along the roadside villages. He'd been travelling for four hours which included a good ten-minute break and he had just changed horses at the chandlery recommended by the Newcastle stables. If he allowed himself to cover just nine miles an hour, which should be more than comfortable for a good strong horse, then he could be at his destination by eleven that evening. *Let's press on*, he thought to himself.

As he trotted along the roads and sometimes the bridlepaths, he found that he was walking more than riding as the light faded. It had now faded so much that he was unable to travel any further.

In the distance, a dim light up front flickered and lit up an old hostelry, offering overnight traveller's accommodation and breakfast, so Joseph stopped and stayed for the night and slept well after supping a couple of beers.

The next morning, he woke at his usual five am, rolled over and re-awoke at seven. He stretched and stepped to the window, wiping the condensation from the pane. He looked out across the yard to see his mount happily ensconced in the open stable and regarded the greying clouds with a hint of light shafts dancing between the clouds. With nervous anticipation, he left the hostelry with just nine miles left to travel. He studied his map, traced his finger along the country roads and looked to travel slightly south of Carlisle to Buckabank. He was at Newby East on the main Carlisle Road and needed to look out for signs for Wetheral, then Carleton and finally Buckabank.

He had eaten a hearty breakfast, bread baked by the landlady, sausages made by the landlord and fresh eggs from their hens. He set off at eight that morning, as the sun was rising. He was rested and had washed with the cold water that was left in a jug in his room. He even managed to shave before thanking and saying goodbye to his hosts, a portly, middle-aged, jolly couple, who had inherited the inn from her parents many years before and managed to eek out a living. Joseph jogged along comfortably on his dapple grey, seventeen-hander. It kicked and bucked every so often, until the horse got used to his rider again. The hamlet of Wetheral with its small church and pretty painted cottages came and went, Carleton another hamlet with equally pretty cottages and a few brick built houses and a village pond, came and went and then here was a sign for Buckabank three miles. His heart started to race, the blood pumping frantically around his vessels and causing him to pull up and take some deep breaths to recover slightly. He had to stop, get of the horse and swig at some beer from his flask. Despite the sun shining, it was a chill morning, at least the grey clouds had cleared. He gave a shudder and told himself to get a grip. He re-mounted.

As he jogged along, the clip-clopping almost help him regain his equilibrium, he was feeling much better now and was pleased to see another rider up ahead. He could see from his saddlebag and then his flat-topped cap with its shiny badge that it was a Royal Mail rider.

Joseph greeted him. "Good morning. Can you help me please? I'm looking for Buckabank Timber Mill. Is it around here and if it is, is it far."

The rider, Albert, replied, "That's easy lad. Just ride alongside me, that's my next stop. We're ten minutes away."

Albert reached for his pocket watch. He pulled the chain from his waistcoat pocket and out popped his shiny silver timepiece, glinting in the sun.

"It's ten to ten, lad, we'll be there for ten. Is that okay for you?"

No sooner had they had that conversation than they were walking their horses down the long uneven cart track towards the mill. Joseph could see a small gathering in the distance. Four figures. What looked like an old man, then a very old man, a young girl and a man with a walking stick, holding the reins of a chestnut horse.

Joseph's heart began to pump again. His blood was running so fast through his veins that he thought his head was going to burst.

He called out, "Bennnnn!" But nothing came out of his mouth, it was dry.

He tried again, "Bennnnnn…" But nothing, just a dry squeak.

The small gathering, turned to see the two figures walking their mounts down the trackway. They recognised Albert straightaway, no mistaking their most regular visitor, but who was the other figure?

Then it struck Ben. He screeched, "My god! It's Joseph! It's my brother Joseph."

With the realisation that they had recognised each other, the two men started walking toward each other, they broke into an intermittent sort of run. They threw their arms around each other and burst into tears.

They hugged each other for what seemed to the onlookers a lifetime, trying to make up for the lost years.

Albert stood by watching. "Don't mind me, but I have a telegram for you Ben."

"Albert, I'm so sorry. This is my brother Ben. We haven't seen each other for three years. Until now, I had no idea where he was or even if he was alive. Sorry, what did you say? A telegram?"

Albert handed Ben the buff paper envelope.

Ben opened the envelope, then started to laugh and then burst into tears again, handing the telegram to Daisy to read.

Daisy started to read the telegram and started to laugh and then burst into tears.

"Give it to me," Samuel demanded. "I'll read it!"

Samuel began:

READ YOUR AD. STOP. YOU HAVE FOUND ME. STOP. WILL BE WITH YOU FRIDAY OR SATURDAY. STOP. YOUR BROTHER JOSEPH. STOP.

There was much hugging and shedding of tears.

CHAPTER 22

2020, Jan and Dale, Carlisle, Investigation continues

The two detectives left the scene. The forensic team were just winding up their on-site investigation, taking photographs from every angle. Each and every corner of the broken-down property, the damaged door and the bolt, apparently having been slid shut from the outside. They had done their best to separate the three sets of skeletal remains, laying them out on plastic sheeting, wrapping them and then committing them to black, zip-up body bags. These would then head back to the forensics labs in Newcastle. They estimated the bodies to have been there for at least twenty to thirty years, possibly more.

It was now up to the detectives to establish, not only who they were, but how they had become locked inside that damp dingy hole and ultimately how they died.

The two detectives climbed into Jerry's Range Rover, though next time they visited this site, they agreed that the beaten-up old tinny blue police Land Rover might be more suitable. Jerry moved off tentatively, but his rear wheels still spun away, having been temporarily semi-submerged in a mud pool. Grass, mud and water spat out over the old barn against which Jerry had parked.

Rob spoke, "First thoughts, Jerry?"

"Not me matey, I'm retired! It's your case, I'm only here at your request as an observer and some-time advisor."

"Well Jerry, some-time advisor. Now is the time for your input, or I will be rejecting your invoice and won't be signing-off any of your expenses claims!"

"News to me young Rob, I didn't know I was getting paid for this! But as you have put it like that, in this case I'd say, with all of my long-years-experience in policing. With this vast knowledge

THE SECRETS OF THE TUMBLEDOWN

and expertise, you claim that I have, I'd just like to say… I haven't a flaming clue! But, let's kick around a few possibilities.

"First look says it's murder. Second look says, it's murder. Third look says it's the same as the first two looks! The obvious clue here is the door to the cellar which was bolted from outside. It's a big old heavy door, so trying to break out through that was an impossibility and the perpetrator must have known that. There is however, the possibility that the door was closed in anger, after say an argument and the guilty party didn't return. That's still murder. One last possibility, is that the door was bolted in anger and the perpetrator intended to come back, but met with an accident or worse, in which case we could be looking at manslaughter. That's of course, if the guilty party is still alive. Now, that's my opening salvo. What do you think?"

"Thank you, Jerry, as ever, I am happy to learn from the master. But my thoughts were exactly the same. We now need to see what Forensics say. The bodies may have been dumped there after being drugged or beaten, let's hope they come up with some clues. Though I think, that that scenario is not likely. To murder each person, while the others were around and dump them one at a time is highly unlikely. The only way that could happen is if they were drugged, so we are back to your initial thoughts. It's murder, no question! Now we have to prove it and find the guilty party."

Jerry drove steadily back to Carlisle Police Station, now DI Rob Wilton's command base. The small station at Denton, his home base for many years was long gone, though most of the staff had been retained, despite the cut-backs. The lovely Julia was now Detective Constable and had done so well that she was soon promoted to sergeant and had now joined his team. She and Grant, the one they always called Mr Front Page, had married, but Grant seemed to spend most of his time in London as a retained Senior Crime Reporter for more than one publication, while continuing to write for the local rag. Jerry was always pleased to see the couple, when they visited his and Gill's pub, The Feathers, on the weekends, usually after a busy week.

As they arrived back at Carlisle Police Station, Jerry parked his car in one of the visitor spaces, next to a disabled bay. He was becoming really precious about looking after his recently acquired big black shiny vehicle.

They climbed the old wooden stairs to the Detectives Office, leaving the 'woodentops' as Jerry would always refer to them, as long as they were out of earshot, to their endeavours on the ground floor.

Rob walked into the centre of the room and addressed the four or five officers there. "Okay, people, listen up. Our new case is The Buckabank Mill Murders. We need to unlock the 'secrets of the tumbledown.' So, Julia, please pull up a crime board and head it up 'Buckabank'. Meantime, I'm sure you all know our colleague DCI Jerry Blake, ex of The Met, who has now retired and lives up here amongst us. He has agreed to helping and giving us his input on this case."

DS Julia Cox dutifully rose from her chair, walked across the room to the far corner and wheeled across a six foot, by four-foot clear perspex magnetic crime board. Each of the men in the room watched Julia as her pretty figure graced the dreary surrounds. They were thinking the same, but nowadays, any comments or even wolf whistles, could be met with a disciplinary, but the boys couldn't be arrested for what they were thinking. She certainly was, and always had been a 'looker'. No one ever forgot when she was first introduced by the Chief-Super as the lovely Julia', when she joined the detective squad, something he, nor she were ever able to live down.

Julia wheeled across the crime board and set it alongside the large white painted wall in the expansive office. It was surrounded with dull grey metallic desks and dark blue fabric seated chairs, somewhat warn at the edges, but perfectly serviceable and adequate given the current cost savings drive by the Superintendent.

"By now," Rob continued, "Forensics will have sent all their photographs across for you to study. There aren't a lot of clues to be gleaned from these, but it makes you aware of the crime scene. At some stage I want you all to go down to Buckabank and familiarise yourselves with the location. If there are any clues you might have as to the owners of this property and in effect who the deceased may be let's hear your thoughts. Say now, or give it some further thought and we can share them and if necessary, add them to the board. Right now, there is nothing to add to the board, unless you can tell me different. Okay. Thoughts please and any questions?"

There was a general hubbub between the officers and a mumbling to each other.

DC Dave Knowles piped up. Putting a finger partially skyward. "Yes, Guv. Just a bit of history. I dug out some old photographs this morning as soon as I heard the news on the grapevine. The mill was part of a massive estate years ago but I believe it was gifted to an old man they called Sammy, short for Samuel, who used to work for the estate. These are some old sepia photographs of him when my Grandad William used to work with him. There is also a photo of him, William that is, with the two brothers who worked there. They're a bit faded, but it might give us a start."

DC Knowles placed them on the table in front of the crime board.

Rob commented, "Thanks Dave. That could be really helpful. I think you should be adding those to the board. They may prove to be significant at some stage. Do we have a date for these?"

"Not an actual date, Guv, but I can look into it a bit further. I would guess that this is about a hundred years ago, or thereabouts."

"So, we could be looking at the parents of the deceased," Rob replied. "We need to establish who they all are. Can someone make a note to check the Land Registry please."

DS Julia Cox interjected. "Yes, Guv. Already have. It's very sketchy. There are no official records showing ownership apart from some old maps, showing Buckabank as part of the old Cardew-Petteril Estate. There is then a huge gap, showing the single owner as Mrs Janine Phillips."

"Okay, well done. It's nice to see that the old machine is well oiled and working!"

"I don't know how to take that Guv," Julia retorted. "Are you saying that I'm an old machine, or that I'm well oiled?"

The room laughed.

"Okay, next steps. I have already briefly interviewed Janine Phillips, she calls herself Jan, by the way, and her partner a Dale Scott at the scene. They were visibly in shock. I will bring them in again tomorrow or the day after, when we have a little more information and when we can get them to throw a little extra light about their acquisition. I understand that the Buckabank Timber Mill was an inheritance, through a Morris family connection. I have asked them to bring in a Family Tree, which once again should help us tie down the identity of the deceased. I have arranged to meet the couple down at the old Mill and let them know how we will be managing the site."

Before they were allowed to leave the scene, Dale asked whether the investigation would last long, and when they would be able to get back to working on their tidy-up plans.

Rob answered. "I'm sorry, Mr Scott, I can't answer that yet. The site as marked, is still required to remain as a crime scene. Perhaps when the forensics team have come back to us and given us the all clear, then we can release the site back to you. Until then, I'm afraid that you will have to work on the clearing of your cart track. That's the best I can do. I'm sorry, if that's not what you wanted to hear, but that's where we're at currently. I will give you a bell when I would like you to come in to the police station. Thank you."

Rob was keen to re-affirm their dialogue. "Okay, Mr Scott, I guess that will suffice for the time being, but we will need the deeds or at least a copy of those deeds to verify the ancestry tree. Thank you. You have been very helpful. We will have to continue to have to cordon-off the majority of this area, until the forensics team have given it the final once over, but I can't see that there will be much to gain, from locking down the complete site. For the meantime, if you could stay completely away, from the area we have marked out today please, I'd appreciate that. We have noted that this will be marked out and detailed as part of an investigation into these deaths.

"We will let you know when you can start clearing your property again, but until then, please do not cross the area which have been marked out, with police tapes. It might not be too long before we can discover and reveal, the 'secrets of your tumbledown', *so once* again, your patience is very much appreciated. And Mr Scott, as soon as you can bring those ancestry details into the station, then the sooner we can start working on that part of the puzzle, which this case is currently presenting. Shall we say the day after tomorrow morning, please? Thank you again for your help."

He nodded to Jan. "Ms. Phillips."

The detectives, DI Rob Wilton and the retired DCI Jerry

Blake, headed back to Carlisle Police Station. Jerry had insisted that Rob clean his shoes off before he climbed back into the Range Rover. Rob made a gesture of cleaning off his muddy brogues, as Jerry laughed at his old pal's predicament.

"Next time young Rob, instead of being so keen to get me involved in a new case, perhaps you should have given the location a little more thought and grabbed some wellies. Next time then!"

Rob grimaced.

As Jerry pulled carefully along the recently made track and out onto the 'B' Road, they pondered the situation of the three sets of skeletal remains. It was almost impossible to come up with a theory of how the three bodies came to be in a cellar. But with what looked like a bolt across the heavy wooden cellar door, then it was easily deduced to be, and both agreed, this could only be classed as a multiple murder.

Rob asked whimsically, "Well, Chief Inspector retired, what are your further thoughts?"

Jerry answered, "Well, I thought that she was a bit of a 'looker' not quite a dumb blonde, just a bit bemused by their situation. Him, he was a bit too quick to bat us off his ancestry details. However, as that was not what you were asking, we'll take it step by step for what it is. Three bodies locked in a cellar. The old house, now a pile of rubble, but from looking through that one old window into the remains of what must have been their kitchen with that rusty old range, I think that we can rule out robbery. Though, if this was a busy mill, they may well have had cash on site, in which case anyone wishing to ransack the place would, or could have, locked them in the cellar. Looking around at the remains of the old vehicles, these people didn't have much worldly-wealth. So, I think robbery is out."

Rob threw in his thoughts. "Okay, that sounds logical. So why were three people locked in a cellar. If they were hiding from someone, then they couldn't have locked the door themselves, so there was another element here. I'm asking myself what was their relationship? Would it have been mother father child? Looking at these photos on my phone, I would say, that this was three adults. Looking closely at these pictures, two of the skeletons had rings on their wedding finger, or there were rings on two of the skeletal remains, so this is two women and a man. My next question would be, where was the fourth figure in this pageant? Was it a jealous husband who locked the threesome in the cellar after he found they were having a ménage-a-trois? But why would they be down there?"

"I think Rob, we'll wait and see what this chap Scott brings in, the day after tomorrow. Meantime, we can look forward to the forensics team's report, not that I think they will; be able to offer very much. Would you like me to drop you off at home, the station, or would you like a quick half with me at The Feathers?"

"Well Jerry, as you're offering, then The Three Feathers sounds good to me."

***

The following day, Jerry was up early and out with the dogs from six-thirty. By eight-thirty, he had been back to the pub, had showered, changed and breakfasted and by nine am, was walking into a much surprised, Rob's office, ready for another look at the pictures from the tumbledown, up at Buckabank Mill.

The office above the station, with their old iron cells, buried in the basement, was full of chat about the sinister find up at Buckabank. It wasn't long before the telephones started ringing. The local rag, the Denbury Gazette had got the news on the grapevine. Their old friend Jenny Southfield who was the editor and additionally, the local funeral director's wife, was in at the enquiry desk, chasing the detectives for details, so that she could get an informed storyline in readiness for next week's paper, with a print headline created by later that day.

The phone constantly rang on Rob's desk. The desk duty sergeant on the downstairs reception spoke to Rob. "Sorry Rob, bonny lad, I've got Jenny Southfield giving me a hard time, down here in reception. She is insisting on speaking to you and she won't take no for an answer, can I send her up to you please?"

"Okay Sarge. I suppose so. Send her up."

Jenny was surprised to see Jerry Blake.

She burst through the admin office door, the tails of her long-skirted linen jacket flying in her self-created breeze that was whirling across the office and headed straight for Rob. He had opened his office door to greet her. Having known Jenny and her husband Richard, since they were kids, he and his wife could often be seen out together, especially up at the 'Feathers', with Jerry and

Gill who had become part of their 'gang'. Even so, it was a rare event when Jerry and Gill were able to leave the very busy country pub for a night off.

As Jenny strode across the office floor, as if her life depended on it, notepad and pen at the ready, Rob put both hands up and announced, "Before you ask, Jen, I can't tell you any more than you already now!"

Jenny snapped back with that sugary sweet smile, part of her investigative style that she had adopted over the years and pleasantly demanded.

"Don't give me that Rob Wilton, there has to be *something* you can 'quote, unquote me', off the record, surely?"

"Look Jen, we have only been up to the site a couple of times and all we have established is the fact that there are three sets of skeletal remains, that have been there for probably over thirty or forty years, maybe more. Until Forensics have given us their findings, we have no means of identifying them. All I can confirm 'off the record' is that we are investigating the suspicious deaths of three persons, as yet unknown and as soon as we have some information on the actual identification of those persons, then I promise I will let you know. I can't say fairer than that, can I?"

That short statement, completely took the wind out of Jenny Southfields sails. "But I need something to tell my readers and if I don't get something in the press by tonight, you know it's a weekly rag, then it'll be yesterday's news, come on Rob, you must have something!"

"Look Jen, this didn't come from me, but we are expecting a couple in for a second interview sometime today. These are the folks who have inherited the old Buckabank Sawmill. They have the ancestry of the previous owners and from that we should have a few more clues as to the identity of the three persons that have been found. That should get your creative editorial juices flowing sufficiently to give your rag a front page exclusive, then you can keep the story going for a few weeks to come. Right. Now that's it. We may be besty-mates, but I can't discuss the case any-more, so off you go. Out, out, out!"

Jenny backed off and backed out, much to the mirth of some of the staff, officers and to Jerry Blake, who were much amused at watching the comic act.

Before he had even had a chance to grab a cup of coffee from the dispensing machine in the corner of the office, Rob's phone rang again. He answered.

"Yes, Sarge. Yes, I'm expecting them. Send them up please."

***

Jan and Dale had had another troubled night's sleep. They were committed to taking the balance of Dale's ancestry notes to the police that next morning, this morning in fact, but were terrified that the police would insist on DNA proof, that they were related to the three bodies in the cellar. Their heads were running away with themselves, putting two and two together and making all sorts of nonsense. As far as they knew, Dale and Jan could have been young enough to have been the perpetrators, the murderers, who could have killed these three people. They were both headed towards their fifties and if this happened twenty or thirty years ago, they were old enough to have carried it out, and they might have been keeping it a secret all of these years. "No, ridiculous." they said to each other. "Ridiculous!"

Dale pulled in the reins. "We'll just give them the ancestry records that we have, and that will be enough. I'm sure we could both prove that neither of us, had even visited this part of the world before. The Family Tree shows that this is likely to be Samuel Morris, AKA Sammy Morris, or the brothers Benjamin and Joseph (Morris or Morritzstein). Therefore, it is likely that one of the corpses could be his wife, Violet Morris. We'll give them that and nothing else. That should be enough."

Jan was nervous as hell and suggested that, "There was another relative who had disappeared from the scene, and that was Bryn Morris. On the Family Tree, he is shown as a cousin. He also had a wife, Mary. I suggest you give them that and they will have plenty to work on. What do you think? You're the expert?"

"Yes Jan, you're right. The more they have the less they will trouble us and, in a few weeks, it'll all blow over. You're right, I'll give them the Family Tree as we have it."

Jan and Dale were escorted up the stairs of the old police station. Each wooden stair creaked as they trod on the painted wooden stair treads. Jan ran her hands along the oak panelling squares as she slowly climbed the weathered oak planks in trepidation, nervously gripping the round wood stair banister, she took in the smell of polished wood, mixed with a feint aroma of coffee coming from the detective's offices. The two sets of stairs seemed as if they would never end, until they reached the top of the landing and DI Rob Wilton, courteously welcomed them and thanked them for coming in. He showed them into his office and offered them coffee or tea, and some biscuits. It was always Rob's way of breaking down any tensions with people he wanted to interview. Just slowly breaking down psychological borders and boundaries. By the time they sat down, Jan and Dale were both relaxed, just as Rob wanted them. Putty in his hands. Jerry sat in the corner of the office, more as an observer than part of the team, but no less, Rob was always pleased to have his presence and experience.

Rob opened. "Well, Jan and Dale, if I may call you by your first names?"

They both nodded in agreement, trying to break a smile. They knew they weren't in the frame for murder or any other serious crime…yet. But if they started to ask about DNA to link them to the three bodies, or skeletal remains in the cellar, then, they would certainly have some explaining to do.

Rob continued, "Firstly, I appreciate that this must have been a shock to you. I know it's a little late, but I would like to say that I am 'sorry for your loss', given that these were your relatives Jan, based on what you have told me, about your ancestry links. So, if we take this slowly. Please just tell me how you came to be at Buckabank Mill, when you found out that you had inherited this property, and when you decided to come up here and investigate."

Jan was hesitant. Dale jumped in. "If I may, officer. I had been researching Jan's ancestry, when I discovered that there was an unclaimed estate bearing the same name as hers. It was just a co-incidence at first, but the more I looked into it and Jan's family tree, there appeared to be a direct link to the family heritage. From that I followed it through on Jan's behalf and the link was proven. The Bona-Vacantia office of the Treasury confirmed the family link and so we decided to take a three-month sabbatical and investigate the property. We have only been here for two weeks, but it has taken us almost all of that amount of time to get organised, buy a tractor and equipment and get started."

Rob continued, "And Jan, tell me what happened when you

got to the clearing and saw the old mill house?"

"We had a copy of the deeds of the property and a map showing the extent of the land and the woods and the house. But when we were able to get through the last bit of overgrowth, we were excited to see the old house, which unfortunately had not weathered well over the years and was quite simply a 'tumbledown' of timber and rubble and slate with elders and ivy and all sorts of stuff, growing all over it. We thought we would try and clear the debris and everything that was growing over the old house, and we had a grand idea of re-using all of the old bricks and stone to rebuild the place."

Dale cut in. "I started pulling at some of the fallen roof timbers. I'd taken out quite a few, pulling them to one side and starting to make a stack. Then I seemed to have pulled one too many and the remainder of the roof, which was already leaning at a forty-five-degree angle, started to collapse. We both ran backwards, as the roof with its heavy stone slates crashed downwards and into what we now know was a cellar."

Jan continued, "It was sort of scary and eerie, that these steps revealed themselves, as the timbers twisted and up-righted themselves, having fallen through the hole in the floor. There was plenty of light in the space, we didn't need a torch. It was spooky, but we wanted to take a look, which is when we saw the skeletons. God it was horrible, it was really upsetting. It was a shock. We did nothing further, but go straight back to the jeep and phone the police. Until you mentioned it, we didn't even give it a thought that these might be my relatives."

"We haven't been near the steps again," Dale added. "We only knew the cellar door had been bolted from the outside, when one of your lads suggested that that was what had happened."

Rob questioned further. "If you inherited this property, and you have a family tree to show me, then you must have a pretty good idea who these people are?"

Dale opened his folder, with all of the work he had done on the Morris family tree, confident that he had tied up the details to an unquestionable level. What he hadn't made provision for was three dead bodies and the possible necessity for Jan to have to have a DNA test at some stage. He spread it out on Rob's old leather topped ink-stained mahogany desk. He ran his finger over the documents and pointed out the ancestry roots, and Jan's family connections. Jerry stood and viewed the documents.

"It looks likely that two of these people could have been Jan's great, great, grandfather, Emmanuel, also known as Manny, and his wife Violet. We have no idea who the other person might be. But then these could be totally unrelated, if they perhaps were renting the property or if they were foreign workers. I don't know, I'm only saying."

"Well, I think that's as far as we can go today," Rob concluded. "You have been very, very helpful. Thank you for your time."

As Jan and Dale left the police station, Jerry commented to Rob, "I'm not a hundred percent sure that these two are telling the truth."

"Why, Jerry, what makes you say that?" Rob asked.

"The pair of them are ridiculously nervous, for a couple who have just inherited a chunk of Cumbrian countryside. They have the paperwork, with the family tree, but they don't seem to want to part with it. That to me says they're hiding something."

Rob acknowledged what Jerry was mooting. "Understood, Jerry. Let's see what comes up in the next few days, The only way of actually proving that they are, or should I say, she is related to the deceased is by a DNA result. We should have something in from Forensics in the next couple of day, that's if there is enough left to scrape it up, so to speak."

Meantime, Julia has taken DC. Knowles up to the Cardew-Petteril Estate offices to see what they can glean from their records. If Dave Knowles has photographs of his grandad from all those years ago, then there must surely be something up at the Estate.

***

Jan and Dale, left the old Carlisle Police Station, feeling slightly less nervous than when they had arrived. Jan's hands had stopped sweating and the nervous tick in Dale's eye, had stopped irritating him, but still occasionally twitching and causing him to rub at his eyebrow, but that *had* relaxed a bit since they left the station. This didn't go unnoticed by either detective. Both Jan and Dale knew that they were far from being in the clear, in fact they were trying to convince themselves that the police wouldn't need a DNA sample. What they had provided should be sufficient. If indeed Jan had to produce a saliva sample at any stage, they would be sunk.

There was always the possibility that Dale's slick, silver-talking tongue, could talk his way out of it. Only time would tell.

The nervous couple sat in their Jeep, trying to regain their composure and equilibrium and wondered whether this journey was worth it. Could they get away with it still, or were they going to end up as prisoners in some miserable gaol somewhere at Her Majesty's pleasure, with a conviction for fraud? *Perish the thought.*

"I need a stiff drink," Jan piped up.

"Me too!" Dale replied in almost perfect harmony. He set their newly acquired Jeep on its way, back to the old town.

"Maybe we could give the money I inherited back, if it'll keep us out of gaol?"

Dale wasn't panicking quite yet. After twenty minutes, they drove into the car park of The Crown & Mitre Hotel in Carlisle and sat in silence, pondering for a few minutes, reflecting on the events of the day.

"It's six o'clock. Let's just have a drink and a meal. Try and relax for the night and not worry about things going wrong tomorrow, when it might not happen. They're not after us. All they want is to find out is who murdered the three bodies we found, who's responsible and why. They don't need to identify us as family. It's not relevant, not relevant at all. I'll speak to Roger down in our office. He's the solicitor, he should be able to advise us. We just need to help them identify the three bodies and that's it. When that's done, we're in the clear. Agreed?"

"Yes, Dale darling, if you say so I agree, I trust you. I have to. You got us into this mess and it's down to you to get us out of this mess. Now, how about that drink. I'm desperate."

CHAPTER 23

DC Julia Cox

It was bucketing with rain as DS Julia Cox accompanied by DC. Dave Knowles arrived at the Cardew-Petteril Estate Office. They had arrived unannounced, but Julia had visited the Cardew offices many times over the years on different matters and in fact the old Lord Cardew was her Godfather, though she very rarely saw him. His Lordship, a lovely gracious, old man, was now bedridden and pretty physically infirm, but still had most of his marbles. Julia didn't want to bother him, or feel the need to at this stage of their enquiries.

The two officers entered the great hall of the Manor House. They walked across the multi-coloured tiled floor, leaving wet footprints as they headed towards the Estate Office, situated behind an oak-panelled wall and a heavy oak-panelled door with huge black iron, circular handles. Below the galleried landing, which overlooked the main entrance hall, were historic paintings of past Lords of the manor and their ladies, or their families. Many of the portraits were now darkened with age and the backgrounds were hardly visible on the older paintings.

Estate Manager Tom Castle welcomed Julia in as an old friend and offered a cup of Earl Grey to his visitors. Tom was brought up in the vein and the ways of a 'gentleman farmer'. His parents farm had been purchased by the current Lord Cardew, many moons ago. Tom dressed the part, with his tweed suits and matching waistcoats and riding boots, a university graduate with a high degree of management skills. Some might say a 'canny lad', but a very nice chap, Julia always found.

"Tom, thank you. That would be very nice."

Tom's young assistant Jeffrey Cardew, who was learning the

ropes was pleased to be helpful.

"Now Julia, how can I help you. If you had telephoned first, I could have prepared whatever you needed. I guess that this is something to do with the bodies that were found at Buckabank Mill?"

Julia replied, "Yes Tom, not rocket science, but well worked out. DC. Knowles here, has some old photographs of his grandfather who we think may be one of the victims. So I thought that you may be able to check your records and give us any more background and perhaps see if there are any photos of them with their spouses, say at fairs or fetes or festivals or hoe-downs. You know, the things they used to do 'back in the day' before television!"

Young Cardew brought in a tray of Earl Grey with some slices of lemon. Tom poured and Julia sipped her clear liquid with a slice of lemon floating nicely on top. DC. Knowles, turned away as he pulled a face of disgust and swallowed the revolting brew down in one gulp, burning his tongue in so doing.

"Not to your liking sir?" asked young Cardew.

Knowles replied, "Been used to builders, all my life. But thank you anyway. It was lovely."

He thought on this occasion, it was courteous and acceptable to lie!

They knew he lied!

***

Julia was revelling in sipping at her aromatic brew from the prettily decorated blue porcelain china cups. She took in the delicate aroma, always having loved the smell of Bergamot since the first time she had enjoyed Earl Grey up at The Manor House, when she was a child. While they savoured their brew, Tom Castle had headed to a closed dark wooden cupboard with scarred, cracked and chipped white china knobs. The cupboard was the size of a large domestic wardrobe and had probably been in place for the last hundred years or so. It creaked as he opened it and he sneezed as the dust fell from the top.

"Bless you!"

"Thank you! Excuse me! …Now, let's see what we can find in here, shall we?"

He passed the large leather folders one at a time over to Julia and Knowles, which Julia had likened to old dusty family bibles, but larger. They thumbed through the pages of photos and letters and agreements and more photos. The nearer they got to present day then the clearer the photos, but the less likely they were to find what they were looking for. After an hour or so, the two officers thanked Tom Castle for his help, but there didn't appear to be any clues in these volumes.

"Are there any more albums anywhere, which might have what we're looking for?" Julia enquired.

"I don't think so Julia. The only other albums are with his Lordship. But unless it's absolutely necessary, I wouldn't want to disturb him, he's not a well man, if that's okay with you?"

"Okay Tom. I understand. However, if you are able to access them, then please let me know as this *is* a murder enquiry. Thank you again. And for the Earl Grey, Jeffery, it was perfect. Thank you."

The two officers left the estate, disappointed that they weren't able to glean any clues and headed back in the rain to a deserted Carlisle Police Station.

***

Julia arrived home and flopped in her favourite armchair as her mobile started ringing.

"Hi, Sweety, it's your favourite husband here. I just phoned to see how the case was going and if I could help."

"Hello favourite husband, yes, I'm fine thank you. And how are you? And no you didn't phone to see how I was…you phoned to see if I could give you an inside story. And that's a *no* then! Unless you want me to get the sack! It's reporter first and husband second. But I'm sure you love me, Grant darling, so I'll forgive you not caring how I am, despite all the pressure. It's no wonder they call you Mr Front Page!"

He retorted, "I'm serious. Of course I love you… Sorry, what did you say your name was??!! Just kidding!! Please don't forget, I have the access to millions of records at my finger-tips. Newspaper headlines, photographs, they go back well before your case. I might just be able to help. You just have to ask. Anyway, I also phoned to say I'll be home tomorrow. Need to go now I'm meeting a Publisher at the Globe Inn in Westminster. He's promised to read through the script of my new novel. Love you."

With that, Grant had gone, blown away like a falling autumn leaf swept up on a swirling, blustery-breeze. Julia poured herself a large glass of cheap Sauvignon from Aldi and settled down in front of the telly, to a Waitrose, Charlie 'big-one' (as Grant called it). It was tray-bake in a wooden tray, that she had taken from the freezer in the morning and placed in the fridge to thaw sufficiently, to cook in the microwave.

"Delicious," she said to herself. "Delicious."

CHAPTER 24

1895-96, Buckabank

After Albert handed Ben the buff paper envelope, with Joseph's telegram in it, they had shed tears for at least ten minutes as well as hugs, kisses and introductions. They read Joseph's telegram again.

PICKED UP YOUR AD. STOP. YOU HAVE FOUND ME. STOP. WILL BE WITH YOU FRIDAY OR SATURDAY. STOP. YOUR BROTHER JOSEPH. STOP.

"I can't believe it, Ben exclaimed again. My brother, my missing brother. My best man!"

Joseph replied and posed the big question, "Best man?"

"Yes, Joseph. This is my Daisy and we are betrothed. The Banns are already being read and I put the Vicar off, until I could find my best man, my own brother. No one else would do. Anyway, we can talk about that again. Tell me all about your travel, how you came to be in this part of the world and how you are doing."

Joseph began his tale of adventures and travels, mainly around the British coastline, but also to the Norwegian coastline countries and their ports as well as Ireland and even France Belgium and North Africa. He was pleased to tell all the tales of a sailor and was pleased that he had had such an experience. But it was time to settle down and he had heard that Newcastle was a growing town, with plenty of work and not only had he settled down, but he also was betrothed.

Joseph relayed to his brother Ben and Daisy, as Samuel and William listened on with amusement and some envy. All sat around the big oak table in the kitchen, enjoying several hours of the two brothers telling amusing stories of Joseph's sea-adventures and Ben at the mines and then meeting Sammy. While catching up, they were enjoying glasses of home brewed beer and Ben's favourite bacon sandwiches, made from great-big thick chunks of Daisy's home-made farmhouse loaves, straight out of the range.

Ben started to think out loud as they talked about their futures.

"We must have a double wedding! Me and Daisy and You and your Alice. We could each be the other's best man and we could have a great big celebration party."

Joseph replied with enthusiasm, but with reservations. "That' a wonderful, wonderful idea Ben, but I think Alice would want to get married in Newcastle, where her family and friends are, *and* my work is there. They are just about to make me a director. I have a great future mapped out. I do have one drawback however, the old man James Wrighton, the owner is not a well man and the only person who could take over the business is his fourteen-year-old grandson, so that won't happen. The other thing I'm bothered about is that the old man's daughter-in-law, who is Wrighton's Son's widow, is being courted by someone who wants to buy the yard. He's a slippery character and she can't see through him. He's only after one thing…and it's not her, it's the yard and the old man's money. So, I need to get back and talk to the daughter and make sure she continues with the business."

Sammy, now almost deaf and poorly sighted spoke quietly, "Joseph, my boy. If you find yourself in need of work, you could always come and take a part of this yard with Benjamin. It's his now. I am not for this world much longer. I've had my time and you are the next best thing I will ever have to a family. Why not come here and live with your brother and Daisy and bring your Alice with you. There is plenty of room."

Joseph was noticeably moved by Sammy's words and thanked him for his kindness and his generosity.

The day at Buckabank mill flew by and soon night fell. The dark clouds tumbled around the skies and thunder rolled in the distance. The wind whipped across the top of the tall pines and whistled through the old cottage windows.

Joseph sadly announced, "I shall have to leave first thing in the morning. I need to get back, ready to open the yard again on Monday morning. Maybe Ben, you could come back with me and meet Alice and her Ma and look at the yard I'm running?"

***

The following morning Joseph and Benjamin wrapped in their long oilskin raincoats set off on horseback to cover the sixty miles to Newcastle. They planned to pick up Joseph's horse from the hostelry and change Ben's over there, which he would return on his return journey. They left Buckabank at nine in the morning and travelling at a steady trot, having changed horses at the roughly half-way point and thanks to improving daylight, then they were back in Newcastle by five in the evening.

They deposited the horses back into the stables and by twenty past five Alice was throwing her arms around Joseph's neck and eventually let him go to be introduced to his big brother Benjamin.

The next day, Monday, Joseph opened the yard and conducted the day's business. Ben helped with some of the unloading. His fitness had improved ten-fold over the last few weeks since his beating.

Daisy and Ma loved Ben. He was so much like his brother Joseph. Kind, considerate, thoughtful, helpful and clearly, a worker. Like two peas in a pod. Alice loved the idea of a double wedding and couldn't wait to meet her new sister-in-law to be, but Joseph was troubled. Payments were still not clearing for some of the new shipments to clear the docks into the yard. Tonight, he would have to go and see old man Wrighton.

He ordered a carriage for 5pm when he had shut the yard gates. The carriage only took ten minutes up to The Grange. He entered the portico and pulled the big brass bell-pull.

The butler answered the door and greeted him. Ben remained in the carriage.

"Good evening, Mr Morris."

Joseph hadn't been greeted by a servant before in that manner. He felt privileged and important and replied, "Good evening, Mayhew, I've come to see your master, Mr Wrighton."

"Oh. I see. Would you be kind enough to wait here in the hall sir, please."

The old man's daughter-in-law Mrs Wrighton entered the hall

from a set of doors to the right. She was dressed in black. When he'd first met her, she was in a pretty blue silk hooped dress with a matching blue and white bonnet, but now she looked very sombre. She spoke.

"Joseph. It's nice to see you again. However, I'm sorry to have to inform you that unfortunately, father is not well enough to take visitors, in fact he is not expected to last much longer. The doctors are with him now, trying to make him comfortable."

Joseph was visibly shocked. He nervously and tentatively enquired. "Please forgive me for asking Ma'am, but what will happen to the yard. Mr Wrighton was to make me a director and allocate some shares to me. I would truly give those things up if it would make him better. He's been very good to me these last many months, since I've managed to help turn the business around?"

"Joseph, I'm so sorry," she replied. "I know father has relied heavily on you since his illness, but he isn't going to get better and I won't want to take responsibility of running the business. It's not ladies' work. I'll have to let you know, and I will do so as soon as I can."

Joseph felt devastated. What was he going to tell Alice and Ma. This could affect their wedding plans and buying a nice little house together.

Joseph climbed back into the carriage and bade the driver to return home.

"Joseph," exclaimed Ben. "You looked like you've seen a ghost."

"Well, I came close to seeing a ghost. The old man is dying and not expected to recover soon and the daughter is going to close the business. All my plans have been dashed. I don't know how I'm going to tell Alice and her Ma. They were counting on me."

Back at Ma's house, most of the evening was spent in silence. Ben was trying to be cheerful by offering Sammy's solution as fate. But nothing would cheer up Joseph.

The following morning Ben made the return journey to Carlisle.

On Monday of the following week. With no warning, Joseph went down to the yard to open up as usual to find slats of timber, from his yard, nailed across the yard gates, with a printed sign saying: Business Closed. By Order of George Milburn. The Tyne and Weir Development Company.

Joseph looked in horror at the notice and noted the contact office address and noted the name.

He left the yard and returned to Ma's house and sat with a mug of tea, until he felt it a suitable hour to visit The Grange. At ten am, he made his way up to the big house, not sure what he might achieve, but visit he must.

He stepped up on to the portico entrance and pulled the bell.

Mayhew, the butler, answered and greeted Joseph courteously as ever, but was told to state that the master had passed and the mistress was not taking visitors, however, he might like to talk to the mistress's fiancé, a Mr George Milburn.

Mr Milburn starchily thanked Joseph for his involvement in the yard, but as the yard was now closed, his services were no longer required and wished him a good day.

Milburn turned to Mayhew and said, "Show the gentleman out Mayhew."

Joseph was dumfounded and speechless. His mouth was dry and he couldn't speak. He just turned on his heels and left The Grange for the last time.

A few days later an envelope was hand delivered to Ma's house for Joseph. It had one hundred pounds in it, accompanied by a polite but pleasant note from the old man's daughter-in-law, thanking him for all of the help he had given her father-in-law. Joseph was very grateful that the daughter had recognised the fact that Joseph had worked hard at her father-in-laws yard and kept it going for so long, or perhaps she was just adhering to old man Wrighton's wishes? Joseph wondered if there was a will and perhaps, he might have been left some shares in the business as the old man had promised. He wondered whether there may have been some interference with any wills by that lizard-like George Milburn. He was the type. But he would probably never find out. Hence the decision was made. Joseph and Alice would move to Buckabank to start their new life together. With Ben and Daisy.

Joseph finished loading the cart that he had borrowed from Ben's mill. They had given it a thorough clean out first and brought it back to Ma's house in Newcastle. Daisy had come along to meet Alice and already the girls were like a couple of excited children off to the may fair. The worldly goods being taken back to Buckabank, were few and with little value, but they were Alice's and she felt the need to have her own bedding and some of her childhood playthings in her new home to make it feel like her space. Joseph carefully loaded a couple of armchairs that Ma had gifted her for her new home and Ma, climbed up on board to make the journey to Carlisle.

Ben was to have his wish. The two couples were to marry on the same day at the same church and at the same time. Each was to be the other's Best Man, though this confused the Vicar, particularly when it came to the exchanging of the rings. There was much merriment in the villages. The bells rang, the folks clapped and threw confetti and rice and the day came and went, with much singing and dancing, eating and drinking, exuberance and high spirits. With part of his hundred pounds, Joseph had booked both couples into The Crown and Mitre for one night. A wedding night in an old, wind-swept, drafty and damp stone cottage, up at the old sawmill, just didn't seem right.

It was money well spent. Nine months later, both girls, young wives, were expecting. Daisy sailed through her pregnancy and produced a lovely boy… Emmanuel. They called him Manny for short, unless he had stepped out of line in any way and then it was Emmanuel!

Alice had had a difficult nine-month passage, with much pain. She also produced a baby boy. Sadly, the baby died a few days later. Joseph and Alice were heartbroken but consoled themselves with the fact that they knew they were still young, fit, and in good health, and that more babies would come in time. Sadly, the years went by and Joseph and Alice accepted that they wouldn't be blessed with children.

Benjamin and Joseph worked happily together, with Emmanuel growing up and working in the family business. Daisy and Alice were great company for each other and made a real home for their men as well as running their market stalls twice a week in Carlisle. The business flourished and the brothers, with the help of Manny, Benjamin and Daisy's son, were able to rebuild the stone and timber mill house so that everyone had a comfortable shared space of their own. Life was good.

Old Samuel Abrahams died in his sleep of old age, a happy man, having had his 'adopted' son working with him for many years and then his lovely family, working around him and caring for him until he passed. Samuel Abrahams would have been overwhelmed by the number of folks that turned out to see his final farewell to the world. It was a grand funeral and was celebrated up at the big house on the Cardew Estate, with much merriment, and dancing. Exactly what old Samuel would have appreciated. Daisy and Alice had been baking for a week to provide for an open-air, sit-down meal of home-made breads and cheeses and all the delights of a home-made country kitchen. Photographers even recorded the event, meant to celebrate Samuel's life and not to be a sombre affair, exactly as he would have wanted.

A few days later, joy of joys. Life could not get better. The couples had been married for almost twenty years when Alice and Joseph announced that Alice was 'with child' and Bryn was the new addition born into the family. They were truly blessed and could not be happier.

As the years went by, Alice, who was never in the greatest of health passed away and within weeks, Joseph pined and pined and willed himself away, refusing to eat or drink or take any medication. Joseph just wanted to be with Alice, the only girl he had ever loved. Alice was sixty-eight and Joseph was just short of seventy years of age, when they passed and were eventually buried together in the chapel gardens, where they had been married.

Benjamin and son Manny carried on the business being helped by cousin Bryn, who never seemed to be the happiest of young men. He liked his beer too much and often overindulged. Things improved somewhat when he met and eventually married Mary Gwenllian Pritchard, a young cousin of Daisy, up from Newport in Wales, visiting family in Carlisle.

Benjamin and Daisy passed away within weeks of each other from what the doctors was saying was Consumption or Tuberculosis. No one knew where it had come from, they just kept coughing and didn't seem to be able to stop. It was a sad drawn-out death and it didn't seem a fair end to their hard, working life. They were buried alongside Joseph and Alice in the chapel gardens, where both grave-stones bore the names Morritzstein and additionally engraved, known as Morris. Benjamin and Daisy. Joseph and Alice.

Meantime, Bryn seemed to jog along together with Mary-Gwen who was generally a passive, docile, happy soul who had the patience of a saint and put up with Bryn's drinking and bad behaviour. But love affects folk in different ways and she always stood by him, through thick and thin, no matter what controversy he might make for himself.

"He does work hard." You would often hear her say.

Sadly, the lion's share of what he earned, most of which came from working with Manny, at Buckabank, went down his neck, much to Mary's despair. But nothing would change him and it seemed his resentment at being poor, his vexation was getting to his deeper roots and turning him into a bitter, angry man. A lot of this was directed towards Manny, as Manny held not only the purse strings, but he owned the mill and its surrounding acreage. To Bryn, this was a small gold mine, waiting to be sold and turned into wealth, a wealth he had never known.

"Why was it just Manny's?" he would continually puzzle and pose the question to Mary.

"Surely, both brothers owned it, and one was my father, so why am I not allowed a share?"

Every time the argument came up, and it raged on for years. Manny would say.

"My father Benjamin, left it to me. It's my inheritance. You're twenty years younger than me. You can have it when I'm gone and not before and that's the end of it."

CHAPTER 25

2020, Carlisle

Grant's parting words to Julia on the telephone a couple of nights ago, kept rolling over in her mind. "I'm serious. Don't forget, I have the access to millions of records at my finger-tips."

As Julia sat at home in her breakfast bar in her crumpled pink dressing gown, her blond hair in disarray after a half-sleepless night, she sat stirring her black coffee, starting to unwind and enjoy her weekend off duty. With Grant home for a few days, she was looking forward to thinking that they could get out and do a bit of hill-walking, when her mobile rang. She answered, "Julia Cox."

"Good morning, Julia, it's Tom Castle. Sorry to trouble you on a Saturday, but I was left puzzled after you were here at the estate office last week with the other officer. I thought to myself, 'why would *he* have photographs of estate workers that I didn't have on file', so I went hunting for what I thought might be another album. Somehow it had found its way into his Lordship's library, so I took it and re-located it in its rightful place, here in my office. And in anticipation of your next question, yes, there are several photos of the Morris's both up here at harvest time, delivering cut timber and some at the sawmill. They're all a bit old and hazy, but you can clearly make out the folks I think you are looking for."

Julia replied, "Tom, thank you so much. I'm sure that this will be helpful to us in identifying our corpses. I will be up to see you some time this morning, if that's okay with you. Thank you again."

"You're welcome."

She shouted out to Grant, who had arrived home late last night, in fact, in the early hours from London. "Grant, get up! We're going up to see Tom Castle up at the Cardew-Petteril Estate.

He has another album for me to look at. Are you coming?"

A dreary looking Grant, emerged from the bedroom rubbing his eyes. Fortunately, despite the cold, it was a bright day, with the sun shining, taking most of the chill away now that the wind had subsided.

"Yes, yes. I'd love to see these photos and then maybe I can work on the old newspaper records and identify some dates and events for you. In my experience, it's amazing what you can turn up when you start digging into the old newspaper files. Now everything is recorded on 'microfiche' and available at the tap of a few buttons, then we might be surprised by the things that may have happened around the years that the photos were taken. I might also look up any headlines in the following years that might reveal something and be relevant to your enquiries. So yes. I'll come with you."

After quickly showering and throwing on some civvies. Julia drove Grant up to the Cardew-Petteril Estate, taking in the beauty of their trip. The soft green rolling hills, the deep valleys, the small pine forest, the stream running through the beck, the lake at the bottom of the land which was fed by the stream and ran back into the river. Past acres of turned fields planted with winter barley and beet. Across two cattle grids and along a long crunching driveway up to the big house.

Julia pulled up outside the house and walked in through the open double doors to be greeted by Tom Castle. There was no need for introductions as Tom and Grant both played for Carlisle Cricket Club's Second team. They shook hands acknowledging each other and headed through to Tom's estate office. The much-worn large suede and brown leather topped album was sat opened on the oak desk.

Julia started to thumb through it, taking photos on her mobile phone. The hand scribbled dates on the top of some of the pages started at 1900 through to 1920, showing a very old man, Samuel Abrahams, together with two other men, alongside timber carts, a tractor, haystacks and what appeared to be some fairground games. Julia assumed these to be photographs from one of the harvest or haymaking fairs, which Tom confirmed. Someone had painted Harvest 1920 in scruffy white letters on an old brown board.

Julia thumbed back as far as 1900, to find photos of what

appeared to be the two brothers, with wives and one couple holding what looked like a new born baby. Someone had scribbled new arrival Emmanuel. There were one or two more photos that bore the same men, but nothing of any more significance. She thumbed forward a few more pages to 1920 to find a photograph of a Funeral procession. This was the funeral of Samuel Abrahams in 1920. Obviously a sombre affair, with everyone dressed in black. The scribble under this was Samuel Abrahams from Buckabank Sawmill. But then, another couple which looked like the younger brother Joseph and Alice with a new born, which they had named Bryn.

After spending a half-an-hour studying the previously missing album and taking endless mobile photos, Julia thanked Tom and she and Grant headed back home. They now had some names and photos that they could work with. Julia was wanting to go into town and into the police station to get to work on the new information that they had gleaned from the missing album, but Grant was hesitant and then insistent that they enjoy their weekend together. Besides that, they had arranged to meet up with Rob and Jacky and Richard and Jenny Southfield at The Feathers and she could tell Rob of her findings then.

Julia commented, "Having said that, I daren't give away too much information while Jenny Southfield is there, she has already been chasing us for quotes for the Denbury Gazette. Remember that little local rag you worked on all those years ago that gave you your first big break?"

"Whatever," Grant replied. "Today is Saturday. Saturday is precious. Saturday is sacrosanct. Yes! It is our day off and a rare day off together! So absolutely not, we are going hiking."

An hour later Julia and Grant were upstairs in the Detectives room at Carlisle Police Station. The sketchy ancestry information that Dale Scott and Jan Phillips had left, didn't really help matters. The majority of the Family Tree showed Jan Phillips as a descendant on the Morris tree, through her grandfather, but no links to other potential persons. After two hours of fairly fruitless time spent, if not wasted, the pair gave up and went home and back to bed, to make up for Grant being away for the last ten days.

Julia and Grant decided not to share their findings with Rob on Saturday evening, though inevitably the case came up. Julia was bursting to tell Rob what she had found but decided to wait until Monday morning, just before the team meeting scheduled for 10am.

Perhaps tomorrow, she could check the local chapel, church and parish records.

On Sunday morning they phoned the Reverend Worthy and asked if they could visit after his morning service.

Julia explained about the photos taken at the church where the couples were married, was incredibly helpful. The reverend studied the photos and the names and took Julia and Grant into the Vestry where he kept all of the local records. The Cumwhinton chapel where they had married had long ago been sold to become a private property so the records were transferred to Cumwhinton Church, nearby. He opened the pages with due care at the dates which Julia had sought. The beautifully hand written records, with calligraphed first letters of the Parish records were helpful. The register revealed the double marriage of the brothers, Benjamin and Joseph Morris who married Daisy and Alice respectively. Nine months later, almost to the day, the birth register showed a baby boy born to Benjamin and Daisy. A week later, the register recorded a funeral for the child of Joseph and Alice, whom they named Albert, apparently after the long deceased Queen Victoria's Prince Consort.

On Sunday evening. Julia and Grant sat at their dining table, with photos and copy records laid out in chronological order.

They believed that they could identify two of the deceased as being Emmanuel Morris, being the son of Benjamin and Daisy and Emmanuel's (Manny) Wife Violet Morris, both born circa 1900 and therefore, both aged around seventy.

The third person would be another female, based on the clothing found wrapped around the skeletal remains.

Julia would present her findings to her boss, DI Rob Wilton and DCI Jerry Blake in the morning. Tomorrow Grant made a commitment to scan the records back to the 1900's through to recent times and see what emerged.

Meantime, Grant and Julia were enjoying what was left of their weekend.

"Another glass of red, Sweety?"

"Mmmm. Go on then, just a large one!" Grant replied.

CHAPTER 26

2020, Carlisle Police Station

Julia was in to the station early, as ever. As her boss Rob arrived, she was quick to head him off and usher him in to his own office. She couldn't get the information out fast enough.

"Woah. Slow down Julia."

Julia started to detail her findings to Rob, with the combination of dates, matched up with the church records and the various photographs.

"Okay, Julia. First, well done, this is very good work, and secondly, you might as well add as much of this information to the crime board as you can. We may well need another board. In this way, the whole team can get their heads around the third person at the mill, if you think you've identified two."

Rob tapped his coffee mug with his pen. "Okay, listen up people. DS Cox has been busy over the weekend, thanks partially to DC Dave Knowles bringing in some old photos. This led Julia up to the Estate and then on to the Parish church. She'll give you all an update… Julia?"

"Good morning, all. With the photographs I am now putting on the board, I will give you what I think is the history of the Morris family and how I believe I have identified two of the three deceased. I apologise if seems a bit long and drawn out, but I think that will help us identify the third person and the perpetrator, of what looks like a triple homicide.

"Now, to summarise, Buckabank Sawmill had been in the Morris family for almost a hundred years. It was originally worked by Benjamin Morris and his brother Joseph from the late 1890's and well into the 1900's. There are no funeral records for either Emmanuel (Manny) or his wife Violet. Neither are there any funeral records for Emmanuel's younger cousin Bryn. So, he may well still be alive. We need to check this. He would be a person of interest and presumably he was married. So, could this have been his wife the other Jane Doe?

"Emmanuel (Manny that is) and his father Benjamin and Benjamin's brother, Joseph, worked for Samuel Abrahams. Sammy, as a Jew fleeing Europe himself, had managed to get a contract to cut timber from the vast Lord Cardew's Estate, to supply timber posts for the mining boom and timbers for the new railways that were being forged across the country. He had occupied the sawmill site for so many years. It was seen as his wood and towards the end of the century when the old Lord died, it was assumed that the woods worked by formerly Samuel Abrahams, together with the brothers Benjamin and Joseph Morritzstein (which had long ago been shortened to Morris), after forty years, were their woods. Nobody questioned it and Samuel had had, a map drawn up together with a Deed that the Solicitor had registered with the Land Registry, confirming that the land was theirs.

"The title had not been disputed, so the land, the woods and the sawmill legally became theirs. The map, showed the mill, and more importantly the land and the woods that they had worked and had been replanted over the many years which amounted to some two hundred acres.

"This brings in another question. This Jan Morris and Dale Scott. We have seen their deeds and they only believe that they have inherited something just over a hundred acres. In which case where have the other hundred or so acres gone?

"I'll continue with more detail as we may also be looking at property fraud here. Samuel Abrahams, together with Benjamin and his brother Joseph, were there, they had become the legal owners, almost by default. When the cutting stocks in the central area of the woods became depleted, Benjamin just expanded their 'claim' as any sitting tenant might, until the total land mass had expanded to around the two hundred acres. No one ever questioned it. This took in timber woods, young saplings and woodlands, several pastures and grazing meadows, which were let out at a peppercorn rent and of course the river, which ran through the whole eastern area of the estate. As he was still giving a good and useful service to the old deceased Lord's estate, then Benjamin continued to expand his area of timber felling and re-planting without any question as to ownership.

"It was always assumed that this was Benjamin's land, inherited from Samuel Abrahams and as it was only a small part of a vast estate, running to thousands of acres. Then its ownership became so insignificant that no one took heed or stock of the land or its value.

"The land itself falls between two rivers. To the west is the River Cardew and to the east was the River Petteril. It sits partially in a valley with undulating areas and soft rolling hills.

"Samuel's business had slowed down over his later years and the staff dwindled to just the two loyal and trusted main employees, Benjamin, whom Samuel regarded as his 'adopted' son and his brother Joseph Morritzstein. Samuel died of old age, with no known relatives to whom to leave his much depleted 'timber empire'. Benjamin and Joseph adopted it as their own, though Samuel on his dying bed had gifted it to Benjamin, who was a young lad when he first helped him and befriended him, all those years ago at the coal mine, when his load had been spilled. Samuel though determined, had underestimated his fitness and was unable to deliver the particular load, single-handed, which was when Ben rushed to help him with his delivery to where it was required, at the pithead.

"There was also some bad blood here between Benjamin and the Tam Lock clan whose father had shares in the Colliery where Tam Lock's father, Thaddeus Lock died in suspicious circumstances. These weren't fully investigated at the time.

"This was the incident, that gave Ben the opportunity to leave the pit and to work with old Samuel (Sammy) Abrahams. Benjamin made sure that the two of them delivered timber to the pit, together, so that the old man wouldn't have to put up with Thaddeus Lock the colliery manager, or trying to deliver another heavy load, on his own and potentially killing himself in the process of delivering those pit-props.

"When finally, the brothers met up and Joseph moved from Newcastle with Alice, they each raised a small family, or at least they had one 'off-spring' each. Ben and Daisy's first born was named Emmanuel and became known as Manny. He was born in

1920. This was the name of the brother's father, back home in Eastern Europe somewhere. They didn't know why they were never blessed with another child. The son of Joseph and Alice expected at roughly the same time as Manny, died a few days after he was born. It was another twenty years before they had another child. Bryn who was, we believe born circa 1940, though we need to further clarify this as the records are a little sketchy.

"We *need* to find Bryn.

"Each son helped in the business, either in the sawmill or clearing and planting new woodlands or delivering to local farmers. They had created new uses for their timber and acquired new steam cutting equipment by Wadkin in the early 1900's, with which they were able to cut to customer's requirements, but as well as their bespoke service, they were creating timbers ready to build barns. Timber ready to assemble as chicken sheds and every manner of timber pre-construction they could conjure-up. The sons of both Benjamin and Joseph were fully integrated in the business, though Manny became the boss as he was twenty years older that Bryn. As they expanded, then so did their land mass which was now headed towards over two hundred acres plus, maybe even up to three hundred acres with at least half of their land planted with saplings for the future generations to cut, harvest and store. When Joseph and Alice moved across to Buckabank they apparently, from the photographs, lived in two wooden caravans while they re-built the stone cottage or mill house, if you prefer. Although there was only a couple of years between them, they were very close, but the younger brother Joseph seemed to take the lead in everything and between them they had slowly built on and extended the stone-built cottage, to create a double dwelling for each of them and their new brides."

Julia continued to spread photographs on the table as if she were revealing the identity of hidden playing card numbers.

"Both their off-spring, Manny married a girl from the neighbouring villages where the weekly dance, hoe down or knees-up held in a large wooden barn, rented from his Lordship's estate, brought in all the local folks, girls and boys. They sat upon straw bales spread around the barn and there was always plenty of home brewed cider and rough beer from barrels laid out on hessian sack-cloth covered tables. Manny married Violet and Bryn, eventually married Violet's sister, who had come up from Newport in Wales on a long-term visit."

Julia continued to place photographs on the table in front of her. She continued, "Again, I want you to study these and look for the two couple we believe to be either the corpses we have found and somewhere along the line, find Bryn Morris. These old photos show that the ladies would always bake game pies with hot-water crusty pastry, or that's what they called them, filled with anything they could trap or forage from the woods around. Invariably the entertainment was by a mix of locals and could vary from just a fiddle and a drum to a veritable orchestra with guitars, fiddle, accordion and bodhran, beaten with a well-worn tipper and, not forgetting old Jed with his Jaws harp."

Julia shuffled the various photographs around again, showing the many events in a country person's life.

From the photographs, it looked as though Manny enjoyed those days with affection and remembered how good they were and how families all helped each other. It was a shame how he and his cousin Bryn had grown so far apart from each other and arguments about the mill and their acreage, always ended any social or family gatherings that they held.

"In the last set of photographs, it looks as if Manny is around seventy and his cousin Bryn is around fifty. I can only guess, that Bryn had a massive falling out with Manny, probably over the fact that they seemed to be struggling financially, yet they were sat on a small fortune in real-estate. Could this be the reason for the three of them being locked in the cellar?"

Rob summed up Julia's good work. "Can we have some comments from the floor then please? Your views. Is this what lead to the bodies in the cellar?"

CHAPTER 27

1970

Manny finished loading the tractor and trailer, ready to take the sawn timbers to Carlisle train station goods yard, to fulfil another order for Allen's Builders Supplies in North London. Violet called him to remind him to take his sandwiches for the hour-long slow-moving tractor journey and his well-worn Thermos flask filled with syrupy sweet tea.

She called out to Manny as he sat up in the tractor. "When you come back, we need to sort out this ongoing dispute between you and your cousin Bryn. It can't go on like this, we need to resolve the issue of who owns what here. We can't continue putting it off. It's stopping us getting on with trying to run the mill and make enough to live on, instead of having to ask the bank for loans all the time. It seems as soon as we pay off one loan, then we need to borrow more money. We have to sort it out, once and for all, I can't cope with all this animosity and the bad blood that is building between you and Bryn. You and I can chat it through and then when they come to us next Sunday, we can sort it out once and for all." She waved him off. "Mind how you go Luv, come back safe. See you later."

Manny returned late in the afternoon, from Carlisle Station goods yard, having dropped off his load for the night train and its London destination. Nowadays he insisted on money up front, times were becoming difficult. He bumped his tractor and trailer down the side track and pulled the tractor in under the covered barn area. He unhooked the trailer and pushed it around to the side of the barn. His tired body strained under the weight of pushing the trailer over the rough yard but he was used to it and for his seventy plus years, though tired, he still felt very fit and capable.

He was a tall wiry man with unusually long legs and a square chest, the length of his arms seemed to balance well with his strong legs, but he was losing his appetite for work through years of constant physical exertion. On his long neck, still sat quite a handsome, if not gnarled rugged looking man with a deep dimple, often hidden under his two or three days of bearded growth. He had steely blue eyes a long forehead and bushy greying eyebrows, with a swathe of light and dark grey hair falling over his forehead almost to his shoulders. Most of the time he wore a very worn tweed cloth cap, with his hair tucked up underneath. His standard working attire were heavy canvas type trousers, collarless shirt with no stud, rolled sleeves and an old striped waistcoat. He felt comfortable in his own skin. It was a rare thing to see him in a suit. The last time was mother Violet's funeral, which was so far back, he couldn't even remember.

Unfortunately, with the small amount of business coming in, there was only enough income for one person to work the mill and it was decided that he being the older member of the business, then he had the choice. In any event, as the mill was his inheritance in line with what his father and his uncle had decreed and willed to them. Occasionally his young cousin Bryn would come in to help if there was a larger order to get out, or there was a lot of cutting to do. But nowadays, so much timber was being imported from the Baltic states as well as Canada, trying to compete to make a living was becoming harder by the hour. Manny, was getting wearier by the day. Unfortunately, his cousin Bryn had taken to drinking and with little money coming in, he wanted a share of the mill. He wanted it sold. But it wasn't his to sell and Manny was resisting Bryn's constant challenges.

1970, Carlisle, Kyle Redford Land Agents

In the meantime. Bryn was off to meet up with Kyle Redford the young up-coming, local auctioneer and land agent, in preparation for his 'showdown' with Manny.

Bryn Morris had been visiting Kyle Redford for some weeks at his office, Redford's Land Agents, in Carlisle. Redford's offices were situated alongside and above the cattle stalls in the centre of Carlisle's busy livestock market. The livestock sales were held three times a week, Mondays, Wednesday and Fridays and business was good. The rail and road links were good to all the major cities and there had been plenty of demand from all over the country, given that the country's birth rate had been exploding after the war years and the demand for food was ever increasing.

Kyle, a handsome young man. For such a young man in his very early twenties, was making a name for himself as not only a good and competent auctioneer but knew how to value and get the best prices for his clients. He had moved into land sales and had been in negotiation with some large London firms who saw the north as a place to expand. With land values less than a tenth of what they were in London the available sites were green and expansive, with little resistance to building development. If anything, local councils were desperate for developers to come north to create work, for the local population as the mining boom seemed to be over and the Lancashire textile industry was also in decline.

Kyle was indeed a handsome young man of mixed-race parents. His father was Irish and his mother was Afro-Caribbean. His father had married his mother when he had sailed to the United States of America many years ago and brought back a Caribbean wife. Kyle was very proud of both his own and his father's and his mother's roots and displayed on the wall, and in wall cabinets, several artefacts of antique African daggers and swords, shields and headwear, some displayed in glass boxes affixed to the wall. When some of his clients came to his offices, they would often bring their children to see Kyle's impressive African weaponry, masks and artefacts collections. Kyle had a manner which pleased everyone. Nothing was too much trouble and if something needed doing, as long as you had him on board, then the job would get done. He was a big man, a broad shouldered, six foot two, with a mop of curly naturally dark and light greying hair, a big smile under brown eyes and a round face which was always smiling. However, under all of that charm lay a very sharp businessman, with an eye for making money. Kyle helped manage many thousands of acres for mainly small farms, where they couldn't afford to employ a farm manager, so he took care of organising their livestock sales, collections and deliveries. He would often negotiate bulk feed deals for the farmers on his list, and from time to time, there was the opportunity to handle the sale of a farm or a piece of land.

It had come to Kyle's notice that there were developers looking for land in his part of the world and he wanted to seize the opportunity. He had also heard that the motorways which they were building down south, would eventually come north and he wanted 'in' on this potentially lucrative real estate.

Kyle was looking out of the window across the livestock market, the large shiny enamel boards spaced out around the concrete walls, between the iron uprights of the large cattle stalls, reflected the sun straight into his office, dancing shadows across the room as the clouds passed through the bright blue sky. 'Spratts' animal feeds, the letters spelling *Spratts* formed in the shape of a Scottie dog, Spratts red and black Chicken and Poultry feed, and signs for 'Spillers' animal feeds in their striking green background and bright yellow lettering and 'Winalot' Greyhound meal, suggesting that the hounds of the buyers of these products would or might *win-a-lot* of races. In fact, there was hardly a concrete panel left around the building, helping to promote the awareness of so many brands, from OXO to Wills Woodbines, Raleigh Bicycles, Mobil Oil, Shell Oil, Blue Bell Tobacco…cool and mello, Bovril and endless others competing for customers' loyal business, subliminally implanted into their buying mindset and deep psyche. The market was quiet today and not in operation again until Wednesday. It was a warm day approaching the afternoon, Kyle could see out across the concrete yard with its rows and rows of cattle stalls and sheep pens, out through the busy town and past the spired church of St. Michaels, and out along the fast-flowing River Eden and to the fields beyond.

He had been speaking to Bryn Morris about the old timber mill, the sawmill, run by him and his ageing, cousin Manny. Manny was a wily old bird when it came to running his timber mill, there was nothing he couldn't make or turn his hand to when it came to lumber or timber or wood. But he was getting older now and though he was still a strong man, who was in his later years, the ways of the world often bettered him. His mind wasn't as strong as it was and he was sometimes becoming forgetful, which often made him angry, argumentative and belligerent. Kyle had explained many times that they could fetch quite a lot of money for their woods, particularly the area beyond the River Petteril and the pasture lands that they had let out for a pittance for years to their neighbour George Bland. George had kept his flocks of sheep on the grazing land for some number of years. George was nearing the end of his innings so he wouldn't necessarily complain if he had to give up sheep farming and there was no son to carry on. He would probably just retire to his grace and favour cottage from the Blackstone Manor Estate for whom he had work for, for probably the last sixty-odd years, allowing him to breed a few sheep as an extra income. Kyle had put it to both Emmanuel and Bryn Morris that there was a substantial plot of land that could be sold off. There was approximately fifty or sixty acres and if he allowed Kyle to handle the sale, then he would negotiate the right price for the property, which would be more than sufficient for them both to retire and live a good life. Frustratingly Manny with his stubborn ways, didn't like being preached to nor told what he could or couldn't do. He didn't want to retire as there was nothing else in his life to occupy it and he was too old to start something new or even travel, so he wouldn't hear of it. Manny had no intention of retiring, or moving from the mill. The only way, as he saw it was out in a wooden box. And for that matter, a fine carved wooden box, crafted by his own hand. And no more was to be said about the matter.

Needless to say, at his age, with very little experience of life, Bryn was keen to listen to Kyle and see what sort of deal he could come up with. Bryn was convinced that if Kyle could come up with a tangible deal, almost a fait-accompli, then Manny would see the sense and 'take the money', which according to Kyle could run into hundreds of thousands of pounds. Bryn salivated at the thought. All that money, what he couldn't do with it, wasn't worth talking about. He would go to Manny with a renewed determination to get his ageing cousin to see sense.

Bryn pulled his battered old green 1957 Morris Minor pick-up truck, streaked with brown rust marks and leaking oil by the gallon, into a space in the livestock yard, secured the brake handle, slammed the door and then kicked it shut for good measure. He was sick of being on his uppers, relying on work which always seemed to be hand to mouth. If his missus didn't work, they wouldn't even have enough food to put on the table. He wandered over to meet up with Kyle. Bryn was excited at the prospect and looking forward to talking to Kyle, just the thought of buying a new pick-up truck for work, maybe with a two bar and a motorized power winch and cable pull fitted to the rear. Bryn parked right under the sign that read 'Kyle Redford Land Agents', set above a large glazed window, half of which was obscured by the etched glass display with a list of the services that Kyle's business offered. The sign had a line in smaller print at the base of the window which brought enquiries from all and sundry.

....

Kyle Redford Land Agency
'Land Management', 'Land Sales', 'Farm Management', 'Livestock Sales'
No contract too small or too large to be undertaken.
Please enquire within.

....

Bryn tentatively opened the half-glazed door in nervous anticipation and entered the unit. Kyle shook his hand warmly, with two hands and spoke, at the same time looking out of the window to see if anyone had accompanied him.

"Bryn, very nice to see you. You didn't manage to persuade your cousin Manny to come along then."

Bryn grimaced and replied, "No Kyle. It's such a touchy subject. We always end up rowing every time I raise the matter. But I am determined this time. I am not going to let it rest. If you can set up some sort of a deal, then I will make the 'old-bugger' sign it if it's the last thing I do. The mill is worthless now. All the equipment is well past its safe and useful limit, a lot of it is unused and so-antiquated and rusted, that if anyone was to take on the mill to run it as a commercial operation, they'd have to invest a fortune in new machinery. And have you seen the prices of saw-mill machinery nowadays, we are talking, not just an arm and a leg, but big loans and bank borrowings. It's an impossible situation. I could never afford to take over from Manny, not that he would be interested anyway, stubborn old bastard."

Kyle stood there listening to Bryn wrenching his hands without realising it and unloading his woes about his disinterested kith and kin. He remarked, "Look Bryn, if I can get some interest from some serious buyers and we can get an indication of a price, as long as it's fairly firm with not too many complicated completion clauses and delays, then we can present Manny with a big fat sum of money to consider. That's surely the way to can turn his head. Let me show you what I've found in the County Records Library, I think you'll find these papers very interesting."

Bryn waited in anticipation.

Kyle stepped over to his metal filing cabinets and fished out some old papers. He shuffled them around and spread the old dusty papers on his well-used, well-worn scratched and stained large oak desk. Amongst the yellowing papers, was an historical map of the counties around Carlisle. Sat around the middle of the aged creased old map was an outline of the land which was occupied by Samuel Abrahams and then Benjamin Morritzstein and passed on to his son Emmanuel. The land shown was under-represented by the old lineage and appeared to have grown over the hundred years that it had been in Samuel and Benjamin's possession, though that wasn't shown on the map. The map was so old it would need updating, unless Kyle could find one at the County records office. Having said that, he might just get away with getting a potential buyer to accept his own re-drawing of boundaries. If he had this professionally re-drawn, probably in London where an Architect or Cartographer might just look on this as a commission to 'tidy up' a counties map, for selling on as an old map. But that was something that could be done if his potential buyer wanted to look at the complete 260acre site, no rush. There was no interest in the sawmill or the woods or the pasture land west of the river. None of that was suitable for industrial development.

The history as Kyle understood it, was that the Timber, or Sawmill as it was known, had been left to Benjamin Morritzstein, when Samuel Abrahams had died at the grand old age of eighty-seven after running the woods and the Timber and Sawmill for maybe fifty or sixty or even 70 years. Benjamin was the first of the two brothers, Benjamin and Joseph used to work for him, then he had bequeathed the sawmill and the woods and the land on which they sat, to the one brother, Benjamin, who had helped him for the two years before Joseph had come to work alongside them both.

Kyle ran his fingers over the map, tracing the faded lines outlining the county borders, down along the rivers Eden and

Petteril and he had pencilled in, where he believed the land belonging to Manny started and stopped and had been extended to. Bryn watched with interest taking in the large area and realising how much work he had put in over the years, from lumber-jacking to cutting and reefing and refining the timber cuts for drying out and selling on. He thought about all of the clearings that he had created and the re-planting which was now looking sufficiently re-grown for cutting again, heavy sweaty work, muscle wearing and back-breaking work. *So much work, so little return for me*, he thought to himself. And then said out loud, just under his breath, "So much fuckin' work and what have I got out of it? Nothing, fuckin' nothing."

"Bryn, look here, I have been looking and studying the old maps of the area which cover your piece of land. It's a fine piece of real estate. From my rough calculations, the total land mass is over two hundred and sixty, maybe three hundred acres, but the most valuable piece of real estate, is beyond the river to the east, where the land is level, or pretty much level with the river running alongside it."

Bryn a relatively simple working man, apologised for his bubbling, simmering and growing anger and for his swearing. With his limited education asked what real estate was.

Kyle was quick to apologise. "Bryn, I understand and I can see where you're coming from, I feel for you. With regard to the term real estate, I'm sorry, I used an American term that seems to be popular amongst our Southern, or London neighbours for land, and that's what you are sitting on. Real estate. That means real money, you know, the stuff you can spend and enjoy your life with, retire, travel, buy a small-holding or a farm, breed prize bulls or prize chickens, whatever you fancy. That's what real estate means and I think that I can sell that piece of real estate for you and Emmanuel as well as what's left of the Timber Mill."

"Okay, okay, Kyle, I've got the message. I just need to convince Manny and Violet. What do we have to do next?" Bryn responded.

Kyle laid out the procedure for getting things in place for a sale. "The most important thing is to have a 'Terms of Contract for Sale' in place as this is a commercial business, showing you and Manny as the Sellers. Now, if we were to create the mill as a company, and then within the company there is an off-shoot that owns the land, the selling of the land would be infinitely easier than trying to sell the company and then have to prove that it owns the land, which any good Solicitor would find when it completes what they call searches. Now, if I complete searches and add them to the land transfer documents, then it cuts out the Solicitors needs to make those searches, and I am guessing that the people that I have been talking to, are so keen to acquire land that they would easily be persuaded to take several short-cuts, just to achieve their goals.

"Now, I can go ahead and do all that, which I am prepared to do at my own expense, but I need some guarantee that we can complete a deal. This part will be down to you getting Emmanuel to sign a 'Contract to Sell.' If you can't do that, then we are both, as they say, 'up the creek, without a paddle'."

Bryn was determined that this was going to work. You didn't have that many opportunities in life to make good for life's poor decisions and past mistakes, and this opportunity, was not going to escape him. It wasn't, no way. It just wasn't. He wanted to underline his determination and spoke with firmness, sufficiently that Kyle knew he was serious and would get this done.

"Kyle, trust me. I'm going to make this work."

"Okay Bryn," Kyle replied. "If you're sure that you can convince Emmanuel, then I will go ahead and create a company. Then with 'my' searches as part of what they call a 'Legal Pack' and add to that as authentic as I can get, a map, showing the boundaries of the Timber Mill, with the woods outlined together with the river and grazing land and the extent of those boundaries. In all I will show a total of about 260acres that's about 105 hectares and though that doesn't sound a lot, the word hectare, comes from the Greek hekaton which means a one hundred, so a hectare is a square measurement, 100 metres times a 100metres, and if you want to further complicate it, that's another ten percent, or so in yards. Anyway, these people, won't be that interested in the woods but we'll do our best to hand them a nice simple deal on a plate."

Bryn understood what needed to happen. "Okay Kyle, I'll be seeing Manny and Violet next Sunday. When can I come in and see this contract?"

"Just give me 'til the end of the week, let's call it Friday afternoon when the livestock auction and all the other trading has finished and I'll have something drawn up for you and Emmanuel to sign. What I suggest is that you sign a sheet and I'll leave a sheet open, ready for him to sign. How does that sound to you?"

Bryn was grateful, the pair shook hands and Bryn walked calmly from Kyle's office knowing that this was his last chance to talk to Manny. As soon as he had that 'Contract of Sale' in black and white, there in his hands he would convince Manny.

As Bryn left Kyle's offices, he spotted Violet, walking back from the market square, so he ducked down behind a sheep pen, hoping she wouldn't see him, but she had. She would store that information for another day.

He should have remembered that she made it a habit to go into town once a week on a Friday Farmers Market-Day, when all the stalls were full of wares for the weekend. She loved the hustle and bustle and the laughter and the stall holders bargaining with shoppers. But most of the shoppers were canny farmers' wives who were used to bargaining and would have no mountebank take their money for shoddy goods. This was always the best day for fresh fruit and vegetables, but she liked to wait until the stall holders were packing up and wanted to get rid of everything, and they would reduce their prices accordingly. She liked to think that she was a canny shopper. Earlier in the day, she had delivered some of her own wares to her regular customers the Grocers, Bakers and Butchers stalls who liked to buy and sell her home-made pies, cakes, jams and poached fruit.

CHAPTER 28

1970, The Sawmill

Manny had been toiling all day. Heavy sweaty, back-breaking work. He had lost track of the many times he had removed his cap, which resembled that of a train driver and mopped his brow with his sodden handkerchief. He knew better than to strip down to his bare waist on a warm day like today, especially as he had spent most of the day slicing larger timbers into planks ready for layering and stacking. Many times, he had seen pieces of loose bark split and fly off, hitting an operative's bare chest and digging into or ripping off flesh. He always made sure that he always had a shirt on and his thick leather waistcoat on, no matter the weather. He had been operating the big steam-driven power-saw which had been playing up from the time he had started at six this morning. It was now seven in the evening and apart from Violet bringing out Thermos flasks of thick brown sweet tea and a sandwich at midday, he had worked through, virtually non-stop.

Business had slowed these past years, mainly because of lack of staff to fulfil the orders they did get. Just his cousin Bryn, helping out when he didn't have other better paid odd-jobs to do. So consequently, if the mill couldn't produce an order to a customer's time requirements, then orders were dwindling. In any event, Manny was getting too old for this work. At seventy-five, even though he still had tremendous upper and lower body strength, he just didn't have the staying power any more. The only day he looked forward to was a Sunday, when he vowed and promised Violet he would rest. Their day, a peaceful quiet reflective day, reading books and eating a nice roast lunch, their day exclusively. If only he could sell the mill as a going concern, he couldn't part with it in any other way. Nothing else would be acceptable. He had spent his life working the sawmill after his father Benjamin, had been gifted it by old Samuel Abrahams almost a hundred years ago. He felt duty bound to spend his days here and be carried out in the coffin that he had carved for himself in solid pine.

It was sad that his only son, David had gone off to do his duty in World War Two, together with Joseph's son Arthur. Manny didn't want either of them to go, but as far as they were concerned, they were fighting for Jewish lives. What they were calling 'The Holocaust' horrified the world and both David and Arthur wanted to go off and do their bit. It broke their parent's hearts, particularly in that they were both killed on the last day of the fighting, before peace was declared, but at least they were together. Neither Manny nor Violet ever got over this. Manny naturally thought that David would take over the sawmill, but it wasn't to be. So, he continued to toil, almost working to forget, but often looking back, remembering the days when David and Arthur would come along into the woods, cutting lumber, hauling the logs with the old shire horse they had had for many years, watching Manny carefully cutting the trees and turning them into so many different things for people.

Manny had had enough for the day. He cleaned all his tools and returned them to the big wooden constructed shed, and hoped that the big steam saw wouldn't play up next time he used it. But at least tomorrow was Sunday, his day of rest, except the cloud on the horizon was that his cousin Bryn and his Wife were coming for supper. Bryn was starting to get on Manny's nerves, every time they visited, he kept wanting to talk about selling the mill and the land so they could retire.

"But it's not his decision," Manny would keep telling Violet. "My father Benjamin left the mill to me. Bryn can have it when I'm gone and not before."

Violet knew not to argue with Manny, he would just go into silent mode and go and hide away in his den in the cellar, below their feet. She would just have to play 'piggy-in-the-middle again and try and keep the peace.

Violet came out to meet him with a large flagon of rough home-made cider drawn from the barrel in the pantry. It was cool and smooth with a rough bite to the after taste. Lovely, just the thing to finish off the day's work. Manny supped the large two-pint glass mug without stopping for breath. He smacked his lips as he finished, wiping his mouth with the back of his hand and belching loudly in appreciation, again removing his hat and wiping his forehead with the same sodden handkerchief.

He thanked Violet who reminded him that cousin Bryn and his wife Mary were coming tomorrow evening after supper as they wanted to discuss what they called family matters. But at least they would have most of the day to themselves. Come Sunday morning, Violet had put some home-made cheeses and fresh baked bread under a slightly damp cloth on the cheese board for them to put in Manny's fishing basket, for them to take down to the river, the only pleasure that seemed left to them. He would always talk about how their son David, who would like to fish when he was just a little fella, and when he was older, would never fail to come back home with a nice trout or two for supper. Ah, if only. But at least they did have him by their sides for twenty-five years, and for that blessing, they were grateful.

Manny and Violet spent most of the day in the warm shade. Violet watching her lovely man stood in the shallows of the cool blue, fast flowing River Petteril a tributary of the River Eden, casting his line, changing the different colour flies on his line, cursing every time he managed to stick one of those sharp little beasts into his thick, work-hardened thumbs. Violet would happily sit knitting winter jumpers for the both of them and just enjoying the sounds of the forest around them, with a gentle warm breeze just rustling the tops of the tall trees from time to time. She wondered, as always at the birds that sang all day, the squirrels that scrambled up and down the trees, squabbling with each other, the distant bleating of George Bland's sheep, the male pigeons cooing and flapping around the female birds, without ever seeming to tire of the chase. How could they ever leave a place like this. Manny was right, this is heaven on earth.

Violet Gwendoline Pritchard had been married to Emmanuel Morris for more years than she could remember. Life had always been tough but they were as happy as a working couple could be. They had managed to raise a son and a daughter, but their daughter died of meningitis when she was only three years old and sadly, heartbreakingly, their son David had been killed in World War

Two.

Manny and Violet met when Violet's parents had died when she was just twelve and she had had to leave her home in Newport in Wales to live with her aunt in Carlisle. That was well over fifty years ago and they met when Violet's uncle had visited the sawmill to repair one of the big chain saws and she came along for the ride on the open cart, pulled by uncle Seb's dappled pony. *Ah, lovely memories*, she thought, reflecting on life more than ever now, in her twilight years.

They sat outside the old stone mill house, on a large rustic bench that always seemed to have graced the front of the building, now covered with ivy and roses and rambling honeysuckle, crawling up the walls and over the grey slate roof and around the stone chimney, flowering all the way up to the chimney stack and around the red earthenware chimney pot. The same old stone house that Manny's father Benjamin and his brother, uncle Joseph, had resurrected almost from rubble, for their boss Samuel Abrahams. The brothers were ever grateful that they could both work together at the sawmill. They were good servants to old Samuel and he showed his appreciation, by gifting the sawmill to Benjamin, who was first on the scene two years before his brother Joseph.

As Violet went in to prepare their supper at five in the evening, the sun was still dancing across the room. It bounced off the Victorian mirror that they had given to them when they first married, Violet looked upon the mirror as a reminder that she had married such a good honest hard working beautiful man, that obviously cherished her so much. He wasn't looking forward to his cousin's visit, because this would always end up in an argument and he was just getting too old and too tired for it all.

Violet looked up the big grandfather clock, set on the grey scrubbed flagstone floor and spoke to Manny. "Now promise me Manny, that you'll try and keep a civil tongue in your head. We can't go on quarrelling with your cousin. This has gone on for long enough, I'm too tired to fight any more, I want some peace and quiet in my old age. I want to sit in the old rocker you made me, all those years ago, and just enjoy my last few years without having to worry about how you and Bryn will be forever arguing about this land. Maybe you should let him take over the sawmill, he is

230

twenty years younger than you and much fitter."

Emmanuel answered indignantly, "Violet, you've missed the point. Firstly, this is my inheritance from my father, not his and secondly, he doesn't want to work the mill, he wants to sell it. It's all I've known all my life and this is where I want to die. He says that there is some property agent saying that he can find a buyer and there would be enough money for us to move to a small cottage and for him to develop the land. How can you develop this land, it's all wooded, apart from the river and the clearing. He doesn't know what he's talking about. Anyway, it's my land not his and I want to live here for the rest of my days, so he'll just have to wait 'til it's passed on to him he'll have to learn to be patient and not be greedy. That's my final word on it."

"Listen Manny, I can hear their car coming. Now try not to argue please, it upsets me."

Bryn and Mary Morris drove carefully into the clearing and parked outside the big wood storage shed. The big shed also housed the tractor and trailer and various other rusted old vehicles and industrial cutting machinery and attachments. They climbed out of their old green battered Morris Minor pick-up truck, Bryn slamming the door to make sure it stayed closed. Violet couldn't help but notice that Bryn looked unsteady on his feet. She suspected that he had been drinking again, much to the annoyance and exasperation of Mary. She had been bickering at him before they left their cottage and much to Mary's chagrin, he annoyingly increased his intake of whisky, just to show her he couldn't be told. It wasn't a good start to the afternoon. A couple of pigeons took flight having been tucked in the eaves of the old barn, feathers fluttered down as the car door slammed. He waited for Mary and they walked over to the stone house walking passed stacks of green timber piled high with boards separating the layers to help them dry out. Emmanuel opened the creaking, weather worn, gnarled oak door that he'd made himself over forty years ago and greeted them. He stretched out his hand to a half-hearted response from his young cousin who shook his hand as if he were not wishing to place any sincerity in his cousin's grasp. He had to sort out this land. He wanted his Manny to accept that they should sell it and sell it off so that Manny and Violet could retire. He and Mary could use the money to start a new life in the city, instead of trying to eke out a life of just struggling to put food on their plates every day.

Bryn and Mary were welcomed into the old stone house to see a roaring fire, even though the weather wasn't that cold. Violet had been using the baking oven to the side of the open fire to bake some fresh Welsh cakes, Manny's favourites loved especially, spread with home-made butter and home-made jams. Mary bade them sit at the big pine table sat in the centre of the kitchen which was set on large rough stone slabs, with the treads of time offering a smooth pathway to the front and back doors the kitchen door and the fireplace. Violet had given the big flagstones their weekly scrub earlier that day and everything was looking immaculately clean, as ever.

They sat at the table Bryn opened the conversation, "Manny, we can't keep going over this, we are missing an opportunity to get a good price for the mill and we can both move on. You and Violet can retire and Mary and I can have a few quid in the bank to start a little shop in Carlisle and not have to work our fingers to the bone anymore. Now come on what do you say. It'd be best for all of us to move on."

Manny was adamant. "How many times have I told you, I'm not discussing it. The mill is in my name, it's my inheritance and when I've gone, you can do what you like with it. It'll be yours then and not before. I'm not telling you again."

Bryn sat there quietly stewing as Violet interrupted with the offer of her plate of Welsh cakes, hot from the oven and a nice good strong cup of English tea, from her best china-teapot which she thought might broker the peace. Mary tried to cut the uncomfortable atmosphere with a little light conversation with Vi. But Vi was up to date with all the news so that fell flat.

Bryn couldn't contain himself. "Look Manny. My father Joseph, your uncle and I worked my butt off for you and this mill. When I was a lad, I even helped you build up this house, brick by brick, boulder by boulder, stone by stone. I remember when we clad the roof with those big flat timbers on top of the timber frame. It was you and me and now you're refusing to let me have a share of the mill that's rightfully mine. If it wasn't for me, you'd have never done it on your own and there wouldn't be a mill. I've cut trees, I've sawn lumber, I've done every labouring job on the site and I've sold timber to merchants and farmers alike, I've done all that, and you're not acknowledging the fact that if it wasn't for me, you'd have nothing. Now I want my dues. I don't think I'm asking for too much. If you're not willing to sell and give me a piece of the mill, then I want you to give me and Mary enough money to be able to settle in Carlisle and set up a shop. It's not asking too much is it."

Emmanuel's response was, "No. I'm not selling for you or anybody and that's the end of it." At that, Manny stood up, knocking his chair over, storming out of the house and around the back of the house and down a flight of rough timber stairs to his workshop, where he kept brushes and paints and tubs of axle grease and a few hand tools for fine carving work. The workshop, which Manny called his den, was situated under the property. He slid the two big bolts across and opened the door. He walked over to the bench and started the generator before he put the lights on.

The workshop was only a small area, where he kept one lathe for completing some of the more delicate jobs that they were occasionally asked to do. The workshop was also well equipped with a fine range of small files, jigs, and all manner of woodworking tools acquired over a life time and a small rack on which to boil a kettle, fired by methane gas. This was also Manny's sanctuary. It was his world that no-one else entered, or did so at their peril. Unless, of course, there was a specific invitation for someone to see when he was working on something special and either needed outside input which was rare, or he wanted to demonstrate or show a new piece of work, particularly the 'Welsh Love Spoons' he liked to make for Violet.

Vi, Mary and Bryn sat in the kitchen.

"Look Violet, can't you see what I am trying to get my thick pig-headed cousin to agree to, to understand. It's not just for our own good, it's for all of us. This is my last attempt I'm going to have to speak to him. He can't just walk off and leave me cold like this, I'm going to see if I can't knock some sense into his head." At that, Bryn stood up in anger and made his way out of the house.

Vi looked at Mary and shrugged her shoulders. "Family!" she said. "More like warring nations."

Bryn stamped around the house and opened the cellar door. He trod carefully down the rickety staircase and confronted Manny. The argument continued and when it reached fever pitch, the girls upstairs could hear the fracas that was going on below stairs. They were screaming abuse at each other but the girls could hear that a scuffle had broken out. Vi rushed out of the door with Mary close behind. They were around the back of the house within seconds. Bryn was brandishing a large mallet and was just about to attack Manny. He in turn had picked up a pick-axe handle and there was a temporary Mexican stand-off, but blows were about to be exchanged and administered.

Mary screamed at Bryn, "Bryn for God's sake, this is getting out of hand, this is your flesh and blood."

Bryn responded with a mouthful of abuse suggesting that she should be on his side. As he swung back around, Manny was swinging the pick-axe handle and hit Bryn across the ribs, under his arm. Bryn swung the large timber mallet and cracked it across Manny's shoulder. Manny fell to the ground in severe pain and before Bryn had a chance to administer another blow, Mary had grabbed his arms, screaming at him to stop. Both Vi and Mary had dropped down on to their knees to help the injured Manny.

Bryn was still screaming blue murder and physically shook Mary off his back. "Fuck the lot of you, fuck you, you deserve each other!" He left the cellar room in tears of fury and anger and slammed the big old oak door behind him, sliding the big iron bolts across, locking the door, firmly shut. 'There!" he shouted. "You can all cool-off and think about what I've said and you can come out when you see sense and agree with me!"

As he left the back of the house, he slammed the top door shut and stomped across the yard and jumped into his pick-up truck. He headed for town. His favourite watering hole was the Black Lion in one of the back streets. This was the sort of place that 'decent' folk wouldn't want to venture. This was the sort of place where you could find a woman if you so desired for a few pounds. You could buy hooky booze or fags, all sorts of 'back-of-the-lorry' contraband or where you could sell your stolen goods for cash, with no questions asked. You could even drop the local bobby a few quid to escape any minor misdemeanours, transgressions, villainy or even sometimes some major misdemeanours.

***

The landlord called out to Bryn, "Usual poison, Bryn?"

"No, George, give me something stronger. I'll take a bottle of whisky and a glass. Cheers."

"No problem, Bryn, coming up."

Bryn sat in the corner of this noisy little back street pub on a table that had seen better days, many better days. It was chipped and stained and had on more than one occasion, found itself as a weapon in a brawl, like many of the patched-up pieces. The atmosphere was thick with smoke and the sawdust on the floor smelled of beer and vomit. But then you weren't expecting to entertain royalty there. It was the sort of place where crooks and vagabonds went to get out of the way knowing their 'own kind' were there around them. Bryn finished the bottle and asked for a top up.

George, the landlord, was happy to serve another bottle of whisky, but hadn't ever seen Bryn going at it like this before. He asked, "Bryn, mate, are you okay, you've already had a bit?"

"Mind your own fucking business," came Bryn's retort, "and just give me a bottle. This is a drinking house isn't it? Then give me a bottle, and give me another one to take home and be done with it."

Bryn emptied his pockets of all the money he had and told the landlord to put the rest on the slate. He took the bottle and crawled into his pick-up parked on the rough ground outside the pub and made for home.

Meantime, Vi and Mary had been trying to force the big cellar door. Manny was in no fit state to help. He had passed out on the floor. He was breathing, but groaning in pain. He couldn't help, he was weak and they needed to get him to a hospital. They kept trying the door but Manny had made the cellar strong enough to ward off any intruders and the door was bolted firmly shut. Solidly shut, no shifting it.

Mary spoke, "He'll come back when he's cooled down. He just wants to teach Manny a lesson. We'll be alright. He gets this way sometimes when he's been drinking."

Violet said nothing, she was too concerned about Manny, and was mopping his brow with a rag that she had found on the workshop bench.

***

Bryn could just about remember his way home through the haze of booze that he had consumed. He clipped his old pick-up on the stone wall that led up to their cottage and left it strewn across the lane, which was a dead end running into a bridleway. He was unrepentant. "That'll teach him to dupe me," he said. "Me, his own flesh and blood, into making his fortune and not sharing it with me."

He crawled up to the single bedroom in the tiny cottage they called home, clutching his bottle in his hand. He collapsed on the bed and passed out. He awoke in the early hours of the following morning, head spinning, not knowing where he was. It seemed familiar, but what was familiar and comforting, was the remains of the bottle of whisky that stood by the side of the bed. He swigged thirstily, heaving out his raw breath as it burned his gullet. He cursed and swigged again until he passed out.

***

Vi and Mary had run out of tears and were running out of energy. Manny was in a poor state. The blow on his shoulder seemed to have navigated itself downward to his lungs and was affecting his breathing. He wheezed and shuddered. They were getting desperate. Their hands were red raw. They were trying to survive, but the air in the cellar was getting stale. They had the idea of setting alight the big old oak door. However, the small pile of sticks and materials in the form of a few old papers and pieces of wood that had been lying on Manny's workbench that they'd placed against the door, soon burnt out. The door was too big and heavy and the flames hardly marked it.

CHAPTER 29

1970

After the fracas with his cousin, Bryn had been in a stupor for the best part of two weeks and was being awakened by the smell of his own vomit down his singlet. He had long run out of whisky and apart from water, there was nothing left in the house that would give him what he needed, so he was slowly coming to. Everything was in a haze, he was getting flash-backs of him in the Black Lion and having a stand-up row with the landlord and being thrown out in the street. But he knew he had the consolation of his whisky which he had put of the front seat of his old pick-up. He half remembers crashing it into his wall in the lane outside his cottage, but his memory was thin. What he needed was a drink!

He sat on the side of their rickety home-made bedstead with its lumpy horsehair mattress and pushed back the stained and ill smelling sheets and eiderdown. He ripped off his singlet and stood up. He was dizzy, not from the booze, but from lack of sustenance, not having eaten anything, apart from a few crusts of bread, since he didn't know or care when. His grubby working hands, found their way down either side of the narrow staircase, remembering not to trip on the last treat which had the threadbare carpet rucked up from years of neglect. He made his way over to the stone sink and lifted the iron handle of the pump to raise some cold water from the well, which was below the old flint cottage. Though it was a warm spring day outside, the water was cold and he shivered as he threw the cold clear stream at his face and over his head and shoulders and rubbed it up and down his arms in a fast motion to relieve the shock and take away the pain in his head.

The events of the last few days, or was it weeks, he had no inkling or measure of time, his mind was a blur. He remembered the screaming match with Manny and his banshee of a wife, Mary, trying to calm him down. He remembered Manny taking a swipe at him and he thought he remembered hitting him with a pick-axe handle. God, his head hurt. He opened the door in the kitchen, where Mary kept the clean laundry and pulled out a crumpled, but clean, blue striped, collarless shirt and buttoned it up. He rolled the sleeves up to his elbows and took off his filthy britches. There was no such luck, looking for clean denim jeans in the laundry cupboard, so he returned upstairs to his wardrobe, where he kept his best (and only) Sunday suit. Even this was a hand-me-down from his father. An old rusty coloured tweed, several sizes too big for him, the jacket hung on him like a shroud, but the trousers and the waistcoat were just about passable. He took off his slacks and rubbed his underbody with the now removed pair of canvas working togs and dressed the rest of his body. He still didn't smell too fresh. The smell of vomit, still held in the air. He went downstairs, sat at a wooden chair put his foot on the gnarled pine table, slipped on his working boots and tied the shredded laces of the tan thin soled scuffed old boots. He stretched and coughed heartily, my, his head hurt, it was banging like the striker on a massive church bell and reverberating around his whole body as if he were in a gale, being buffeted back and forth by his own motion.

I need a drink, hair of the dog, that'll sort me out, he thought. He opened the door of the cottage, managing to remember to duck or else he would bang his head on the low-lying doorway, but he didn't manage to miss the ragged dog-roses. The times he'd told Mary to cut these down, particularly the ones that fell around the top of the porch's threshold. It caught his hair and hands, and in the effort to free himself he drew blood on the backs of both of his hands, wiping them without thinking in his fresh shirt.

"Fuck-it!" he howled in anger. "Fuck-it, fuck her, fuck the lot of them."

He stopped dead in his tracks, blood still dripping from the back of his hands, it stung even through the wound-up grubby handkerchief he had wrapped around the superficial wounds, to stem the flow. He went back inside to wash off his blood-stained hands and to find another rag to dress his minor wounds.

Then it hit him. *I locked the door. I bolted it. I bolted it, locked shut. Shut. I shut them in. I locked it. I locked it shut. Shit, when was that? Oh, whenever it was, fuck-it, they'd be out by now, Manny would be able to open the door from the inside. Yeah, they'd be out by now. They must be. Christ, I'll have to go and see. Yes, I'll go and see straight away, or they could still be there, but I need a drink first, I can't go without a drink. They'll have to wait. I'll go when I've had a drink.*

Bryn looked around the kitchen to see where Mary had put the housekeeping and the rent. "Where's that cow put it?" his foul mouth muttered, under his foul-smelling breath. He stood on a kitchen chair which turned out to be one of the less fragile shaky kitchen chairs and reached up for the earthenware jug, he managed to touch the wooden lidded blue and white striped jar. As he reached it and slid it along the shelf, towards himself, he managed to tip it off its home on the top shelf and it crashed to the floor smashing into a thousand pieces, spraying the contents. A couple of notes floated down to the floor, and the small amount of change that was inside went pinging, bouncing, spinning and rolling under the table and the big kitchen dresser.

The chair broke under his weight sending him crashing to the floor, and he cursed yet again. On his knees, he now managed to rescue all of the coins and notes he could see, certainly enough for a couple of bottles of Johnnie Walker's best scotch. He looked around in utter disappointment at the poorly furnished small rented cottage, with its tiny windows dressed with pretty floral cotton curtains which Mary had made from an old dress. The few wheel-back chairs, some patched up, the gnarled pine table and the iron kitchen range, an iron water-well pump and a stone sink. He asked himself out loud, his anger and bitterness continued to boil over "Is this all I've got for a lifetimes work? Nothing!" he screamed. "Fucking nothing! I need a drink."

He gathered the notes and the change and put it into his trousers pocket pulling his frayed black braces over his shoulders and stormed outside again, this time avoiding the pretty, flower-filled vines that were around the cottage doorway. He stepped the three paces to his broken-down gate, the one that that bloody woman was always whingeing about him not mending, and stepped outside the wall to see his damaged pick-up truck. Studying it, he realised that he must have hit the wall, knocking part of it down and bending the offside wheel arch of the truck into the tyre the other evening, when he might have been trying to drown his sorrows after that miserable bastard of a cousin of his, refused to talk about his legacy, a share in the sawmill. No wonder I locked the bastard in, he deserved it. That'll teach the mean old buzzard.

Bryn went to the shed at the back of the cottage and came back with a large iron 'jemmie' with which to prize the truck's bent mudguard. He managed with a bit of sweating to prize the metal away from the tyre, which had damaged the tyre beyond repair. Fortunately for him, he had a spare on the back of the truck and after a half an hour in which he had struggled to change the wheel. He then trundled off down the unmade lane towards the village and the grocers, with the off-licence. His mind was so stressed and clouded with the events of the last couple of days and his recollection them that he couldn't begin to take in the beautiful countryside that surrounded him. The trees were heavy with leaves, the undulating fields and soft flowing meadows, which were the view from the top of the hill where the cottage was situated, were bursting with wild flowers. The birds sang, the Red Kites whistled, the sunlight danced across the fields as the Sun lay golden shafts across the planted soil. Sadly, all Bryn could see was the bonnet of his truck, bouncing up and down on the rough road.

He reached Edenbrook Village and parked awkwardly abandoned on the road, causing one or two 'old-fashioned' looks, from passers-by and other road users alike, but he didn't care. He marched into the grocery store, where he was greeted. "Good day, Mr Morris, how are you and Mary, we haven't seen her for a while?"

Bryn wasn't in the mood for pleasantries. He spoke abruptly to Josie Brown, the shopkeeper. "Just give me a couple of bottles of Johnnie Walker, or whatever you've got."

"I'm sorry Mr Morris," she replied. "We don't have a licence any more. We let it drop because the cost of keeping sufficient stock, wasn't worth the return, so I'm sorry, you'll have to go in to town if you need some spirits." She hesitated, but then jumped in. "And while you're here, perhaps you would like to settle your account. It's way overdue?"

Bryn turned without saying a word of thanks, apart from grumbling under his breath, "And fuck you too," Much to the disgust of Josie Brown, a pleasant and helpful lady, in most instances. But not today.

"Mhm, no call for that attitude," she mumbled.

Bryn jumped in his truck and after a couple of false starts he set off again, in search of his downfall, the demon booze, his undoing, his ruination. He set his sights on The Black Lion, his second home, where he knew he was always welcome. *Yeah, my mate Jimmy the landlord will be pleased to see me. He's got whisky, that's what I need.*

Bryn arrived at the Black Lion and started another marathon drinking session. After consuming his first two bottles of scotch in the first hour at the pub, Bryn's plans were beginning to overtake him and he had been boasting about how he and his miserable old buzzard of an uncle were going to be rich when they had sold the sawmill to some London big man. After a couple of hours, his loose talk was half way around Carlisle and half the county. Bryn owed money all over thanks to his drinking and gambling habits and soon there would be one or two unsavoury characters coming out of the woodwork, after these 'millions' he kept bragging about.

Meantime, Kyle was getting more anxious about Bryn's ability to deliver the signed contract with his and Manny's signatures. The rumours had quickly circulated around town about Bryn's drunken rantings and at around six thirty on Friday evening, two weeks after Kyle was expecting Bryn Morris back in his offices, Kyle decided to visit Bryn at his home. He knew that Bryn and Mary lived in a small stone cottage about three miles outside Carlisle in a hamlet called Edenbrook. Their old stone cottage was part of the Blackstone Estate and Bryn and Mary had occupied it for over twenty years. Bryn had decided long ago that he could never ever save enough to put a deposit on a property, so most of his spare money went down his gullet. Kyle had decided that if Bryn wouldn't come to him, then he would go to Bryn. This was too big a deal for it not to go through. He had already created a company as a vehicle to buy the land and mill. His underlying thoughts were to be able him to buy the mill and its surrounding land as cheaply as he could from Manny and Bryn and then sell it on to the London Land operators, as his own. This was going to make Kyle a huge amount of money and he wasn't about to let a couple of country folk spoil his plans. They would still have a relatively sizeable amount of money, certainly more than their needs and certainly more than they had ever been used to and in the event, be able to retire in some sort of comfort.

Kyle drove his new, green coloured, two-seater Land Rover, that seemed to be the vehicular badge of choice of the local farmers, along the narrow lanes and up along the rough tracks out to Bryn and Mary's semi-detached cottage. It sat high on the hill, with magnificent views overlooking the countryside, just outside the hamlet of Edenbrook. There was no sign of anyone in the adjoining cottage, in fact it didn't look as if it had been occupied for some years by the cobwebs hanging at the cracked window panes and the rotted window-sills alone. It was just after six thirty, but there was no sign of Bryn. After nosing around for ten minutes or so, Kyle pulled up an old rocking chair as the sun still shone brightly into the cottage through the small windows. There was an unhealthy smell in the house of stale body odour coupled with a smell of spirits and what smelled like stale vomit in the air. He settled down to wait for Bryn.

Looking out of the small side window he could see all the way across the vale, down to the Eden River where a huge oak tree spread its ancient branches, like limbs of an aged old man embracing all below it. A pair of chestnut horses wallowed in the shallow waters, sharing the river bank with a few Friesian cattle, below in the shade of the ancient tree. The sheep and cows roamed freely keeping the rolling pastures looking used, trimmed and maintained and cared for. He sat quietly contemplating what he might say to Bryn. He needed this. This was going to be the start of an empire he had dreamed of from his humble beginnings. He had sparred and parried, bobbed and weaved, ducked and dived and schemed and planned. He had to use every bit of his cunning and guile to reach where he was today, and what he had done at the tender age of twenty-two. He was becoming a successful land and farm agent and auctioneer and was gaining the respect of the local farming community as a 'man who can' and he went out of his way to maintain that aura. But now, here was the chance to take his ambitions beyond the horizons and over the hill to the rainbow he had always sought. This was where he should be, this was how he was going to do it and no-one was going to stop him.

By ten in the evening with the last glow of the sun wavering on the horizon, he heard the rattling sound of Bryn's boneshaking old banger bouncing up and down the track towards the cottage.

He could hear Bryn's awful singing. He was without doubt well stoned, but no matter what, Kyle was going to have it out with Bryn and get the matter settled, by hook or by crook. He waited in anticipation of Bryn's arrival. He heard the slam of the door of the pick-up truck, then the thud of a boot against the door and the cursing of Bryn when the door fell open again. Then he heard Bryn's words, "Oh fuck, I've pissed myself, fuck."

Kyle watched as Bryn Morris staggered and lurched into the garden, his stumbling footsteps, following his hands grasping along the wall. Kyle wondered how he ever arrived home in one piece, having driven the three miles or so from town. Bryn pushed the door open and fell on to the floor, cursing. As he looked up, he saw a pair of hand-made leather brogue-ankle boots, in front of him at the base of his rocking chair.

"What the?" was Bryn's exclamation. His eyes, in a blur, followed the line of the boots upwards, brown socks, brown tweed plus-fours, green suede waistcoat and a matching hacking jacket. He strained his neck upwards but he had to take a breath to help generate the strength. He rolled over and sat on his backside. Kyle noticed the wet patch on the floor and a large circle of damp around the crutch of his pants. Kyle stood up to help him get to a chair. Bryn sunk into the old wing-back chair that had been given to him and Mary as a wedding present twenty years ago. He slumped there, with his head falling forward, until he straightened it and then it fell forward again.

Kyle needed his attention. He went over to the scullery, in the corner of the kitchen, pumped the iron handle and drew a pitcher of cold water from the mouth of the iron pipe set on the side of the stone sink. He walked over to Bryn and threw the complete pitcher into his face and emptied the last drop over his now soaking wet hair. Bryn shook, almost uncontrollably and let off a mouthful of obscenities and venomous abuse at Kyle, 'til Kyle slapped him on the face and told him to, "Shut the fuck up and listen." But Bryn was in no fit state to listen, nor was he in a fit state to argue, but he was in his mind, in a fit state to pick a fight, and Kyle was there in front of him. In his aggravation, he realised that he was the complete opposite of what Kyle was. Kyle was successful and he was a failure. Kyle was young and he was old. Kyle was rich and he was cold stone broke.

Out of nowhere, Bryn screamed, "When are you going to get me my money?"

Kyle had no idea why Bryn had asked such a bizarre question. Nothing was settled yet and replied, "I'll get you 'your money' as soon as you get Manny to sign a contract of sale for me to *negotiate* your money. Until then nothing can happen."

Bryn replied in his drunken stupor, "Well, you won't have to worry about Manny anymore he's gone away. He ain't never coming back. Him and Violet have gone back to Wales. They left in a hurry and they took my Mary with them, and good riddance to the lot of them."

"Well, I can't sell the property without signatures," Kyle replied. "So it looks like you're never going to get your money."

Bryn was furious and frothing at the mouth like a mad dog about to attack. "No money! You've lied to me, you bastard. You're trying to con me out of what's rightfully mine, my inheritance, like that tight-arsed bastard of a relative of mine. You're cheating me…you fucking thieving bastard…"

With a fierce, angry intense sense of outrage, together with the exasperated realisation at the forefront of his addled mind, that he was never going to get any money out of this so-called deal, it was more than his head could cope with and he struck out wildly at Kyle. Even though Kyle had come here to help him, his arms thrashed out randomly, missing Kyle with his right swing, but catching him with his left. It stung. Kyle was trying to calm Bryn, but he was having none of it. He took another swing as Kyle was trying to calm him down. This time, he was bang on target, even though he was well-drunk, his fists were still hard and strong, though they lacked the weight behind them. Kyle fell backwards against the Welsh Dresser, his face stinging from the blow, knocking cheap china cups, saucers and plates flying onto the floor, smashing and adding to the debris of the striped jar, that Bryn had broken earlier in the day.

The table in the kitchen toppled over as Bryn lost his balance and fell into it, the contents of the kitchen drawers spewed out across the stone flagstones as Bryn recovered and pushed himself upwards. He took another swing, and Kyle took a swing back, his fist hitting its target full on in his face, sending Bryn sprawling on the floor. Bryn was screaming mad, he picked up one of the kitchen knives and lunged at Kyle, ripping through his hacking jacket. Kyle was now turning to his childhood roots, where in the playgrounds, the streets and the gutters, he'd had to fight for every penny he made, every inch of gain, every morsel of food. He kicked Bryn in the shins and as Bryn dropped the knife, Kyle picked it up and plunged it into Bryn's chest. Bryn's eyes bulged, and the shocked wide-eyed expression on his face grasped him as he felt something pumping in his chest. In his head the realisation of what his assailant had just done struck fear in his mind as he went to stand up again, to strike Kyle. But it was too late, Kyle stabbed again into Bryn's chest, again and again. The knife must have struck a bone as it refused to pull out again.

Bryn fell to the floor, blood oozing out onto the cold flagstones. But he kept shouting and trying to grab at Kyle. Kyle laid his hands on a stone pestle that had fallen from a shelf with its mortar. The mortar was see-sawing back and forth as it fell. Kyle brought down the pestle like a hammer on Bryn's skull and with two blows, there would be no reviving him. He realised that these wounds would be fatal. He was losing consciousness fast. He realised that he was a dead man, a corpse in waiting, and it was going to happen sooner rather than later. He cried out for Mary, but she wasn't there to comfort him.

The realisation of what he had just done, was hitting Kyle hard. He was in a panic and sweating. He looked at the scene around him. Broken chairs, broken china and glassware all over the floor. Knives and forks and a mixture of kitchen gadget spilled all over the floor and Bryn, now lifeless, just lying there in a pool of blood. Dead. And Kyle had killed him. There was blood all over his clothes and his hands, from the blood which spurted out as he stabbed Bryn.

Kyle stood a kitchen chair upright and sat on it, sinking his head into his hands, regarding his actions and trying to think straight. He drew a cup of water and quenched his dry mouth and throat.

He started to analyse the situation. Who knew he was there? No one. Had anyone seen him arrive or had he seen anyone on the way up to Bryn's cottage? No. Had anyone seen his Land Rover en-route? No. There are plenty of dark green Land Rovers out here in the countryside. He drew another cup of water from the pump and poured it in his hand and swilled it around his face. He took out his handkerchief and wiped his face and his hands. He pondered further. *So, who is going to miss Bryn? Mary? He said she had gone away. What did he mean by that? People just don't 'go away' as he suggested. Perhaps I should take a look up at the sawmill?*

In the meantime, I need to get away. Thank God it's dark. I'll leave Bryn where he is and hope he doesn't get discovered for a while. There's nothing to tie me in to this, no one knows I'm here. I'll be okay.

Kyle, having convinced himself that he would be in the clear with nothing to tie him to Bryn's death, slowly closed the front door of the cottage and walked the few steps to the wall and shut the gate. He climbed up into his Land Rover, pulled the door shut, quietly, just in case there was anyone at all about in the area. He knew the local gamekeeper was always on the lookout for poachers. He turned the engine over and switched on his side lights and started to make his way down the lane which ran alongside the fields over which the cottage looked.

Kyle gripped the wheel of the vehicle as if it were going to buck out of his hands. His head was spinning, with what he'd done, going over, and over and over it in his mind. Reliving the argument, Bryn's behaviour and the way in which Bryn just attacked him, completely out of the blue. *I had to defend myself, otherwise it could be me lying on the cold grey flagstones.* "Oh God, what have I done?" he kept asking himself. He drove steadily, down the lanes and along the country roads, only putting his headlights on when he thought he was out of any sightings by any would-be witness to him leaving Edenbrook.

He was on the main road now, headed back to his home in Carlisle, a small terraced cottage he had bought from some of the commissions he had had from profitable land sales. He parked the Land Rover outside his house as usual. Nobody appeared to be around, so he finally felt as if he were safe, now he was home. He went to his cabinet and pulled out a bottle of twelve-year-old malt whisky and poured several fingers into a glass and threw it to the back of his throat, smarting as the fiery liquid 'hit the mark'. He poured and took another and slunk into a soft chair to again try and clear his mind as to what happened and what should be his next move.

His memory went back to Bryn's comment about Manny,

Violet and Mary leaving in a hurry and going back to Wales. To Kyle, knowing that Manny wasn't exactly a dynamic decision maker, he couldn't see how or why Manny would leave the sawmill, and certainly not so suddenly, as Bryn had indicated.

Kyle undressed and fell into bed, dropping his clothes on the floor where he stood. When he did sleep, he slept heavily, but every so often he would awake with a start and relive the scene again. He woke early with the headache of all headaches. It was five in the morning, just dawn with the blinding sunlight stinging his eyes. He looked at his clothes in a heap on the floor and saw the blood stains. He decided that he needed to get his suit to the cleaners that morning. He would have to say that the stains were incurred when handling some of the livestock.

Kyle kept turning over in his mind the missed opportunity to make a huge commission from the selling of the sawmill and all the adjacent land. Out of the nearly three hundred acres, one hundred acres were woodland and sixty acres were potential building land. Perhaps this was too good an opportunity to miss. He needed to go up and see if Manny had taken flight as Bryn had suggested, though he found it hard to reconcile. I'll give it a couple of weeks and see what emerges.

It took two weeks before the images in Kyle's mind started to fade, though he would still wake up, bolt upright and see Bryn with the kitchen knife sticking out of his body and lying in a pool of blood on that kitchen floor. But nothing had been reported. If he had been discovered, someone would have said something by now. It would be all over town. But nothing. *It is very remote out there,* he thought, *but surely the landlord would want his rent, it has only been two weeks though. I'll have to be patient and bide my time. I'll give it another week, maybe two and then go and see if I can talk to Manny.*

CHAPTER 30

1970, London Land Management Ltd

James Goodrich was chasing up his colleague Charles Dartington, about the potential sixty-acre site up in Cumbria which he had been tentatively offered by a local land agent, '*Kyle somebody or other*'. As usual, he found Charles in the typing pool, chatting up one of the long-legged young girls, trying to impress them with his posh accent and his family's sprawling estate in Devon. He invited them, to see his magnificent herd of South Devon cattle and his parents' stable of thoroughbreds.

But alas, to an East-End girl it fell on stoney ground. She'd rather go out for a pint and a jug of cockles and a good old knees-up. I'm afraid that that, wasn't in Charlie's repertoire at all, no way, heaven forbid.

James found Charlie and managed to drag him away from staring down the embarrassed girl's blouse. "Charlie, for God's sake man, leave the poor girl alone, you're far too old for her. Now I want to get up to the north and look at some properties. The one that looks the most likely is your one, where that local land agent has a 60acre site for us and possibly some more, and at what we would regards as a reasonable figure. I think you said that we would be prepared to go up to £5,000 per acre, so the deal would be circa £300k, am I right?"

"Yes, James, well remembered," Charlie answered. "Our client is prepared to pay substantially more for that site based on the map references I have given him, provided he can build on it. As he builds rather grand houses, on largish plots, that would be a good deal for him. So, if we want to get this deal done, then we had better get in touch with 'my man' in, Carlisle, and sign him up. I'll get on the phone and arrange to view as soon as possible. I'll let you know as soon as I have something arranged."

"Ideal, Charlie, perhaps we can make a weekend of it and get a bit of shooting in."

CHAPTER 31

1970, Edenbrook

It was now six weeks since the unfortunate incident up at Edenbrook Cottage. Kyle could only assume that Bryn's body was still there lying on the floor, deteriorating in ways he didn't want to imagine. Perhaps the foxes or badgers, or maybe rats and mice, could get in and see off the corpse. Obviously, no one had discovered anything or talk would be all over the county. Kyle was feeling as if he had literally gotten away with murder. Though to Kyle it was totally self-defence and nothing else.

Perhaps now was the time to go and see what Manny had to say.

Kyle left various instructions with his office staff to do with last week's livestock sales and some interest being shown in the old Cartwright Smallholding up for sale out on the moors. He would be out for the next hour or two seeing clients.

He stepped outside into the warm sunshine taking in the late afternoon sun and looked around at his small empire. His office and buildings, the cattle and sheep rails, the couple of smaller working machines which he hired out with his two tractors, all paid for, he satisfied himself, from the commissions from my land sales. As he stepped up into the Land Rover, he noticed the stain on his jacket as well as the waistcoat and his trousers, that didn't completely come out of the tweed material of his suit as promised by the cleaners. But he didn't pay too much attention to that, and anyway, it was too expensive a garment to throw away yet. He set his Land Rover off in the direction of Manny's sawmill. A half an hour later he was rumbling along down the bumpy path, over stumps and bumps and grass growing in the centre of a relatively narrow track. It was just enough to get a tractor and trailer load of timber off the site and out into the main thoroughfare and main road. Kyle changed down into second gear and drove very slowly, for almost fifteen minutes along the track, before he saw the clearing with the old stone mill house set to the back of it. He pulled up in front of the big wood timber shed, with stacks of planks piled and carefully slatted out, for drying and ageing. There was an old open backed truck, with no sides to it, just metal uprights to hold timber, when the old lorry was fully loaded. There was an old black Ford car tucked under the tall shed, an old Massey Ferguson and an even older, Fordson tractor, partially covered with a tarpaulin and the place seemed deathly quiet. There was certainly no one around. Perhaps Bryn was right, Manny and the two women had in fact gone away, or even 'done a runner'. There didn't look as if there had been any movement around the sawmill for many a week. The grass was long all around and hadn't been trodden down or cut. It really was quite eerie, Kyle decided. Very eerie. He alighted his vehicle and walked over to the house. Not a sign of anyone, but the farm house door was slightly ajar. Kyle entered. As he walked into the kitchen he heard a scampering of mice, running for their lives. As he entered the kitchen, he could see the remains of what must have been an afternoon meal with now empty and overturned pots of Violet's home-made jams, on the table and on the floor. Mice scurried away.

The windows were still open, so he closed them. He could only assume that Bryn had driven the couple and his wife away, perhaps with a threat or perhaps there was some emergency and they did go to Wales as Bryn had said. Or maybe Bryn murdered them to try and claim the land for himself.

Kyle's mind was ticking. He assumed that the missing three people were in fact in all probability dead, maybe buried in the grounds somewhere, but he was neither going to look for graves, nor report it to the police. Instead, he was going to close the house up, as best he could and chain the double five bar gate at the front entrance. It was the only way of accessing the property, so that any visitors or customers would assume the place was closed down and not open for business any more.

He left the sawmill with a plan in his mind of what his next move would be.

CHAPTER 32

1970, Police Enquiry

At 10am on Monday morning, the telephone rang at Carlisle Police Station. The rain drizzled down the red brick Victorian building set in the centre of the town amongst the mish mash of higgledy-piggledy roofscapes. It stood out like a sore thumb alongside timbered Tudor houses and stuccoed and half-tiled cottages that leaned forward into the street scene, with cream and green painted terraces, filling the spaces between bow fronted shops. The stained and unkempt town houses looking like a row of bad teeth. Inside the police station, the metal framed windows, an abomination from the 1940's, misted up and streamed a steady trickle of beads of water onto the window sill and down the wall forming cloud shapes of damp and salt white patches adding to the already dreariness of this old building. All who passed through agreed it was badly in need of modernisation.

As the phone started ringing, the duty officer swivelled around on his chair to reach the incoming call, stretching across his heavily worn mahogany desk, laden with papers and case notes, with its roll top half open and answered the phone.

"Good morning, Carlisle Police Station, Sergeant Stevens speaking, how can we help?" answered Jim Stevens.

"Good morning, Jim. It's Estate Manager Pat Mellish, I hope you've eaten your breakfast and have digested it sufficiently. I've found a dead body up at Edenbrook and it's not a pretty sight."

"Good morning, Pat," Jim greeted. "A dead body you say? How do you know it's a dead body, is there any life in it at all? Sheep, cow, horse, human?"

"Trust me Jim, it's a dead body," Pat replied. "It's human, or was. I've seen one or two, in fact more than one or two from my time in the French trenches. But there's not much left of this one, basically it's not quite a bag of bones in a shirt and trousers, but the foxes and rats have been all over it and there's not much left. You need to send someone up straight away. On second thoughts, there's no rush, because the poor chap isn't going anywhere in a hurry!"

"Fine Pat, understood. How did you discover it?"

"Well, I went looking for one of our tenants today, Bryn Morris, up at Edenbrook Cottage. He and Mary were well behind with their rent. Bryn Morris has never been that reliable, but he always pays, thanks to his wife Mary being a bit more on the ball. He hadn't paid for a few weeks, but I wasn't that bothered as Mary always pays eventually. And when he's run out of money for booze, she has to go and get some work to pay his bills. So, I drove up there at 8am this morning to see if I could catch him. His vehicle was there, so I knocked on the door. Nobody answered, so I knocked a couple more times and then opened the door, which wasn't locked, in fact it was partially ajar. Now, animals don't need much space or encouragement to get through a partially open door. He, Bryn that is, was there lying on the floor, dead as a dodo, with a kitchen knife protruding from his chest. Additionally, it looks as though his head is caved in. There wasn't that much left of the body, it wasn't a pretty site, I can tell you. So, I'm back at Holme Farm phoning you, so that you can send a detective up there to view the scene and investigate. If you want me to be there, or meet your chaps, please let me know. Otherwise, I will just go about my business and not mention this to anyone until the police announce it and the locals spread the bad news."

Sergeant Jim Stevens was grateful for the report from Mellish and thanked him for his efficiency and promised discretion.

Jim Stevens replaced the receiver and re-dialled. The phone, located on the next floor, was answered almost immediately by Police Detective John Livermore.

"John Livermore," he answered.

"John, it's Jim downstairs on the desk. I've just taken a call from Pat Mellish, the estate manager at Edenbrook Manor. He's reported a dead body up at Edenbrook Cottage."

John Livermore interjected, "That's Bryn Morris's place, isn't it? Big drink problem. Always getting thrown out of the Black Lion, if I'm not mistaken. Got real problems that fella!"

"Well, John," Jim replied. "It sounds like his problems are over. You'd better get up there before the locals do. I get the impression from Pat Mellish that it's a pretty macabre sight and site, as the body's been up there for several weeks and has a kitchen knife still stuck in the middle of his chest."

Detective Inspector John Livermore thanked Jim and called out across the office to rally two of his detective colleagues and to organise a couple of uniforms to get up to the location straight away.

John left his office to go down to see Jim Stevens and get some more details of the notes that Jim had taken when Pat Mellish called it in. He also took Pat Mellish's phone number up at Edenbrook Manor House and Holme Farm from where he had called, both on the Cardew-Petteril estate.

As soon as John's colleagues, Robert Bainbridge and Ralph Noble, rattled themselves down the old dry, creaking wooden stairs, they walked out and around the building to the police car compound and climbed into a police Land Rover. Two uniformed officers followed a marked Morris van with all the necessary paraphernalia for marking out the scene. The weather had eased and the sun was warming the street paving slabs, as they left the town and a heat mist was rising off the pavements and the rooftops and car bonnets alike. They took a steady drive south from Carlisle town, down through Dalston, turning east off at Buckabank and out further eastwards towards Reay. They had arrived at Edenbrook within a half an hour, the Land Rover making light of the lanes and unmade track up to Edenbrook Cottage. The dark blue Morris van arrived almost ten minutes later, struggling with the rough tracks up the hillside.

John Livermore parked behind Bryn's rusted old Morris Minor pick-up truck. The three detectives alighted the vehicle. John opened the door and was first into the cottage to view the badly savaged and decayed corpse of Bryn Morris, lying there as was reported, with a kitchen knife stood erect and firmly embedded in his chest.

The body larvae and the mites had long since left the body and given the lack of prevention to keep out the cold, the mice and rats had had a field day, with very little left of the Bryn Morris that everyone knew. The combination of decay, decomposition and rodent infestation, left little evidence for the detectives to work on. The Morris Van arrived and the two uniforms stepped out into the sunshine stretched their long legs and took in the views, high up on the hillside.

The taller older bobby put his head in through the doorway, viewed the corpse and asked, "Guv, how do you want the site marked and cordoned off? Do you want it around the whole cottage and the van, or just the front path and cottage? And apart from that, is there anything else you want us to do?"

DI John Livermore answered his helpful colleague, Sergeant Jim Stevens. "Jim, thank you for that. I think that we are going to have to call in our forensic friends from police headquarters in Newcastle. This is definitely one for them. So, I think that you and your young colleague ought to cordon off the whole site, all around the cottage as well as the old pick-up, so that it is clear to anyone that they shouldn't cross the line. I think this may well be one for the forensic team to try out this recently introduced finger printing technique, NAFIS, I think they call it. Something like that, that we have been hearing about, 'National Automated Fingerprint Identification Systems', no wonder they shortened it to NAFIS. I guess they will especially want to take anything off the knife, which is pretty clearly the murder weapon, assuming that with all this mess here, he didn't commit suicide!"

"Okay, John. We'll cordon off the whole site, no problem."

John replied calmly to Sergeant Stevens in a matter-of-fact way, as if this scene was an everyday occurrence. "Jim, I'll call the forensics team in Newcastle and get them out here as soon as I can. In the meantime, I'll need you two to stay here and ensure that there are no visitors and if there are make sure they don't cross your lines. Particularly the local 'Rag'."

"Got it Guv, no sooner said than done. If we need to pee, we'll go in the wood. We won't go in the cottage and as soon as we are back, I'll organise a house to house, which might just take a while as these dwellings are so few and far between out here, but someone may have seen something."

John replied with gratitude, "Ideal Jim, many thanks."

CHAPTER 33

1970, Carlisle, Offices of Kyle Redford

Kyle sat in his office at the back of the building, with the door firmly shut, so that there were no inquisitive ears overhearing his telephone conversation with James Goodrich, one of the partners of London Land Estates Ltd. His anticipation and rising excitement were hard to contain. He would soon have a company, completely separate to his land management, livestock and auctioneering business, with funds amounting to the greater part of a many hundreds of thousands of pounds.

"Yes, James, we are good to go on the sixty acres. Everything is mapped out and I have the Contract of Sale and the Heads of Agreement here as the addendum to the contract. So we can exchange and complete in one transaction, as long as we are agreed on the final figure of £5,000 per acre, then that is £300k in total. This of course is payable to Sawmill Estates Ltd. with my client's signatures already on the documents, signed and witnessed by me. So, my next question is, when can I expect you, and when can I let my clients have a completion date, and when is the company likely to be in funds?"

"Well, Kyle. From our perspective, we see no hold-ups at all. We have already applied for outline planning permission, on behalf of our clients and there have been no objections from any of your Parish or local Councils, so we are set to go. We will be up to see you this weekend and with a bit of luck, we might get a bit of shooting in and perhaps a bit of riding. My pal Charles, knows a couple of stable owners not too far from you, so we are looking forward to combining a bit of business and pleasure. However, as a final part of the deal, we would like to meet the sellers of the site to assure them that their land is in good hands. Otherwise, we look forward to seeing you this weekend. Cheerio old chap, see you on the weekend, we'll give you a bell from our hotel and you can bring your clients along and we can have a glass of the old bubbles in celebration. How does that sound?"

Kyle was lost for words. He could only spit out, "Yes, yes, yes of course, whatever you say. Bubbles. Hotel. Yes, give me a bell. Thank you. Next weekend. Thank you. Yes, I'll see you then."

Christ, he thought. *What the hell am I going to do, they want to meet the owners. Shit!*

I'll have to get someone to stand in for them. Jesus, who is going to do that and what shall I tell them. Maybe I could get some actors and pay them. No that wouldn't work. Maybe I could get my girlfriend, Bella. Or Annie my secretary. No, she'd be too suspicious, having said that it was her brother that drew up my contracts, without asking too many questions, he never even blinked at the fat fee I gave him. Maybe I could get both of them to come to the hotel for that drink, I might otherwise not get my sale completed. Bugger! Why did they want to meet the owners of the land?

***

Once Kyle had left, James turned to Charles to confirm that all was okay with collecting the signed contract for the sixty-acre site as agreed. They decided they should arrange some accommodation in Carlisle for next weekend. "I'm told that The Crown and Mitre in the centre of town is very good," James suggested.

"Okay, I'll book that. Strange young man that Kyle Redford chappie. All he could do was keep repeating 'yes, yes' to my suggestions to go up and collect the signed contract and have a celebration drink. Kept saying 'yes, yes, yes' as if that was the extent of his vocabulary. Strange fellows these Northerners. Anyway, it's all fixed. Next weekend it is then. If you can speak to your pal up there so that we can get some shooting and riding in, then that would be very good, business and pleasure combined, can't beat it."

"Brilliant, looking forward to it."

CHAPTER 34

1970, Edenbrook, Police Enquiry

Sergeant Stevens together with his young constable, had stayed in his vehicle at Edenbrook cottage until late that evening, to ensure that no inquisitive folk turned up to view the crime-scene, which they had cordoned off. He had decided that at almost midnight, it was safe to go home, get a good night's rest and return to the cottage at 7am, to continue their guarding of the site. John Livermore had spoken to the forensics team at Newcastle headquarters, and they were expected to be on site at around 8am.

Jim Stevens' thoughtful wife Molly, had packed a sandwich for him and his young PC and also filled two flasks of tea, knowing that the young man, who was living on his own, would not have been that organised. As planned, they pulled up bang on time at 7am. It was a morning full of the joys of spring and summer, with the sun coming up to greet them. The birds were singing. Squirrels were running up and down the trees, chasing each other, or chasing a mate, or chasing a potential mate. Bryn Morris's old truck was covered in morning dew, which dripped down the side of the rusted old vehicle like a leaking tap. A soft mist lifted off the body of the old truck as the sun warmed the painted metallic frame. Underneath the truck, a large grey rat scurried along in the hedgerow, followed by another, Jim shuddered. He didn't like rats, couldn't abide them. One or two mice could be seen darting out from under the badly fitting cottage door, having given up on what remained of the corpse, that was assumed to be Bryn Morris.

Jim and William, his young PC speculated on what happened to 'poor old Bryn'.

"He wasn't a bad bloke really," commented Jim Stevens. "I've known him, well, knew him, for probably forty years or more, since school. Hard worker, but boy, he liked to knock it back."

William, not quite awake yet, asked, "What, knocked back work, you mean he didn't like to work?"

"No, young man," Jim replied. "He knocked back the booze. He loved his whisky. Many's the night I rescued him in years gone by from a fracas with other fellas, usually on a Saturday night in the middle of town, because he'd had too much to drink. He settled down when he married Mary, lovely Welsh girl. Her cousin Violet was married to his cousin Manny, who ran the sawmill, over at Buckabank, which is where he got all his work. It's funny how his wife Mary has apparently disappeared too. Word has it, that she has gone back to Wales with Manny and Violet. Maybe this is why. Perhaps Mary had had enough of him and decided to bump him off?"

Will added his 'five-penneth', "Well Sarge, if you look at the crime scene, with all that mess everywhere in that kitchen, I reckon that there was a big bust-up, someone drew a knife and it looks like Bryn came off worst. Whoever it was, they must have wanted him dead as they took the trouble to do the job properly and bash his head in as well. Or maybe…"

At that moment, as young Will was about to give his dissertation on how to solve the murder, the forensics team rattled their van up the hill and pulled up directly outside the cottage, leaving enough room to get personnel, in and out.

Jim recognised the doctor and her assistant, a very pleasant lady in her early thirties, demure, plain faced, but attractive in her own way, and her tall similarly pale gangly assistant, wearing round-framed National Health specs, with a pink tinge. As pale as they both were, they resembled some of their latter-day clients. The doctor acknowledged Jim Stevens and asked for a very brief resume of the scene, they gowned up and then entered the cottage. The last mouse briefly looked up at the visitors as they entered and then scurried off through the open door.

Ten minutes after the forensics truck arrived, so did DI Livermore and his sidekick Sergeant Bob Bainbridge. They entered the cottage.

They greeted the doctor and her assistant and enquired.

"Good morning, ladies. Any conclusions yet?"

"Good morning, John… Yes, I trust you're well too!" was the

sarcastic response. Detective John Livermore apologised. The doctor continued, "John, we have been here ten minutes and we can confirm that the corpse is definitely going nowhere. And yes, it is dead, and yes, there was a long-handled kitchen knife protruding from the remains of the body, held upright between the ribs, having penetrated the bone. The head has also received blunt trauma. In other words, someone has also hit the poor man over the head, I would assume with a pestle, as there is a mortar bowl on the floor, but the pestle is missing. And yes, we suspect that it could only be murder. Based on the state of the decomposition and decay of the torso in particular, we are probably looking at a minimum of eight to twelve weeks, so that is where your timeline finishes or starts, dependent upon the way in which you approach this investigation."

She stopped and took another breath and re-commenced her soliloquy. "Yes, I'd say eight to twelve weeks. We will take our usual photographs of the corpse and the scene, but I don't think that we will be able to glean much more from the site. We will transport the remains back to the lab and do our best to identify the body from the remains. We won't be able to take fingerprints, as there are no fingers left, or at least there is no skin left on the bones. There is a name tag sewn into the lining of the shirt collar, 'Joseph Morris'. There was a gold band around what was the third finger of his left hand, so we could assume he was married, or at least married at some stage. We have bagged the knife and we might be able to lift finger-prints off the murder weapon. Last but not least, we may be able to identify the body by the dental records, but from what I can see there hasn't been any work done on the set of teeth. That on first observation, either of us could see, we might be able to glean more on further examination… "Now, does that help you, John?" she concluded.

John Livermore answered in calmed tones, almost sarcastically, but not enough to injure his very close relationship with his pal, Angela. "Yes Angela, thank you. That was more than I could have asked for. So, it looks like the dearly departed is one Joseph Morris, based on the name tag sewn onto the shirt collar? Or at least that's a place to start. Thank you, Doctor, that's excellent. When can I expect to get a full, written up report?"

"Well, if we're still on for lunch on Wednesday, as you

promised, then I'll have the report for you then. How does that sound?"

John answered in the affirmative. "Doc, that's brilliant, thank you. And if we can get an ID on the fingerprints, then that would be even better. Thanks, Ange. I'll see you in a couple of days then."

Detective Livermore left the two forensics ladies to bag and lift the remains, with the help of William, the young PC.

John Livermore spoke to Sergeant Jim Stevens. "Jim, thanks for looking after the site. There's not much else to glean from the cottage now, so the cordon can come down, and you can let Pat Mellish know that we've cleared the scene and he can have his cottage back. If you can just get your young PC to have a sweep and tidy up inside the cottage, that would be helpful."

"Any clues John? Murder as we suspected?" Jim Stevens enquired.

"Yes, Jim. One Joseph Morris it would seem is the corpse, from the name tag on his shirt. The doctor is going to try and lift some fingerprints from the knife and check a new national database to try and identify the killer."

Jim responded, "Well before you go any further with your Joseph Morris, let me tell you now, that Joseph Morris died, probably twenty years back. He was a pal of mine, we used to go fishing together up at Buckabank. This will be his son Bryn, who has occupied this cottage since his father died. I can only assume that Bryn was wearing one of his father's old shirts, if that helps."

John was grateful. "Jim, thank you. That has saved me a lot of work. I'll try and establish who might have been visiting *Bryn,* Bryn Morris, you say, and therefore more than likely the last person to see him alive and therefore the person that probably murdered him. Is there anything else you can tell me?"

"Yes, John. His wife Mary hasn't been heard of for a while. There was talk of her going back to Wales with her cousin Violet and her husband Manny. They run the big old sawmill up off the Buckabank road. Perhaps that's your first stop. If Manny and Violet aren't there, then perhaps Mary really has gone back to Wales. But they've been here for years, I can't see them going back for any good reason and I'm sure that Violet would have mentioned going away to some of her stallholder friends, who she supplies with home-made jams, honey and bakes bread for. Maybe she did 'do for him' and went running off to Wales, but then why would Manny and Violet disappear off at the same time, unless of course, they were trying to escape something? Makes you wonder, doesn't it?"

John replied, grateful for the information. "Yes Jim, it does make you wonder. Perhaps she did 'do for him' as you suggested. I think my first call needs to be up at the old sawmill. Thank you, Jim, very helpful. I'll see you back at the Nick, later today perhaps. Once again, thanks for the local knowledge, it might prove invaluable. I'll keep you in touch. Cheers."

Detective Livermore climbed back into the police Land Rover, with his sergeant, Bob Bainbridge, and headed back to Carlisle Police Station to report to the superintendent and the team, and to formulate a plan of action.

CHAPTER 35

1970, Carlisle, The Crown and Mitre Hotel

Charles Dartington and James Goodrich from London Estates, stepped down on to the platform from the London to Carlisle train. It was two o'clock in the afternoon on a particularly rainy day. The rain lashed the windows of the carriages as it had sped along, making the journey particularly disappointing when they were told by colleagues, that the journey up to Cumbria would allow them to see some of the most stunning countryside they had ever seen. A far cry from London, they were told, green fields, magnificent trees, sheep grazing in fields, cows chewing the cud. Pretty little villages and altogether a thoroughly nice journey, but alas no. Nothing but rain lashed carriage windows obscured what little there were or even, next to no views. The only consolation, was that they had booked the first-class buffet car for the journey and had enjoyed British Rail's quality service, wines and cuisine, with a pretty, and chatty little buffet-car waitress. She kept them well fed, watered, and entertained for their journey of several hours.

Carlisle Station was a disappointment in itself. It seemed to have lost its magnificence, from the days when the Victorian's built monuments, to the engineers who created these remarkable steam engines. They pulled their suitcases down from the netted luggage racks and opened the carriage door. The building was grey, grubby and gloomy. The platforms looked as if they needed a good sweeping, scrubbing and a wash-down. There were swirls of discarded rubbish flying around the platform with every breeze that blew and occasionally settling in corners, as the wind and drafts subsided. It didn't help that the day was so gloomy. There was a cattle truck in the process of disgorging its load of beasts onto a goods train on the opposite platform. There were sheep bleating in the carriages that had already been loaded, ready to go down to a slaughter house in Birmingham, they were told. Thankfully, the rain was easing and they stepped outside the building and hailed a taxi to their final destination for the day, The Crown and Mitre Hotel in Carlisle centre.

The journey took just ten minutes and they stepped out to view another magnificent relic of the Victorian age. *This is definitely not London*, Charlie thought, *but business is business and this will be a nice piece of business.*

A porter scurried out with an umbrella to meet the two new guests. Another young man in a blue suited uniform with a flat box hat, with a gold strap under his chin, stepped out with a sack barrow to collect the suitcases that had been dropped by the taxi.

The two London gentlemen were ushered through the revolving glass and highly polished mahogany doors and walked across the thick carpeted floor to the reception desk. They each signed the register and were handed a key.

James asked the girl behind the reception desk, "Are these your best rooms, young lady? I did book two suites."

She answered patiently, despite the overbearing attitude of the new guest. "Yes, sir. Your two rooms, are our very best two rooms. They each have separate bathrooms and a small sitting area, within the room. We are listed by the RAC as having Four Stars, and we are pleased to be the only hotel with that rating between here and Newcastle-upon-Tyne. We will also endeavour to do our best to look after you, during your stay."

Charles chipped in. "I hope so, but oh dear, only four stars? Well, I suppose that will have to do. But it's not the Ritz is it!"

The porter waited faithfully and cheerfully for the guests then showed them the way to the lift. The lad then followed with their cases.

On arrival at their room, the young porter placed their cases on the luggage stand in each room and then Charles tipped the lad five crisp green pound notes, a relatively small-fortune, in relation to the lad's wages. The lad then asked if they would like to order anything, perhaps some afternoon tea, or something from the bar.

"Send up a bottle of your best Champagne and a couple of glasses and a couple of Cuban cigars. And lad, make sure it's well chilled."

The lad answered courteously, "Yes, sir, straight away."

James chipped in, "And make that some coffee and some pastries, lad."

"Yes, sir, straight away, sir. Thank you."

Charles and James went to their respective rooms and unpacked their suitcases, hanging up their shirts and spare suit and their hacking clothes.

Charles walked around to James's room and looked out at the dreary day, hoping for better weather for the rest of their five-day business trip and adventurous, countryside weekend away. James joined Charles at the window.

"God, this is a depressing place. This guy Redford had better come up with the goods."

Charles answered, "There's no reason why he shouldn't and he's bringing the owners with him this evening, so the lure of our bank draft, if they understand that this is real money, should turn their heads nicely then, you and I Jamie, my boy, will be on our way to our property empire. Thank God your father is in banking in the City, otherwise we wouldn't have been able to get started. It'll be interesting to see these owners tonight, I guess they're just a bunch of country bumpkins."

There was a knock on the door and two waitresses, dressed immaculately in black and white, delivered the items they ordered. Fresh coffee and pastries together with an ice bucket containing a bottle of Bollinger Champagne.

Again, Charles tipped five, crisp one-pound notes. If there is anything else you require sir, please don't hesitate to ask. My name is Virginia. Both waitresses semi-curtsied and left the room, with James lightly slapping the last girl out of the room, on the bottom. There was no objection from the girl. In fact, she rather liked it. She liked that the well-dressed young man, to her imagination, of obvious wealth and breeding with a posh accent, took a fancy to her, or so she liked to believe. "Ooooh," could be heard as she left the room and walked down the corridor.

James remarked, with some satisfaction, commenting, "I think I'm beginning to like it here in the north, some of the girls seem quite friendly!"

"I knew a girl called Virginia once. Yes, Virgin for short…but not for long!" Charles scoffed!

James then picked up the room phone and asked to be put through to Kyle Redford Land Agents. The phone rang. Kyle answered.

James spoke. "Ahh, Mr Redford. It's James Goodrich here. Charles Dartington and I are at The Crown and Mitre Hotel, I trust that you are still okay for tonight. Shall we say 7pm for dinner, with your guests. If you could inform me how many will there be, then I can book a table of accordingly?"

Kyle stuttered a response, knowing that there were no owners of the site, apart from him, or the company in whose name he had placed the sawmill and its surrounding acres.

"Oh, yes, hello James. The owners seem to be a bit reluctant to meet anyone outside of their own circle. You must understand that these are country folk and are not used to handling money. I'm not even sure that they understand the sums that we are dealing with. They have asked me to act as their representative, which I am happy to do. I am sure that we can complete the transaction this evening, without any delays or hiccups. As for table numbers, I will bring my secretary along with me and my fiancé, who are both chatty and are good company. I trust you are happy with that?"

James wasn't happy with that. He wanted to meet the owners to ask about the land and its history, but he seemed to have been presented with a fait accompli, which he had to accept. This was too important a deal to go wrong now. So, he might have to put up with giving a free meal to a couple of local girls. It might turn out to be fun, as long as they get the business done. He replied to Kyle, "Okay, Kyle, so be it. We would have liked to have met the owners but if you are their representative, so be it. So, it'll be five for supper then. I will book a table at Queen's Restaurant, we'll see you at seven. Cheerio for now. Toodle-pip."

Kyle was mightily relieved. Meantime, James and Charles finished the coffee and pastries. They washed down the Bollinger and sat in arm chairs in the sitting area of Charles's suite, puffing away on their Winston Churchill Havana cigars.

By seven o'clock, both Charles and James had bathed and changed ready for dinner and had wandered down to the bar. Serving behind the bar, was the young waitress that had delivered them their champagne in the afternoon, Virginia.

James was very taken with Virginia and she, clearly, with him. He beamed a boyish smile, which she returned, aplenty. He spoke. "Well hello Virginia, how very nice to see you again." He leaned across the bar and in a quieter than his usual voice, asked, "Virginia, you said earlier, if there was anything else I wanted, I shouldn't hesitate to ask."

Virginia looked coyly at James. Looking to either side of her and over her shoulder, to make sure that no member of staff was overhearing their conversation. "Well, yes, sir. What did you have in mind?"

James replied, watched by Charles who was full of intrigue and admiration, for James's subtle approach to making a date. "We have to entertain some people here for dinner, but perhaps after that say around probably eight-thirty, you would like to join me for a drink, in my suite. What time do you finish work?"

Virginia was more than flattered. She replied, "I finish this shift at eight, so that would be very nice. Just so you know. I do like champagne. It's my favourite, but I don't have it that often!"

James was quick to reply. "Well, it looks like, tonight is your night. Meantime, young lady, I'll have a gin and tonic and my pal, Charlie, will have the same. Make them doubles. Thank you, Virginia. Here's to later." James lifted his glass in a toast to her. She curtsied and smiled a beamish, knowing smile.

Kyle arrived in his Land Rover, with his fiancé Margaret and his secretary, Madeline. He parked his vehicle up in front of the hotel, under the now lit, large brass and copper, coaching lamps, which were positioned either side of the open archway entrance, before they walked through the revolving doors.

The rain had stopped, but the ladies were wearing raincoats and these were taken by the porter on duty. They were shown through to a table in the bar, where James and Charles, were seated in the corner.

The chap's eyes lit up to see Kyle, with such attractive company and were pleased to shake hands and be introduced. Charles was mesmerised by Madeline, who was tall, blond and statuesque, with large watchful blue eyes. These ladies were not what they anticipated, but their first priorities of the two gentlemen from London, was to get the deal done.

After the niceties of introductions and the serving of drinks,

James asked Kyle if he had bought the paperwork for them to read. Kyle handed over a leather document case and confirmed, that all the signatures were in place and all they had to do was sign their parts of the simple transaction document, agree it and pay by draft, as agreed.

The maître d' asked if James and his guests were ready to come through and escorted the party through to the restaurant.

The restaurant was a very grand affair. It reminded the visitors of a bygone era, when everything was very grand and opulent, with an overabundance of waiting staff, a Sommelier, a wine waiter, and all matter of serving assistants. But looking around, on closer inspection, the Londoners could see that what was once a hotel that was the essence of quality, was very much headed towards faded glory.

The party of five were seated in a quiet booth on the side of the restaurant, which was stepped up slightly from the main floor, giving guests a pleasant view of the grand dining room with its swags and tails and impressive chandeliers. All around them, there was a rich and sumptuous ambience, with coloured glazed leaded windows throwing shards of coloured light across the room.

After the third bottle of Bollinger the party were relaxed, with the ladies somewhat giggly. Kyle made his excuses and left with his girlfriend, leaving Madeline to the mercy of James and Charles, though she seemed to know what was expected of her and was happy enough to go along with events as they happened. Though Madeline was introduced as Kyle's secretary, it was slightly more obvious that she was there for a good time. Kyle had made her a promise that if all went well, then there would be a nice envelope for her handbag in the morning. When James suggested that they all retired to his suite, there was no hesitation. Madeline was keen and by the time that they had reached the room, Virginia was already there, sitting there against puffed-up pillows, completely naked, in the big four-poster that dominated the room, with the covers pulled up to her chin, exposing her soft pink naked shoulders.

As James closed the door behind them, Madeline said, "Oh, if it's that kind of a party, then I'd better get into the bed." Without batting an eyelid Medeline stripped off her flimsy top garment and climbed in next to the naked and giggly Virginia.

James and Charles looked at each other in blank amazement, thinking, *Well if that's how it's done in the north, then who are we to argue!*

CHAPTER 36

1970, the investigation of Bryn's Murder continues…

DI John Livermore arrived back at his base at Carlisle Police Station. He called all available personnel into the detective suite, a grand name for an open plan office, upstairs in the old red-brick building. When the team of six men and two female officers were assembled, he called them to order.

The warm weather continued, much to everyone's delight, with talk of trips to the beach and cheap holidays abroad, thanks to the likes of Monarch, Thomsons, and several others. Alternatively, if you wanted cheap with no frills, well, bring back Freddie Laker.

Someone shouted from the back of the room.

"Ladies and gentlemen. Settle down please. I'm sure you all know by now about the body up at Edenbrook Cottage. We have already established the identity, more or less, of the deceased, subject to confirmation by Doctor Angela, at Forensics. We should have that within the next twenty-four hours. But at this moment in time, we believe the deceased to be a Bryn Morris. Male around fifty years of age. Tenant of the Lord Cardew-Petteril Estate up at Edenbrook Top that borders with the Blackstone Estate.

"Pat Mellish, the estate manager, has confirmed that this was their tenant and it seems that he was pretty unreliable. His wife Mary controlled the purse strings. I have heard from various sources, that he liked his drink and he liked to pick fights with anyone who took his fancy. Favourite haunts were few. The Black Lion pub, was about it. There was evidence that he liked fishing. There were some rods and reels tucked in one corner and a battered fishing basket, hung behind a door.

"Most of his employment or work, seemed to come mainly

from what we now know is his cousin Emmanuel, known as Manny, up at the old Sawmill. Some of us know it as the old Timber Mill, where the majority of their work used to come from making 'pit-props', but more latterly, the tall pines were sold as telegraph poles.

"That, is about all we have gathered for now, but I'm sure we'll learn more about Bryn Morris, if it is in fact Bryn Morris, as the days go on.

"Now, listen up gentlemen. Bob Bainbridge has produced a work plan for everybody. I expect you to be vigilant in your part of these enquiries, and remember, that the smallest details can often be the key to solving a crime, in this case a murder.

"I can see hands going up, so I will take questions, shortly.

"I just want to say, that at the top of our list of people of interest are Bryn's wife, Mary. The only other people of interest are Bryn's cousin Manny, and we would like to talk to his wife, Violet. These are the only potential leads we have so far.

"Now, questions, please."

Several hands were raised to ask questions that could not be answered.

"Motive?"

"Sorry, no idea."

"Where are Manny, Violet and Mary?"

"Again, no idea, your job is to find them."

"Someone suggested they had gone back to Newport in Wales. Will someone need to go down to Wales?"

"We need to see how the case develops, I'll let you know." He paused. "Now, we need to get on with this case as quickly as we can, please don't forget, detail can often be the solution to cracking a case. We will meet here again at 4pm and progress our findings. Let's go please."

DI John Livermore's first stop was to visit the old Timbermill, with Sergeant Bob Bainbridge. It was an obvious first stop to try and make contact with Manny and his wife Violet, and to establish the whereabouts of Bryn's wife Mary. They took the two-seater, short-wheelbase Land Rover, out of Carlisle and all the way to Buckabank, turning off onto the Wreay Road and out into the wilderness of the southern Carlisle borders. The lanes criss-crossed each other and the road signs were few and far between. Dead ends were a given, with nothing at the end other than an unused style, and though they were marked as footpaths, there was only the odd indicator, that these were rarely used by walkers and hikers alike. Eventually, they came across a timber, tall, seven-bar gate, with barbed wire affixed to the top and sides. The gate had a heavy chain wrapped around the post and was well bolted, with a big padlock securing the chain. There weren't many options for the two detectives. Find another entrance, somewhere. Scale the apparently impenetrable gate, clearly meant to keep people out, or go back to base and get a 'chain-cutter'. The latter appeared to be the best option, though they would try and find another route through the heavily-timbered, overgrown woods.

Finding a needle in a haystack, would have been easier than finding a way into these woods, so it was back to base.

After the abortive visit to try and find Bryn's nearest and dearest, John Livermore decided that he would re-convene his meeting at 4pm as arranged and get an up-date from the crew. He wanted to see what had been learned. He and Bob Bainbridge were wasting their time, up at Buckabank, trying to enter the Morris timber mill, the old sawmill.

Back at Carlisle Police Station, the scheduled meeting for 4pm didn't reveal a lot apart from, some histrionics about Bryn's drinking. The landlord of the Black Lion, said, that as long as he contained his drink level, then he was perfectly normal and social. Unfortunately, he wasn't always able to control his drinking habits and had to be physically ejected from the pub, on many occasions, but he would always come back for more. He had been banned from most of the other ale-houses in the town, but the landlord, a Welshman, took pity on him. It also helped that he was a big spender.

His wife Mary, was a meek and mild, but lovely pretty, dark-haired lady, up from Wales. She was related somewhere to Violet Morris, Manny's wife. Otherwise, her only work was on the three market days in town, when she ran a stall of fresh products for Violet. Theirs was a meagre existence and they were always short of money, the feedback was that they could only barely eek out a living, apparently. No frills, no extras, just a day to day existence.

There were no leads whatsoever, just conjecture from Pat Mellish, the estate manager up at Blackstone Manor, on the

Cardew-Petteril estate, where Pat would often have to threaten eviction for non-payment of rent. But in the end, Mary always paid up. Pat Mellish did say that and the quote was, "One day I'll swing for that man."

Otherwise, nothing else came out of the local door to door search. Unfortunately, the nearest 'door', Crockleford Farm, is a mile and a half away and no one there or in between, or anywhere in fact, heard or saw anything. All dead ends. Down in Edenbrook Village, which is nearly two miles away, the local shopkeeper, Becka Lawlor, said that she saw Bryn about six weeks ago. He came in and was very abusive to her, because she had closed her Off Licence department, and he couldn't buy any whisky. She also asked him to settle Mary's account, which was well overdue, to which he refused and started cursing Mary as he left the shop, stating, "That woman needs a good thrashing." Mrs Lawlor was horrified, as you might gather.

DI John Livermore addressed the task force, summing up the little evidence they had gathered to date. "Ladies and gentlemen. It seems that all we have so far is a circumstantial chat. We can't get far on that. At this moment in time however, what we have building up, is a case of financial misery, struggling or hardship. What income they had was going down the throat of Bryn Morris. It looks as if Bryn Morris was an overbearing bully, often taking to striking his wife Mary. We then have Mary, probably sick of this man drinking away probably, all of her menial amount of hard-earned cash and a potential row of cataclysmic proportions, building up into a fight in their kitchen. Clearly, Bryn didn't come off very well, as he is the body in our morgue.

"So, we can possibly come to the initial conclusion, that during a fight in their kitchen, Mary Morris killed her husband and hasn't seen since. Is that how everyone sees this case, or is that just my conclusion?"

After a brief pause, he asked, "Comments from the floor please? And don't be shy. If we cannot see any other route, then we will be looking for Mary Morris as our prime suspect. In which case, that is where we now need to focus. We need to find Mary Morris."

There were no questions from the floor, so the room was dismissed, having been given their tasks for the following day.

276

***

The following day, John Livermore and Bob Bainbridge acquired a bolt cutter from the vehicle workshops and headed up to Buckabank, to Morris's Timbermill.

The day was growing very warm, but despite being in shirtsleeves and driving along with the windows of the Land Rover open, both men were perspiring, with large damp patches on their shirts. They eventually arrived at the gates of Morris's timber-mill and saw, what they hadn't noticed when they were at the site the day before, mainly covered by overgrowth. Nailed to the timbered seven bar gate, was a sign written in rough hand, red-painted on a sheet of thick plywood.

>>>

BUCKABANK TIMBERMILL

CLOSED DOWN.

NO FURTHER ORDERS ACCEPTED.

GONE AWAY. KEEP OUT.

TRESPASSERS WILL BE PROSECUTED.

By Order: E.Morris. Owner.

>>>

The Carlisle detectives were a little bemused at seeing the sign that they hadn't seen the day before. They looked more closely to see that the nails used to affix the sign-board to the gate were new. The hand-painted sign was crude and appeared to be a last-minute thing, done in a hurry. It definitely wasn't there yesterday and the detectives were partially convinced that there was some collusion, between Bryn's wife Mary and Violet, whom they believed to be her younger sister, possibly together with Manny Morris, Violet's husband. In any event they needed to get into the grounds and view the mill-house. It looked as if they had done a runner.

"Admission of guilt?" Bob Bainbridge queried.

DI John Livermore answered, "Possibly, Bob. We'll get a better idea when we can get past this gate and see if there's anyone hiding away in the mill house. This might just be a smokescreen and there are people hiding away. Particularly if someone has killed Bryn Morris and are being harboured in the depths of this property somewhere. Let's just cut through the chain and we can get this gate open."

Bob Bainbridge, reached in the back of the Land Rover and picked up the bolt cutters. They walked up to the gate, having parked the vehicle on the overgrown verge. Bob, eventually managed to cut a link of the chain, in two places and the chain fell to the ground. They unwound it from around the post and dropped it to the floor. The gate was so heavy, it took the two of them to lift it up and push it across sufficient enough to drive the Land Rover through onto the rough track.

The track was bumpy and uneven and the brambles had overtaken the hedgerows along the track. They had to stop occasionally and hack back the overgrowth of brambles to be able to get through, but get through they did. About a quarter of a mile down the rough track, was a clearing with several outbuildings, stables and timber storage areas. Parts of the clearing were given over to stacks of timber, being seasoned for use in years to come and opposite some of the cut wood sheds, much further down, was a stone-built house. The house wasn't a sophisticated affair. It had been made from a mixture of boulders, large and small, red and grey bricks and granite cornerstones. The windows looked as if they had been hand-hewn and the door was as solid as a rock, with a massive rusted iron ring for a door knocker. The detectives assumed it to be solid oak. The door was secured by a large rusted hinge and bolted with a padlock. The roof was thick grey slate and flat cut stones, with a tall single red brick chimney. Virginia creeper had partially covered the wall with the chimney on the outside. It had climbed up and was spreading its thick, vinaceous tentacles up across the roof-line and over the other side.

The sunlight streamed through the tall pines and the birdsong was something to behold. Swallows, swooped around the house, wood-pigeons cooed, woodpeckers could be heard pecking, sparrows, starlings, blackbirds, song-thrush were singing, and you could hear a solitary cuckoo, somewhere, not too far away, probably trying to take over another bird's nest.

They parked their vehicle in the clearing and walked across to the house. There were several wooden bars nailed into the door frame and again wooden bars across the few windows, all around the house. The vegetation, grass, brambles, weeds, woodland flowers had taken over the areas which would normally have been trodden down by the movement of people moving around a property, while they worked. But this was eery. No folks around. Everything locked up. Everything overgrown. No animals about, cats mewing or dog's barking as you might expect on a working farmhouse, or mill house as this was. Nothing. They peered through the windows between the wooden bars. The kitchen table was clear, no signs of life. The chairs were set tidily and orderly around the table. In fact everything looked perfectly normal, apart from the fact that the house was deserted.

"Like the Marie Celeste," Bob muttered. John Livermore agreed.

"You're right Bob. Just like the 'Marie Celeste', just a couple of old bangers rotting away in the yard and an ancient rusted 'Fordson' open back truck, with flat tyres. It looks like they've fled this place, and probably legged it to Wales, like one of the team suggested. I don't think that there's any point in breaking the door down just to look around."

They peered through the dirty windows to see a relatively neat kitchen and bedrooms through the neat windows. Nothing out of place. Nothing untoward as far as they could see.

"Everything looks perfectly normal, so I think it's back to the station for us, and we'll move our search to the family homes in Newport, in Wales."

Bob Bainbridge nodded approval and they turned and walked back to their vehicle. They alighted their vehicle at the entrance gate, pulled the big gate shut, wrapped the chain around the post as securely as they could and headed back to Carlisle Police Station.

1971, Unsolved Case

After six months of investigation, with no leads, despite two forays into South Wales looking for the Morrises, on instruction from his Superintendent, DI John Livermore, with no leads, the DI reluctantly signed off the case and wound down the investigation and the file was marked accordingly.

The assumption and conclusion was that Bryn had been killed by his wife, Mary Gwen Morris. She had gone back to the mill and her sister Violet Morris and her brother-in-law Emmanuel (Manny) Morris had helped her escape back to Wales.

CHAPTER 37

2020, UK Heir Hunters Office

Tuesday morning came around again, and Dale was putting the finishing touches to his 'masterpiece' of ancestry juggling. He had managed to create an off-spring of the Morritzstein family, that led straight to Jan's own bloodline and ancestry. It was just a case of 'cutting and pasting' genuine birth, marriage and death certificates, from old records, altering names and occupations, as well as noting offspring, places of birth and death that needed to make the documents appear to be absolutely genuine. He had spent so much time on this project that the newly created 'family' felt genuine, believable, and credible.

Dale sat back in his chair, fingers entwined and stretching his arms outward. His partner, Roger viewed him across the office and asked, "Well, Mr Scott, partner, you look very pleased with yourself, have you found us a nice fat commission?"

Dale coughed, trying to buy himself a few seconds of thinking time and answered. Richard the other partner looked up from his PC, his half-rimmed glasses perched perfectly on his sharp nose, waiting for something exciting to be revealed.

"Ah, Roger, it's something I've been working on for a few weeks. I won't fill you in yet, as I haven't quite tied it up. But watch this space, I'll let you know as soon as I can."

"So young Dale, is there anything I, or Richard, can research through for you, size of estate or possible commission for our humble company of heir hunters?"

"No Rog, it's a work in progress, I'm okay thank you. I'll let you know when you can help."

Roger's curiosity was appeased and Dale breathed an inward sigh of relief. They had run a few of their 'estates' a bit close to the wind sometimes, but this was quite a departure from bending a few facts to make sure an inheritor got a share of a distant will, from a very distant, more often than not, unknown relative that they were totally unaware of. So, what's the difference if Jan's family turn out to have a link to a distant relative and they have a bit of land to pass on? There's no money that the Treasury are missing out on, just a bit of land that nobody, apart from me, knows about. And of course, a fee would be due to the company.

For Jan, the day was dragging by. She was looking forward to another of her 'nights-off', a third Tuesday night in a row, a night away from Phil, thanks to his 'Forty-One Club' mates and a night with Dale. It was exciting. It was clandestine, which made it feel dangerous and even more exciting. Forbidden fruit always tasted sweeter, if it was stolen, and squirrelled away. She seemed to be looking up at the clock every five minutes and the hands didn't move. She was checking her watch and then her mobile phone. She couldn't keep still. Meantime Phil plodded on doing the VAT and the monthly management accounts that kept an eye on their sales, costs and cash-flow. Things were okay. They had been better, but they had been a lot worse in years gone by, but they had kept the whole business rolling and growing slowly. Fits and starts, but growing slowly.

Phil was still puzzling with how this new company, London Land Agents, this Goodrich and Dartington, having taken over the main contract from their largest client, the 'High Street Bank'. Its group companies, was going to affect their day-to-day trading. When he visited the new regional manager, the chap, a bland faced, anonymous being, with a personality by-pass, suggested that nothing was to change. They would still have all of the servicing contracts for cleaning, inventories and painting and decorating etc., but there was no written agreement. The new company, was almost impossible to get hold of, so he was nervous, to say the least. Last evening, he had banged off an email to Goodrich & Dartington, trying to clarify Camden Estates position, but as yet this morning, there was no reply. Not even the courtesy of an automatic reply. In his mind he would wait until, say, the end of the week and then try and phone and speak to a director of the company. Otherwise, all of this sudden change was all a bit open-ended, and Phil didn't like open-ended.

Meanwhile, Jan was stalking up and down, like a caged animal and suddenly announced, "I'm going out for lunch. Phil, do you want me to bring something back for you?"

The answer came back. "No Jan. I'll get something from the Tesco Metro. I'm okay thanks."

At that, Jan left the office. It was just twelve o'clock. She stepped outside, on to the pavement, into the fresh warm air. It was yet another busy day at Camden Lock. It was mid-summer and the place was heaving with visitors, all sat around, on benches, on the grass, on the side of the canal. Narrow boats were stacked three deep, waiting their turn to go through the locks. The birds were chirping overhead and the starlings in particular were making a nuisance of themselves, squabbling in the trees. To everyone's amusement, a family of ducks waddled up from the back end of a narrowboat and up on to the quay, stopping for the odd piece of bread that was thrown by folks eating their lunches and enjoying the busy scene.

Jan picked up a salad sandwich from the kiosk with the candy-striped pink canopy, that had seen better days, but this was a regular stop for Jan and the fayre was always fresh and tasty. She managed to squeeze on the end of a bench as an older couple moved on. She removed the plastic top from her coffee cup, a Mexican latte, an ordinary latte, with a hint of spicy-chilli, and took a few sips of the too hot, rich swirling liquid. She finally started to relax. This was the first time in many weeks that she felt good about life, particularly about Dale. The guilt was beginning to wear off and she was looking forward to this evening. She had for the first time in a long time, put on a dress, instead of her normal, formal business suit. The dress, a pretty Laura Ashley style floral of subtle, pinks and greens brought the colour out in her soft pink cheeks. Today, she hadn't clipped her hair back in a small pleat, which she had always felt was more business-like, instead she had let it down onto her shoulders, which enhanced her appearance. Today, Jan wore a pretty matching ribbon in her hair and she felt, light of foot and light-headed and elated and she didn't know why, or didn't want to admit to herself, that Dale, might be the reason.

She dialled Dale. Knowing it was Jan, he picked up straight away.

"Jan, you lovely thing, how are you?" she answered coyly.

"Well, young man, I hate to admit it, but I'm really looking forward to seeing you this evening. I also hate to admit it, but I've been looking forward to it, since last Wednesday. I feel like a different woman. I'm also intrigued to find out, how you are getting on with my family tree and when I can claim my inheritance, well the one you have created for me. Crikey Dale, I hope we are not digging a big hole for ourselves. I hope you know what you're doing, I don't want to end up in gaol, for fraud or whatever."

Dale assured Jan. "Jan, don't be so nervous, I've been doing this job for over twenty years and I have tied up every loose end. Nothing can go wrong. You'll have to trust me. Nothing can go wrong."

"Oh Dale," Jan answered. "I hope you're right, it sounds so exciting. I can't wait to see you tonight. I need to go now, otherwise Phil and the staff will think that I've run off. See you later, so looking forward to it. Byee!"

Jan finished her sandwich and now, lukewarm coffee and wandered back to the office, filling her lungs with fresh warm air and breathing out heavily. She felt good.

Jan arrived back at the office to find Phil in pensive mood. He had been pawing over the accounts and slowly moving his head back and forth. The girls in the office had noticed his apparent despondency and low mood. Jan had breezed back into the office to a sombre atmosphere and called Phil in to the closed office. She put the small white fan on the corner of her desk, which whirred slowly around, every so often creating a breeze which caused the blind to wave in a forward motion and relax, back into position. Phil placed some of his notes on the desk, pointing at some areas for concern.

Phil spoke. "Jan, I'm worried. These people that have taken over the rental contracts on the bank's properties, which as you well know, we have looked after since time immemorial. I am quite worried that this transfer of properties out of our portfolio for the bank, to these new people could do us or our business, irreparable damage. I knew we should have had a contract in place for ongoing business, and I couldn't really understand, why the bank was stalling us. But now we know why. Unless we get the servicing business from this new company, we are potentially up to our eyes in the 'mire'."

Jan retorted. "Just say it like it is, Phil. You mean, we're *'in the shit'!*"

"Yes, Jan. As you say. *'In the shit.'* I am going to see what happens this week. I have emailed the new company, with not even the courtesy of a response, so I will wait a few more days and then start ringing them, to organise a meeting, to clarify our position, if that's okay with you?"

Jan was pre-occupied in her mind, but answered in the positive. "Of course, Phil, if you think you've got a handle on it, then it's over to you to sort it."

Phil left Jan's office and placed his note book back in the drawer of his desk, then called out, "I'm just popping out to the Tesco Metro for a sandwich. Won't be long."

He closed the door behind him as he left the office and skipped down the stairs.

Phil couldn't wait to speak to Samantha. He weaved his way through the holidaymakers crowding the pavements and spilling over into the roads. People eating everything from ice creams, hot-dogs, sandwiches, and dipping into bags of nauseous-smelling, salt and vinegar-soaked fish and chips. Kids stuffing themselves with bags of sweets, folks with boxes of pizza sat upon their knees as a temporary table, kids were screaming, dogs getting stepped upon under foot and yelping in protest. There were dogs barking at each other, and getting pulled back on their leads by their angry owners. He pushed his way down on to the quay and walked a few hundred yards up stream, to a quiet spot, away from the smell of the vendors selling food and drink. The smell of fried onions, and chips, and burgers, did nothing for his asthma. He found a quiet space and dialled Sam.

She answered while sat at her office desk at the firm of solicitors where she was a partner. "Hi Phil. I'm having a rubbish-day, it was so nice to see your number come up on my phone. I am so looking forward to seeing you tonight. How are you?"

Phil answered, pleased to receive the warm response from Sam. "Yes. Hi Sam, I am really looking forward to seeing you tonight as well. I've also had a rubbish day. I might have to take some legal advice from your firm, but I won't let that spoil dinner. I just wanted to know that you were still up for us meeting tonight, and sharing some time together, as we did last week. It was so wonderful."

"Oh yes, Phil, I'm not only looking forward to it, but I've treated myself to some new clothes, if you know what I mean. I hope you'll like them," Sam answered.

Phil sat slightly uncomfortably on his seat, in quiet expectation. "Oh Sam. You really don't have to look any more alluring than you did last week, I thought you looked absolutely perfect as you were, but I am intrigued. I can't wait to see you. Anyway, enough of that for the time being, I need to get back to work, I have an impending crisis to fend off, or try and take control of. I'll see you at seven in the bar, as last time, if that's okay?"

"Yes Phil, that will be lovely. See you later."

Sam was mildly intrigued to hear about Phil's rubbish day and that he might need some legal advice from her firm. She thought no more about it and settled back into the dreariness of her working day.

Phil headed back to the office, after 2pm, having quickly digested his tuna sandwich in a few large bites. He swirled the last dregs of his Costa coffee, stretched as he got up from the bench and headed back to the office.

The rest of the day for Phil, was spent on researching the facts and figures, studying all of the historic records of work they had carried out for the bank contract over the years. As far as Phil was concerned, they had done an exemplary job of running the bank's tenancies and the servicing of all of their properties, with the minimum of fuss and involvement for the bank, and a steady flow of business for themselves. So to lose that contract, was leaving Phil peeved, to say the least.

As for Jan, she just couldn't concentrate on work. Her head was far, far away, dreaming of a life in the countryside and wondering how Dale was progressing with this wonderful estate, he kept talking about and was creating for her. Five o'clock couldn't come fast enough for her. Eventually, when the large hands turned to five on the office wall-clock, and the girls were leaving the office, Jan sat in her chair and started to relax, in anticipation of spending some time with Dale.

Phil stood up from his desk and announced that he was going for a walk. He wanted to clear his head, and give some more thought to their position at Camden Estates and the portfolio of rental properties, that they had just unwittingly relinquished. He felt that they had been duped, by some sharp organisation, with no scruples, these 'Goodrich and Dartington' people.

Jan was still in another world and answered, not having taken in the enormity of what Phil was trying to convey to her. "Okay Phil, I'll see you tomorrow, around midday, I guess if you're meeting up with you drinking buddies tonight. I'll be here in the office a bit longer, then I'll be on my way home. Do have a nice evening, won't you. See you tomorrow. Goodnight."

***

Sam sat at her desk, glancing up at the clock on the town hall building just across the road. It was always a bit fast, but on checking her own watch and then her mobile, five-thirty finally ticked over. She picked up either side of her large green leather-covered desk diary, and slapped the both sides together. It settled on the desk blotter, with its gnarled leather-bound corners, giving the scribbled pad a touch of sartorial, professional credibility. She then placed it all in the drawer, turned the key in the desk and stood up, finally finding it to be the right time to say goodnight to her partners and those staff still remaining, who were working on unfinished or urgent cases.

In less than thirty minutes, she would be luxuriating in a foam bath, with a glass of Sauvignon in her hand, purchased earlier from Sainsbury's, and nicely chilled, thanks to the fridge in her room. Relaxing in her room at the Holiday Inn, waiting to meet Phil, for dinner. *A fitting end to a 'rubbish' day,* she thought.

***

Dale had been busy all day. Not only was he and the other two partners very busy with new cases, but he had spent a lot of time on the phone, speaking to Brian, their 'Case-maker', the name they gave to their man 'on the road'. His sole responsibility, was to make face to face contact with the beneficiaries, they had found at the end of an estate search. These were the people that they would have to sign-up, before another heir hunter's company, who were also on the scent and potentially, researching the same estate, were to turn up and offer more favourable terms. They had signed three large estates this week already, and were searching at least another three, with as many new cases in hand. They were doing extremely well. Before he even realised it, his day was drawing to an end, or at least his day at the office. He still had a little work to do to present to Jan, but that was just fine detail. Most of the bulk of the work had been done, and he was ready to press the button to get the ball rolling and claim the estate through the Bona-Vacantia office at The Treasury. He was really looking forward to seeing Jan, to give her the good news. And that wasn't the only reason.

By six o'clock, Jan had locked up the office, strolled down the canal for a while and back, still with the warm evening sun beating down on her shoulders. At lunchtime, she had had time to nip down to M&S, just a few hundred yards in the centre of the village at Camden. She had decided that Dale's shirts, as alluring as Dale may have found them draped on her body, that she would make the effort and, buy something more befitting. She was excited, she felt like a modern-day 'Matahari', luring her man with her feminine guiles, it felt fun. It felt powerful, it was exciting and she wondered if she had *ever* felt like this before. Like a spider, weaving her web to catch its prey. She had been married so long, that when it came to romantic moments with Phil, well, now she started to recount them, they were a bit of a damp squid, and not that exciting. Nothing was spontaneous, looking back. So, this was a new experience and she was loving it.

***

She knocked on the door to Dale's flat. He called out, "Come in gorgeous. It's open!"

Wow. She was taken aback. Flowers! Flowers everywhere! They took her breath away!

"Dale Scott! What are all of these flowers doing here, I'm counting three, four, five, six lovely bouquets and covering all the available shelf-space and a couple of very nice floor displays! What are you up to? What's the occasion and why the extravagance, these must have cost you a fortune!"

"My lovely, lovely Jan. They're all for you. I was so excited to tell you about the inheritance that I thought flowers and champagne were the order of the day. And here Jan is a bottle of Mr Moet's finest. Come over here, I want a hug!" Dale answered.

Jan obliged, without hesitation. "Dale, you are naughty."

They exchanged a long warm embrace, which took on several extra hugs and squeezing each other, allowing their hands to wander along shoulders and arms and backs and backsides, almost smothering each other in long lingering kisses.

They came up for air with Dale saying, "Come on, enough of that now, plenty of time later. Let me show you your ancestral inheritance. I have done a complete family tree and can prove how your family are related to this estate. I have traced the family back to the 1890's when two Jewish brothers came across from Ukraine, looking for work. I have a complete history of where they worked, their off-spring, the death certificates, the Marriage certificates, the birth certificates and when those children died in adult life. I have yet to fill in a few dates on the birth, death and marriage certificates, but that won't take me long. There were a couple of hiccups, in that three of the owners disappeared without trace and another was murdered, but no-one was ever charged. This chap was called Bryn Morris and this is where your Great Grandfather came into the family, by some very skilful, grafting on my behalf."

Jan studied the ancestry and the family tree which Dale had created and Jan was beginning to see that there was a connection, even though in her heart, there was none. But she accepted Dale's enthusiasm and the dream, that was fast becoming a reality.

"Oh Dale. It all sounds too good to be true."

They sipped at their glass of chilled champagne, excited at the prospect of actually inheriting, such a vast estate. Dale commented, "I had estimated that there was no serious value to the estate, maybe a few hundred thousand, as it appeared to be an estate of mainly timber and some meadowlands, with a river running through it. It had been a working estate back 'in the day', but as there appeared to be no family after the 1970's, that's over fifty years of growth and probable neglect, then the woods will probably be much overgrown, and I guess someone will have just let sheep, or even cows or horses roam the meadows as there would have been no-one to object."

"If that were the case," Jan wondered, "will someone have cut down all the timber and sold it all off?"

"Mmm. Unlikely," Dale replied. He continued, "I have looked on Google Earth at the site and most of it looks almost beyond redemption, not accessible at all. Over to the east side there is a freeway and a trading estate, beyond a river, which seems to divide the properties.

Anyway, I have put a claim in to the Bona-Vacantia office at The Treasury and claimed the estate on your behalf. I did that this morning and my man 'inside' briefly looked at my submission and saw no problems, as the period for claim is almost up to its fourteen year 'run-out date'. There has been no other interest or enquiry in all of that time, so it looks like it will be ours…well yours, within weeks. What I will have to do is get a local land valuation and then submit an offer to The Crown Treasury on the inheritance value and therefore taxation value of the estate, to be paid to the Crown."

They embraced again, Dale lifting Jan off the ground and spinning them around in a couple of circles, getting dizzier and dizzier, with the moment and with the intoxication of each other helped on by the champagne. Dale put Jan down and they embraced again.

"Dale, take me to bed!"

Dale needed no encouragement. He swung his arms around Jan's back and under her legs and lifted her in his arms. Just a few steps and they were in the bedroom. Their previous meetings were cool and romantic. Supper, a few glasses of wine, slip into bed and enjoy a soft warm liaison. This time it was different. They were both excited and intoxicated, not just with the sparkling wine but the thought of a new phase in an otherwise mundane working life. They stood opposite each other at the foot of the bed, tearing at each other's clothing. Jan's dress sipped quickly to the floor as Dale pushed the straps off her shoulder and pulled her zip down at the back. They were kissing. Not passionately, but furiously. It was fast. It was all consuming. It was over in minutes. It was wonderful. They collapsed in a heap, hot and sticky and laughing and giggling. Ecstatic. They hugged, a long warm hug. They kissed long warm and romantic kisses.

"Well, Mrs Phillips, or rather Miss Morris, how was that for you? It was bloody marvellous for me! Now let's have some supper."

2020, Holiday Inn

Samantha had been luxuriating in a warm soapy bath in her room. She couldn't remember the last time she felt this relaxed. Phil was such a lovely man and a real old-fashioned gentleman. Kind courteous, thoughtful, loving, considerate, prepared to listen to her letting off a bit of steam after a rubbish day as she called it. *Mmmm*, she thought to herself. *I think I could be a Mrs Phil Phillips, he's such a nice man.*

Sam climbed out of the bath and wrapped the white towelling bath robe around her, emblazoned with a large 'HI' for Holiday Inn, which amused her. It seemed almost like an invitation, *to what*, however, she hadn't figured. It was still a lovely warm evening and having padded herself down with the robe, she let it slip to her ankles, feeling very care-free, with a touch of wild abandon creeping into her psyche. She looked out of the window to see the people walking in the gardens, around the large ornamental pond, with its weeping willows skirting the water, the white and purples of the flowering water-lilies reflecting elongated dabs of colour on the water. It was lovely to see moorhens and ducks paddling around the pond and children sat on the bank, trying to feed them bits of bread or biscuits that they had saved from the afternoon tea they had just enjoyed. Cars slowly filled the car parking areas, arriving one after the other for the night, or for a conference, or for a secret liaison, just like Phil, coming in to see her.

She dipped into her shopping bag from Victoria's Secrets, her lunchtime shopping excursion and pulled out a lacy, lilac coloured underwear set and slipped them on. She was *so* looking to see Phil's face when she started to disrobe, later in the evening.

For this evening, she had chosen one of her favourite dresses. This was a multi-coloured, vintage Nina Ricci floral, with splashes of lilac, to enhance her underwear. It was thin enough to almost see through, but just left enough for Phil's imagination to work a little overtime. Glancing at her watch, she noted the time as seven pm. She ran a brush through her hair, picked up the hair spray and despatched a cloud over her locks, followed by an over abundant haze of Channel, slipped on her mules and she was ready!

Phil had entered the hotel, nodding to some of his Forty-One Club 'mates', then making excuses, as he did last week, at having to miss the meeting. He ducked around the corner and ordered a G&T and sat waiting for Sam. A few minutes later, Sam swept in, like a woman with every confidence in the world, though Phil knew that a lot of this was bravado on her behalf. Phil knew she was vulnerable, not having been treated very well by previous partners, including their business neighbour Dale Scott. But now, here was he, having a passionate affair with Sam and to date he had hardly given a thought to the longer-term consequences. He had just been caught up in the moment, well, three weeks of 'moment' and now it was beginning to sink in, that he was in deep and didn't know how to end it, or how it was going to end. He didn't like to admit it to himself, but he was falling for Sam, big-time and couldn't let her down. But right now, his heart started to thump as she walked into the bar, looking absolutely stunning, just like something out of Vogue magazine. He knew she was beautiful, but wow, until now, he hadn't realised how beautiful. He was smitten and stuttering like a love-sick school boy.

They hugged, a long hug as they greeted each other, her delicate perfume wafted across him like a summer scented breeze. He took it in and the emotion of the moment, brought a tear to his eye. He pulled away momentarily and wiped his eye with the serviette from his drink.

Sam spoke. "Oh, you dear, sweet man. I think that you're feeling the same way about me, as I do about you. I know that this is only the third time that we've met up, but I feel so close to you. Do you feel the same?"

Phil responded, "Yes, Sam. I know I am falling for you and there's nothing I can do about it. But I am a married man, as you know and I am going to have to resolve this sooner or later. For the time being, can we just enjoy each other's company. Let's have a nice meal and some nice conversation and then go to your room, without having to feel overburdened by where we are in this romance, or affair, as it really is."

"Yes, Phil," Sam answered. "Wherever we are in this romance or affair, as you probably so rightly called it, let's enjoy what we have, right now. Come on, let's get off to the restaurant. I booked for 7pm and it's that time now."

Sam tucked her arm under Phil's arm and they strolled happily towards the restaurant for dinner.

***

At Dale's apartment, he and Jan were letting things get ahead of them. But reality was creeping in and the surreal dream, was about to become a real situation. Jan started to question herself and Dale.

"Christ, Dale. Three weeks ago, this was all a bit of a

pipedream, a bit of fun, a bit of frivolity, but now, I'm nervous. I don't know if what we are doing is what we should be doing with our lives. It's alright for you, you're a single man, with no commitments, you can go anywhere you like at any time you like, and you have partners that can run your business for you. But my business is just Phil and me and if I left, the whole thing would collapse in a heap, as it is the business is in a period of transition, with new people muscling in on our contracts. And, you and me? Where are we going with this? It started off as a bit of a flirtation and a bit of sex on the side, and it's been exciting, I've loved it. I haven't felt this good for years, you really have given me my life back. I feel like a young girl again. But I think that we are both thinking that it should be something else? But I've been married to Phil for over twenty years and I can't keep this going for ever, this thing between us. How do I tell Phil? He'd be devastated."

Dale responded as best he could, given that the reality of the situation was finally finding its way to the surface. "Jan. Whether you like it or not, I think you know that I am in love with you and have been for as many years as I can remember. You do-it for me, like no other woman ever has and I would drop everything for you. But you're right. We can't go on forever like this. This is not just a three-week romance, for me this would be for life. And now, here we are with a unique opportunity, to break away from the chains that keep us here. I know you've not been happy. You told me yourself, that things between you and Phil, have become stale. This is our opportunity to break away from it all and start a new life, out in the countryside, on 'your own estate.' But let's not spoil the evening, let's give it some thought. The practicalities, the realities. Maybe we could take a trip up to Cumbria as soon as we've claimed the state and all the paperwork has come through and had been cleared. Tell me that you'll think about it and then we'll sleep on it. Yes?"

Jan feeling slightly less pressured, decided that buying a little thinking time was the best way to go. "Yes Dale. We'll both think on it! Now how about this 'special pasta dish' you say you have created for me 'Chef'. I'm hungry. I'm looking forward to this. Not too much garlic I hope. Then I was thinking, that after that bit of excitement we had earlier when I arrived, we might have a half an hour in your Jacuzzi, to relax us and in my bag, I have a very nice bottle of massage oil to try out."

Dale's mind was working overtime again. "How about we skip the pasta?"

"No, Dale. Settle down. It'll be worth the wait, I promise you.

2020, Holiday Inn

Sam and Phil were basking in each other's company. They neither of them felt ravenous enough to eat a big meal, both opting for salads, a 'Salad Nicoise' for Sam and a 'Waldorf- Salad', for Phil with some chicken, followed by a lime and coconut panna-cotta. For most of the meal they chatted like old friends. Holding hands between eating and talking about anything and everything, though it was obvious that Phil was worried about some of the legal to-ing's and fro-ing's, with his and Jan's business Camden Estates. He felt absolutely hand-tied, with a new company having been awarded, what had been their contracts, for year after year, 'til the bank's new regime stepped in. Anyway, this evening was not the evening for business discussions, tonight was all about them. Them being together, which made all the world seem a better place. They finished their meal and Sam signed the check, with Phil protesting. They strolled through the foyer, and Phil turned away as he saw some of his club members headed his towards him. The lift pinged and he and Sam entered, alighting on the third floor, just a few doors from Sam's bedroom. Sam opened the door and they stepped in, the door automatically closing shut behind them.

Phil swept Sam in his arms. "Oh, Samantha. I can't help it. I hope you won't mind me saying this, but I'm in love with you. Absolutely in love with you, hook, line and sinker."

Sam sighed deeply. They held each other for several minutes, just enjoying the moment, 'til Sam said, "Phil, undress me. Take your time, I want to enjoy every minute. I want you to enjoy every second, every minute that we're together."

Phil obliged. It was no hardship, though slowly was a challenge as he was trying to control his natural physical need. Button, by button, he revealed the prettiest underwear that he had ever seen on a woman, revealing soft smooth warm, creamy white porcelain skin. The dress fell to the floor, in a heap. They were locked together in an embrace with both their hearts pulsating in anticipation. They moved to the king-sized bed. She wrapped her legs around his body and they melted together, enjoying each other until they fell asleep, exhausted, but very happy.

CHAPTER 38

2020, Camden Estates

At Camden estates, the 'shit' seemed to be 'hitting the fan'.

On Wednesday morning, neither Jan, nor Phil had arrived in the office before midday. The girls had opened up the office. Usually, the phones were ringing off the wall, but today, for no apparent reason, they appeared to be very quiet. In fact, the office staff had wondered, whether there had been a break in the telephone lines. Betty had phoned BT, to check if there was a breakdown locally, and received the answer. 'No madam, all up and running, no local-works'. And Maisie had checked the internet for an up-date. But nothing. The phones had stopped ringing. They were mystified.

As soon as Jan arrived at the office the girls brought the telephones situation, or lack of them to her attention. She turned on her PC to find several urgent messages, from clients, asking what was happening with the rentals and why had they been given a 'Section 21. Notice to Quit', what had they done wrong and what was the problem? Were their rents unpaid? Why had they not been given proper notice?

On studying the addresses from where the enquiries had come from, a pattern was emerging. The messages were coming from two rows of Victorian red-brick, 'back-to-back' houses in nearby Kentish Town and Paddington.

This was an area where developers were desperate to buy up these old properties, knock them down and replace them with very expensive, high-rise office blocks and apartments, with fancy boutiques on the ground level, generating substantial rental income.

Jan had known some of these tenants for nearly twenty years

and her father had looked after them for at least ten years before that. She picked up the phone to one of them, an old lady in her nineties, it rang and a frail voice answered, simply, with a, "Yes?"

Jan spoke. "Hello, is that Mabel? Mabel, it's Jan. Jan Phillips from Camden Rentals. Have you had a letter to quit your premises?"

The old lady answered. "Yes, Janet. How could you do this to me, I've been here for over sixty years, ever since I got married. I raised my family here, all my friends are here and now, you're kicking me out and your letter says that it's final and that I shouldn't phone you. I should only reply by email. Well, that's impossible. I don't have one of those computer things. I refuse to. So why are you kicking me out?"

Jan was shell-shocked. "Mabel, can I come around straight away. There has to be some misunderstanding here. I haven't sent out any such letter. I'll be around this afternoon and we'll sort this out, if that's okay with you?"

"Yes dear. I hope you will. I'm nearly ninety and I'm too old to move out now, so I hope you can sort it. I'll put the kettle on the stove."

Jan was peeved, to say the least. The girls, as well as Phil, had been listening to the conversation, or at least, one side of the conversation, but could easily work out what appeared to be going on here. Jan needed to see the 'letter to quit', herself, to see exactly where it had come from, the exact wording and by whose authority. She was getting angry, and suspecting that the new company that had taken over the bank portfolio, which included the double row of Victorian properties, were up to no good. The research that she had previously carried out on them, through Companies House, showed that they were a Land and Development company, with a base here in London, but with links all across the country. The Directors, were a James Goodrich and a Charles Dartington. Homes in London and abroad. A Shooting Estate in Cumberland and a very large portfolio of domestic and commercial rental properties, in more than one city, since the establishment of the business in the early 1970's.

Jan set out to see Mabel Jeggs in Kentish Town. She hailed a black cab and gave the address. Within twenty minutes, Jan was knocking on Mabel's small terraced two up and two down red-bricked terrace, with its faded red door and yellowing nets at the single bow window. A call came from within, "Come in love, it's open."

Jan walked the few steps down the passageway, to the scullery to be offered a cup of tea. The old lady had been shedding tears, from the streaks down her face. She took a damp handkerchief from up her sleeve and had a good blow of her nose, sniffing and wiping the drip from the end.

Jan sat down, and as Mabel made a cup of tea, she slid the letter in front of Jan, on the scrubbed pine table in the kitchen.

The headed paper read:

==

Goodrich & Dartington Ltd.
King's Chambers, London Bridge, London. EC4R 9HA
Date as postmark.
Dear Sir or Madam,

'SECTION 21 NOTICE TO QUIT'
We have recently acquired the rental portfolio which includes yours and other properties. We note that there is no bona-fide current contract in place for you to continue renting this property.

We therefore regretfully hereby give you this legal 'Notice to Quit' and for you to remove yourself from the property forthwith.

However, as you have been a long-term tenant, we will allow a period of 28 days for you to leave the premises.

Yours faithfully,
For Charles-James Company Ltd.
JG
Chief Executive.
==

Jan read the letter and then read it again. Then she read it out loud and mouthed every single word, with absolute dismay. The dismay was growing to incredulity and a growing anger. She looked at the notice that was attached to the letter.

--//--
NOTICE OF INTENTION TO BRING PROCEEDINGS FOR POSSESSION.

Housing Act 1988. Section 8. Section 21 Notice. Etc.

---//---

Jan studied the letter.

It was something that she had seen before, many times, and had to use herself, when they had a non-paying tenant, or a disruptive tenant, or a tenant that was damaging the property. She knew the words well. But it didn't seem relative to this situation, whatsoever.

She was hopping mad. She voiced it loudly. "You just can't kick people out, just because you want to develop the land. That was definitely not on."

Jan was cross, but she explained carefully to Mabel, what was happening.

She spoke to the old lady. "Mabel, this is not from me. This is from a company that has taken over the portfolio that we have looked after for the bank, for probably thirty years, that's me and Phil and my father before me. This is awful. I shall be at the bank tomorrow to get this annulled. It needs to be rescinded and undone. It's just not on!"

She thanked Mabel for the tea and took the letters with her. She hailed a black cab and was back at the office within twenty minutes. By the time Jan returned, the office was empty, apart from Phil, who had been waiting anxiously for Jan's return.

She sat down at her desk and as she was starting to talk to Phil about the letter, from these dreadful 'new people', she glanced at her emails and noticed a mail from 'Goodrich and Dartington', at the base of her messages.

=======================================

From: Charles-James and Co. Ltd.
(Incorporating: Goodrich & Dartington). The London Land Agents Since 1988.

To: Camden Estates Ltd.

Re: Bank Servicing Contracts.

It is with regret, that we are not renewing the Servicing Contract for your company, Camden Estates. We have made the decision on a cost analysis basis. It does not reflect on your quality or ability, but we have for the sake of economy, to complete all of these servicing requirements in house, with immediate effect.

Yours regretfully,
The Charles-James Property Company.
(Incorporating: Goodrich & Dartington). The London Land Agents since 1988.

==

Jan let off steam, screaming, "Jesus Christ! What have we done to deserve this? These people have taken over most of our contracts, they are upsetting all of our old letting tenants and now, they are trying to ruin us. Jesus Christ almighty, this is twenty years hard work, down the drain! Christ almighty!"

She sat for a second and drew breath. "Right Phil, before we get off home, we'll get a letter out to all our clients and then we need to see the bank and tell them what's going on. We'll get down here early in the morning and get these people sorted out. Better still, we'll stay over at the Holiday Inn and be here first thing."

At that, Jan got up. Closed the blinds, pulled the key out of her bag, ushered Phil out of the building and slammed the door shut, locking it behind her. They headed for the Holiday Inn, in Camden.

On arrival at the Holiday Inn, Jan couldn't understand why, and how many staff were saying either hello Mr Phillips, or nodding and smiling as if he were an acquaintance. Phil, tried to keep his head down as they booked in at the hotel's reception desks. One of the Receptionists on the counter greeted them.

"Good evening, Mr Phillips, how are you?" she asked as she looked Jan up and down in disapproval and greeted her less warmly. "Good evening, madam," she said with a slight intonation on 'madam'. Having seen Phil with Samantha for the last few weeks, she had been very happy and smiley.

Jan gave Phil an old fashioned look and as she was about to ask him why so many of the staff seemed to acknowledge him… Samantha walked up towards them.

Jan noticed her and gave her a big wide smile as she came closer. They kissed cheeks as Phil turned all the colours of red and pink within seconds of her kissing Phil on the cheek.

Jan offered a greeting. "Sam, how are you? We haven't seen

anything of you since you broke up with Dale. Are things okay for you now?"

Sam replied in a relaxed manner far away from her usual frenetic self, that Jan didn't recognise. "Oh yes, Jan. This is my last night here. I have had my apartment completely re-furbished. I move back in tomorrow, so things are much, much better now. I'm over the moon. I have a new romance and he is wonderful. I couldn't be happier. He's kind and considerate and witty and loving. He's a marvellous and considerate lover. I just couldn't be happier. You could probably say I'm in love."

Phil continued to blush. Jan noticed. "Phil, are you okay, you look very hot?"

Sam was thinking, *Oh yes, he's hot, so hot, if only she knew.*

"No, no, I'm fine. It's just very warm in here, very warm." Phil replied.

Jan dismissed it as she had other things on her mind. "Well, must go Samantha, lovely to see you. Glad you're doing okay. Bye."

Jan strode across to the lifts, with Phil in toe like a lap-dog, looking very sheepish after the near fatal exchange with Sam. *Thank god she didn't say anything*, he thought to himself. *I'm going to have to say something to Jan soon.*

Jan had an agitated night's sleep, tossing and turning, not being able to relax with the Section 21 Notices to quit, that her old established clients had been receiving from this Goodrich and Dartington company. Not only that, but they had given her company, notice that they were to keep all of her previous cleaning, painting and maintenance contracts in-house within their own company. Talk about not just 'pulling the rug' from underneath their feet, but more likely, picking it up and dumping it in the skip, there was no denying it.

Jan had been down and had breakfast before Phil had woken, having had a peaceful night's sleep with sweet dreams of him and Samantha. *God, that was a lucky escape*, he thought. On the dot of 9am Jan started making calls… to the bank, to their Solicitors, to the Rental Association and then eventually as the morning wore on, to Goodrich and Dartington.

She had returned to the office and had spoken to Charles Dartington, with James Goodrich on an open line. They didn't seem in the least bothered that overnight, they virtually stripped her of her business, the rental clients, the contracts and her income. By four o'clock she was devastated, she felt wrung out and had been hung out to dry. No matter what she did to try and persuade these people, the snooty bastards weren't having it. One had commented, "All's fair in love and war, deary. You'll have to do something else with your dreary little life. Let's face it, we're probably doing you a favour."

Jan could hear sniggering and muffled guffawing in the background. At that, Jan slammed the phone down on her mahogany desk, the desk that her father first purchased when he set up the business, so hard that she cracked the mouth-piece, which hung from its cable, swinging back and forth.

"Bastards! Effing bastards. Who are these people, Dartington and Goodrich, to treat us like this. I'm not happy, what a dreadful way to treat us. I'll get to the bottom of this if it kills me!"

She was cross and whatever Phil had said or was trying to say was going straight over her head. Phil had escaped earlier in the day, knowing that Jan would want to make all the calls herself. He had sneaked back to Samantha's room at the Holiday Inn, after receiving a text, saying she was working from her hotel room today on several client files.

Needless to say, there was a short interlude from work, where Sam jumped on Phil, to his absolute delight. Phil had returned to the room by 4pm as Jan was packing up ready to go home for the weekend.

Jan phoned Phil. It went into message mode.

Jan was in need of some comforting and it seemed that her first choice nowadays, was not Phil.

"Phil, love. I am going to stay another night down here. I need to be going through all of our books and records in the office, to see exactly how this is going to affect our business. You go home love. I've booked another night here."

Phil didn't bat an eyelid. *Well, should I tell her now? No, that would be the last straw, she couldn't cope with me leaving too. No. I'll leave it for a bit,* he thought.

As Phil left the room, Jan picked up her mobile and dialled Dale. His phone rang. Jan spoke. "God! I never ever thought I'd hear myself saying this, but I'm desperate for a glass of red and to see you!"

Dale almost dropped the phone. "But Jan. It's the weekend, how are you going to get away?"

"Is that a yes? You'll be pleased to see me, and have I just given you a gun in your pocket?"

"My, Jan. How things have changed, it was always me doing the chasing and now, well, your guard seems to be completely down. When will you be here, I can't wait to see you."

***

Phil dialled Sam. "Hi Sam, it's me."

"Yes, Phil, I know it's you. Your name comes up on my dial."

"Samantha… I have to ask. Did you really mean all those nice things you said about me when we ran into each other last evening with Jan? You did make me blush."

"Yes, Philip. I meant every word of it. And, I might have some interesting news for you. I hope you're going to be pleased. I certainly am, it's all I ever wanted."

The line went quiet.

"Well, I'm free this weekend. I can help you move into the new apartment. We can have the whole weekend together if you would like?"

"Oh yes. I would very much like."

The weekend seemed to come and go in a few hours.

***

Jan and Dale spent most of their weekend in bed, going out for supper at their favourite Italian fish restaurant, Mussellini, just off the Regents Canal where Vittorio would always find them a nice quiet table and a good bottle of Valpolicella, some Marsala with their Espresso and then back to bed, or the sofa or the thick floor-rug or the shower. It was an exhausting, but an uplifting, happy and exciting weekend, where Jan had dumped all her woes and Dale had finally persuaded her that she was going to inherit up to three hundred acres of Cumbrian countryside.

The biggest challenge would be to tell Phil. He was going to be heart broken. Surely, he would understand that they had drifted apart. But Dale, their neighbour, he didn't like him at the best of times. She wondered if he would take a swipe at him.

Oh crikey, she thought. *I'm not going to like doing this.*

***

Samantha's apartment, after a few hours, was looking well

organised. She had always planned to start again after the break-up with Dale. She had abandoned most of her old furniture that she had put into a lock-up and got house clearance people in to clear it. Besides, one of her bedrooms was now designated as a nursery, for a little Philip or perhaps Philipa to occupy. She swept around the apartment in a translucent dress and a dream for most of the time, apart from when she had draped herself around Phil's shoulders and various parts of his body, enjoying just being with someone she felt at total ease with. It was the nicest weekend that either of them could remember, ever, in their lives.

But now comes the hard part.

"Phil, darling, you said that you would tell Jan. When do you think you might pluck up the courage? I know you said that your business was going through a very difficult time, these last few weeks, but if you say it could end up in collapse, perhaps now is a good time to wind everything up. As a Solicitor, in my business I see it all the time. The business goes bust and the partners fall out and that's it, the end of the line. You don't need to salvage much. I have my parent's inheritance and the apartment and a good income. And… I don't know what you might think of this…but I've always wanted to run a nursery and we could create something really, really good down here. Nurseries are in big demand and our little off-spring will have so much care and from both parents. Whew! Did I really say all that without taking a breath?"

Phil sat on the sofa, somewhat bemused, but pleased to have had an escape route 'master-planned' out for him. He wondered whether he had heard that correctly, 'offspring'.

"I'm not sure Sam. Jan and I have been married for quite a few years, I don't want to leave her on her own. I have no idea how she would cope, and can you imagine how we would both feel if something happened to her? If we have to wind-up the business then I would continue in the same premises that we would still own and try and re-build that business. Let's see what happens."

***

Jan sat contemplating her situation. Dale tabled an idea. "Jan, can I make a small suggestion. My ex, Samantha, is a Solicitor and a very good solicitor. I think that given the situation with your business as it stands right now, there is only one way out and that is to wind it up. It's part of what Sam's practise does and she would be very discreet. You would be able to walk away, with no black marks on your sheet, so to speak. I think that this would be the best solution for you and Phil. You would still have the few flats you have bought from the business over the years and these would not be affected. You would have income, without hassle and of course we can go up and develop your Cumbrian inheritance. Now what do you say. Good suggestion or not?"

Phil sipped at a cup of black coffee. Sam gently kissed his forehead.

"Phil, I know I've given you a lot of food for thought, but I want to just add another idea, if you're not fed up with me by now?"

Phil responded, "Sam, I'm in love with you now, more than ever, so I could never be fed up with you. Tell me what you are thinking."

Sam started to map out a few thoughts for consideration. "My practise deals with all aspects of business from Start-ups' to expansion, mortgages, acquisitions and 'wind-up'. After all of the information you have given me this weekend. It strikes me that the best solution for your business is to close it down, before *it* closes *you* down. I can create a clean break with not much aggravation. You have your properties running as a separate company, so they would not be affected and you could just close the doors and walk away. I can handle all that for you and Jan, and not charge you a fortune, call it 'mates-rates'. What do you think?"

"Okay Sam, thank you. Let me think about it for a few hours please."

***

Jan and Dale sat facing each other in the dining area at Dale's flat overlooking the canal boats as they chugged by, having just negotiated the upward lock. Dale spoke. "Jan. I'm going to phone Samantha and make an appointment with her so you can have a chat about your business. It's Monday today, shall I try for Wednesday? I'll come with you if you like. It can be just the three of us if you like. You can tell Phil that you've had an exploratory meeting after the event, then at least you will know what your options are. What do you think?"

Jan was hesitant. "Mmmm, I'm really not sure. Will you come with me? If you will, then okay, Wednesday if you can. Thank you."

Samantha's work mobile rang. Dale's name showed on the dial.

"Samantha, it's Dale. I'm with our friend Jan Philips from Camden Estates. She'd like to come and see you about her business, on Wednesday if you can fit her in. I said I would come with her, if that's okay with you. She's naturally a bit nervous."

Sam was a little taken aback. For two reasons. *Firstly*, she thought, *why no Phil, and secondly, why Dale?*

"Yes, Dale. That's fine. I can fit you in at 2pm, if that's okay with you two?"

She had gone fishing, by putting the emphasis on 'you two'.

She called out to Phil who was in the kitchen. "Phil darling, I have just arranged a meeting on Wednesday for your wife to come along to discuss your business. I find it hard to believe that you weren't included. The other strange thing is that Dale Scott, my ex, whom you know of course, will be accompanying her."

Phil was puzzled and intrigued. With the traumas of the last several days, he knew Jan was going to be seeking legal advice, but it was half of his business, so he wondered why she hadn't phoned and informed him of what she was arranging. *Well*, he thought, *we shall have to see.*

***

Wednesday came around and Phil hadn't been home. He didn't realise that neither had Jan. They had both been tucked away in their individual bolt-holes, their respective new partners' flats.

Jan and Phil arrived at the offices of Cohen, Green and Southwell and were shown into the Conference Room. Samantha watched them on the internal security cameras and was a little taken aback to see them cosying-up to each other and then Dale stealing a kiss from Jan. The kiss was reciprocated and some.

Aha, Sam thought. *The game's up!*

They were offered the customary tray of tea or coffee and biscuits with bottled water. They sat for ten minutes and watched the clock tick around 2pm. From the back-office, Sam phoned Phil to come in to her offices. Meantime, the three politely greeted each other and then discussed the situation facing the business. After an hour, a simple solution was arrived at, reached without too many objections and Samantha asked if she should put the 'wind-up' proceedings in motion. Then she delivered the next question.

"And where is Mr Phillips in all of this?" Without waiting for an answer, she said, "Perhaps we should ask him?"

Jan and Dale looked at each other bemused.

Samantha pressed the intercom.

"Could you send in Mr Phillips please?"

CHAPTER 39

2020, Carlisle, Police Search for Bryn Morris

Julia's discussion with her boss Rob Wilton and Jerry Blake over the weekend, regarding the delivery of photographic links showing the Morris family over various periods in the mill's and the estate's history, prompted an early Monday morning meeting with the detective squad.

In the meantime, Julia's husband Grant was doing what he had promised and that was to search the newspaper records and files for any incidents or relevant history, that might help with the current enquiry.

He entered Buckabank Mill into the search. There were some ancient adverts that had been placed looking for staff and equipment sales. A couple more offered 'Timber Services', from cutting down woods to tree felling, firewood for sale and several other insignificant 'for sale' type adverts. As he thumbed through the Carlisle Gazettes year's, back-catalogue of news, he entered a further search for Morris and bingo!

"Wow," Grant exclaimed to himself. "This is more like it."

He started to read headlines in the Carlisle Gazette July 1970.

'Local Resident Found Dead in Cottage Home.' The date on the paper was July 28th 1970. The report was very sketchy, but was the first hint about a dead body being found in a Cottage up at Edenbrook. A DI Livermore was only able to quote: 'Unable to give any details at this stage as an investigation is ongoing'.

'Murder Victim Named.' July 30th 1970. Sketchy details again emerging. 'It is believed that the body of a Bryn Morris, a local wood-cutter and craftsman has been found at Edenbrook Cottage on the Cardew-Petteril Estate. The information available to us at The Gazette, received last evening, indicates that this death may have been the result of a fracas at the cottage. The police are unable to further quote.

'Wife of Murder Victim Urgently Sought.' July 31st 1970. It is understood that the police are seeking to find the Wife of Bryn Morris, named as the murder victim at Edenbrook Cottage earlier this week. Police are searching for Mrs Mary Gwen Morris who may be able to help them with their enquiries. It is believed that she may be headed to her former home in Wales.

'Search for Murderer Continues.' August 3rd 1970. The search for Mrs Mary Gwen Morris, the wife of the murdered Bryn Morris continues. The search has been extended up to Buckabank Sawmill, where Mrs Morris's sister Violet and her husband Emmanuel Morris (known locally as Manny Morris), run the 100-year-old established but now declining mill business. It is understood that Mr & Mrs Emmanuel Morris have also disappeared and are suspected to be assisting Mary Gwen Morris in her wishing to avoid questioning in connection with her husband's murder. The police are unable to give any further updates, only to say that their inquiries have been extended to South Wales and that they are receiving assistance from Cardiff Police.

'Unsolved Murder Case Closed.' March 1st 1971. It is ironic, that the search for the murder suspect of Bryn Morris, has ended after six months on St. David's Day. It was assumed that the perpetrator a Mrs Mary Gwenllian Morris had returned to her home town of Newport in Wales. She has not been seen since. DI James Livermore commented that the case would be assigned as unsolved but remain open.

Further back in the records Grant found a headline from the main Carlisle Colliery:

'Accident or Murder?' July 1895. Thaddeus Lock, manager and

shareholder at Carlisle Colliery, known to be a hard task-master at
the colliery, was pronounced dead yesterday, having fallen to his
death down a disused mine-shaft. The police refused to comment,
other than they were treating the death as an accident. The Gazette
was unable to receive further comment.

"Wow! This is what we were looking for!" Grant picked up his
phone and dialled Julia. It went into answer mode.

After a half a dozen tries, Grant dialled Carlisle Police Station.
After two rings the phone answered.

"Good morning, Carlisle Police. Duty Sergeant here. How
may I help?"

"Good morning, Robert. It's Grant here, Julia's husband,
could you put me through please."

"Good morning, Grant. I'm sorry, I was told to not put any
calls through to the detective room, and if I did it would be on pain
of death!"

"Robert, trust me on this one. This is very urgent. I have some
highly significant information for the team. I will take the rap if
you get into trouble, but believe me you won't, in fact neither of
us will. Trust me."

"Okay, Grant. If you say so!"
***
The phone rang upstairs in the team room. Julia went to answer it.

Rob shouted, "No! I said no calls. No matter what. What does
that sergeant think an order is, something that needs ignoring? No,
pick it up and put it down again."
***
After three attempts to put Grant through, the duty sergeant
clunked up the creaking wooden stairs and knocked heavily on the
door. Rob Wilton opened the door.

"Well, Sergeant Robert, I hope you have a good reason for
this interruption."

"It's DS Cox's husband, Grant. He says he has significant
information on the murders!"

Rob was slightly taken aback after his normal calm approach
to the job had temporarily exploded in angry frustration. "Fine. Put
him through then."

The phone rang. Rob answered, "Grant. This had better be

good!"

Grant spoke for just a few seconds, before Rob asked him to hold, while he placed the phone on loudspeaker.

After Grant stopped speaking there ensued a general hubbub of conversation around the room.

Rob spoke. "Okay folks. From what we have just heard, we might have found our three bodies. If Bryn Morris was murdered, there is the indication that he was murdered by his wife Mary Gwen Morris. However, if the three bodies in the cellar are Mary and her sister Violet and her husband Emmanuel, which is highly likely, then how did they get there and who locked them in and therefore surely murdered them. I suggest that we raise the old 1970/71 records for this case, which I understand has an 'UNSOLVED' designation and from that we might be able to piece something a bit more positive together.

"Julia, speak to your old man and ask him to email copies of the headlines to us and get them printed off and added to the crime board. Meantime, I am going to take another look at our current crime scene with DCI Blake."

***

Rob and Jerry arrived at Buckabank mill. The scene hadn't changed. The yellow and blue tapes still cordoned-off what has been designated as the crime scene, though one or two had blown away from their ties.

"Well Rob, my old friend, nothing has changed. What did you have in your mind for this re-visit?"

"Jerry, I just wanted to re-acquaint myself with the cellar and the heavy lock on the door."

The two detectives strolled over to the tumbledown. The grass and overgrowth were now well trodden down with the movement of a range of police vehicles, vans, cars and forensics. The wind was blowing through the woodland-copse below them, leading down to the stream and the stiff breeze was blowing at the tops of the tall pines in the forestry beyond. The scent from the pines filled the air with a sweetness he remembered as a boy playing in these woods. He could only remember the sounds of timber being cut and the mill's heavy machinery sawing timber for hours. He remembered him and his pals playing in the streams and rivulets that led down to the river, Cops and Robbers, Cowboys and

Indians, and all the games that kids play for hours on end when they are left to their own devices.

"I still have vivid memories of those days," Rob reminisced. "It seemed that when the spring erupted, so did the wildlife. The birds would sing, the squirrels would run up and down the trees leaping, almost flying from branch to branch, the deer and muntjac would be leaping and frolicking through the trees and foxes would sit and stare at the antics, as they taught their offspring to hunt mice and vole and rabbits. Brown hares with their distinctive long ears with black tips, would 'box' other males for the hand of a 'fair-maiden' doe. I don't think until now that I really appreciated the freedoms we enjoyed as kids.

"But here I am now forty years later, wondering whether I was around when these murders were committed."

Jerry brought Rob back to reality. "Snap out of it, Rob, you're day-dreaming!"

"Sorry, Jerry. Happy times. Just thinking that I might have even been around at the time these murders were committed is scary. Anyway, I just wanted to look at the scene again."

They viewed the scene again and pondered.

"Okay young Robert, let's hear your theory."

"Well, I think the clue to this is Bryn Morris. Here's what I think may have happened. Bryn and Mary Morris went to visit their relations, her sister Violet and her husband Emmanuel, also known as Manny Morris, for let's say Sunday lunch or tea. I think there may have been a massive row and we know now from the old case files that Bryn had a temper. I think the row got out of hand and Mary, Violet and Manny scurried down into the cellar, which was a sort of safe haven. The very angry Bryn then bolted the door and went on his way, either thinking he would free them later, having taught them a lesson, or that they could get out themselves after they had learned their lesson. I think the argument would have been about finance, or in simple terms, money or Bryn's lack of it once again, given the feed-back from the old case files. They all seemed to be living on fresh air, yet the mill and all of this acreage must have been worth a fortune, even back in those days.

"With regards to the cold case where it was suspected that Mary killed Bryn up at the cottage, then if Mary is (or was) down in the cellar, then who killed Bryn. My guess is that they are still alive and walking around freely."

"Yes, Rob, I can see all of that," Jerry replied. "That makes sense, good logic. Now that we have all those photographs and the garments that Mary and Violet were wearing at the time, then Forensics need copies of those so they can match then up. The other thing we must do is go to the Land Registry and look at who is the current owner of the land and see what, if any, sales and transfers have been made over the years. That might just open up another can of worms."

"Mmmmm, yes. This case gets more interesting every day!"

With these conclusions in mind, the pals climbed back into the old Land Rover and rattled their way back down the long, overgrown driveway to the main road.

"I need to get the couple in again, Jan Morris and Dale Scott."

As soon as Rob returned to the office, he phoned Dale Scott's mobile and asked them to attend Carlisle Police Station again in the morning.

Jan and Dale duly arrived as requested.

CHAPTER 40

2020, Offices of Cohen, Southwell and Green

Sam pressed the intercom. "Could you send in Mr Phillips please?"

Phil walked into the office to see Jan and Dale sitting there, looking like a couple. They shuffled apart, though it was obvious to Phil that this wasn't just Dale accompanying Jan on a business meeting. To him, they looked as if they were together.

He didn't speak. He just calmly took a seat at the side of the table where Sam had been sitting. Of course, he knew that they were there together as Sam had relayed the conversation that she had had with Dale on the Monday, two days before, about the proposed winding up of the company. So, he was totally au fait with the content of the meeting. Not only that, he agreed that that was the best course of action. He was disappointed however, that Jan saw to seek the advice of their neighbour and it suddenly struck alarm bells that there was something going on between these two. It had finally clicked. All the guilty feelings that he had been harbouring suddenly disappeared like a sack of coal being taken off his shoulder.

Suddenly he felt relaxed and started to enjoy the almost tactile power he felt that he now might hold over Jan. He felt a surge of superiority, knowing that they were starting to squirm, there, right in front of him and they had no idea about him and Samantha.

Sam went to talk. Phil pulled her hand backwards and hushed her. He spoke, "Well, this is a fine state of affairs. It's fairly certain to me that you have been seeing each other, perhaps you would like to explain yourselves."

Jan started to speak. She stuttered, "I, I, I don't know what to say Phil."

Dale butted in. "Phil, mate—"

Phil gave a quick shake of the head. "*Mate?* I don't think so, *mate*! I'm not your *mate*, far from it!"

"Phil, it's all my fault. Let me explain, please. In my weekly searches, an estate came up with the name Morris on it and I said to Jan, if nobody claims it, then maybe I could claim it for you. And that's how it started. I'm sorry mate, it was all my fault."

Phil, acting calmly and trying to feign a little indignance said, "So, Dale. I guess you've been shagging my wife. I thought she was acting differently lately, always making excuses to stay at work late and not worrying about me. And, while I think about it, suggesting that I go home to Huntingdon alone. Yes, it all fits now." Jan tried to interject. "Shut up, Jan, let me have my say!"

"But, but, but–"

"No buts, Jan, this is serious stuff. I'm not prepared to accept anything you say. In fact, I think our next discussion in this office, is to talk to a divorce lawyer, I'm sure that Sam can organise that. Sam?"

Samantha replied, somewhat stunned by the turn of events, which seemed to be playing right into Phil's hands. No confessions, no admissions, no repercussions. Jan had done Phil's dirty work for him and Samantha. How well did that work out. How happy could she be. Sam, was mightily pleased. Now she had everything she wanted. A man, a baby on the way, her lifetime's wish fulfilled, her home back and a new and exciting future.

I'm sure Jan and Dale will have worked something out for themselves. Something already long-term planned. Yes, and I suppose they did look suited, even good together. She smiled sweetly, and responded to Phil. "Well, yes of course. If you're sure?"

Phil regarded Sam's question and answered, simply and succinctly, "Yes, I'm sure."

He then stood up and left the meeting, no one saw him smirking as he left the room, leaving everyone dumfounded at the speed of the decision making and how a simple business meeting panned out to be life-changing.

"That," Phil said to himself, "was very satisfying." *That was the simplest game of chess I have ever played. They fell like pawns to my Knight and I didn't even need my King or Queen. Lambs to the slaughter. My god, that felt good.*

Jan and Dale rose from the table feeing shell-shocked, but as they left the premises and returned to Dale's flat, they started to appreciate where this had left them in the scheme of things. In fact, in the scheme of them being together. As they briskly stepped along Camden High Road, Dale in particular, was not only mightily relieved at where they now were, in his relationship with Jan, but was feeling overjoyed that everything had come to a head between them and Phil and was now in the open.

They sat back in the flat, having opened a bottle of rose and poured two large glasses and were pondering why all of that was so easy. Dale asked Jan, "I don't get it Jan. Why was all that so easy? How come your Phil just accepted that we were not only together, but he didn't even blink when Sam said she was going to wind up the business? I am thinking that Sam had already filled him in on the meeting."

Jan topped their glasses, emptying the bottle. "You don't think that they have been at it, all the time that we have, do you?"

Dale opened another sweet Zinfandel Rose. "Well, from what you have told me, particularly of the events of the past few days, particularly your overnighter at the Holiday Inn, where so many staff seemed to recognise him…and…thinking about it, Sam has been holed up there since I kicked her out. All those months ago, while she had been refurbishing her flat, you don't think that they may have gotten together, do you?"

"Bingo!" Jan exclaimed, having solved the puzzle. "You're absolutely on the money. They've been at it all the time that we have. The supercilious, bombastic, condescending, patronising, flaming hypocrites!"

"Steady on Jan, say it like it is then!" Dale interjected.

"And I was feeling *so* guilty. Well, I think we'll store that for another day. At least we can now get on with our plans to go up to Cumbria and takeover 'my' inheritance. Wow, now I can get excited without feeling any more guilt! Over to you Mr Heir Hunter, when do we go?"

"But what about your business and its winding-up?" Dale asked.

Jan replied with some relief. "Well, that's now down to the solicitors. They can inform everybody. Clients, customers, debtors, creditors etc., etc. Let someone else worry about it all. I'd just about had enough anyway, though I will continue to harass this London

Estates about the Section 21 notices. I don't mind going to court to fight the corner for some of my old tenants. What they are doing to some of those old folks is just not on."

CHAPTER 41

2020, Carlisle Police Station

Jan and Dale drew up to the police station in a very nervous state. Jan was shaking. Dale squeezed her hand.

"Jan, come on, relax. It'll be alright. I have written and re-written these documents. It would take a real expert, even more experienced than me to figure out that this was a made-up claim. Trust me, we'll be fine."

Jan still hands shaking nervously. "But what if they want our DNA?"

"There is no reason for them to want our DNA. All we have done is inherit some land. Please stop putting hurdles in front of us, it'll be okay…and if it's not, I will take the rap!"

The desk sergeant phoned upstairs to announce the arrival of Jan Morris and her partner. Julia Cox came down, greeted them and ushered them upstairs to Rob's office, where he and Jerry waited. Rob greeted them and offered tea or coffee, which helped Jan relax a little.

"Now, may I call you Jan?"

Jan nodded in acceptance.

"Did you bring with you the land maps we asked for outlining the land you have inherited, as you understand it?"

Dale replied, "Yes."

"And did you bring wellington boots or walking shoes as I asked?"

"Well, yes!"

Dale pulled the papers from his old leather attaché case and presented them on Rob's desk, carefully unfolding the old papers, tattered and having much faded over the years.

Rob pulled a wodge of papers out from a file in his drawer

and laid the maps out together. Then pointed out, the observations that he Julia and Jerry had made in relation to the parcels of land. Jerry spoke, "Just as we thought."

He pondered over the maps with his fore-finger, pointing out some substantial differences between the drawings. "Here, look at these border lines."

Jan and Dale sat quietly, trying to work out what the two detectives and their sergeant were hinting at.

Dale was curious. "May I ask why you are making comparisons between these sets of maps?"

Jerry started to point out the differences. "Looking back on the Estate records, the land worked by Samuel Abrahams on behalf of Lord Cardew-Petteril, eventually totalled some three hundred acres. This included Buckabank Sawmill and its surrounds, but also included the woodlands and surrounding acres and the forestry, all marked. A portion of that land was sold off by Emmanuel Morris and sold to a company called Dartington and Goodrich, a London based company. Now, this is why we are interested in your old maps. Detective Wilton can continue."

Rob was pleased to talk through the next piece of their puzzle. As soon as Jan heard the name Dartington and Goodrich, her ears pricked up. Rob continued, "The agent for this land sale was a firm called Kyle Redford, whose signature is here, as a witness to a second signature Bryn Morris, who died on the same day that the documents were signed. The signature of Emmanuel Morris (sometimes known as Manny) from other paperwork we have found, thanks to the bank, is seen to be fake. From the research we have done, it seems that this was a fraudulent transaction. If this is in fact the case, yet to be proven, then your hundred or so acres, is not a hundred or so acres as you thought, but more like three hundred acres."

Jan was white faced by this time in the proceedings, she didn't know whether she was in the right or wrong and asked, "I'm sorry, but I'm not sure what you are saying. Are you saying that the estate should be three hundred acres and that my inheritance has been defrauded by, what a hundred and sixty odd acres, and by these Goodrich people from London?"

"If you'll let me, I'll continue. This we will not be able to establish until we speak to them, but what has helped this morning, thanks to you, is we believe we now have sufficient evidence on whom to place the responsibility for these deaths."

"Well, who was it then, or who were they?" Dale asked.

Julia chipped in. "Well sir, that is for us still to determine, but there is now a much bigger question for you. That is, where is your land and can you claim it back?"

"Well, does it matter that much? If it's a hundred acres or so of farmland, the value won't be that great, at least not in this part of the world, will it?" Dale asked.

"I think that we need to show you something. Come on, let's go. I'll take the maps," Rob commented.

Rob and Jerry jumped into the Land Rover and Jan and Dale jumped up into the back. They headed out south of Carlisle for Buckabank, arriving at the property and bumping along the long still much overgrown cart track, to the clearing outside the tumbledown property.

The four alighted the vehicle. Rob donned his wellies and started to walk away from the tumbledown, heading eastward. The land dropped down a modest hill and further down towards the river. Fortunately, the tracks were good, sheep having regularly passed this way. They climbed further down a bank and crossed the river on some very large stepping stones.

The scenery through the year rarely changed, in that the woods were made up mainly of tall pines with small areas of older deciduous trees becoming skeletal-like through the winter months. This was a calm and magical place, perfectly peaceful, but for the sound of the saws spinning and cutting timber in the sawmill all day long, but long, long ago. Three quarters of the way into the mill's acreage was a fast-flowing brook running into the river Petteril to the east of the land and from the old photographs that had come to light, the brothers would spend many hours on a Sunday, their one day of rest just sat on the banks, casting their lines. No time for church, much to the local minister's chagrin and vexatious scolding, water off a duck's back. They worked hard and decided that Sunday was their day to spend either fishing or with the family. But that was many years ago. The brothers were now very long gone.

The three followed Rob as he climbed the east bank of the river and finally arrived at the top of the hill. The four stood looking out from the top of the hill.

Rob spoke. "You might be interested to know that all you see down there in the valley *is, or was, or* probably legally *is,* all yours."

Jan and Dale were aghast! After several minutes silence. Jan spoke. Her mouth was so dry, she could just about manage a squeak. "But there's a huge industrial estate down there and a ring road. That's not possible surely?"

"Yes, from the records, it seems that what we are looking at was acquired illegally, in which case, in all probability, then the property should be a part of your inheritance, after all, they may be distant, but it was your relatives that owned the land and the land should be rightfully yours."

Jerry suggested that they need a good, very sharp lawyer and an even sharper barrister. They may well have a legal fight on their hands.

The group re-traced their steps and Rob dropped Jan and Dale back at the police station, leaving them with plenty to think about.

CHAPTER 42

2020, The Three Feathers

Rob, Julia and Jerry sat in the snug at The Feathers. Gill, the Landlady, greeted the others and gave Jerry a kiss on the forehead, before heading back to the bar, which produced a beaming smile. Rob and Julia sat with a half pint of Carlisle Best and a couple of packets of Cheese and Onion and Jerry with non-alcoholic lager and a packet of mixed nuts and a packet of pork scratchings. As soon as the dogs heard Jerry's voice at the bar, they were at his feet and of course, slobbering over the pork scratchings.

Rob opened up the conversation. "Well, that's a fine can of worms we've opened up for those two. To be honest, I'm still a touch uncertain about this inheritance of Jan's. But, their problem, not ours. Ours is to tie up these murders, so let's have a sum up of where we are. Julia?"

"Yes, Guv. I think that the photographs, together with the garments, or the remains of the garments pretty conclusively ties the bodies down to Mary-Gwen Morris and Violet and Emmanuel Morris. It is probably fair to assume that Bryn, Mary-Gwen's husband locked the three of them in the cellar, after a row. Now whether or not he intended to come back or not, is probably immaterial, as they died anyway, so that has become murder, maybe manslaughter."

Jerry added, "From what Grant has managed to glean from the old Gazette headlines, which reported the death of Bryn Morris and the old case report, it was assumed that Mary had done the deed and escaped to Wales with Violet and Manny. But of course, we now know that that is blown apart as they all ended up in the cellar."

Rob entered the conversation. "That means, that we are now

looking for the person who killed Bryn Morris. We need to look at why someone would take the trouble to go all the way up to Edenbrook Cottage, which is way out on the moors to see Bryn. I think our next step is to try and establish to whom he owed money. I can't think of any other reason why someone would go up there to see him. Julia, Jerry? What do you think?"

"Well, Guv. I think it could be about money, but not just money per-say, but about the value of Buckabank mill as a property. I think that Bryn might have been trying to do some sort of deal to sell the property and perhaps that's why he locked the others up in the cellar?"

"So, are we looking for say, a land agent, or estate agent, maybe a gamekeeper or estate manager who wanted to cut a deal somewhere along the line," Rob surmised. "We need to go back fifty years and see if we can find interested parties."

Jerry cut in again. "I think that whoever bought the land fifty years ago, might have had a hand in all of this. I think we need to look again at the Land transfer documents. That will surely give us some names to follow up on."

It was agreed that next week would reveal some interested parties. But for now, the weekend was theirs to enjoy.

The Crown and Mitre

Jan and Dale had returned to the Crown & Mitre and had had another sleepless night after the revelation that Jan's 'inheritance' could be creating more trouble than it was worth. Now that they had claimed the mill and its hundred and thirty acres, they now knew that the estate had been 'robbed' of over a further hundred and sixty acres. Not only that, but the company that appeared to have purchased all of this contentious land, was known to them. Dartington and Goodrich, The London Real Estate Company, was currently doing huge damage to Jan and Phil's estates and lettings business, that's if it was the same people. But how could they make a fuss. They would have to prove that the land had been illegally sold all of those years ago. They tentatively agonised over the potential cost of employing firms to fight something as contentious as this, a transaction that had taken place over fifty years ago, then the cost could be enormously prohibitive. Not only that, if they had to prove who they were, and the only foolproof way was through DNA, then the game would be up!

They woke, bleary eyed. It was 8am at the Crown and Mitre Hotel in Carlisle. The traffic had started to move and the streets began to bustle on another busy Saturday market day. Jan stretched, yawned, stripped off her nightdress and threw it on the bed. Dale, bleary eyed soon woke up seeing Jan's lovely shape walk across to the bathroom.

Jan teased, "C'mon lazy bones. Breakfast, and then I want to go down and look at this Trading Estate."

Dale wandered across to the bathroom and peered in the mirror. He didn't particularly like what he saw. I can see my father looking back at me! It was too early for him. He needed a shower. That, would wake him up, he hoped.

He replied to Jan's plan. "Okay, Sweety, whatever you say. But I don't know what you are going to achieve by that, but whatever you say."

Breakfast for Jan was never a marathon. It was a yoghurt and a slice of toast with a smear of marmalade. For Dale, well if it was in the price, it had to be eaten.

He gestured to the waitress. "Full English please, two eggs, builder's tea and white toast, with plenty of butter please. Thank you."

When Dale had finished his fourth piece of buttered toast, they rose from the table and headed for the car park. Jan knew that the Industrial estate was easily visible from the sawmill site, but was slightly more-tricky to access. Before she had started the car, she had checked her phone on the easiest route they needed to take. Their journey involved leaving Carlisle on the north bound road to then access a slip to take them back on themselves, through a series of roundabouts and then turn into the industrial estate.

Jan drove slowly along a two-way side road, fenced with chain link. Ahead were various company signs and one huge sign-board on tall concrete posts.

Carlisle Trading Estate
Quarry Road, Carlisle. Established 1970.
All enquiries: Kyle Redford Estate Agency. 01228. 026620
Developers: Dartington & Goodrich Ltd.

In association with: The London Real Estate Company Ltd.

Jan stopped the car in front of the sign-board. Speechless.

"Jan, why have you stopped and why have you not uttered a word?"

"Why? Because I *am* speechless! I cannot believe that these are the same people that are trying to ruin my business in Camden. I just can't believe it. The co-incidence is remarkable. My problem with this is, how can I bring a case against these people for stealing 'my' land, when this inheritance has been created for me by my boyfriend's cunning ways. This would be one fraud, trying to out-do another fraud! The trouble is, everything I know about these people say that they are incredibly successful, which makes them rich, and rich makes them powerful. So, it's a dilemma. How do you think we could approach this? I would like to see them sued for…well, I don't know what. Fraud, misappropriation, theft. I just don't know what. Maybe even assisting in murder. Who knows what they had to do to be able to buy that land from the folks that were probably already dead?"

Dale sat rubbing his finger and thumb up and down on his chin. Then scratching his head, he ventured a few words.

"I am wondering, whether the two detectives might want to pursue the case. After all, it looks like fraud, with a capital 'F'. Not only that, but there may be some collusion, with these murders in the background. I think we need to be talking to the police."

"Okay. I suggest that we have a nice weekend here and speak to either DS Julia Cox or DI Rob Wilton. I think that they are the main players here."

"Agreed!"

As Jan drove back into the town, a car parking sign offered additional and overflow parking at the Cattle Market. The Cattle Market sign showed its opening times for Auctions as Mondays, Wednesdays and Fridays.

Jan pulled up into a space and noticed that in one of the windows overlooking the cattle market stalls was a board offering units in the Carlisle Trading Estate. Phone or Apply-within. At the top of the red brick building was a long signboard perhaps two feet in depth and twenty feet long across the top of the building, reading:

'KYLE REDFORD' Auctioneers, Land Agents, Land & Property Management.

"Look, Dale, that's the name that's on the sign down at the trading estate. Maybe this is the key? C'mon let's go in and see if we can find out a bit more about how this firm are the agents for London Estates."

"Woah. Stop! If we go in there, we don't know what we are going in to. Before we do that, we should go back to the hotel and do a bit of research. The two might not be related at all, but if they are, don't forget we are looking at potentially exposing serious fraud and I can't see anyone taking to talking to us too kindly. Not only that, but these people could have been involved in the murder of our three dead bodies and even this Bryn, who seems to have been the 'last man standing' as well as a fraudster who may have helped perceive and even perpetuate these land transfers. It seems that he might be another murder victim. No! Not our job. Let's do a bit of research then if we can find anything interesting, hand it to the police on Monday as soon as we can."

"Yes, Dale. You're right, of course. They're the police, they can go in and ask whatever questions they like and expect to get answers. Okay we will have to be patient and wait until Monday. Monday it is then. Back to the hotel bar then. I need a stiff one."

"Wow, Jan, does that constitute an offer. If it does, then count me in!"

Finally, a little levity. The first laugh broke the tension of the last few days.

"Yes, darling, okay. Why not!"

CHAPTER 43

2020, Carlisle Police Station

Julia was in the office early on Monday morning. She and Grant had dared to have the Sunday off together and went walking over onto the moors. Grant had to catch the early train from Carlisle to Euston for a midday editorial meeting to update his editor on several stories he was working on. But now he had a new story. 'The Secrets of the Tumbledown.' Julia had forbidden him to release the story until her boss, Detective Inspector Rob Wilton, was satisfied that any publicity wouldn't have the 'world and his wife' trampling over their crime scene. But he'd kick the story 'round until it was in a nice readable format and they could make several days headlines from it. He loved it. He'd been known as Mr Front Page and Mr Exclusive, thanks to the several headliners he had brought in over the years and here was another one.

But there had been some rattling's from the tiny Dunsford Bugle, Grant had worked with Jenny Southfield when he was a local reporter and knew her to be a sharp cookie when it came to a story. Her paper was just a weekly local rag, full of mainly adverts for Care Homes, Gardening and Landscaping firms and all that periphery stuff. The sort of stuff that keeps local rags with enough income to breakeven and give the villages a feeling that they are still in the current century. When they aren't in profit the mother-ship keeps them going thanks to a feeling of responsibility, towards the local community's news market. Being part of the Newcastle Times Group sometimes has its positives and Jenny Southfield, the rag's editor had already hinted at a multiple murder site. The buzz 'round 'The Street' was that this could be a big story, which the Newspaper Group would love to run with. So, Grant was trying to keep his head down. Difficult, with an investigative team of reporters ready to light the touch-paper on this story.

Rob arrived in the Office followed by Jerry Blake. Even though Jerry was retired, he was enjoying being in on a case that seemed to keep on giving. Rob called a team meeting.

The team sat around on desks, chairs, and on the cushioned bench that was set against one of the walls. The office had only been refurbished in the last couple of years. It was completed in varying shades of grey, with dark blue office chairs and a grey flecked carpet tile floor covering.

The crime board was looking busy now with photographs of the crime scene, old photographs of the mill and many photographs from over the years from the Cardew-Petteril estate records.

There were the names of the deceased. Mary Morris, Violet Morris and Emmanuel Morris, all linked by a thick black felt-pen marker and below that the name of Bryn Morris as the probable perpetrator of the crime of murdering the above three Morris's.

But the large red felt-pen mark showing a big question mark hung over Bryn Morris.

The detective team, needed to tie up the details of the last movements of Bryn Morris, which was proving extremely difficult as the case was over fifty years old.

"Julia, where are we with the Estate records, please? At our last meeting you said that you were hopeful that the estate would let you have the payment records for Bryn Morris's home, Edenbrook Cottage. Regretfully, the bank that Bryn was registered with, the records don't go back that far. So that's a dead end."

"Yes, Guv. The estate records show that the rental payments were very hit and miss. The Morris's were always being chased and there are several notations that Mary, Bryn's wife always ended up paying the bills. So yes, they were always under pressure for money."

Jerry had been listening to everything that had been put forward and discussed. His conclusion as to the next logical move was to track down the agents who facilitated the sale.

"I think our next stop is to visit Kyle Redford Land Agents. His signature is against the Witness Signature to that of the main signatures on the document itself. For all we know he could have written the whole document himself. Before we go, I think that we need to raise a search warrant for his premises as well as his home. The reason for this, is that I believe that at least one of the signatures, which we believe to be fake, will be his."

Rob chipped in. "And perhaps all the signatures? It could be that Bryn Morris either signed the documents himself, or forced Manny to sign and then locked them all in the cellar. We will need a handwriting expert to prove that. A Graphologist or a Forensic Handwriting expert. We just need to visit these premises. Julia?"

"Yes, Guv, their offices are alongside and above the Cattle Market. We're just two minutes away. I can get an emergency warrant from our favourite Magistrate Martin Gurry, he'll be sitting today and if we say that this is urgent, he'll always oblige, provided that he thinks it's all above board."

"Okay Julia. Over to you. Tomorrow is Market Day, so I think we shall pay Mr Redford a surprise visit, perhaps while he is at Auction and has to come back. That should knock him off balance!"

2020, Crown & Mitre

Jan and Dale before taking the step of approaching Kyle Redford, decided to do a bit of research. Each tapped away at their laptops. The focus was on the names on the Trading Estate sign boards. A Companies House search revealed that London Property Company employed a board of six Directors. There were two named Dartington and two named Goodrich as well as two others. There were four directors who were under the age of forty and two who were over seventy. It seemed that both Dartington and Goodrich had their off-springs on the board, but the two older guys were the founders of the business, whilst still in their very early twenties, straight out of university.

"Jan, look at this! Never mind Kyle Redford Agents, The London Real Estate Company is a PLC. It's a public company, supported by shareholders. That means if there was some sort of enquiry into their dealings and these were seen to be fraudulent, particularly if it was hinted that it was fraudulently set up with a dirty deal from day one, when the company was first traded, then we might not have to go to court at all."

Jan was puzzled. She wasn't sure what Dale was saying, or even hinting at. "Well, why not. Why would we not have to go to court?"

"Shares Jan, shares. You know how fickle the stocks and shares market is. It can be up one day and down another. So many of the times when a company gets into trouble, is when its publicity machine loses traction. Or in other words, if there is ever any bad press, then shares are sold off, they sell, sell, sell, just like rats, leave a sinking ship. When there's a shares slide, people follow like lemmings jumping off a cliff!"

Jan was still puzzled.

"That means Jan, that if we could create a bit of bad press, then the company's value could fall, big time, and they would have to draw in their reins. If we got really lucky, for example they might have to give up any recent acquisitions like your Estates Portfolio. If we look at that longer term, that means that Phil can still have a business and we can carry on with our plans up here."

Jan finally got it. "Got it. Yeah, sorry, got it. A little slow but I've got it now. So, what's our next move Dale, you clever boy!?"

"Well my next move is…come here and give me a hug!"

"Yes, yes, yes, but first I think we ought to take our findings to that DI Wilton and maybe that bright Sergeant Julia Cox. If they start looking into it, then they are the people who can follow it through. Meantime, the other name that was on the Carlisle Trading Estate name board was Kyle Redford Land Agents. If he was in at the start, then he could be up to his neck in it too!"

Dale continued, "I think that we should take our findings in to the police station and see if we can glean anything from these detectives. If we are capable of working this all out, then so must they be. What do you think?"

Jan was impressed by Dale's deductions and agreed that the next step was to contact Carlisle Police. "Do you know what Dale, I think that there is no time like the present."

Jan fished her mobile phone from her hand bag, at the same time rummaging for the card that DS Julia Cox had given her. She dialled Julia's number. It answered.

"Julia speaking."

As soon as Jan heard a voice on the end of the line, she handed the phone to Dale. Dale stuttered into action.

"Oh, hello. Is that DS Cox please?"

"Yes. Who's calling?"

"It's Dale Scott, we are the couple–"

"Yes sir, I know who you are. How can I help?"

"Well, we have been doing some research that we thought might help you in your investigations."

"Yes, Mr Scott. What would that be, that you think it might help us?"

"Well, maybe it would be better if we met and we can show you our findings."

"Can you give me a hint Mr Scott, Dale, isn't it?"

"Yes, Dale. Please do call me Dale. Well, it's about The London Real Estate Company. They are a PLC and they have been set up since your Bryn Morris went missing and Kyle Scott came on the scene. Well, we have been putting two and two together and there seems to be a connection. We have it all on our lap-tops."

"That's very interesting Dale. Thank you for that, but we have already made the connection. However, if you would like to come along on Monday, ask for me, sometime after ten in the morning, I will be happy to chat it through with you, if that's alright?"

The wind was taken out of Dale's sails, but he was grateful for Julia's ear.

"Yes, okay detective, we will come in on Monday. Thank you."

***

"Who was that Jules, sounded interesting?" Grant asked.

Julia answered, "It was the couple who have inherited Buckabank mill. They have been doing some research and seem to think that there is a connection between Kyle Redford, the people who originally bought the mill property, or most of it, and The London Real Estate Company PLC, and the death of Bryn Morris. Well, we've made similar connections, but we haven't looked deeply into The London Real Estate Company PLC. I guess there could be a direct connection, but I haven't got time to research it. We'll be visiting Kyle Redford's offices as soon as we can get a warrant. But that's all about hand writing and potentially fake signatures on the mill's sale contracts."

Grant's ears had pricked up. "Mmm, LRC, PLC, they're a massive property company. I even had some of their shares at one time. Wish I had some now, they are really riding high. Do you know what, there has always been some sort of mystery around their two main board directors. A couple of la-di-dahs. Family estates in the Westcountry and riding and horses. You know, all that hoi-polloi stuff. There was some trouble a few years ago, I remember reading. One of them had had an affair up here in Carlisle, funny enough, and there was a big paternity suite. There was a toss-up as to which one of them it was. Seems they had both been at it with the same girl on the same night. I am sure they settled out of court, but my, didn't the shares take a tumble back then. I might just look into that, might make a good story. Do you know what, if my memory serves me right, that girl or woman as she had become turned up dead in France or Spain or somewhere like that and no-one connected her to Dartington or Goodrich. Far too powerful."

Grant picked up the phone and dialled his secretary's mobile. She answered.

"Hi Katey. I think I have a nice little story, just being hatched, but I need a bit of research done first please. It's anything you can find on Dartington and Goodrich and The London Real Estate Company PLC. Usual stuff related companies, directorships of other companies, personal history, scandal, schools, family, launch of company. All the usual stuff please. I'm sure there was a bit of a scandal ten or twelve years ago, involving a paternity suite. I'll be down on Monday, late, so whatever you can do before I get there would be good. You might also speak to our man Tristan, at the stock exchange and get a bit of history on LRC, PLC's recent trading history. Thanks Katey. See you Monday."

CHAPTER 44

2020

Market day in Carlisle was always a busy affair. At six thirty in the morning, most of the stallholders had already set up. Three streets were lined with metal frames which were covered in a multi-colour of canvasses. At seven thirty the market saw people coming into town off the buses and walking up from the railway station and the town was starting to buzz. The cattle and sheep auctions were due to start at eight and farmers, both local and from many miles around, had already delivered their prime stock to their allocated pens in readiness for the Auctioneer to start his calling. The market was full to bursting with enthusiastic buyers and sellers, all anticipating a good day's trading. Kyle Redford had been the main auctioneer at the Carlisle auctions for over fifty years, was a popular character and was well respected by the farming folk that brought their stock for sale. But there was always an air of superiority about Redford. Talk was, that he had come into money at a very early age, but he had no family as such, and in the early days, there were doubts to his credibility. At twenty years of age, he had bought several properties in the town as well as land outside the town, much of which had now been developed into housing and Trading Estates. Folks had long ceased worrying about Redford and his wealth. He was wealthy and that was that. He'd been married a couple of times, which didn't last very long and he had a couple of wayward children by each marriage, but they had obviously chosen to live with their respective mothers. He now had a 'fancy piece' as the locals called her, who ran an expensive sports car and spent his money as fast as she could.

Julia had listened to what a couple of the older bobbies had said about Redford, which as far as she was concerned, was good background information.

DC Julia Cox had secured a search warrant from Magistrate Martin Gurry, at the request of her boss, to enable them to search the land agent's premises. Rob had previously taken a drive-by look at Kyle Redford's offices and could see that these were extensive. He had also asked Julia to secure a warrant for his main property, a large Victorian house, set high above the town in several manicured acres. He created a team of six as well as himself, Julia and Jerry to attend the premises. Julia had completed several background checks on Kyle Redford to establish several things, including whether he was still alive and kicking, if he was, was he still active in the business. If that were the case, what was the financial state of the business and the state of Reford's personal wealth, his bank account status and its history.

The team assembled in the Detectives Room at the police station at 7am. The plan was to serve the warrant at 8am as the auction began and Kyle Redford was just starting the auctions. In that way, they would have no resistance when presenting the warrant to office staff and there would be no time for anyone to go destroying any old paperwork or file. Neither would they be able to interrupt Redford on the auctioneer's rostrum.

DI Rob Wilton gave the instructions to his assembled colleagues, his chosen team and they left the station, six in the mini-bus and he and Jerry in Rob's Audi. Julia took two uniforms up to Redford's large Victorian house on the edge of town. At 8am as Redford kicked off the cattle auction, the team opened the door of Redford's offices entered the premises piled in and served the warrant to an indignant, haughty looking lady with a metal badge on her jacket that stated, 'Sylvia, Manager'. She protested vehemently, until she was told by Rob, that if she didn't shut up and sit down, she would be arrested. *That* soon shut her up.

Simultaneously, Julia knocked on the door of Redford's house, which was opened by a bleary eyed 'brassy-looking piece', probably in her late forties or fifties, who was served with the warrant.

CHAPTER 45

2020

Grant tapped away furiously on his computer keyboard. Most of the story was established, but it was important to get facts and details correct before he consulted the Legal Dept. Had one of the most successful property companies in the country, been set up on a fraudulent transaction and if so, how many more of this highly successful company's dealing's, were conducted in the same way?

This, The London Real Estate Company PLC was a publicly quoted company, with hundreds, if not thousands of shareholders and if Grant breaks this story, the knock-on effects and subsequent fall out could be devastating with the potential to see the company collapse, with no hope of recovery.

The two main board directors, Charles Dartington and James Goodrich who formed the company around fifty years ago, may have conducted their first transactions by falsifying, or being party to falsifying Land Registry documents

Grant phoned Julia. "Julia, I'm up to my neck in it down here. My editor is breathing heavily over my shoulder, waiting for you to make arrests. He wants me to 'go' on the story, but the legal department are holding me back 'til Rob makes the arrests. Where are you with *that* please?"

Julia responded, "Grant, you ought to know better than to ask me something I can't give you a definitive on, any arrests, until we've actually done the deed, and as yet we haven't. I'll let you know when I have something a bit more concrete. Right now, I am exercising a warrant, which we are hoping will reveal documents confirming our suspicions. But even then, we can only arrest suspects. We will have to go through the process of which you are well aware, before we can even look at charging them. And I'm sure you are aware, our three main collaborators in these frauds, our suspects are very high-profile, wealthy people and will have very expensive lawyers on board, so there might well be weeks of wrangling yet. So please, *do not* and to make it clear I will repeat it, *do not* print anything that could possibly damage our case, as they will quickly work out the source of your information and story and my bosses will know who let the cat out of the bag, and I will be hauled over the coals, or even get dismissed."

Grant was pleading for something, anything that would enable him to kick off the story, fearing that the local rag would beat him to it. "Jules, c'mon sweetheart, I need something, anything. Please?"

Julia answered, "Sorry Grant. My first loyalty in this instance is my job, not my husband. However, if I can give you anything by this evening I will. But at this moment in time, it looks like tomorrow is going to be the earliest. Sorry, but I can't do any better than that. Now please let me get on with my job of searching these premises."

Julia was having to put up with 'the fancy piece' walking behind her protesting at every corner. Her name was Nancy, and Nancy had tried phoning Kyle Redford's office, to no avail. Meantime Rob and Jerry and their team were steadily going through filing cabinets, drawers, box files and any records that they could lay their hands on. The largest free-standing metal cabinet, held all the lease agreements for the Carlisle Trading Estate, many of them going back as far as 1972, when the first warehouse buildings had been completed and let. There had been many changes in tenants, but the site was almost always fully occupied, due mainly to its ease of access to the newly built ring-road which led out to the motorway.

The manager, Sylvia, had managed to slip out and make her way to the auctioneer's rostrum and above all the noise of bleating sheep and lowing cattle, speak to her boss, Kyle Redford. Redford was now seventy-two years of age, and though he had become a little portly, still looked fit and well. He was dressed smartly in a tweed suit with matching waistcoat, which was flecked with red. This was poorly chosen as it seemed to highlight the red thread-veins in his red and blue cheeks and his mixed family blood had given him a tanned hue. His greying curly hair seemed out of place with his attempt to present himself as if he were of farming stock.

He left the rostrum, handing the next auction lot over to a younger assistant and hurried back the few minutes to his office, to find arms full of boxes of files being carried by uniformed police officers and loaded into a police van, stacked right up to the roof.

Redford stormed in and demanded to speak to the senior person here. Rob was on his knees, looking through more filing cabinets, but stood up and came forward and spoke.

"Mr Redford. We have a search warrant for your premises, both here and at 'Hartop' your family home. I am arresting you in connection with the fraudulent acquisition of properties, dating back to 1970. You do not have to say anything. But it may harm your defence if you do not mention when questioned, something which you later rely on in court. Anything you say may be given in evidence, either during your arrest or before questioning."

Kyle Redford tried to argue, but Rob told the uniforms to take him away. As Redford writhed and wriggled demanding to know where their proof of what they were saying was.

Rob just replied, "We will be interviewing you later in the day, Sir. You may have one telephone call, which the duty officer will make for you, and oversee. Take him away."

Jerry telephoned Julia who hadn't found much in the way of files at Redford's home.

"Julia, how are you doing? We are about to wind things up here. We've arrested Redford and Rob is going to start interviewing him later, when we get back."

Julia replied in the affirmative, "Yes, Guv." Though Jerry was now retired, Julia still looked on him as a senior superior officer, respecting his years as a detective and acknowledging him by calling him 'Guv'. "We've completed the searches as the DI instructed and not found anything that might help our investigation. However, there was a fairly large safe in the basement, for which there appeared to be no key. It was covered up by an old blanket, but didn't look as though it had been opened for years. Nancy, the girlfriend, had no idea. She was clearly not in the know about anything, apart from spending money. She did however, reveal an expensive apartment in London and another in Spain, pointing out the photographs on the wall. I'll wind it up now and leave a uniform here to keep an eye on the house. I have asked for a locksmith to attend with me tomorrow."

"Okay Julia, well done, I'll let Rob know and we'll see you back at the nick."

CHAPTER 46

2020, Carlisle Police Station

The 'troops' arrived back at the station, hauling box after box, file after file, up to the detective's room. Rob and Jerry mounted the stairs after they had booked-in Kyle Redford, confirming to the Duty Sargeant the reason for the arrest on suspicion of fraud, under the Fraud Act 2006 and the Theft Act 1978 and False Accounting (Section 17 Theft Act 1968). DI Rob Wilton wished to ensure that all of these acts were noted to cover the alleged offences committed, dated back to circa 1970. Rob also wished to further ensure that there would be no technical or legal loopholes in this case, given that they were allegedly perpetrated before the later acts became law. Rob asked for Redford to be placed in a cell, until they were able to interview him. Rob assembled his team around the crime board.

Rob addressed the assembled team of detectives and uniforms. "Ladies and gentlemen. Firstly, thank you for today, I could not have wished for a more efficient operation, in that we commenced the serving of the search warrants, both here and at Redford's home, bang on 8am as planned. We encountered no resistance and I believe that we have all of the files that we required to commence a thorough investigation of fraud going back fifty years. All that, I thank you for, well done. However, this is now where the hard work begins."

As Rob was about to hand over to DS Julia Cox to organise the paper searches, as he looked around the room, her absence was noted, as she breezed into the room, apologising for her late arrival, just having returned from Redford's house.

"Ah DS Cox. Just the person I need. Please take charge of the distribution of the files from Redford's offices. Everything needs

THE SECRETS OF THE TUMBLEDOWN

to be catalogued, client companies, alpha-sequentially and then by date. Please allocate a number of boxes to each officer and give them an indication of what they should be looking for as we discussed. As soon as you can give me a starter list of transactions, with particular reference to the Carlisle Trading Estate, and The London Real Estate Company Ltd. the sooner we can start to interview Mr Redford. But before you allocate the work, how did you get on at Redford's home?"

Julia answered, "Well, Guv, apart from having to deal with that scrawny Barbie-Doll girlfriend of his, there didn't appear to be anything at the house in terms of files. My two uniforms and I completed the usual search areas, from drawers to behind paintings, cabinets in the garage, bedroom furniture, kitchen area, toilets and cisterns. Nothing. No clues and I don't think that if we were to re-visit those areas we would come up with anything. However, there was one real area of interest. It's a big old Victorian house, with a set of stairs, half-hidden, behind a large wooden cabinet, which had a fancy antique wall hanging, a sort of tapestry I guess, which led down to a cellar. It clearly hadn't been used for I'd say, years. There was a Chubb antique safe with a double key opening. There were no keys about and it was a waste of time asking Barbie. I wouldn't like to guess how many years the cellar had been closed up and sealed. There were cobwebs everywhere, the lights weren't working, and it was dark and damp. We found the safe hidden, or at least concealed under an old blanket. I called a Locksmith and he will meet me there at 8.30am tomorrow."

"Excellent Julia, as ever. Thank you. Sounds very interesting, I wonder what that will reveal. Meantime let's say for the next hour or so, if you can dig anything of interest out for my interview with Redford, that would be very helpful," Rob replied.

Rob gestured to Jerry and they returned downstairs to the desk sergeant and asked for Kyle Redford to be taken along to an interview room.

Like all prison cells in all old police stations, these spaces were meant to be intimidating. They were invariably dark, with dark coloured painted walls, could be grey, or dark blue or perhaps dark green. In the case of Carlisle their cells were painted in a depressing shade of burgundy. That's not bright and cheerful like a Burgundy wine, but dull and flat more like dried-blood.

Psychologically, these dark colours are meant to depress. They are meant to give the residents or temporary residents a platform in their minds to repent, confess and give up all of their dark secrets, when interviewed by a skilled trained interviewer. Unfortunately, nowadays, once a client, or in this case, prisoner, is met by his brief, then invariably he, or she, are advised to say nothing or plead 'no-comment'.

✳✳✳

By contrast to the confined isolation of the cell, the walk along the corridor to the new wing on the rear of the station was clean, light and bright. The interview room was just a box, of limited proportions and housed the bare minimum for its job, a basic metal legged table with a hardwood top. No windows. A large one-way mirror. A facility to record and four one-hour chairs, placed two either side. They called them one-hour chairs because after an hour of being interviewed, the interviewee starts to shift around on the seat, becoming uncomfortable and hopefully will start to unload, because they want to be somewhere else. Well, at least, that's what the psychologists say.

Rob and Jerry sat at the table. An indignant Kyle Redford sat at the table. He had been offered a telephone call, to phone a solicitor, but refused. "Why do I need a solicitor? I shouldn't even be here."

He continued to protest until Rob reminded him of his rights and that they would be recording this interview. Rob stated who he was and stated who Jerry was. He then continued, "Mr Redford, you are here because, while investigating an incident up at the old Buckabank Sawmill, a chain of events has led our investigations to your door."

Redford was quick to jump in. "Well, that was nothing to do with me! I didn't leave them there to die. Nothing to do with me!"

"Thank you for that in-put, Kyle. Is it alright if I call you Kyle?" Rob asked.

Kyle Redford nodded an okay.

"You are not being interviewed in relation to that incident, but I would be interested to hear any other comments you may wish to add, regarding that matter. I will tell you however, that we are treating these deaths as murder or manslaughter at the very minimum. So, any help you can give us on these deaths would be helpful."

Redford nervously shifted about on his chair and responded. "I don't know anything about what went on up there and I am not prepared to answer any further questions, until my solicitor is here."

"That's no problem, sir," Rob replied. "The desk sergeant will allow you to make a call and we will be holding you overnight, until we can resume our conversation. Interview suspended at 6pm."

The duty sergeant duly arrived from further down the corridor and escorted the suspect back to his cell, after he had made one call to his bemused, agitated girlfriend and had instructed her to phone his solicitor.

Rob and Jerry knew that there was a lot more information to be gleaned from speaking to Kyle Redford and were looking forward to interviewing their prisoner in the morning, subject to Redford's solicitor being on the scene.

"Mine's a pint then Jerry. Feathers?"

"Yes Rob, where else."

On Wednesday morning, bright and early the team were in sorting, and shuffling through endless papers. Over the almost fifty years since the trading estate was built and expanded, there had been hundreds of tenants and of course hundreds of leases. Given that Rob and Jerry believed that Kyle Redford's very first transaction was fraudulent then all of these transactions would therefore be seen as dishonest and corrupt, given that any monies generated from the first perfidious transaction would be just piling fraud upon fraud. However, a good Barrister would probably argue differently. But then, if you were leasing property on a trading estate, that had been purchased through massive deception, then surely, the transactions would or should be voided and the property returned to the rightful owners.

The duty sergeant informed Rob as he arrived at 9am, that a Gordon Goodwin, Mr Redford's solicitor, would be attending the station at 10am and trusted that that would be convenient.

Meanwhile Julia had arranged for a Locksmith to be up at Kyle Redford's house at 8.30am to open the safe, which was discovered in the basement of Redford's home.

The scatty girlfriend opened the door in a house coat, looking as if she hadn't slept all night. Her dyed blond hair looking like a bird's nest and with no make-up, she was looking like a cross between a blond scarecrow and something that had just had a big fight with a hurricane which had finally blown her backwards through her own hedge.

Julia and the Locksmith carefully picked their way down the stairs. Julia had had the foresight to bring a pack of bulbs, knowing that the cellar had been in absolute darkness, when carrying out their search the previous day. They picked their way down the stairs, descending very slowly until Julia could find a socket in which to place a bulb. They located the safe and the Locksmith commenced trying to open the huge chunk of ancient steel box.

Rob and Jerry began interviewing Kyle Redford and after the preliminary opening, outlining Redford's continuing rights, Rob commenced the interview.

"Kyle, you said I may call you Kyle. Yesterday we exercised and served a warrant on your premises, both business and home. We have obtained many documents in our search of your premises which has led us to believe that you have been fraudulently trading in property, for many years. Perhaps you would like to comment?"

Kyle turned to his solicitor and whispered. Goodwin, a smartly dressed man in his seventies, wearing a well-cut, hand-made grey worsted chalk-striped suit, a rotund overweight red-faced figure, with thinning grey-hair, sat there quietly taking everything in that Rob was suggesting. His half-buttoned waistcoat seemed to be splitting open on his bulk as he leant forward and advised Redford. Redford heeded his solicitor's advice. He turned back to Rob and uttered, "No comment."

Both Rob and Jerry tried to persuade Kyle to answer some of their questions, but to no avail. Goodwin asked to have a private consultation with his client, to which Rob agreed, but unless he was able to help them with their enquiries, they would have to hold him for a further twenty-four hours.

Rob was insistent, despite the protests of his Solicitor and the Solicitor's threats to speak to his friend the Chief Constable. Rob and Jerry had heard it all before. They were stirred, but not shaken.

Meantime, the team continued to log companies who had leased units at the trading estate over the last almost fifty years and Julia was persevering with the locksmith, trying to open the rusted-out safe in Redford's basement. Alas, the safe was locked solid, the mechanism had rusted and collapsed inside the steel door.

"How are you fixed for tomorrow? Can you get hold of some cutting gear to open the safe?" Julia enquired.

"Yes, Sarge. No problem. We'll resume tomorrow."

Grant's story, headlined: A Business Built on Fraud

Grant copied in his editor and followed up with a conversation.

"What do you think Mike? I've run this past Legal and they say that there is nothing in there that directly points a finger at the Company. Can we go with it?"

"I'm not happy Grant. Not sure about the headline. Try something else. We need some more details, some more proof."

"Sorry Mike, I've got more, but I am having to wait until I see some incriminating documents. I know it's border line, but if I don't get this story out soon, then someone will bribe a cop somewhere and we'll get pipped to the post. And no, I didn't mean the Newcastle Post, but you know where I'm coming from."

"Okay Grant, get it scripted up and if we have nothing better, it can go front page. But you are going to need some pretty convincing follow up material, because the phones are going to start ringing and they'll be mainly from expensive lawyers."

Grant phoned Julia. The phone went to answer. Grant phoned Rob. Rob picked up.

"Grant, Julia's not here can I take a message?"

Grant answered slightly nervously, not wanting to spoil a long-standing friendship. "No, Rob. I wanted to speak to you. I am about to run a story, which is going to hit the front page, if there's nothing better tomorrow. I don't actually have any detail other than, shall we say, common hearsay. But I do want you to know that Julia has been absolutely tight-lipped about your case, she wouldn't tell me anything, so this is me doing my journalistic take on things, to come up with this story. Before I *go*, with it, I'd like to run it past you before you see it in tomorrow's papers. Can I email it over?"

"Christ Grant," Rob answered. "You do stretch my patience sometimes. Yes, okay send it over, I guess you'll want me to read it straight away."

At that Rob's email inbox pinged. He regarded the email. He showed it to Jerry. They both smiled.

Jerry commented, "Well, he's said nothing, but everything. It won't take the rest of the media long to work it out."

Rob sat there sipping away at a thick brown cup of tea contemplating, smiling and remarked, "Do you know what Jerry. I think that this could flush out Mister Kyle Redford and might open up another can of worms for us. Frankly I have enough on my plate to have to take on a major fraud case, we can leave that to your mates at the Met, can't we? I'll phone Grant and tell him to go ahead."

Rob phoned Grant's mobile which Grant answered in trepidation.

"Yes Grant. Go with it. Good article, says nothing but everything and they'll be suing you not me. So yes, go ahead. Actually, it might help us. Thanks, for letting me know. See you at The Feathers on the weekend."

Grant's article was set to go.

PROPERTY FRAUD. A business built on a lie.

Today it was revealed that one of the largest property groups in the country, were being investigated into allegations of long term and historic fraudulent trading. The company known for their dynamic growth, some say through unscrupulous, bullying and pressure tactics. The Company had recently set out on a journey to clear vast swathes of their properties in the East End of London, of tenants who had been renting from the company, many of these for over thirty years. However, it has now come to light, that the origins of the empire are questionable and it is being heavily rumoured that the company was set up on a web of fabricated and falsified documents.

Around fifty years ago the two founding and long serving directors of the company, purchased a large amount of acreage of land in Cumbria and developed a substantial part of this land into a vast trading estate. The development included link roads and motorway access roads. It has come to this paper's notice, that the process and transfer of this acreage, was not as clear as it should have been and there was no verification as to the true owners of the land. Nevertheless, a sale went forward and a purchase made. The land was then developed and is now part of a vast property empire and Public Company.

We are unable to give further details of the company at this moment in time as investigations are ongoing.

Grant Hooper.
Award Winning Journalist.

CHAPTER 47

2020, Crown and Mitre

Jan and Dale woke to a knock on their bedroom door at The Crown and Mitre. Their wake-up call, with one pot of English Breakfast and one pot of Earl Grey with sliced lemon, and the daily paper.

Jan poured their cups of tea, while Dale swilled some cold water over his face. They kept beating themselves up and kept wondering if this self-made nightmare would ever end.

Jan sipped away at her cup, while Dale skated through the cricket results on the back page. Jan suddenly coughed and tea sprayed all down the bedding, like a woman 'wild-swimming' but drowning in a deep wave, spluttering and spitting out a mouth of sea water.

"Christ Jan, are you alright?"

"Look, look, look." She couldn't say anything else other than 'look' as she pointed at the front of the paper.

"What, what, what is it?"

"Look, look, look."

Then he saw the headlines.

"Shit! That's us. Look it mentions Cumbria. Oh my god. People will find out and this story will lead to us. Shit!"

He threw the paper down on the bed as if to dismiss it from his mind, as if that act of attempted destruction of the newspaper headlines would work!

"Hang on Dale, let me read it. Hold on sweetheart, I like this."

Dale retorted, "What are you talking about, how could you like it?"

"Well, do you remember a couple of weeks ago, you told me that there had been a paternity suit, some years ago and they didn't know whether it was Goodrich or Dartington who was the father. You said that they settled out of court. But what interested me about what you said, was that their shares took a tumble and it took quite a time to rebuild the company. So, if this all comes out as a company who have always been into, let's say crooked dealing, then this could see their shares taking a massive tumble and the company collapsing, in which case Camden Estates will still keep running and Phil will have a job for life and we can carry on with my inheritance. Not only that but all my renters, my tenants, who were going to get Section 21 Notices to quit, will not now have to move."

***

Julia had seen the email from Grant and after she had given him hell and slammed the phone down. She phoned her boss, Rob, to apologise.

"Guv, it's me, Julia."

"Hi Julia, are you okay?"

Julia wondered why she didn't straight away get a blast from her senior officer.

"There's an article about to…"

"Yes Julia, Grant phoned me and I gave my approval. Jerry and I think that it might help us flush out Kyle Redford, who at this moment in time is saying absolutely nothing. We shall see."

"Oh, so you're not cross then?"

"No Julia, anything but. So why have you phoned?"

"Oh. Umm. Nothing Guv, just to give you an update on Redford's safe. It's completely rusted out and we're going back tomorrow with some cutting gear."

"Okay. Thanks for the update, I'll see you tomorrow."

Julia was bemused but relieved.

***

The following morning, the team trooped into the station and began shuffling and listing, deciphering and noting endless transactions, worth hundreds of thousands of pounds over several years.

Kyle Redford's Solicitor arrived at 10am again and the interview began just after.

Rob opened, "Good morning, Kyle. I trust you slept well. We have now sifted not only through many hundreds of your files, but we have managed to find the original sale documents for the Buckabank Sawmill and its surrounding land. The thing that bothers us most Kyle are the signatures on the document. More particularly, the witness signatures. Would you like to comment?"

Kyle shook his head and as advised just said, "No comment."

Rob pushed various copies of letters towards Redford.

"These, Kyle, are copies of original letters written by Bryn Morris to his cousin, Emmanuel Morris. We have had a handwriting expert compare these with the sale documents to the mill, which you completed and they bear no resemblance to those on the transfer documents. Do you have anything you would like to add?"

"No comment."

"Further to that, even though they appear to be slightly different, two of the signatures have been made by you. But these do not bare your name. You appear to have signed these as Bryn Morris and it appears that Bryn Morris signed on behalf of his cousin, Emmanuel Morris. But our hand writing expert says, though they have been disguised, or there has been an attempt to disguise the handwriting, they are actually both yours. What would you like to say about that, having compared like for like against your own witness signature?"

"No comment."

"Kyle. This evidence is inescapable. If you are not prepared to help us further, we have nothing left, no other course of action but to charge you."

Rob's phone rang. A text was received simultaneously, so Rob knew if Julia was trying to contact him, it would be urgent.

"Julia?"

"Guv. Sorry to disturb you, but we've just opened the safe in Redford's house. In a tin box at the bottom of the safe was a much-faded bloodied rag which was wrapped around a pestle. The pestle had hairs and blood still attached to it and if I'm not mistaken, Forensics suggested, apart from the obvious knife sticking out of the chap's ribs all those years ago, that it was the probable additional murder weapon, up at Edenbrook Cottage. I hope that helps you with your interview."

Rob was temporarily speechless, but thanked Julia.

"To continue, Kyle Redford. We will be charging you with

Fraud under The Fraud Act 2006, additionally, Property Theft, under the Theft Act 1978 and False Accounting. Section 17 Theft Act 1968.

"We will be also be charging you with the Murder of Bryn Morris at Edenbrook Cottage in 1970. Do you understand the charges, and do you have anything that you would like to say?"

Kyle's face went purple, his heart beat so fast he thought it was going to burst, he gasped for breath, then wet himself, leaving a trickle of urine running down the leg of his chair and forming a pool on the floor.

Rob nodded to the waiting officer to take him away.

CHAPTER 48

2020, London Property Company PLC

"Jesus Christ, Charles, have you seen this?"

James Goodrich threw the newspaper down across the board room table with such force that it slid across the table into a cut glass decanter knocking over several glasses which crashed to the floor and splintered everywhere.

"Hang on a minute James, it doesn't actually mention our names or the company, does it?"

"No, but it's not going to take much of a genius to work it out, is it?"

"Fuck! You're right. We need to get on to our legal department and put some sort of a block on it. We'll sue the bastard. Who's written it? Look, it says here Grant Hooper, little shit. He hasn't got any facts in this load of old tosh, he's just flying a kite and hoping something will stick. I'll issue a writ against him and sue for damages. You don't mess with us, young man!"

Carlisle Police Station

Jerry arrived at the nick, with a copy of Grant's front page headlines.

"Have you seen this article, Rob, Julia?"

Julia almost fainted with the shock of seeing Grant's article and had to get the sudden rush of guilt and responsibility off her chest. "Look, Guv, honestly, I haven't told Grant anything. He asked but I said no and that it was more than my job's worth to give him any information."

Rob replied, "Julia, it's okay, it's okay, don't panic. You explained perfectly well yesterday, I'm okay with it. Honestly. If you actually read the article, all he has written, is conjecture, pure journalese. Any of that could have been gleaned from just listening to the local gossip. When you think, given that we have solved the puzzle of the murders in the cellar and we have now arrested Kyle Redford for Bryn's murder then people would soon put two and two together, which is basically what Grant has done. Additionally, together with the people up at the big house, looking back through historic photographs, then it was all there to be worked out. Don't worry, I know you wouldn't let us down, you're a good copper. In any event, what it seems to have done, is open up a potentially very big high-profile fraud case for London Met."

Jerry chipped in. "If anything, Julia, I think you should congratulate Grant on doing us a big favour. Who knows what he will come up with as a follow on, now that we have arrested and charged Kyle Redford. I think we should buy him a drink at The Feathers this weekend. Or better still, given that we have given him another scoop, he should be buying us champagne."

London, Grant's Office

Grant's editor, Mike Chandler, an experienced 'hack' himself in years gone by, but now a wise old operator, had an inbuilt instinct into knowing what stories he could get away with and which ones were sailing a touch close to the wind. This was an in-betweener. Mike knocked on the open door of Grant's office. Grant was sat completely relaxed, sipping black coffee from a plastic cup, his sleeves rolled up and his feet resting on his desk.

"Good morning, Grant. Don't get up. It seems that you've hit a nerve with your headlines this morning. Legal have been inundated with messages to return the calls from the Lawyers for Dartington and Goodrich. But as editor of this paper, and given the fact that I like your article, my decision is to put a hold on replying for twenty-four hours. I have instructed them not to reply, until, maybe tomorrow afternoon. I'm hoping that you might have a follow-up to your story that will, blow this company completely out of the water and shut these people up? They have always been seen to be a company that sails close to the wind. Perhaps this will expose them for what they are. As far as I'm concerned, the two main directors who run this company have always been a disgrace to the City. I'm amazed they've lasted this long."

Grant replied, "Well, boss, there is nothing in the article that actually says anything. But clearly, they must think that there is, or they wouldn't be making such a fuss, and you know what they say…there's no smoke without fire. And yes, I'm half-way through a follow up. I just need some confirmation from my source."

Mike was quick to answer. "I guess you mean your missus, Julia, at Carlisle nick? Say no more."

"Well spotted Mike, I'm just waiting for confirmation of the one suspect, that I believe is going to be charged with murder or even multiple murders, but until I get that confirmation, I am a bit hands-tied. My story will be headed… ***'The Secrets of the Tumbledown'***. I think you'll like it! It might even make a book…watch this space."

CHAPTER 49

2020, London Stock Exchange

"Yes, sell!" This instruction could be heard, several times a minute, for the next half an hour and then steadily throughout the day.

"LREC. PLC. Yes sell."

"Yes, sell."

"Yes, sell."

"Dropping like a stone. Yes, sell."

"They're trying to prop it up you say? No, just sell."

"Yes, sell."

"Yes, sell."

London Real Estate Company PLC

"Christ Charles, have you seen the share price?"

"Yes, James. I've instructed our broker to buy as many as he can, otherwise the shares will collapse like the last time we had a bit of trouble, I'm sure you will remember over that girl we both screwed. That was a minor scandal, then, but we got over it. The thing is to not panic. I've put some of our own properties up to the bank, so we can keep funding purchases. We can't afford the price to completely collapse or the house will tumble like a pack of cards. I've also put a hold on a couple of those last proposals, you know, the Camden Project where we were going to develop a lot of those old properties that were managed by that piddling Camden Estates business."

"Okay Charles, well done. We'll get through this. We've been here before. Pass me the Scotch, don't bother with the soda!"

2020, Crown and Mitre Carlisle

"Shit Jan, have you seen this?"

Dale passed the newspaper to Jan who was in shock after reading the first few lines.

"This is us. This is because of us. If we hadn't come up here in search of the inheritance, none of this would have happened. No estate, no bodies, no murder investigations, no history, no one would have known anything. You know that this is going to affect those two hyenas that were laughing at me when I was chasing them over their virtual takeover of mine and Phil's business. Now it looks like they've got their comeuppance. I tell you what, Dale, check their share prices, The London Real Estate Company."

Dale tapped away on his shares site and there was an immediate notice about LREC. PLC share trading.

"Christ Jan, you're right, their shares are dropping like a stone."

"Dale, honey, check the BBC news headlines, see if there is anything about it on the website."

London Real Estate Company PLC

"Christ Charles, have you seen the share price?"

"Yes James, it's dropping like a stone. I suggest you get on to some of your institutions and tell them to buy a few blocks of shares or we are going to be up to our eyes in shit soon."

"Yes, Charles, I'm on it."

"Christ, it doesn't seem to be making any difference to the share price. We'll need to throw some more cash at it. I'll speak to our banks."

James dialled the Internationale Bank of Europe, their main funders. "Put me through to Robert Hartley-Jennings, straight away."

"Yes sir…" After a short delay, "I'm sorry, there's no answer from his line. Would you like to leave a voice message?"

"No! I flaming wouldn't. Put me through to his PA."

"Yes sir…" Another pause. "I'm sorry sir, she isn't answering either. Would you like to leave a voice message?"

"No, I do not want to leave a bloody voice message! I want you to get hold of him straight away, it's urgent."

"Yes, sir. Who is speaking please? Did you say Mr Dartington? Oh, I'm sorry sir, I was told to say that Mr Hartley-Jennings was in a meeting all day and would not be available until tomorrow." The receptionist heard the phone being slammed down with some force.

"Christ James, that bastard Jennings has blocked me. All that I've done for that little shit. I saved his arse when he was my Fag at Eaton, the endless gifts I've bestowed on him. The slimy little turd. I've introduced him to endless totty and now the little shit has turned his back on us. I think he's trying to get back at me for when he found out I shagged his wife. He'll be sorry."

"Charles, this is not looking good. It must be one of our board that has temporarily put a stop on our trading. No, look at these emails, the Securities Exchange Commission has suspended our trading. Shit. I've got emails galore coming through."

"Who the bloody hell has done that? That means we will have up to ten days to come up with an explanation, or we could be taken completely off the trading floor. Shit!"

2020, Crown and Mitre Carlisle

"C'mon Jan, let's go down and have some breakfast. I'm feeling quite positive today. I'm getting the feeling that things might just work out okay. I've just got that feeling, you know. Look, it's a nice sunny day out there and we'll go and have a look at the mill now that the police seem to have finished their investigation down there. C'mon, let's go."

Jan and Dale sat at the breakfast table, tapping away at their iPads, checking the up-to-date headlines as well as the daily share trading and the news of the apparent collapse of The London Real Estate Company, with the knock on affects for Charles Dartington and James Goodrich, reaching fever pitch. It seems that anyone who had a grudge against this pair are now getting in and having their say.

The Hotel Receptionist approached the couple with a pile of re-addressed letters for Dale. Dale thanked her and reminded Jan that he had organised his mail to be forwarded to Carlisle.

He looked at the pile of mail and sifted through it, pushing most of the envelopes to one side and placing one in front of him.

He stared at it, wondering whether to open it or not. Jan looked at him pondering the affect that it appeared to be having on Dale and his hesitation in opening the single envelope that was sitting in front of him.

"Dale, what is it?"

"Well, you remember I said that I was going to send away for a DNA test for you, just for the fun of it, before we even embarked upon your 'inheritance', or should I say the inheritance that I created for you. Well, that's it there, right in front of me," Dale answered, nervously.

"Oh! I'm not sure I want to know. You can either chuck it in the bin or open it."

"Eeee, Jan. Not sure."

"Well, why are you waiting? We can't be any deeper in the mire than we already are. Go on open it."

Dale took a knife from the table and slid it slowly along the top join, opening the letter with their results. He looked at Jan's DNA origins in disbelief.

"No, it's not possible. I don't believe it!"

"What Dale, what is it? What don't you believe?"

Dale pushed the letter showing the results of Jan's test, across and in front of Jan to read for herself.

"No, Dale, I don't believe it. It's not possible, is it? You've fiddled it haven't you!"

"Well Jan, my lovely, there it is in black and white. And *no,* I have definitely not fiddled it. Go on read it out."

Jan started to read out her DNA result and started to laugh and then the tears started rolling down her cheeks.

"It says here, I am 25% Ashkenatzi from Eastern Europe, I guess from my grandfather, or great grandfather, 8% Irish, 10% Welsh and 13% Scottish. Christ, someone had a bike! The rest is a mixture of Baltic States and English. And…my family name is Moritzstein…and I have over 4,000 ancestry matches!"

"You know what, Jan? This means that the estate that we conjured into your name is actually yours! Yes, yours! It's your true inheritance. And if you think I'm writing to 4,000 ancestry matches to offer them a share then you're very much mistaken! What we do about the 'stolen' acreage, is another question for another day."

Dale then called out to the waitress, "Young lady, I think we'll have a bottle of your best champagne. We have something to celebrate!"

Printed in Great Britain
by Amazon

60845657R00208